THE VEILED ASSASSIN

A NOVEL OF THE LATE ROMAN EMPIRE

EMBERS OF EMPIRE
VOL. I

Q. V. HUNTER

130 E. 63rd St., Suite 6F
New York, New York,
USA 10065-7334

Copyright © 2013 Q. V. Hunter
⚚⚚⚚

ISBN 978-2-9700889-0-5

This novel is entirely a work of fiction. The names, characters
and incidents portrayed in it, while at times based on
historical figures, are the work of the author's imagination.

Q.V. Hunter has asserted the right under the Copyright,
Design and Patents Act, 1988, to be identified as the author
of this work.

eyesandears.editions@gmail.com

1. Hunter, Q.V. 2. Circumcellions 4. Late Roman Empire 5.
Historical Fiction 6. Numidia 7. Action adventure 8. Early
Christians 9. Donatism 10. Espionage
I Title

TO OUR ROCK, 'P.'

Also by Q. V. Hunter

Mediterranean Sea

Icosium
Cisi
Rusuccuru
Iomnium
Tigisi
Rusubbicari
Centenarium
Tubusuptu
Ad Olkuam
Igilgili
Tucca
Chully
Ruskade
Hippo Regius
Muslubio
Horrea
Codamusa?
Tucca
Saltus
Bagatensis
Calama
Lepti
Satafi
Cuicul
Milev
Constantina
Thibilis
Zattara
Thagastis
Thuburslu N.
Ad Sava
Sertei
Stufis
Horrea
Idicra
Rotaria?
Thigillava
Cirta
Sila
Tigisis
Madaurus
MAURETANIA
SITIFENSIS
Med(iana)
Gemellas?
Sigus
N U M I D I A
Equizeto
Thamascani
Vartani
Nova
Petra?
Diana V.
Macomades
Aras
Zabi
Lamellaf
Thamallula
Iulian
Zaral
Gibba
Ad Centenarium
Ad Capsum
Lamiggiga
Macri
Collas
Lamasba
Lamsorti
Casae
Bagai
Aquae
Caesaris
Niovibus
Lambiridi
Lambaesis
Thamugadi
Masculi
Aquae
Flavianae
Vegesela
Shott el Hodna
Tubunae
Thacarata?
Cedias
Leges Maiores
Mesarfelta
Ubaza
Vescera
Thabudeos
Badias
Gemellae
Ad Malores
Ad Turres

Shott Melrhir

Neps?
(Nepte)

● Catholic bishopric
△ Dissident ('Donatist' bishopric)
▣ Catholic and 'Donatist' bishoprics

0 25 50 75 100 125 150 km
0 25 50 75 100 miles

LEO'S MAP

TABLE OF CONTENTS

Chapter 1, The Attack 1

Chapter 2, Wedding Crashers 17

Chapter 3, Mission to Martyrs 33

Chapter 4, Meeting Apodemius 45

Chapter 5, Leo's Briefing 55

Chapter 6, One Man Too Many 65

Chapter 7, Conversion 73

Chapter 8, Interrogation 85

Chapter 9, The Martyrs Prepare 95

Chapter 10, Another's Bride 109

Chapter 11, Kahina's Secret 123

Chapter 12, Leaps of Faith 139

Chapter 13, Almighty Bludgeons 153

Chapter 14, Leo's Secret 167

Chapter 15, Branding Irons 179

Chapter 16, A Priest from Heaven 193

Chapter 17, Sounding the Alarm 209

Chapter 18, Negotiations 221

Chapter 19, *Laudate Deum* 231

Chapter 20, A Servants' Entrance 243

Chapter 21, The Priest from Hell 255

Chapter 22, One Man Too Few 267

Chapter 23, *Agentes in Rebus* 277

Chapter 24, The Long Game 287

Places and Glossary 293

Historical Notes 297

Acknowledgements 301

About the Author 305

CHAPTER 1, THE ATTACK

—THE GARRISON SOUTH OF LAMBAESIS—

My people were mule traders. My mother would say, 'Mules are loaded with personality. Yes, don't laugh! They're intelligent. They know what they want. Don't ever pit your strength against a mule—you'll lose. Out-think him. Use a rope or a twitch to call his bluff. Stay calm and firm. Don't lose your temper and don't push too hard until you're sure you can make it stick.'

Why was she saying this, over and over? She'd look up from her mending basket and smile with sad eyes at her only son. 'Because you're my little mule. You're good and strong. You'll go far if you're careful. Don't be so stubborn. If someone's trying to out-think you, don't kick. Be a clever fighter, like your father.'

I always found that last phrase reassuring—but odd. I remembered my father, left behind in Numidia, as a stooped and silent man. Humbled by his trade and bankrupted by drought, he'd ended his days tending another man's herd.

My mother was wrong. Being stubborn pays off. Like that particular Wednesday when I was standing guard at headquarters in the last scorching rays of the North African sun. Since we'd first made camp next to some tumbling ruins left by soldiers centuries before us, holding your ground under that sun had become a matter of survival.

Even hardened battle veterans couldn't handle this heat because most of them had been transferred from the north.

Given their rank, I cringed when I saw them drink too much and then march out into the sun to exercise as if they were still on some leafy peacekeeping tour north of the Alps.

They gagged in the dust. Their bodies sprouted drops of sweat that became pools and then rivers before breakfast. After an hour of flexing their muscles and testing their weapons in the shimmering air, they'd shed their armor and head back to their tents for cover, dragging their weapons through the shifting sand.

The boredom down here was the worst. At least the engineers, the medics, the transport and laundry detail had chores to keep their minds off the desert. The infantry just went through the motions of routine, glancing hour after hour with sunken eyes at the horizon. They counted off the minutes until the slanting rays painted the Aurès slopes turmeric and a purple cool crept across the desert sand to their blistered feet.

We were into our third week on this mission. Some had learned to tie wet rags under their helmets or soak their armor padding in water. Some were still passing out from dehydration like dogs.

Me, I was stubborn. I was still standing stiff as ever that afternoon, facing that pitiless disk of fire as it sank behind the peaks. I was the only man the Commander trusted to guard his tent door. If I was sweating, I didn't let it get to me. I wouldn't flinch or faint, even if I was the last man between him and the enemy.

You might say I belonged to him, body and soul.

A stranger, a civilian, approached me across the parade ground with a light step, as if he'd spent the whole day in a cool marble bathhouse.

'I'm here to see the Commander.'

'Did they give you a pass at the perimeter? Thank you.'

I looked over his permission to enter our camp without scrutinizing him up and down, but I could take in a lot with a glance. When he handed over his pass, I spotted a year's worth of pay in gold rings. This middle-aged civilian was rich. He'd driven, not walked, from Theveste to our camp. His leather shoes were soft and polished. The linen covering his thickset shoulders was fresh and pressed, as if it were six in the morning, not sundown.

'I'll tell the Commander you're here. He's finishing up a meeting with the tribal elders.'

'A get-together to meet the locals?'

'That's right.' I gave him a respectful nod.

'Then I'll just wait over here.' He flattened his thinning reddish hair across a bronzed pate and took a stool in the shade and sighed, 'I've waited more than ten years.'

I kept my eyes trained on the neat rows of tents beyond the parade ground. Every army camp looked alike. It was no coincidence—our engineers were trained that way. Within a day, our unit could set up our small world behind its protective palisades, no matter where in the world they dragged us. Every soldier knew where to pitch his tent with his seven mates, where the medical officer Ari's infirmary stood, where the transport experts had stationed our vehicles and where our weapons would be repaired.

Our discipline was good but in the old days, they say, the troops were even faster—making camp in a morning and fighting new enemies by noon. Either way, by the end of Day One, camp felt like home. If we settled down without any hiccoughs, that left Day Two for finding out where the easy women were.

'I'll need your full name, if you don't mine.'

'Please, just say Leo. Tell him I brought my marbles. Go ahead, search me.' The stranger laughed a little, enjoying his private joke.

He'd been patted down for weapons at the entry and cleared again at the second perimeter before crossing the empty yard in front of the Commander's tent at the very center of a camp of over four hundred armed men. I patted him down as a formality. Security had to stay tight out here.

No marbles.

Three, maybe five minutes passed in silence. I kept my eyes locked forward, right hand crossed over to my weapon, back braced.

'Like it here, soldier?' He wanted to chat me up.

'Peaceful, sure.' I knew there was a famous poet who once said, 'Avoid people who ask too many questions. They're sure to be gossips.' I couldn't remember his name.

'So what's with all that gear? Isn't it uncomfortable in this weather?'

'Yes.'

'Not meant for down here.'

'I'm used to it. You know what they say. Safer on than off. I'd be dead by now without it.'

'You served with the Commander a long time?'

'Yes.' I kept my eyes trained on the row of tents stretching beyond the parade ground.

'Seen a lot of action together?'

I took a patient breath but didn't look him in the eyes. 'Yes.'

'Some of my dockworkers up at Rusicada—loading oil and clearing customs—they watched you men disembarking. They certainly noticed the Commander.' Leo cleared his throat. 'He's badly wounded? He didn't say anything in his letters.'

'He doesn't like to talk about it,' I cut the man off. It wasn't my place to tell this civilian that soldiers don't whine.

'No, he wouldn't.'

A cohort passed through the parade ground. They were on their way to change guard at the corners and gates that protected our camp on all four sides. Beyond our camp was an abandoned garrison of stone, brought down by an earthquake generations ago.

The visitor gazed at them as they moved past in formation. 'Give those boys a few more months in the high desert and their marching won't be so crisp.' Leo faced me square, 'But he always gives credit where it's due. Right, Marcus?'

'Absolutely.' He knew my name.

'You don't mind me asking, you are Marcus? I've heard a lot about you.'

'I'm sure there's nothing about me to hear.'

At this he threw his head back in laughter and rubbed his clean-shaven chin. 'Oh, I wouldn't say that. I certainly wouldn't say that.'

4

I didn't like being distracted on guard duty. I tried to focus on the pinkish streak of cloud hovering in the sky behind Leo's bench.

'I'm just doing my job. The field medics took pretty good care of him up there. Then he had home leave. He'll be all right here. It's quiet.'

'Well, certainly quieter than fighting Persians.' Leo nodded. 'Although that's hardly saying much.'

I knew this Leo's type—the chatty salesman who always bought low and sold high, a man who could afford the best plumbing for two baths a day, who could cross a town of swirling dust to wait uncomplaining at the compound gate for clearance and navigate the hundred yards of rough compound, all without creasing his Egyptian linen.

This kind of man greased palms to make sure his oil moved on to cargo boats before any other trader's, and passed his nights secure from attack behind his own high walls manned with private security.

We were the foot soldiers who kept his oil shipments safe from sabotage.

In short, this 'Leo' wouldn't give my commander any trouble—though that didn't mean he was harmless. I didn't know what he was selling but I wasn't sure I liked him. He knew too much and he acted like it.

'You know, your boss was the tallest and handsomest boy in our school.'

'Well, he's certainly still tall.' He was probing for sore spots, but I was a guard, not a diplomat.

The hubbub inside was breaking up at last. The tent flap opened and I took two neat steps to one side. Some dozen men trailed a cloud of sandalwood, jasmine and the fustiness of dried wool past the salesman and me. They adjusted their robes and replaced headdresses of gold braid or simple leather. Only the faintest trace of sweat laced the air—the plateau's dry air evaporated all the usual stinks.

Leo rose from his bench and nodded to one or two, even shook the hand of the eldest, then without further ceremony yelled, 'Atticus, show yourself!'

'Who's that?'

I interjected, 'A man named Leo—with marbles—to see you, Commander—'

'LEO!'

The Commander rushed past me. The two men embraced, arms flailing and pounding at the other's chunky backs, like two ageing bulls locking horns. The Commander pushed Leo back with hands firmly gripped on his biceps.

'So, show me your marbles, you old crook.'

'What have they done? Look at you.'

'Left me one good eye. All I need. I could still win back all those marbles you stole off me.'

To see the disfigurement and to be seen as so changed—I watched them and saw this was tough for both old friends. I would have laid down my life for the Commander, if it came to that, but it was many a day I recalled carrying him across my shoulders toward the triage tent wondering if he'd thank me afterwards.

The salesman forced himself to look straight at the ghastly changes to his childhood playmate's face—at the cauterized eye socket, the lid closed for good, the shiny burnt skin sewn down on the outskirts of a battle still raging, and the taut scar tissue where the medics had forced the last of the missing cheek to connect somehow with the front of the left ear lobe.

The handsome half of his face mocked the mutilated half with what was left of his dazzling smile, and he smiled at best he could now at Leo—it was what a career soldier did. I'd seen that determined smile on dozens of wounded men by now. I'd only been serving under the Commander as his body guard for a few years, but at nineteen, I'd already witnessed how battle left the field strewn with severed limbs, decapitations, and disembowelments. If you could manage a smile after a day of battle, it was your duty to do so.

The Commander showed Leo the stumps left of the last two fingers of his left hand. 'He got to my face first and then I tried to push the bastard away. You'd think I'd know better. Anyway, you've just met my good right hand here. Marcus, my oldest friend, Leo.'

'I guessed this was the boy. What did Laetitia say when she saw you?'

'My dear Leo, Laetitia's not just a well-born lady. She's an army wife. She said it had always been her curse to be married to a man prettier than her. Now she'll stop worrying about me flirting with some servant girl half her age.'

'Good for Laetitia! But I hope that doesn't stop you trying!' Leo winked.

The Commander winced and his razor-thin scar wrinkled into folds. 'Good isn't the half of it. She's no longer the child you kissed on our wedding day, Leo. I'm no longer her god. She's been sick for years now.'

'Sorry to hear that.'

'But in her suffering, she's discovered Christ! She's reborn, she says. Worse, she had discovered charity and sold off all her jewels, even that diamond I bought in the Jerusalem market after the eastern campaign. Go ahead. Laugh.'

'She was always a sweet girl.'

'I'm taking about "Charity." Fund-raisers, donations, and pledges for "The Lord." She's even tried to get me started.' The Commander made the Sign of the Cross with his good hand but Leo wasn't impressed.

'Nice try. Left side first, then right.'

'So, what'll we do tonight, Leo?'

'Stuff ourselves with lamb and vegetables, drink ourselves into the ground, and then who knows?' The chunky trader elbowed the Commander and glanced at his trousers, 'I trust they didn't wound anything essential?'

'Marcus, get us fresh drinks, will you?'

Chatting, the men settled down in two camp chairs at the back of the council tent. I couldn't believe it. The Commander— all tension, anger and frustration since his disfigurement—was a man transformed.

Making sure the parade ground outside was clear, I crossed to the Commander's private tent and the outdoor kitchen beyond, no more than a lean-to shaded against the burning sun.

Hamzah, the new local cook, was curled up and snoring, his bent bones slumped against a pole propping up the rough hemp sunroof. He wasn't even much of a cook but he knew the local markets. I suspected he took a steep commission off every fig and date.

'Squeeze them some juice. I'll take it in myself.' I ignored his annoyance at a break in his siesta. Either you understood military life or you didn't. Wherever we were posted, locals attached themselves like grinning parasites, passing from one menial job to another with no more weight or responsibility than a tumbleweed or desert breeze. I didn't want to be associated with that type. I was as low-ranked as Hamzah—actually lower—but I'd been with the Commander too long to consider myself anything less than a member of his family.

I was his man.

I waited and was gazing through the late afternoon at the traffic of men and vehicles, the usual evening business when I squinted again at the pounded ground in front of the headquarters.

A woman was hurrying toward the council tent. I took a deep breath and bracing my shoulders, I trotted to the closed flap of the council tent to bar any interruption. We didn't search women for weapons—neither at the gates nor even the second checkpoint—but only because village females never penetrated our camps.

Something was wrong with her gait, but I couldn't make out what. Perhaps she was hurt. Her hips hardly moved and she held herself strangely upright under her long, humble dress. I could just make out her dark eyes, large and determined, but little else underneath the folds of brown homespun.

Like most of her desert sisters, she wore a veil tight across her nose and mouth to keep out the dust.

Once she got within a few feet of me, I caught wafts of cloying perfume.

'I want to see your commander,' she said, catching her breath. 'I come from the northern hills. I must see him.'

My boyhood dialect was rusty, but good enough. 'He's finished for the day. Come back tomorrow.'

'There's an emergency in our village. People are dying. They sent me. I've been running since just after midday.'

'Sickness?' I stepped back by instinct and gripped the lucky amulet underneath my shirt as if it could protect me against contagion. It was a weak, childish gesture and I flushed when she noticed.

'Not sickness. No. More secret, more violent. I *must* speak with him. Lives in danger. Just five minutes with him—or later he'll regret he didn't listen to me.'

I detected the same guttural inflections my long-abandoned father used to make.

Maybe because of that familiar accent, I wavered. How had the Commander put it? 'I'm taking you home, Marcus. You'll be my spare eyes and hands more than ever before. It's a lucky break for both us, isn't it? You back at last among your mother's people and me off the battlefield for the first time in ten years!'

This from a man who lived for battle, a man trying to make light of being shunted off with a shabby border command into an imperial backwater. Paunchy senators who'd never lost so much as a drop of blood for the Empire and politicians chortling over their long lunches in the shadow of the capitol building had questioned our Commander's strategy, even pointing to his wounds as proof of failure.

'Just five minutes,' the woman pleaded. 'I've got to be home before the curfew falls. Please.'

A respectable peasant woman couldn't spend the night in a strange town alone, no matter how urgent her message. Surely she knew someone in Lambaesis or Theveste? A vendor's wife? A cousin? Her sweet perfume pierced my nostrils. I tried not to inhale this sickly sweet cloud. Maybe I was just too worn out. I'd been on guard duty some fourteen hours now. No one else took my detail.

I decided to shake her off and clear her out—accent or no.

'Tomorrow. Come back tomorrow.'

'No!

'What's happening out here?' The Commander's head appeared under the tent flap, the last orange daylight catching his 'good side.' For a moment, I remembered him as he looked only three years ago. His half-smile shining in the blindingly low sun seemed to soothe the excited intruder.

'This woman says she has an urgent message from the foothills, Commander.'

'Come in.' He disappeared to rejoin Leo and together they would hear her out.

Later, I relived the next few seconds in my mind like separate sketches drawn in the sand. First, I glanced at the woman's calloused heel passing me. Her feminine sandal didn't match the bunions and thick, hard sole. Then a hairy wrist emerged from under the folds of thick skirt and I just caught the glint of a silver herder's knife soaring up, up, up and swinging around toward the Commander's sunburnt throat.

Animal instinct moved faster than reason. I lurched at the peasant's shoulders and ripped off the face veil, head scarf and shawl to reveal a rough-shaven leer. I wrapped my bare forearm tight around the man's collarbone and shoulders. Now I smelled his fear. I had my army-issue dagger already unsheathed with my right hand clenched over the hilt and then, I reached around his neck and pulled hard down and across, even as his steely fingers fought to loosen my grip on his shoulders.

My blade slid deep and hard across his voice box to the back of his jaw, the rasp of metal scraping bone followed by an explosion of blood. His knife dropped from his hand.

I let the man fall, twitching, to the pounded dirt floor. I kept one boot on his chest while we watched his life drain away.

'Guards! Alarm!' I shouted and kept shouting it until I heard the horns start up outside and the pounding of hundreds of feet.

'Get down! Get down!' Lieutenant Barbatio was yelling over the scream of signals outside. 'To the perimeter! Move your asses!'

'I couldn't see him in the shadow,' Commander Gregorius coughed out. He tried to stand up straight, but his maimed hand lost its grip off the edge of the primitive table we used as his desk. He stumbled and fell back.

Leo helped him up again, covering his own shirt in the Commander's blood.

'Damn, Leo, I should have seen it coming. Before, I would've seen it coming . . . I *should* have seen it coming . . .'

Leo ignored the Commander's anguish. 'Thanks, Marcus. I see why you come highly recommended.'

'It was just my duty.'

We three stood together, chests heaving with relief, watching the killer's blood pooling at our feet and listening to the camp go on full alert outside. The Commander was holding his neck. Blood was seeping through his fingers.

In the far distance, over the horns, I heard chanting. It was so vague at first. It could have been no more than an imagined elegy riding the breezes for the madman whose spirit was leaching into the soil beneath my boots.

But the Commander had heard it, too. 'Strange song,' he gasped through his pain. 'Marcus, you'll have to take this out of here.' He kicked the body with his boot. 'Get Hamzah to clean up this mess.'

I shouted for help. Footsteps marched on the hard-packed ground near our tent. The chanting drew nearer.

'Where's the problem here?' It was a short surveyor named Linus who reached us first. I didn't take offense when he stared right through me. It was the order of things.

'An attempt on the Commander's life,' Leo said.

'Who was manning the gates?' The Commander sounded angry and shaken and I understood why—not by any attempt on his life, which was daily fare in battle, but by his failure to see danger coming at him from his left side. He could accept disfigurement, but not incapacity.

'Commander, there's a procession—'

'Speak up, Linus! I can't hear you over that damned noise.'

The rhythmic singing had risen into a chant of hundreds of voices.

'That's it. There's a mob outside the barrier. Their leaders are demanding a body.'

Leo jerked around. 'What are they singing, soldier?'

'I can't make it out. They're a rough bunch. They say we're withholding their friend's body. Is that it?' Linus pointed with his measuring stick at the corpse's blood cutting rivulets through the dirt toward his neat shoes.

'I was afraid of this.' Leo turned back to us. 'Give them the body, fast.'

The Commander was still holding his neck and the blood flow hadn't eased off. I'd been too slow. The assassin's knife had more than just grazed him.

'Tell the doctor,' I shouted to the departing Linus.

'There's no way they're getting that body while I'm in command,' the Commander said to Leo. 'What's going on, anyway? Who are these people who already know what happened in here? How can they know he's dead? If it hadn't been for Marcus, that would be me lying on the floor.'

Leo lowered his voice. 'I'm telling you, hand the body over.' I could hardly hear his warning for the creepy wailing beyond the camp's fence.

The Commander struggled to keep his balance. No! I'm in charge here. I'll burn it right in front of them!'

'Get a medic here, NOW!' I shouted across the parade ground. 'Sit down, Commander.' I practically had to push him into a chair. This oil trader should know when to shut up and leave but he kept insisting.

'It wasn't an attempt on your life, my old friend.'

'You were standing right here!'

'No,' Leo said. 'This man wanted *you* to kill *him*. And the people outside that wall expected his death. I came here to warn you. I just didn't think they'd move so fast.'

All the bonhomie and self-assurance faded from the oil trader's expression. 'Those are *Circumcellions* out there. Thousands of them sit out in the desert beyond the town walls. They plot and feed harvesters' discontent like festering rats run amok on a rubbish tip. But they're smarter than rats, my old friend. They are organized militants spreading terror across every village and transport route under your occupation.

'What do they want?'

'To purify the province of your so-called polluting troops. To govern it with an intolerant fanaticism that allows no room for us. Listen to them out there. Listen to that chanting.'

We helped the Commander steady himself and led him to the tent door to wait for medical help. Hundreds of troops were dropping their chores to trot down the tent alleys to get a view of the outer perimeter demarcating the camp from the old ruins in the sweeping sands beyond.

I strained my ears through the cacophony. Like an image coming back into focus after staring too hard at the sun, the words of the chant coalesced into, 'Praise be to God.'

'I don't understand.' The Commander still held his neck with his half-hand but blood escaped the stumps of his missing fingers. The first shock had subsided, and now he grimaced with pain. The assassin's knife has sliced deeper than we realized.

'Didn't your headquarters brief you?'

'My orders are to monitor the southern edge of the province, fend off Berbers, and expand the pacified territory. You know, Leo, bring them rule of law, road building, schools and water systems, *civilization*. Small beer after real fighting, body by body.'

Leo's disbelief burst out in a cynical laugh.

The Commander looked like he would bust an artery. 'You've got no right to look down your nose at me like that! If I do my job, the markets are stable and all your damn oil sails out of port on time. You're the one making a fortune, Leo, not me.'

'Well, your bastard generals conveniently forgot to mention one thing.'

'What's that?' The Commander's face was draining to the color of dead ashes.

'You can explain it later,' I interrupted. I slung the Commander's good arm over my shoulder and started with him for Ari's tent. 'Can I have some help here, dammit?' I couldn't tell if anyone heard me over that racket of deafening chant.

Leo half-trotted, half-waddled after us. 'They've assigned you to clean up the West's hotbed of religious suicide martyrs.'

'Suicide *what*?'

'Somebody get a stretcher?' I bellowed down the next alley of tents. We'd crossed half the length of the entire camp when I saw the doctor hurrying toward us on his bandy legs along a row of tents. He carried his kit of painkillers, vicious-looking tools and boiled bandages. Two runners brought up a stretcher right behind.

We settled the wounded man into the surgical tent, upwind of the usual camp stinks and the Greek got to work disinfecting the wound.

Leo wasn't giving up. 'Return the body to the mob.'

'I refuse,' the Commander gagged back at him. 'Burn that body where those buggers can see it. Marcus, take my order to Barbatio. I'll be all right now.'

Lieutenant Barbatio was a huge man, born next to the Drava River. He and an auxiliary dragged the corpse within view of the palisades to give the chanting horde an eyeful of their 'martyr' for themselves.

Screams of recognition pierced our ears but to me they all looked alike, dressed in hooded rags and robes of brown or black. Then the horde abandoned words for a vibrating animal shriek that chilled my blood. I saw at least two of them drop faint from excitement but most of them vented their mounting fury with more foul curses and threatening fists.

We avoided their eyes. It took ages for Linus and his fellow surveyor Lepidus to muster enough firewood from the sparse brush within our barricades. They were used to finding sources of fodder and water for the camp and marking out perimeters, not whisking up instant pyres.

A select band of tall, hooded leaders stepped up close to the gates and intoned, 'Masgava, Masgava.'

Glancing nervously at the throng behind the wooden posts, Linus fanned the flames to get the fire going until the kindling took. Sparks scattered in the rising breeze across the corpse's peasant dress and flames licked his toes and sandals.

Lieutenant Barbatio ordered the rest of the gaping troops back to their routines. Half a dozen of us kept watch by the pyre. We stole uneasy glances at the wailing peasants beyond the ditch.

'Listen to them,' Linus muttered. 'They're capable of anything.' So many hundreds of crazed vagrants made him tremble. The Commander said no one was better than Linus at calculating barrier lengths but he was indeed very short for a soldier. Recruitment standards weren't so strict these days.

'Bastard infidels!' we could make out. 'Lord, take our servant Masgava! Blessed be his martyred soul!'

Their hungry expressions twisted with loathing for us. There were fewer than five hundred of us and maybe seven hundred of them. Our sentries had turned from curious to wary. They braced themselves along the entire length of the outer ditch in case the demonstrators tried to breach the gap. At least our men were properly armed. Their side brandished nothing but clubs of gnarled olive wood.

The creepy chanting died down as our signaler from the island of Britannia, Felix, blew 'lights out.' The hooded rabble stayed where they were, huddled against the desert chill moving down from the mountains. To a man, they didn't take their eyes off the pyre as the would-be murderer they called 'Saint Masgava' roasted down to charcoal and grease.

Barbatio trebled the evening guard.

I had too much to do the rest of the evening, especially with the Commander to nurse all night, to linger near the pyre. I headed back to check on his evening meal and bedding and then laid my thin bedroll just inside the flap of his private tent. I crossed the yard back to the headquarters' council tent. With Hamzah's sullen help, I finished preparing it for tomorrow's regular officers' meeting. It was a mess, but we got most of it neatened up.

Then I remembered. The wise man who warned against people who asked too many questions was Horatius.

What was Horatius trying to tell me about that oil trader Leo? And why did Leo give off the air of knowing more about me than I knew about myself? There was nothing to know. I just did my job.

Hamzah kept on sprinkling and raking fresh dirt over the soiled floor. I straightened the furniture and glanced at the report that should have been dispatched by sunset up to the officers in Lambaesis. Blood had spurted all over the desk, ruining the pages. There was no way I could salvage anything from that smeared mess.

Some other officer would have to copy out and update the report. Through the blood, the date was barely legible—*Dies*

Iovis Non. Ian. MXI, January 5, 1011 on our old-style imperial calendar.

I'd ask Albanus, our aristocratic trainee deputy, to supervise the secretaries in the copying of a new report. I could be determined as a mule, but no matter how I phrased it, it was better coming from Albanus. They would never take an order from a slave like me.

CHAPTER 2, WEDDING CRASHERS

—ONE WEEK LATER—

Thanks to a diet of gentle chickpea stew and Ari's linen bandages soaked in acetum, the Commander's neck wound closed up clean. Army food was decent enough—meat, bread and veg every day, but more important, our soldiers got the best medical care in the Roman world.

I'm not saying it was always *easy* to watch Ari work, but I spent hours of my free time in his tent. Old and young, Ari and I were both slaves using education to advance ourselves.

I was fascinated by what I learned from the hardworking Greek. I once witnessed a tall blond cavalryman stumble into surgery with an arrow gone straight into his head just a whisker from his right eye. I would have sworn that eye was doomed, if not the rider. But Ari broke off the shaft and told us to flip the victim over.

'But you can't see anything from the rear,' I said, helping his medical assistant remove the armor and settle the man back down on his stomach.

'You'll see, young Marcus, you'll see...Where are you from, soldier?'

'Noricum,' the wounded man mumbled.

The doctor nodded, 'Good, he's still conscious.' He prodded around for a minute or two and then started humming. He made a slit at the base of the man's skull with a razor, and I saw the enemy's iron barb gleaming up at us through the blood. Damned if Ari didn't take his pincers and just pull that barb and half the shaft clean out of the soldier's head through the back of his neck.

I'll never forget the expression on that soldier's face as he felt the remainder of the arrow dragging its way through his brains. To my surprise, the cavalryman not only survived, but thrived. I saw him just the other day by the stables with hardly a scar on his face.

Of course, most of our casualties weren't that lucky. But Ari's team did their best. If you'd caught it under our eagle standard, the medics didn't care whether you were a Roman officer like the Commander or a barbarian recruit. It sure didn't matter to the soldiers lying on the surgical table that Ari himself was nothing more than property of the imperial government.

'Another beauty mark to show Laetitia, eh, Marcus?' the Commander asked a week later, fingering Ari's stitches clotted with blackened scabs around his neck.

The sun was low in the east, lighting up the Commander's 'good side' and he was in a mood to match. The newly installed Provincial Governor Silvester had asked Leo to convey an invitation to our men to come into town for a wedding. Governor Silvester wanted to show us off—reinforcements to bulk up the remnants of the once-great Legio III Augusta who now lived like suburban commuters in town with their families, turning up at the military base only for exercises and clerical work.

Leo, or Leontus Longus Flavius as he was to the wider world, had delivered the governor's invitation to our camp headquarters in person, adding his own comment, 'Silvester is nervous. The last governor, Taurinus, got recalled for blundering with these locals. So get ready for a shameless bit of public relations. Dress *formal*.'

The Commander tossed the invitation back at Leo. 'I'm not marching four hundred men in full kit through the sand just to carouse at a wedding of *nouveau riche* farmers.'

'Careful, my friend. You're talking to one of those *nouveau riche* farmers.'

'You don't fool me, Leo. You're wasted in this backwater.'

I caught Leo smile from behind the Commander's blind side. 'Oh, I keep busy.'

In the end, we all looked pretty armored up, weapons polished with sand, helmets buffed and clean tunics and northern-style riding trousers.

Our cavalrymen were already mounted and lined up in the purple dawn spreading across the sand around the crumbling ruins of Hadrian's abandoned garrison nearby.

Over the abandoned walls next to our tents, a single archway had survived the decades' winds. Its engraving read, *Iterum Pia, Iterum Vindex*, 'Faithful Again, Avenger Again.' It referred to a century ago when the Legio IIIA had backed a local governor against the Emperor himself. The legion was disbanded in disgrace and even though it got reconstituted after fifteen years, the Third Augustan had never returned to the fighting force of old.

But our boys were fresh from real battle up on the other side of the *Mare Nostrum*. They joked and jostled at the gate with impatience, their pockets and purses jingling with spending money. Reinforcing the old Third Augustan was a choice posting as far as they were concerned and few of these soldiers would be returning north when their stint was up, however intense the heat.

The Empire had cannily dotted all of Numidia with veterans' colonies. Lambaesis, Theveste, Thurburbo Maius and Cuicul—they were all were peopled with the descendants of soldiers who'd taken their pensions in three acres for a farm to share with a local woman.

The morning air was still cool enough for steady peacetime travel in light armor. We hoped to reach Lambaesis before the real heat hit. Occupying army or no—at the other end we expected a welcome laced with wine and feisty Roman colonial girls who, unlike desert women in veils, knew what lonely fighters liked.

We were still half an hour now from our destination and the sun was halfway to its zenith when I heard one of the men riding behind me mutter, 'Will you look at that!'

We were moving out of the brush-swept sands and into cultivated fields. Thousands of other Romans had come before us. The Legio III Augusta had sweated to build these roads and garrisons for Emperor Hadrian himself just over a century before. Those soldiers never went home and we could see how some of them had been downright lucky.

Soon we were passing imposing estates anchored by whitewashed villas dripping with bougainvillea that glittered in the morning dew. Somehow in our exhaustion on the march south from the coast we hadn't taken in this neighborhood, but now our northern auxiliaries gawped at North Africa's luxury—miles and miles of olive orchards and wheat fields—sprawling on both sides of the state highway.

Closer to Lambaesis, we passed even grander two-storied mansions protected against Berber raids by fortified walls and towers.

'You sure don't see that up in Lugdunum!'

'These bastards must be rolling in gold.'

Thousands of farmworkers—whether blackened by sun or dirt wasn't clear—worked the orchards and fields marked out by regular irrigation ditches fanning out to the horizon.

Even I didn't remember it like this. When I left as a little boy, this part of the country was for grazing and mule breeding—not even arable. But then I hadn't lived in Africa for more than a decade and even when I was here, I was only an illiterate, scrawny brat mending harnesses and hauling water buckets for my father.

What had happened to the herds and the barley of my early days? That's what farmers fell back on when the wheat crop failed. Everywhere we looked today we saw cisterns, basins, and irrigation—with wheels, buckets, gears and miles of canals pushing farther and farther south. It looked like the markets up north were trying to suck unlimited oil and grain right out of the desert under our feet.

And African landlords were defying Nature's stingy rainfall to deliver just that.

I kept my mouth shut, but I knew what was running through the minds of our envious fighters—that Roma's lazy welfare rats ate up the riches that we were protecting down here with our own skins. Any soldier knew North Africa fed the Western empire's layabouts while Egypt fed the East. But to listen to the ranks grumbling away this morning, some of these boys had never considered that somebody actually got paid for it at this end.

'These are fucking fortresses. What are they so scared of?'

The last couple of miles of our march were a stretch as we mounted one slope after another for the cooler air of the terraced foothills underneath the Aurès peaks.

Soon we could spot Lambaesis' triumphal arches catching the sun about a quarter of a mile away. I was looking forward to seeing Leo again today. I'd warmed to him since our first encounter because so far, at least, the trader didn't treat me like a lowly slave. He not only looked me in the eye—he sometimes looked at me longer than necessary.

At times I had asked myself, what was he looking at? What was he looking for?

Ordinary Roman soldiers liked kicking around a *volo* like me but they weren't the worst. It wasn't like the old days, with Romans and 'barbs' in separate legions. We were a mixed bunch now. When the Commander wasn't around, nothing was more fun to some illiterate barbarian bruiser to abuse somebody even lower—a slave volunteer.

It was ironic—as long as I guarded the Commander, he protected me.

Felix pulled his horse up next to mine and sounded the notes that would direct our perspiring column in a switch over to parade cadence. He was our youngest *cornicen* and he felt his junior status too keenly.

'Someday I'd like to sound something more important than a parade,' he said to me. I nodded but knew that the likelihood of a major battle for the Legio IIIA had died in the desert decades ago.

'Never seen action?' I asked him.

'Not yet.' He was a recruit from western Gallia, his pale cheeks freckling in the sun even as I watched. 'But if that time ever comes, you'll hear my horn over all the din.'

He reined in and fell back as the lower officers tightened up our line before we passed through a cemetery west of town.

A welcome party filtered out through Lambaesis' famous arches. There were about thirty of them, all in clean whites hemmed with embroidered bands or fancy trim and topped by various sunhats and caps. Festive music inside the town walls melded with the unimaginative pounding of our drummers.

Trumpets blew down the line. Pennants drooped in the sun as the sergeants shouted their command.

'Halt!'

Even the angle of our eagle standard looked a little off-center in the shimmering warmth. The adjutants trotted up and down the trailing column to bring our formation into order.

Hundreds of townsfolk, 'Romans' who'd never seen the Tiber, peered at us over the wall and through the gates. They looked friendly enough. We didn't expect trouble from landlords and traders—taxpayers to a dog.

But surely word had got out that a local hood had tried to murder the new commander. What if some of the killer's grimy friends lay in wait for us, hidden down the alleyways, right now?

The Commander adjusted his green felt dress hat from Pannonia, a forgivable break with form. He'd left his round metal ridge-helmet back at camp. He tipped the jaunty headgear at an angle across his face, shading his shiny scars and blank eye socket. How would the people of Lambaesis react to their first good look at their disfigured protector in his light Gallic woolen cloak fastened with a German filigree brooch?

Shining in glory, Gregorius had survived Aquileia in 340 leading troops to defend the Emperor Constans against his elder brother Constantine II's greedy land grab. Medals and praise had rained down on him and the handsome Gregorius earned the prefecture of Italy.

But that's how war goes. You can survive the big battle, keeping tight shield formation, watching your cavalry wings and signaling clear changes for the divisions for days on end. Then four years later, you find yourself bleeding to death on a stretcher on the dangerous side of the Rhône. You're mutilated for life just because you walked into the ambush set by some half-wild forest dweller cursing the Empire through his greasy beard.

Lieutenant Barbatio gave the signal and Felix's horn sent us threading four abreast through the first arch dedicated to Commodus, its colored marble base ringed with carvings depicting all the wonderful things that the famously vicious emperor never really did.

Then ducking our heads, we negotiated the other arch for Commodus' successor, Septimus Severus. Not that Severus was any Pompey, but he'd scrambled through a bloody civil war to found his own dynasty. He'd decreed that soldiers could marry. And best of all, he was born in Leptis Magna, Numidia's main port, so Severus was a local boy made good.

Lambaesis was little more than two hundred years old—a smart new town that mushroomed over Trajan's permanent Roman army fort.

We marched past theatres, bathhouses and military burial clubs, all built by the early settlers from the Legio IIIA. I smiled as we crossed one straight junction after another in our progression to the central forum They could build all the fancy townhouses, temples and theatres they liked, but underneath this town any soldier could make out the telltale grid of an army base as regular as those of the barebones tent camp we'd just left.

About a quarter of a mile beyond, we could see the solid two-story arched headquarters that housed the archives, armory and engraved pagan dedications of the original Roman pioneer soldiers. Its sleepy offices housed no one but bureaucrats now.

We positioned our ranks around the spacious forum in front of the Aesculapius temple converted to a Christian basilica not so long ago. Under the garlands of wedding flowers looping across the proscenium in honor of today's fun, the Greek letters, *Chi Rho*, standing for the Christ of Constantine's new religion looked freshly carved.

'Greetings, people of Lambaesis! Welcome friends of the wedding celebrants!'

This new governor wasn't much to look at. Silvester was a small pale man with squinty blue eyes and a paunch. His aquiline nose was blistered and peeling. He squinted at us across the forum with the air of a man waiting for a rescue litter. A slave holding his gold-tasseled umbrella scuttled behind him as he threaded through the crowds of local bigwigs but the sun protection was too late for the back of his neck, already burnt a painful maroon. You could see the way he grimaced in the bright glare that so far into his new post, he didn't much like Africa—no matter how rich the pickings.

'Keep a cool drink waiting for me,' Commander muttered as I helped him unfasten his dress cloak. Now Gregorius, his officers and even Barbatio greeted the Lambaesis elders and then the beaming bridal party in turn. Finally—with as much pagan enthusiasm as Gregorius could muster—he greeted the two imperial Christian priests who would preside over the coming vows.

With the heavy cloak in my arms, I waited some fifty feet away, but even from a distance, these clergymen looked a jittery duo. The tall one with receding hair and high wide cheekbones kept clutching at his crucifix and pulling at his robes. His very short and bald clerical partner twisted his hands together like an old woman kneading bread.

You had to wonder what made those fellows so nervous within the walls of a thriving colony like Lambaesis. Religious tolerance had been official policy ever since the late Emperor Constantine's conversion. Two years ago, the boy emperor Constans had banned public pagan sacrifice, so at least this share of the empire—from his own Africa to his late brother's spread of Hispania, Britannia and Gallia—was supposedly just one big happy Christian family now—with the pagans free to continue their rituals, minus the sheep guts.

I strained from behind the Commander's horse to see if Leo was anywhere among the hundreds of well-oiled grandees lining the forum steps. I caught sight of him just as he crossed the forum to join the lucky few hundred heading into the basilica's cool marble interior.

Leo caught the Commander's shoulder. Gregorius rolled his good eye and smiled hello. He was bracing himself for a long hour of Christian mumblings. He'd confided to me once that the Nazarene's cult lacked all the ritual, blood sacrifice or propitious gestures that made religious observance worthwhile.

I saw Barbatio take a swig of liquor from a flask hidden under his sword-belt as he followed Commander Gregorius over the threshold.

Then to my surprise, Leo turned away from the basilica, trotted back down the steps and disappeared into the crowd.

The last to go inside was the bridal couple. The groom faced the townspeople and lifted the hand of his skinny bride hidden under her flame-colored veil to signal their consent to the onlookers. At least the Christians weren't changing that hallowed routine. We all cheered as the nervous youngsters disappeared into the dark recesses to get hitched.

'Looking forward to the reception, Marcus?'

Here was Leo now, standing at my side with two lively twin daughters followed by their maids. As a slave, I didn't dare scrutinize any of these females too closely. I kept my gaze averted. But I'd noticed that the girls were just coming of age— twin pixies with heads bristling with the same crinkly hair as the remaining strands on Leo's pate.

They kept fiddling with the jeweled combs holding up their 'grown-up' braids and curls. They wore exactly matching sets of gold and garnet earrings. Even when it came to family gifts, it seemed, the trader Leo only bought wholesale.

'Yes. The men expect a pretty good knees-up.'

'And they'll get it, Marcus! See the wine vats under that sunshade in the pavilion down at that end? That's for you boys.' He leaned out of his daughters' earshot, 'And the cheaper houses are down that street, over there, behind the council building.' He winked at me. 'A few *nummi* is the going rate. Ask for Abelia. Say I sent you.'

'I'll keep a watch over the Commander. But I'll let my friends know about Miss Honeysuckle.'

'Of course.' His eyes narrowed as he took me in. Was Leo running a character check on me?

'Where will you be?' I asked him.

'I'll be with the happy taxpayers, over there.'

He pointed at the opposite side of the long rectangular forum where a couple hundred well-fed matrons squatted on stools in the shade. Their heavy-set husbands chatted in bunches behind them next to slaves with fans, satchels and bags of sweetmeats at the ready.

These fat merchants and their wives looked exactly like the kind of distant relatives and business associates slapped onto the bottom of a long wedding reception list. I saw one little girl about eight or nine staring goggle-eyed at our imposing ranks. When I winked at her, she frowned and concentrated on a tiny pet rabbit sitting in her lap and leashed to her wrist with a red ribbon.

Later, when I revisited that peaceful scene, I remembered the mingling sounds—the chitchat across the forum over the occasional hum of religious song coming from inside the basilica and above all, the buzzing of insects flitting from piles of donkey dung to the platters of honeyed meats. The caterers weren't exactly quiet either, shouting orders to the servers and trundling heavy *amphorae* across the polished stones of the colonnade arcade.

Just when some of the guests seemed ready to head home from impatience, cymbals crashed from inside the basilica giving the wedding musicians outside their cue.

The wedding celebrants poured back into the forum, the pair of priests running alongside. The two patriarchs of the conjoined clans beamed and waved to their constituents.

We all looked on, some of us with maybe a little wistfulness. Sure, soldiers could get married now. These were modern times and the law had changed. A foot soldier might find himself a mate, a good woman who'd trail after him. When he fell in battle, she might even pay for an engraved burial stone—but their union could never be top-drawer affair like this one.

For slaves—forget it. We just lived through others, like teenagers mooning over some celebrity gladiator. Right then, I felt as excited as anybody else for the trembling, happy pair.

The Commander emerged from the church in conversation with Governor Silvester. A cheer went up around the forum—

more for the spigots of wine that were being opened than for the poor bride with her groom who would untie the ceremonial 'Hercules knot' in her tunic belt later this evening.

Of course, none of us in uniform knew these families, but compared to fighting fellow Romans in a civil war between Constantine's spoiled imperial brats, our ranks were happy to do their duty today. I spotted Felix, the great spiral of his *buccina* tucked under one arm, heading with his mates for the food baskets piled high behind the bathhouse. Ari and his medical orderlies were washing their hands at the public fountain before tucking into skewered lamb kidneys from a roaring spitfire beyond the forum in the amphitheater pit.

Hamzah and I pushed and elbowed our way through hundreds of servants until we had got packets of meat, some fruit, and drink for the Commander and the senior officers. As usual I couldn't count on that lazy fart. One minute, Hamzah was stuffing his own face and the next, he shoved our collection of snacks into my arms and dashed off in a hail of shouts toward a rough-looking town fellow he knew.

The newlyweds presided at the head table in front of the tall basilica doors. I positioned myself behind Deputy Albanus' chair where I could back up the Commander's bad side and scan the crowd for troublemakers. The party was well under way. It looked as though there might be food even for the lowliest of us once our betters had feasted. I'd pinned my eye on the pastries stuffed with raisins and lamb.

'Odd music,' I overheard Gregorius shout to Silvester.

'Local tastes,' the governor shook his head. 'It's like their food, too full of this fashionable new Persian spice. Everything is yellow as monkey shit.'

I cocked an ear toward the band, picking up some insistent bass running below the tinny horns and snap of the drums. They made a thrumming that collided badly with the jolly marriage song. The carousing locals didn't notice. After all, it was their music.

I was wrong. The wine was running freely and already the guests were too 'happy' to notice, but those of us on duty weren't the only ones stone cold sober. That strange drumming wasn't coming from the band and the musicians knew it damn well. A few lowered their drumsticks. Leo and three or four other men rose from their stools and hurried toward the head table.

Then we all heard it plain—that same chilling chant of the threatening ghouls outside the camp ditch howling for the attacker's corpse. Their song rose, louder and louder until even the drunkest revelers paused and turned from their partying.

We heard a scream at the far end of the forum, then two, and then a dozen.

A wave of hooded creatures in their stinking rags broke through a seated wedding group. They overturned a caterer's stall, sending melons and pastries flying. Like dark pus bursting from an infected wound, they roared into the forum, heading straight for the tables under the temple proscenium.

Gregorius gave the attack signal and Felix raised his horn, but it was hardly needed. Some of the men had already tossed aside their grub and grabbed a position. Others were racing back for their horses to clear the crowd.

My job was to protect the Commander's weak side, running with him as he dashed toward his horse harnessed over near the baths. He threw himself into the saddle and rode, sword swinging, headlong into the snake's head of the column of rioters. Riding above the attackers, he was safe enough. I instinctively turned and searched for Leo and his little girls and maids. They were speeding into the basilica with dozens of others for safety, but the foul demonstrators were close on their heels.

I heard the cries of people stumbling into the lethal reach of the rioters' clubs and falling on the pavement with smashed faces and broken limbs. At a blow from a Circumcellion, the bridegroom fell from the steps, one eye knocking out and hanging from his beardless face. His bride already lay motionless, a heap of flaming silk in the shadow of the tall basilica door.

Within seconds, the stench of blood rose from the hot stones around us. I raced forward.

—THE VEILED ASSASSIN—

The dark cold of the church's interior sent a chill up my sweating back. Leo was sheltering his twins behind the wide column of a side altar along with their weeping, cowering attendants. I threw him my *spatha*, knowing its length could keep back one or two Circumcellions at a time. I drew my short dagger to back him up, but the horde storming into the basilica right behind me raced past our group. They rushed over to the side altars, bashing heads off statues and defacing exquisite carved wooden guardrails, but ignoring us.

They were aiming now straight for the two panicked priests. The tall priest braced himself and clenched his defiant jaw in front of the main altar still draped with gold cloths and fresh flowers. The small priest had armed himself rather ridiculously with an incense-burner on a chain, swinging it wildly to defend the baptismal font, with its various accessories, and the gilt cabinet housing the chalice and relics.

It was too late to save the bigger man. I was used to the skilled thrust of the trained soldier, even the furious wild stabs of the barbarian warrior, but not the way this gang set on the priest ten against one like a pack of animals, their senseless bashing turning his head to a pulpy mass.

I took up a position in front of the smaller priest. The howling attackers seized gold ceremonial bowls from the altar and threw them at us. I crouched low and flinging myself at the knees of their leader just as he raised his club, I ducked and shoved my *pugio*'s blade between one testicle and his thigh. He staggered and dropped his club.

I leaped backwards and kicked him in the stomach, sending his flailing into the path of the hooded fiends right behind him. I had held them off long enough for the priest to dash for safety into the inner recesses of the basilica with the chalice.

Leo was coming up the main aisle to attack from behind. He peeled off two before they realized the trader was there. We might have had the rest of them trapped, but to our astonishment, the Circumcellions lifted up their dying and made straight past Leo for the basilica door, shouting, 'We have new martyrs! *Laudate Deum*! Praise be to God! *Laudate Deum*!'

Outside similar cries of so-called victory rose up from the hooded killers. Leo and I dashed after them but already the rioters had swooped up their dead under the continuing attack of our men. Like sinister footpads, the cowards melted down Lambaesis' empty alleys, dodging our horses and hiding in secret places beyond our reach.

I stood in the forum, taking in the carnage. A girl a little younger than Leo's daughters lay bleeding a few feet away from where I stood. Her hair was mashed in, wet with blood and flaked with white bits of shattered skull. A red ribbon was tied to her wrist. From under the long hem of festive tunic, I saw a ball of trembling white fur. It was the gawking child I'd smiled at before the festival began.

Perhaps Ari could save her, if not the dozens of others lying lifeless and draining white onto the pavement all around us.

I lifted the child up in my arms, pet rabbit and all. One arm dangled away. The bone was broken and jutting right out of her skin.

She was still breathing.

I rushed with her toward the stall where Ari and his assistants were tending to dozens of wailing citizens. Survivors ran for hot water and bandages under his calm but imperious orders. I felt the little girl's life ebbing out of my arms and shouted for the crowd to let me through.

Someone pulled at my shoulder. Annoyed, I glanced back.

It was the short bald priest.

'You saved my life. God bless you,' he said.

'My duty, Father. Sorry, I'm in a hurry.'

He made a slow Sign of the Cross over the girl's brow and shook his head.

'Give little Tasia to me.'

I looked down at her face. She had stopped breathing. I was no help to her now. I handed her over into his outstretched arms.

'And those bastards call *us* impure. 'You're our only hope, Soldier. Wipe out this madness. It's not Christianity. It's— it's . . .' He fumbled under Tasia's limp body and extended his hand, with a thick and furtive grip, to give me a token of thanks.

These Christians were famous for ignoring social barriers. That's probably why their churches were filling up so fast. Even so, I was touched that an educated man of God would shake the bloodied hand of a lowly slave. He walked back to the basilica with his pitiful bundle.

Something in my hand moved. He'd just given me the baby rabbit.

CHAPTER 3, MISSION TO MARTYRS

—CAMP HEADQUARTERS—

'You want me to give you a *what*?' The Commander stared over the leftovers of his breakfast at his two visitors—first at Governor Silvester with anger and then at Leo with amused disbelief.

Silvester slammed his pudgy hand on the wooden table. 'A scout or an observer of some kind! I have to know who's behind these attacks. I have to behead their movement immediately or this province will descend into civil war. And I won't have civil war on my watch, Gregorius. I won't be recalled back to Emperor Constans' court for mismanagement, like that dolt Taurinus.'

'You make this sounds like the work of a week rather than months. Why?' With difficulty, Commander ripped the last flatbread into two pieces and wrapped one half around a juicy fig.

'Two imperial envoys land at Carthago in about a week's time with bags of *solidi* for the poor.'

'Gold coins? Aid for the poor? I don't see the problem.' Gregorius glanced at Leo.

'Because it's not *aid*,' Leo explained. 'More a poisoned chalice. These toadies offer debt relief to small landlords suffering crop failures over the last year as long as—'

'Aid is good. As long as *what*?'

'In exchange, Emperor Constans orders his envoys to force through immediate reconciliation of all Numidian Christians to the *imperial* Church.'

'They all believe in this Christ preacher, so what's the problem?' Gregorius didn't have to spell out his private pagan sympathies.

Silvester heaved back in his camp chair with impatience. He looked to Leo for backup. 'Commander, am I to understand you know nothing about our religious schism down here and don't even care?'

Barely an hour after dawn the day after the Lambaesis massacre, Governor Silvester and two notaries had cantered up to our gates. The death toll of townspeople came to the dozens. As for the rioters, they'd carried off all their dead, acclaiming them as martyrs and saints even as they fled.

Gregorius had barely finished shaving when Silvester and his arrogant minions brushed me aside and trod on my still-warm bedroll as they entered Gregorius' private tent.

We managed to shift them to the council tent and got Hamzah running for some sweet buns and fruit. Amidst all this bustle, a startled Ari arrived as usual to cleanse Gregorius' neck wound while I buckled him into full uniform. Minutes after Silvester's arrival, Leo wheeled up to the camp's perimeter in a wagon steered by a house servant called Nico. He was a sprightly Numidian in a bright red tunic. I noticed he managed a clubfoot pretty well.

Now Nico, Hamzah and I stood in attendance as a full-fledged council, including Barbatio and half a dozen higher officers got their briefing underway in the long meeting tent. The Roman trainee-deputy Albanus agreed to take notes with an ivory stylus on his elegant wax tablet.

Leo turned to the Commander to explain the situation: 'Gregorius. A religious rift divides Numidia Militaris between the imperial church of Constans and the followers of one Father Donatus, a puritan miracle-worker who harks back to the old persecutions. Donatus lost his parish when the state Church was restored to favor. Unable to forgive cruelties of the past and the priests who compromised to survive, he set up a renegade faction. Now there are Donatist parishes competing with state churches across this whole province.'

'Rift. Rift?' Silvester exploded with impatience. 'We have a crisis! It's an all-out standoff!'

Clearly, the new governor thought our commander a waste of his time—just a worn-out military veteran better employed fighting Alemanni brutes in the snowcapped Alps. Nobody had to spell out for him that if Commander Gregorius was half a Roman aristocrat by name, he was Gallic provincial on his mother's side, complete with brownish red stubble, a long jaw, high forehead and unruly hair.

Silvester himself might sport a Dacian silver shoulder clasp and a German buckle of cloisonné gold, but he was unveiling himself as one hundred percent Roman snob, complete with signet ring, haughty profile and neat little haircut.

I'd grown up in the Manlius dining rooms, serving officers and politicians as a favored slave. I knew the petty social games these men played to gain the upper hand. On seeing the generous breakfast spread, Silvester had tossed the Commander a few words of greeting in Greek, 'Friends show their love,' to test Gregorius' education. Gregorius had met the challenge, finishing the Euripides quote, 'In times of trouble,' then switched back into Latin.

The book-loving old Senator Manlius back in Roma had made sure of his son's education.

Clearly, this morning Governor Silvester wanted to be the one giving orders, not the other way around. As the briefing progressed, Silvester failed to hide his mounting irritation. He wanted Gregorius' forces to squash the Circumcellions' movement while he took the credit when the two envoys sailed into port.

He tried flattery next. 'You're a soldier, Gregorius, a wounded hero no less, but you've spent your whole life on the battlefield. I've studied the politics of this regime firsthand. I've done time in the corridors of Mediolanum and Treverorum. Paul and Macarius are powerful *civilians*. Unfortunately one is brutal and the other stupid.' He whipped around to Albanus and said, 'Leave that out of the minutes, if you don't mind.'

Gregorius had taken to sucking the pits out of the last of the dates and licking his fingers just to irritate his guest. 'So stupid they've reached the high position of imperial notaries?'

'You're missing the point. I know these throne lickers. They're going to make everything worse for me down here. They'll browbeat and whip people into their official churches if they have to. They think they can buy poor people off with a bag of coins—'

'Can't they?'

Leo broke in. 'The fundamentalists stir up the locals, Gregorius. They will say the aid money is corrupting. They want to end Roman occupation, run all us colonials off our farms, cut off the transport routes to the coast, in short, do whatever they can to have Numidia back to themselves.'

'The idiots will turn this province back into parched desert,' Silvester said. 'They'll free the slaves and drain our labor force out of the olive groves.'

The Commander sighed and looked at Leo. 'The Governor and I are new boys, Leo. You were here. What exactly did Governor Taurinus do that killed his career?'

'A few years ago, the Circumcellions printed out phony certificates of debt cancellation. Taurinus caught their leaders,' Leo said.

'Axido and Fasir, they called themselves "Commanders of the Saints".' Silvester said.

Leo continued, 'Taurinus tortured Axido and Fasir to death, then "cleansed" their strongholds Subbellensis and Vicot ab Octavu. He refused the rebels and their followers decent burials.'

'Ah,' the Commander pressed his scarred lips together. From stable groom to tribune, a Roman citizen craved and saved for a decent burial.

Leo went on, 'Taurinus left hundreds of corpses stinking and bleaching in the sun and where Roma had had two rebels, she now had two famous martyrs to the Donatist uprising against imperial exploitation, thank you very much.'

Silvester gulped down his thick fruit juice with a disgusted cough. 'Now the countryside is littered with blasted plaques and shrines erected to these idiots. We take down one and two more sprout up overnight like weeds after a rainfall.' He barked at us, 'Someone bring me some watered wine.'

Commander Gregorius' face twisted crookedly as he digested Silvester's summing up. He sent Hamzah for more sweet buns and drink. Nico and I went to get a gulp of water for ourselves as much as to help. When we returned with fresh platters, the lower officers were weighing in:

'So now Paul and Macarius buy them off. Who can't be bought these days?' the slow-witted Lieutenant Barbatio was asking. The other officers chortled. Money in the right hands was usually a part of any military promotion.

'The Donatist priests,' Leo corrected them. 'They survived The Great Persecution down here without handing over the sacraments or Scriptures.'

'Still smarting after so many decades? These people must have dull lives and long memories.' Barbatio's jibe told us he wasn't impressed with Christians facing down dumb hungry beasts in the arena, and why not? Barbatio sometimes acted like a dumb hungry beast himself.

Leo was quietly firm. 'My good lieutenant friend, imagine this. These Catholic leaders like Donatus—for indeed they consider themselves the last and only vanguard of the *true* Catholic faith—they know their elders submitted to the lions and the fiery stake. Now you expect them to swallow imperial bribes so that Constantine's son can hand over their flocks to the heirs of clergymen that betrayed their Lord?'

That was way too many words for Barbatio. The giant illiterate gave a dismissive grunt.

'Let me put it more simply, lieutenant. Would you ride into battle behind a man who'd betrayed your eagle standard?'

Leo lost patience with Barbatio's scowl.

'If your *vexillatio* is going to be any use here in Numidia, you all have to learn the lingo. The Donatists call such priests *traditores*, men who "handed over",' he told the council. 'The good priest who died in the basilica was their prime target yesterday. He was branded a state *traditor*. So was the assistant priest I saw saved by that brave slave standing back there.' Leo pointed at me. 'Both priests were labeled puppets of the Roman occupiers. The townspeople were just collateral victims.'

'Leo! Such rhetoric! If I hadn't known you as a boy, I'd suspect you sympathized!'

'Gregorius, this is serious. The Donatist priests are vying neck and neck with imperial clergy for control of Numidia—town by town and village by village. Unfortunately the Donatists have friends that our side lacks. These crazed Circumcellions step in as executors, secret death squads, so-called suicide martyrs who provoke their own deaths—'

'Suicide martyrs—?'

The two words sent chills down my spine as I listened.

'Staging attacks on us landlords. It's not just churches that fall under their clubs. They sabotage the roads we use to send our oil shipments to the coast, disrupt our labor and provoke us into killing them.'

'Why?' one of the centurions demanded.

'They provoke their own suicides to build fervor for rebellions among the pickers and oil pressers.'

'But who's *really* behind them?' Silvester practically spit his question at Leo across the table.

There was a long silence. We heard an *ala*—some forty or so—of cavalrymen trotting back from their morning exercises, following their noses as the camp filled with aromas of cooking pots. The perfume of a spicy African stew wafted through the flap of our tent on the dying morning breeze.

'I've heard enough. I agree we've got to do something.' The Commander nodded to Leo and avoided Silvester's imperious glare.

How did Gregorius dare defer to the oil trader over the authority of a governor, even a newly arrived one? I sensed more underneath this conversation than a mere slave like me could fathom, but I was so eager to catch subtle signals, perhaps I read too much into that glance.

Silvester was having no more of Leo's political subtleties. 'Cut off their supplies—behead the serpent and leave the tail to wither is what I say. Governor Taurinus had the right idea. He just went about it too *publicly*. These gangsters keep their followers loyal with drink—you can smell it on their breath when they attack. They hold orgies before they throw themselves into a fight—some Christians! Find out, who's supplying them with food and drink?'

Leo added his more measured opinion. 'The Circumcellions pretend to subsist on begging but they're fed and watered by someone, Commander, or they wouldn't have multiplied like the Hydra year by year. We merchants and landlords fear them. *We* certainly don't feed them.'

'Surely this priest, what was his name, Donatus—?' The Commander mused.

'The old man insists that he has no control over these extremists. He condemns them in public and private. He's a gentle holy man, horrified by their violence. He washed his hands of them long ago.'

The meeting had worn on too long and the sun was clear of the horizon. Silvester was losing patience.

'Infiltrate them now,' Silvester barked. 'Send in your scouts, your *speculatores*, your *exploratores*! What are they trained for? Identify the leaders behind these bandits and pull them out of the ground by the roots. Do it before those idiots Paul and Macarius blow this whole province up in our face with their insulting bribes and bully swords!'

Our officers looked at each other. If I felt hungry, I could only imagine Lieutenant Barbatio's mood. His stomach was growling now as loud as Silvester.

'Army scouts?' Gregorius dipped his chin in disbelief. 'Did you ever serve in the military, Governor? No? Scouts could locate these bands, even observe them at a distance, but they couldn't penetrate any native cult. Their army tattoos would be spotted within an hour.' Gregorius stretched out his left arm and above his mangled hand was his own wrist tattoo, a Silesian eagle from his first legion, the Herculiani.

'Then send in a spy,' Silvester insisted.

'A spy?' Leo smiled to himself as he ran his hand in thought across the rough surface of the table.

'Oh, don't deny the empire has such men,' Silvester sneered. 'We all know the *agentes* are more than the messengers and escorts they claim to be. Use one of them.'

The Commander shook his head. 'The imperial government doesn't assign *agentes* to a minor border garrison like this. Besides, we've only just arrived as reinforcements. Those riders outside don't even speak Punic. Most of our strength is an army clerk's fantasy. And all the Legio IIIA regulars within reach may look like locals, but they're descended from Roman veteran fathers. They're city boys now—tax collectors, surveyors and water engineers—speaking Latin. They do their military exercises, but they haven't seen combat in at least two generations.'

Silvester slammed his hand again on the table with frustration.

The Commander fought to keep the upper hand. 'You liaise with the offices up in Lambaesis, Lieutenant Barbatio. Where are the regular Legio IIIA border patrols right now?'

'The mounted forces who do speak Punic are out patrolling for Berbers west of Mauretania, Commander.'

'And the dromedary units check in for supplies at Rusibbicari or Aras only once a month,' Albanus added.

'There isn't time for them,' Silvester butted in. 'I told you. Paul and Macarius will be landing in a week, maybe ten days if there's a lucky storm. If you don't help me, I swear, I'll take you down with me, Manlius or no.'

My master raised his eyebrows at this threat, took a deep breath and looked around the tent. 'Well, you don't think I'm going to send in Hamzah here?' He gestured with his wounded hand at the servant waiting with Nico and me along the back wall. 'I couldn't possibly spare *him*.'

Around the table, the heavy-set Barbatio led the lower officers in laughter. The natty Albanus dutifully copied down the joke. Hamzah heard his name punctuate the rapid Latin he couldn't follow, so he grinned with toothless gums and bowed at the council table.

'You do have one good man who could do it, Commander.' Leo scanned the faces around the table. The officers looked at each other and waited, confused and wary.

Leo slowly turned his gaze up at me standing there at the far end, a kitchen rag over my arm, my back scraping the goatskin wall.

'Marcus' mother was a Numidian seamstress, gentlemen.'

How could this oil trader Leo have known that? The Commander's face drained pale beneath its livid scars. He snorted a little and shrugged. Then the amusement died on his lips as he realized the oil trader wasn't joking.

Leo waved to me. 'Marcus?'

'Yes, Leontus Flavius?' I took a few steps forward into the room, the ridiculous stained dishcloth still drooping off my arm.

'Leo, he's just my slave. Been ours since he was a little boy.'

'Didn't he volunteer?' Leo was oddly insistent.

'He offered to train up as my aide and bodyguard. He's my good side! I couldn't spare him!'

Governor Silvester saw Commander Gregorius' dismay and smelled an unexpected opening. 'You're a *voluntarius*, boy?'

'Yes, Governor.'

'And you must speak Punic. Even I can hear the way you say your 's' as 'sh.' It's your mother tongue, right?'

'Pretty rusty.' I glanced at the Commander for a signal, but he was glaring across the table at Leo.

'Any army tattoos?'

'Slaves aren't allowed army tattoos, as you know, Governor. The only mark for a slave would be an iron brand on the forehead as a runaway, something that will never happen to me.'

The leather seats creaked around the table through the uneasy pause. Barbatio and his superior officers witnessed the rising tension between their commander, his merchant friend, and the Governor.

'Then it's my request that this boy penetrate the suicide cells, identify their true leader, and report back to us.'

'That's a suicide mission!' Gregorius exploded.

'Of course. If he fails, he'll end up a martyr, maybe even get a shrine to his name.' Silvester smiled with cruel irony. 'But I need him to try, *now*.'

A cold shiver coursed down my spine at the memory of those fiends and their deadly shrieks.

'He's not trained for that kind of work!' Gregorius protested.

'We must send in someone who can pass as one of them, but carries no risk that he *is* one of them,' Silvester insisted, looking me up and down. 'Apparently, he's all you've got.'

'Why—? The Commander appealed with bewilderment at Leo. 'But *you* know what he means to me!'

Leo nodded, but he wasn't giving into to his friend's objections. 'If this mission is as important as Silvester says it is, Gregorius, it's your duty to let Marcus try.'

I pictured myself howling '*Laudate Deum*' alongside those wild men just to get run through by an imperial sword. It seemed to me that the suicide fanatics were more mindless and vicious than any enemy we'd faced in the civil war between Constans and his older brother, Constantine II.

And I could still feel the feathery weight of the little girl dying in my arms. These cultists stopped at nobody.

'So that settles it!' Silvester beamed. He stood up and adjusted his light travel cloak back into place.

'Not quite,' Leo said, his index finger raised for attention. 'I have two important things to say.'

'This boy has got to have every chance for success, starting with a good cover story. I'll issue a poster for a runaway slave this afternoon to be displayed throughout the province. I'll take him with me now to my estate. We'll get him ready to infiltrate the Circumcellions.'

The farm driver Nico standing nearby tossed me a welcoming smile.

Leo stood up and looked us all in the face, one by one, starting with Hamzah and Nico and ending with his eyes resting on his old friend.

The Commander had covered his mutilated face with his battered hands but undeterred, Leo continued:

'The second thing is this. If Marcus here returns in time with his mission completed, he has a right enshrined in Roman law that we must honor now with a pledge before witnesses. It would be best to hear the Commander say it for himself.'

Gregorius lifted a face filled with bitterness. I could hardly believe the words his twisted lips spoke next. 'If a *volo* takes up arms on a dangerous military mission, his owner is obliged to relinquish him.'

'I'd be *freed*?' I even forgot to ask permission to speak.

'The Commander must now say it in the correct legal form while we witness his oath.'

There was a long pause before Commander Gregorius managed, '*Servos ad pileum vocare.*'

'I'll speak it plainer for some of you,' Leo looked at Barbatio and his mates and then got up and walked over to me. 'Marcus. If you return with the information we need to stamp out this wave of violence, your head will be shaved and you'll don the *pileus*, the brimless felt hat of the *libertus*, the freed man.'

Leo returned to the council table and put his hand on Gregorius' bent shoulder and muttered, 'I'm sorry, old friend, but it's best for everyone's future.'

My master shook him off and stalked out of the council tent, heading back to his private quarters without a glance in my direction.

As the sunburned little governor and his arrogant minions rode in style back out our perimeter gates and down the desert track we could hear them still laughing at the Commander's defeat.

Whether it would be defeat or victory for myself, I had no idea.

CHAPTER 4, MEETING APODEMIUS

—LEO'S ESTATE—

'Get him to chat, Nico. Work the rust out of his Punic.' Leo patted me on the back as we exited the meeting tent. I collected my bedroll and packed my little bowl, spoon and shaving gear into my sack.

Nico drove the wagon through the gates of the outer perimeter. I sat on the bench next to him. One of the sentries waved me off and went back to his dice game as if I were going to buy the Commander a new pair of bootlaces.

I returned his farewell with a sinking sense of abandonment. I gazed back as the camp's palisades receded from sight. Once we hit the smooth paving of the imperial trunk route, Leo settled down for a doze on silken pillows under a sunshade on the flatbed. I glanced down at his complacent features, the spotless tunic and the golden chains around his neck glinting in the mid-morning blaze.

Could anyone, especially the man responsible, imagine my shock at this turn of events?

Until this morning, I couldn't remember ever being separated from some member of the Manlius family. Could it be that if masters took the presence of their slaves for granted— even in the bath and bedroom—we too took for granted that we could always shelter under our owner's protection?

If not the Commander's man, who was I?

'We'll reach the farm in a couple of hours,' Nico said in the rough Punic of his village, 'It's not far from Thamugadi. Time enough to tell me about yourself. Remember much of this country?'

'Not really. I remember the smell of my father's mules—the stables, the harness leather, and the feed. After he lost his herd in a drought, he took a job in the south and sold my mother and me to a slave trader from up in Carthago. The trader took us to the central slave market in Roma. The Commander bought us.'

'Lucky break. Roma—the big city, huh?' Nico was a few years older than me, I guessed, but I felt a lot more experienced than any Numidian farmhand this morning. Not only had he not seen Roma, he'd never confronted the hardened Alemanni, nor the northern Roman troops fighting for Constantine II at Aquileia.

With that lump of a foot, the poor man never would.

I shrugged it off to make him feel better. 'Roma? You're not missing anything. Rotting from the inside out since the imperial courts relocated to Mediolanum and other capitals. But the Manlius townhouse on the Esquiline Hill still stands proud. The old Senator sits in his library all day, reciting Homer from memory.'

'Well, still, someday maybe I'll get to go there.' Nico's tone of envy lingered in the air.

And here I was. Though I was riding toward a chance at freedom through my native countryside, I felt a wave of homesickness for Roma, thanks to Nico's question. I thought of my late mother huddled over the mending and my childhood days romping under the Manlius tables, teased and coddled by the Commander like a puppy. I'd had an idyllic existence until Lady Laetitia reminded her husband that my upper lip was too fuzzy to continue serving as his *delicatus*, a sort of spoiled toy.

I'd reached the awkward age. From that day on, I was rarely called to the dining room. Even then, I'd been treated well. The Senator's eyesight was suffering and I spent most of my time attending the old man among his books.

'Tough what happened to your Commander. I could hardly look at him, this morning, all burned shiny and stitched up like that.'

'He can still fight well enough with one good hand if he ties the shield tight to the other.'

'I guess you were there, huh?'

I'd lurched off the battlefield with Gregorius in my arms, slipping and sliding in other men's guts and blood. We got him across the pontoon bridge over the Rhône to the medical tent only just in time.

While the injured all around us screamed, festered and died, I'd watched over the Commander hour by hour, bathing his wounds in strong vinegar and reporting any changes that might signal gangrene to Ari. Luckily, there were none.

Finally came the night our service wagon trundled up through the Esquiline neighborhood in Roma to where the houseman Verus waited next to the fig tree hanging over our front gate. Lady Laetitia made the Sign of the Cross over her husband as we carried him under the oak lintels into the atrium. She nearly fainted as the evening lamps lit up what remained of her husband's face but her noble blood kept her on her feet.

The old Senator had descended from his library to take command of his son's care. Maybe he was able to sustain the family's morale only because he was already too blind to see his son's wounds clearly for himself. He summoned medical experts from all corners of the ancient city. But it was soon clear that the Greek medical slaves were the match of any society specialist. All we could give the Commander from now on was rest and moral support.

I nodded to Nico as we drove along. 'Yes. I was there.'

Leo's wagon rolled past grand African plantations set safely back from the road. Nico named the families who owned them, all of them Roman citizens, though most of third or fourth generation African residence. I listened with half an ear while the rest of my mind took in Leo's promise.

'Marcus, you're a freed man—'

Only there was a big 'if' attached.

Between the great estates and their miles of well-watered fields lay wild brush and merciless rocky soil. From time to time, we rattled past a shrine adorned with sun-faded rags and wilted flowers. Some stood near substantial grain storehouses, others were mere lean-tos or cells of stone in which someone had left pottery bowls. Some showed traces of offerings pilfered by hungry thieves.

'Martyrs' shrines,' Nico pointed with his whip. 'You see them all over the place, if you know to look.'

'From the crackdown by Taurinus?'

'Mostly. His soldiers hunted the supporters of Fasir and Axido for miles into these wilds and right up into the mountains over there. Left their bodies for the birds, but the Donatist priests took pity on them, collected their dead and covered the countryside with markers where they fell.'

'Which are you, Nico, Donatist or imperial Christian?'

'What makes you think I'm a Christian at all?'

'The crucifix hanging under your shirt, man.'

'Even pagans believe that behind their gods stands the One Unified God, right?' he parried.

'Sorry, none of my business.'

We reached a junction. Nico took a sharp right. Deliveries of Leo's oil, dates, figs and wheat heading northwards to the ports had pounded this private driveway almost as smooth as the *Cursus Publicus*. The chubby trader dozed on in the back. We neared his property now. Dozens of men and women in plain cotton tunics worked the olive orchards on both sides of the road. They straightened up, tipped a hat or hand in our direction, and then labored on, carting, climbing, picking and weeding.

If my father hadn't sold me, that would be me out there— burnt mahogany, illiterate, stinky and calloused.

And now?

I let myself daydream a little. A freedman stood only one generation away from citizenship with unrestricted rights. As a *libertus*, I might marry someday and my son—why, that poet Horatius had been the son of a freedman, an army officer serving Marcus Junius Brutus. He might have risen even higher if Brutus hadn't killed Julius Caesar and lost to Octavian and Marcus Antonius.

And then there was the emperor Diocletian—he'd been the son of a freedman from Dalmatia. And now, only a century later, the entire Roman army marched according to Diocletian's military reforms.

My son might one day hold his head up at an imperial court—or I might wake up from this strange dream and find myself harvesting Leo's fields where I belonged.

Anything seemed possible this dizzy morning.

Leo roused himself from his nap. 'You'll start working after lunch. Get rid of that uniform. Expose yourself to the sun as many hours as there is daylight. Leave off your boots. We've got no time to waste. From this point on, you're forbidden to speak a word of Latin with anyone but me or you'll be whipped. I mean it. Lash marks would round off your disguise nicely.'

'There are many sides to Leo,' Nico said. We dumped my bedroll and sack near a barn. I hid my boots and shed my army tunic. I assumed I should head off to eat with the field workers or follow Nico to the servants' table in the kitchen.

Instead I was called half-dressed into Leo's study. We'd only arrived at the estate, but to my surprise he wasn't alone.

'Tell me who this is, Marcus.' Leo gestured at his guest. A white-haired man in an elegant bleached tunic and northern-style travelling trousers sat in a wide leather-backed reading chair.

'With respect, how can I?'

'Just guess.'

'Well, he looks an elderly man of about sixty—pardon me—with all respect, your feet are painfully deformed by arthritis. But despite any inclination to rest his troubled feet at home, he travels, perhaps alone. Instead of soft slippers, he is wearing shoes of extremely durable, well-polished leather with marching studs on the soles. A soldier could walk pretty far in those.'

'My goodness, Leo, do all our slaves watch us with such hawk eyes? And where do I travel, boy?'

'I'd say you stick to the coasts rather than inland—far from the danger of battlefield and barbarian plains. You don't smell like or look like a meat-eater so perhaps you spend most of your time in ports or coastal cities offering fresh catch.'

'What else?'

'You might be a conservative official with heavy responsibilities over others at a great distance. Also you are a man who might have enemies. But I'm just guessing.'

'How do you know all that about me, young man?'

'You're wearing very practical trousers derived from the Germanic style, but you scorn the barbarian jewelry of the fashionable Roman official and I see a well-worn family signet ring just like the one worn by Senator Manlius, plus a seal on that second ring for authenticating documents. The fingers of your right hand show the ink stains and bunions of a man who writes many, many letters, but surely you could afford a scribe, so your letters are too sensitive to entrust to anyone else.'

He chuckled. 'And why should an arthritic old man like myself have enemies?'

'I can't say, but you're carrying a concealed weapon on a belt underneath your clothing. You adjusted it through that slit in your tunic disguised as a pocket just as I came in. Normally a man in your position would rely on a young secretary or bodyguard like me—unless he wanted to travel alone and obscurely.'

The older man nodded. 'My name is Apodemius, boy.'

I watched the two men pour themselves some diluted wine. Leo invited me to join them. I was dying of thirst but I took the elaborate goblet from Leo's extended hand with hesitation.

'What's wrong, Marcus?'

'I . . . I may be mistaken, but perhaps I have the wrong cup?'

'You see, Apo! What did I tell you? He's a natural!'

The older man peered at me. 'Why do you say that, slave?'

'Because I believe this is meant for Leontus Flavius. He added some medicine to this drink.'

'Yes, I did, but it might have been poison. You spotted it. The morning we met in the camp, Marcus, you kept your eyes straight ahead but you saw a lot. Don't think I didn't watch you as closely as you examined me. Little escapes you, does it?'

'Slaves are the eyes and ears of their masters.'

'Too bad the eyes are illiterate and the ears can't fathom Greek,' Apo muttered. He rose stiffly from his chair and carried his drink over to gaze through the wide shutters at Leo's busy groves outside.

'Excuse me, *Magister* Apodemius, but I'm not—not illiterate, I mean.'

Apodemius turned, eyebrows raised.

Going to his desk, Leo unrolled a parchment lying among his files and handed it to me. 'Read this.'

'Yes, *Magister. Twenty-two amphorae virgin-press, forty-four amphorae—*'

'Now this—'

'*I regret to inform you that due to a breakage in the irrigation canal at a point twelve miles west of—*'

Leo hesitated before lifting a heavy codex off a bookshelf. He turned a page or two. 'And this?'

'*From Britain he went to Roma to go through the regular course of office and there allied himself with Domitia Decidiana, a lady of illustrious birth. The marriage was one which gave a man ambitious of advancement both distinction and support. They lived in singular harmony, through their mutual affection and preference of each other to self. However, the good wife deserves the greater praise, just as the bad incurs a heavier censure—*'

'My God!'

'I told you, Apo. This Numidian slave is wasted on our friend Gregorius.'

Apodemius' eyes narrowed with suspicion. 'You've read that before, boy, haven't you?'

'Yes, of course. It's Tacitus describing his father, Julius Agricola. I read it to the blind Senator. No one else in the house had time to read to him all day, so he taught me as his sight was fading.'

'It's too good to be true, Leo. Now read something else, boy. Let's see . . .'

Apodemius scanned Leo's shelves. He pulled an older tome down from a high shelf. Amusing himself at the oil trader's expense, he ostentatiously wiped a layer of thick dust off the leather-bound cover. Then turning the text *upside down*, he pointed out a passage in Greek.

I deciphered the words so beloved to Senator Manlius and once I got through the first sentence, almost had to pretend that it was hard. '*For my mother Thetis, the goddess of silver feet, tells me I carry two sorts of destiny toward the day of my death. Either, if I stay here and fight beside the city of the Trojans, my return home is gone, but my glory shall be everlasting. But if I return home to the beloved land of my fathers, the excellence of my glory is gone, but there will be a long life left for me, and my end in death will not come to me quickly.'*

I looked up from the book. 'Please turn the page if you want me to continue. It's Homer quoting Achilles.'

Apodemius laid down the heavy volume and the two men retired to their seats and stared across the mosaic floor at me as they sipped their wine. I stood, breathing as slowly as I could to focus on the next test to come.

'I'm not surprised, Apo. I thought I caught him scanning the Commander's private documents upside down in the tent before the attack.'

'I have to file or deliver them to the army scribes.'

'Yes, yes, of course. That'll be all, Marcus. Go eat with Nico and the others, *in Punic*, mind you.'

Women and men ate together in this household at a shaded table behind the kitchen. Nico had saved a special place on the bench for some housemaid who hadn't turned up yet. After many minutes of ill-disguised hope and irritation, he wriggled to make extra room for me between him and the stable boss, Mastanabal.

'Probably kept inside waiting on those bratty twins.'

'Sure. You know women.'

'You're working the fields this afternoon,' he said. 'I work in the main house because of my leg, but you've got to look like *them*.'

I glanced at other tables set out in the stark sun where rows of seasonal workers wolfed down thin soup and rough flatbread. They were bronzed near to black and their gnarled hands were worse than any barbarian soldier's. Even the little kids were scarred by years of pulling at fruit thorns and hacking branches with blunt iron blades. I listened to the chat bubbling around me. My Punic ears were still good, if I didn't yet trust my tongue.

Yet how could I pass as one of them? It would take months—and I had only days.

We pulled and bashed at olives all afternoon, loading baskets of the oily stuff onto carts and returning for more. There wasn't much Punic of any dialect to imitate. When one man tried to start up a song, another grunted, 'Oh, shut up, save your breath in this heat.'

My hands were worn rough and hard from weapons practice but this was different. After a few hours, bleeding scratches scored my arms. My left hand blistered from gripping too hard to the crude ladder propped against the trees. I wasn't used to twisting my head upwards for hours on end and my shoulders ached from swinging baskets back and forth.

By sundown, I was collapsing with exhaustion and still trying to digest the day's strange turnings. But I was too stubborn to let the others see a military man falter, so I laughed along with their vulgar jokes and headed for more flatbread and olive paste near the house.

I would have thought field workers on a farm like this would eat better, but I was wrong. Leo ran an economic machine and counted his coins down to the last little *nummus.*

Nico limped off to his pallet in the servants' quarters under a proper roof. I was sent off with the temporary harvesters beyond the estate half an acre away. The women and children were sheltered inside a low-slung open-air barn. They huddled around a fire using straw for bedding. Each man found a patch of ground for himself outside.

My bedroll stood out next to their pathetic sacks but I didn't want to give it up. I was used to sleeping rough but not naked to the waist right on the dirt. The bedroll would be some comfort against the cold night. It was one of the Commander's cast-offs—his souvenir of a short stint across the Channel to clean up a mob of Picts.

'Nice,' said a toothless wraith, fingering its soft wool. He peered at me with such evil curiosity, I assumed a shifty look of my own and mumbled, 'Stole it.'

I shuffled off and settled on the outskirts of the crowd, far from the pitiful fires they built with dung and dry twigs collected during stolen minutes of the long workday. I feigned sleep but watched the men clustering into packs around their different leaders, like wolves. From time to time, one would gesture at me or shrug. Within half an hour of nightfall, huddled bodies stretched away from the tiny fires and emptied drinking flasks. After a while, my eyes dropped shut for real.

᚛᚛᚛

I heard a footfall in the soft dirt behind me. I felt for my *pugio*, a trusty triangular dagger four inches long. I waited. When the man got within a yard of my head, I rolled over and threw myself against his shins. He went down over me. We both recovered fast, leaping to our feet and facing off. It was almost pitch black out there, but for a sliver of moon and some oil lamps twinkling from the windows of the distant villa. There were two of them, no more than silent shadows.

The only way I was going to beat both of them off was to use the smaller one as a weapon against the bigger man right behind. I grabbed up my sack to protect my left hand and crouched low. Aiming with the knife in my right, I prepared to take an upward stab at the first stranger's thighs. He lifted a bludgeon and took good aim, but I was too quick for him, pivoting fast to bring myself around to his side. I was about to get a good dig into his ribs when—

'That's enough. Stop.'

I made out the figure of Leo, wrapped in a long cloak and standing in the darkness behind his two thugs. He smiled at me. He gestured the servants away, and now I recognized the first man as his stable boss, Mastanabal, sweating hard.

'Good,' he smiled. 'You're a light sleeper. We wouldn't want a Circumcellion spilling your brains all over the desert your first night on the job.'

'No, no,' I panted with relief.

'Go to sleep now. Don't worry. That's enough games for one day. You'll work a full day tomorrow. Come to my study after dusk.'

Chapter 5, Leo's Briefing

—THE STUDY—

By the time I'd finished ten hours in the harvest sun, the last thing I wanted was to start a fresh shift as the butt of Leo's games. Soldiers have their own ways of blowing off steam after a day's march or a savage battle. All I could do here was keep my head low and ears open.

Three more days in the fields had given me a lot to think about. The grimy laborers next to me had never seen Leo's affable side. They hated him, his daughters and all his Roman friends. One local had failed to meet his taxes. He could even point out the small landholding far in the distance that used to be his property before the hard times hit. He had sold out to Leo and had become just another laboring soul moving from one field to another. I'd spent morning, afternoon and evening hearing curses over Leo's low wages.

Was this the conversation I was supposed to pick up?

Nevertheless, at the end of the day I rinsed off my face, while the filthy workers stared after me with hostile curiosity. The large villa with its bright windows beckoned me across the darkening fields.

I climbed the orchard slopes and crossed the kitchen gardens and found my way by a side door past the wine closet and laundry looking for Leo's study. At any country villa outside Roma, I would have known where I was right way, but African mansions seemed different. Instead of having its garden atrium inside the villa walls, the house had open views to elaborate flowered terraces on three sides. I crossed the dining room, lined with fashionable curved couches and passed an entryway lined with towels and toilette articles that led to the family baths.

Leo's mansion was easily three times as large and irregular as the Manlius townhouse. I moved carefully, confused by unfamiliar passages leading off to spare wings, *trompe-l'oeil* murals depicting vistas of greenery where there was only plaster, rainbow-colored mosaic floors of gods and dancing girls and marble arcades draped with heavy tapestries hemmed in gold embroidery.

I reached the large peristyle garden lined with columns and an ivy'ed portico casting evening shade on three sides.

The twins were laughing off in the distance. Their carefree giggles echoed down one corridor connecting this courtyard to the women's wing. I walked past marble benches set around a fountain trickling into a fishpond under a shrine for the *Lares*, the household gods. I rounded the corner of the courtyard and ignored the smiles on the busts of Tacitus, Livy and Sallust that mocked my confusion. Leo seemed to have a nostalgic weakness for historians of the classical past.

'Tired?' he asked.

There he stood, freshly bathed and waiting for me at the far end of the courtyard. He beckoned me into his study. The room was cool and orderly. Opposite were the two huge windows overlooking the distant olive groves I'd just slogged my sweaty limbs through.

This time, we two were alone.

'It's no worse than a day's march. At least no one attacked me.'

'Sarcasm doesn't suit a slave. Here, slake your thirst.'

'Thank you.' I drank deeply of the pomegranate juice.

'Do you remember when we first met?'

'Of course. It's hard to forget an assassination attempt like that.'

He chuckled. 'No you don't. You were five years old, maybe six, and your master Gregorius was debating anti-Persian tactics after dinner in Roma with a group of his army buddies. He was absent-mindedly twisting your curls and feeding you scraps from the banquet table. He treated you like the family puppy you were.'

What did this have to do with my suicide mission? I waited with curiosity.

'Do you remember Gregorius used to invite the guests to set you riddles?'

'Did you set me riddles with the others?'

'No. But I watched you with great interest. You were a quick little bugger who could parrot anything back from memory or mimic the most pompous of his guests for a laugh.'

'Well, it stopped being funny as I grew older. Apparently my jokes struck too close to the bone. Some guests took offense. I was kept in the kitchen or the library after my beard sprouted.'

'I recognized you that first day in camp, not because of any letter Gregorius had written me about the battle—oh, he did write, of course—but I recognized you straight off because I remembered you as a child. I'm sure I'd recognize Clodius, too. People don't change that much.'

Clodius was the nephew whom Lady Laetitia's brother offered up for adoption when Laetitia failed to provide an heir for the Manlius family. The adoption hadn't been finalized yet but we all assumed that someday the Manlius townhouse, vineyards, bee farms, oyster beds, cattle herds as well as the Ostia apartments and docks would fall into his spoiled lap.

'Fond of Clodius, were you?'

I said nothing. Clodius had not been kind to me.

'Playmate and slave boy? Chummy as rascals?' Leo stared me in the eye. What was he testing? If he remembered me as an obscure slave child scampering out of his path into the shadows, then surely he would have remembered Clodius as a sour boy squirming under the spotlight as intended heir.

'There was hardly time to play. Most days Clodius studied with his tutor. I attended the old gentleman upstairs.'

'Yes. Viewed in one light, a curious arrangement.'

'It seemed natural enough at the time.'

Leo said nothing. Perhaps he was turning over memories of long ago.

He turned to his desk and shuffled through a pile of documents on his desk. When he spoke, he used a less insinuating tone.

'We're in luck, Marcus. This morning a band of Circumcellions attacked a merchant caravan making its way to Rusicada. The barrels were emptied, the slaves freed and driven off, and the two drivers viciously battered.'

'It hardly sounds lucky.'

'Lucky for your mission, I meant. When one driver defended himself by sword, one of the fanatics was fatally wounded and carried off in triumph by his loony companions and the skirmish ended. We think it's the same group that upended a magistrate's bench last week and succeeded in braining the poor judge before his court guards could fight them off.'

'I take it you want me to join this band.'

'Yes, before they vanish back south into the Gaetulian foothills without trace. I'm waiting to hear reports of their exact location. Meanwhile, you keep on working in the fields but be ready to leave—barefoot and friendless—without baggage, knife or *bulla*, on a moment's notice.'

His eyes rested on the coarse cord from which my amulet hung on my breast. My hand rose to protect it, just as the spirit of the *bulla* had always protected me. It was an ill-wrought lump of bronze-covered pottery, not the gold ornament of a society child.

'I can't take it off. The old Senator gave it to me. It's the only object I value.'

'And well you should. But you're too old to wear such a thing. It betrays you as a member of the Roman community. I want you to hand it over to me.'

'It protects me!'

'Pagan *and* slave! You're so superstitious? I credited you with more intelligence, but perhaps you *are* subhuman like most slaves . . .'

'The Senator himself told me never to let it go.'

'You're disobeying? You'll leave it with me!'

'But, it's my *protection*.'

He reached forward and jerked hard, the cord cutting into my stiff, stubborn neck. The knot snapped and the *bulla* dangled in his hand.

'Don't you understand? From now on, your wits are your protection!'

I stood at attention, hating this man and feeling betrayed by my master for relinquishing me to his vulgar indifference. He may have been a schoolmate of the Commander's, but his act was typical of a *nouveau riche* colonial—a gesture of disrespect to one of the most venerated senators of Roma's dying aristocracy and an insult to me, the property of the esteemed house of Manlius.

Leo didn't take much notice my contempt. 'When we know where the band is headed, Nico will call you from the fields. He'll guide you near to the shrine or wherever they're camped and then he'll slip back here.'

'I see.'

'Oh, stop sulking. You'll approach them on your knees, begging to be admitted to their circle. You'll claim to have worked for me but thanks to my constant beatings and mistreatment, you've fled to their promise of freedom from slavery, salvation in the Lord, glory in a martyr's death, *et cetera, et cetera*. Of course, we'll ensure that you bear the marks of such a beating.'

'Of course.'

'They'll ask why you're prepared to die. You'll tell them your family was one of the Donatist faithful slaughtered by Governor Taurinus. Be as vague as you can about that—you might be unlucky if there are old veterans of that battle among this band. Say your father was a—was a—'

'My father was a mule trader. I thought you knew.' If he knew my mother was a seamstress, I allowed myself that little hint of sarcasm.

For a moment Leo looked confused. Then he recovered and said, 'Yes, of course. Your mother's husband. Well, use his story as best fits.'

He reached into a box on his desk and took out a drawstring burlap pouch on a woven belt of hemp. He cinched

59

it around my waist. 'That's all you take. Inside there's a bronze mirror, like the ones soldiers use to relay signals off the sun between fortress towers across the desert.'

'I've seen them do it.'

'If you have information or need to meet Nico, signal in our direction at sundown reflecting this mirror from the highest hill you can find. But until you have firm proof of who's the mastermind behind these killers, lie low.'

'What if I can't get any information?'

'There's bound to be some frantic movement on their side. The envoys Paul and Macarius mean to buy or browbeat this entire province back into the arms of the official Church, and if there was any time the leaders behind these extremists might show their hand, that time is now.'

'I'll do my best.'

'How much do you know about Christians?'

'Lady Laetitia tried hard to convert everyone in the Manlius household. She says that salvation is within the reach of all of us because we're all equal before the Lord—except when it comes to changing dirty bed sheets.'

Leo raised an eyebrow.

'Her little joke, not mine.'

'I see. Well, this is no joke to the Christians following Donatus. They claim the high ground—to be the only true Christians left. They worship anybody who stood fast and died during the Diocletian persecutions—fair enough—but they refuse to forgive clergymen who weren't so brave and who handed over the sacraments and Scriptures under torture, the so-called *traditores*. And while Roma calls for tolerance and forgiveness of past weaknesses, these diehards refuse to worship under any priest ordained in the imperial church.'

'Yes, I heard your briefing to the Commander.'

'Good. Some slaves daydream through the day.'

'Not I.'

'Now, look over here.' Leo pulled me over to a wide table near the window overlooking the fields. I was astonished to see a large map of Numidia Militaris disfigured by black triangles, dots and squares.

'Where's our camp?'

'Here, next to what's left of Hadrian's temporary garrison ruins, the one that was destroyed by an earthquake.'

'Yes, we've explored the ruins nearby on our time off duty.'

'The biggest and richest city is Lambaesis, up here. It grew on top of the permanent military base, but after centuries, it's thoroughly civilianized.'

'Where the wedding was.'

'Right. Now here's Theveste, the main communication hub, with eight imperial roads leading in all directions. Here's Rusicada, the port serving the capital and here's the city of Constantina, over here. I go up to Rusicada every two weeks to supervise shipments of olive oil. The state pays for the transport of the grain, but if my men are quick, there's extra space on board for our red pottery wares and ground *mulex* shells for purple dye—at no shipping cost to me. I also have to meet my banker.'

He cleared his throat and patted his thinning hair. It was none of my business, but that vain gesture might mean there was also some society matron up in Rusicada for the widower Leo.

I focused on the map, looking for anything marking the simple village my homesick mother had spoken of during her long evenings of service in Roma, but I saw none.

'Pay attention, boy. These black dots represent the bishops professing loyalty to Roma. The squares are peaceful dioceses where there are two churches—one for imperial Catholics and the other for the Donatists. Now these triangles are one hundred percent Donatist. Any of them could be the headquarters of the extremists costing us blood and treasure.'

'But that's half the province!' At a glance, triangles dominated dots and squares all up and down the eastern side of our territory.

'Now you understand better. Only Numidia is left to feed Roma and these crazy Circumcellions want to rob us of Numidia.' He rolled up the map and stored it carefully out of sight on the highest bookshelf behind a bust of Virgil. He hid my *bulla* there as well.

I'd seen the poor in ragged queues up in Roma waiting for their welfare. They lined the streets and public squares every morning with their outstretched hands. A well-fed slave in a respected household never envied those wretches, but they enjoyed one form of power. When the Roman rabble starved, chaos broke out and imperial heads rolled.

Leo collapsed down on the old chair behind his desk as if the battle was already lost. 'Political control of the economy which produces Roma's weekly meals guarantees the survival of the entire Roman Empire. Governor Silvester knows it, the Emperor Constans knows it, and now you know it.'

'I realize this is an important mission.'

'We're relying on you, Marcus. You speak their language, but can you read their hearts? Have no fear, they'll be quick to read yours. Under the cover of faith, they'll indoctrinate you with political poison. They'll complain of colonial abuse, exploitation, tax farming, and hardship—you name it. In two hundred years we've turned this province from marginal desert to profitable agriculture, but that doesn't impress them.'

He walked over to where I stood and pressed his thick finger into my chest. 'And you must play along with them. We can only keep up Roma's food shipments by discrediting whoever is using the extremists for political purposes.'

'I'm sorry, but I don't see how my becoming a martyr can possibly help Roma in time. The envoys will be pass through the province with their bribes in no time.'

'You're strong and quick. Offer to fight, offer to *lead*. Ask how they survive. Monitor food and drink to see who supplies it. Our only excuse to the Donatist congregations for a political crackdown would be hard proof that one of their own high and mighty saint-like priests is responsible for the bloodshed.'

'But the Donatists say they have no control over the extremists. Perhaps the Donatists are not lying. Perhaps don't control the Circumcellions?'

'Well, someone does.'

'How can I fool them?'

'You do everything their meanest followers do. By all accounts, that includes drinking their rotgut wine and fornicating with their women in the mud. And for the gods' sake, *don't show off*—pickers on my farm don't read Livy and Sallust between harvests.'

'Yes, Leontus Flavius.'

'There's other one thing you'll find hard,' Leo added. 'You've been trained all your life to be loyal to your master. Luckily for you, Commander Gregorius is a good officer. You love him as every slave loves his owner. You live *through* him.'

'I understand. Now I must be loyal to the Circumcellions.'

'No. This is different! You will not be loyal to any person or any group. You must be loyal to a *mission*, an ideal. You must do whatever necessary to maintain your cover, even if it goes against every grain of your conscience, even if it means attacking *the Commander himself,* like that veiled assassin.'

'I take your point, but it won't come to that.'

'This is a rare opportunity. Doesn't every slave dream of freedom?'

Leo didn't have to drum that in. How often did a slave get sent on a mission that might rescue an imperial province from the clutches of religious rebels? Nothing would go wrong, if I could help it.

'There's one more thing, Marcus. Along with the signal mirror, I put a vial in that pouch.'

I fished out a small blue glass bottle filigreed in gold.

'It was part of Aemilia's toilette,' he chuckled. 'How my wife loved her vanity box full of all its trifles—her combs, her brooches! And the rouges and powders! The twins are turning out just as bad and double the expense!'

'Why would I need scent?'

'I refilled it with *herba Apollinaris*. Ever heard of it?'

'Henbane? It dulls the senses. Ari uses it during operations.'

'Yes, but you're holding a *lethal* dose. If there's any danger of leaking your true purpose, we expect you to use it—all of it—on yourself.'

'But poison is a woman's weapon.'

'Without your *spatha* and *pugio*, you will have no other on hand.'

I tossed the suicide vial back into the pouch. I was sure to return it untouched. I was a survivor.

Nevertheless, his gesture filled me with a flush of pride that few Roman citizens would understand. I knew it was against imperial law for slaves to commit suicide—it was robbing an owner of his property. Leo may not have realized it, but with the gift of that suicidal dose followed by a solid slap on my shoulder, he had just promoted me from slave to man.

Unfortunately, to everyone else, I was still just a slave.

CHAPTER 6, ONE MAN TOO MANY

—NIGHTFALL—

Days of backbreaking harvesting crawled by. In the evenings, Nico and I practiced with our mirrors, devising clever codes for 'New information,' or 'Meet at ten.' Compared to real army signals, it was child's play to me, but it amused Nico no end. Showing me around the estate was an excuse for him to slack off his usual chores around the bathhouse and kitchen where he limped back and forth with laundry towels, baskets, and buckets. Because of his bad foot, he was stuck helping the women and old men on the estate.

Sometimes he sneered at the pickers. He made out he was lucky but I could tell his foot bothered him.

'It's easy work and I save up my coins. I have my eye on a particular girl and if I win her over,' he boasted, 'we'll move on together where nobody knows us, maybe up to Carthago where a guy like me can find work in a tavern.'

'Don't be an ass. They'll find you within a week with a limp like that.'

'You forget, I'm not a slave,' he sneered. 'If I leave, I leave. I belong to nobody.'

'So what's stopping you? Apart from your foot, you're handsome enough.'

'Fear. She's afraid. Doesn't think I could protect her from her family's retribution. But I could. If I get enough together, she'll go with me.'

'Well, good luck with that.'

Just because Nico knew why I was there, didn't mean I had to put up with his snide contempt. I was a slave, but I was a

Roman aristocrat's property, not some backyard drudge clearing out slops. Obviously, Nico knew he was supposed to get me into and out of the Circumcellions' clutches but he didn't really understand any more than he'd heard back in the council tent. If Leo didn't confide in him, I didn't have to.

'Hunting the bandit chief out in the desert, huh?'

'That's the idea.'

'They're a pretty nasty bunch and two-faced in the bargain. All full of holiness until the night before an attack.'

'What then?'

He turned confiding and suggestive. 'Well, what I hear is that the future martyrs have themselves one hell of an drunken orgy, a kind of "Last Supper," you know what I mean?' Nico winked at me. 'People say they've got women followers who do *anything* you want—if you're going to die the next day.'

'Well, I gather you've already got your girl,' I shrugged.

His face darkened a little. 'Hope so.'

'Where is she? Point her out to me tomorrow.'

'Haven't seen her for a couple of days.' He shrugged. 'She often gets dragged into Lambaesis on shopping trips with the twins.'

⚥⚥⚥

I began to think that Numidia was nothing but scorching sun, backache, and baskets slippery with olive oil. I missed the army camp. Believe it or not, I even missed army food. Nothing felt so alone as lying on the hard ground with no tent flap over my head, just the stars above, and no amulet around my neck calling on the gods to watch over my fate.

I was losing count of the days, but could mark time passing as my skin bronzed and my blisters swelled, burst and hardened.

One night I went to sleep and for the first time, almost forgot the tension of waiting for my mission to start. The next thing I knew, Nico was shaking me awake. I realized I hadn't heard him approach. If he'd been a killer, I would already be dead.

'It's on,' he whispered.

He carried no lantern. We tread carefully through the black night. I threaded my way behind his limping silhouette, between the sleeping clusters of exhausted harvesters and toward the long drive that led up to the villa's gardens. I turned toward the house, but he yanked me in the other direction, toward the stable.

Of course—I'd forgotten—there was still the matter of the beating to make my flight believable. In the dark recesses behind some bales of straw, waited the brutish Mastanabal who'd attacked me on orders from Leo and nearly lost his manhood in the process.

'The master told me to make it convincing.' Leo's instructions were unnecessary—the man looked keen to redress his defeat.

Nico limped out of the whip's path. I found the back wall, took hold of two harness hooks and braced my bare shoulders.

Those two weren't going to see me wince. I wasn't just stubborn, but also proud. Since leaving Roma for the field in the Commander's personal service, enemies had tried to kill me, though I was only a slave. They had even left me with the odd slice or slit to be bandaged up in Ari's tent.

But no one had ever beaten me—or for that matter—branded or scarred me. It's no vanity to state facts—in a patrician Roman household, a slave is as valuable for his bearing and good looks as for his talent for stabbing a *pugio* into a barbarian's groin.

Mastanabal took ten lashes, hard and fast. Like searing bolts from Zeus, the open welts rose up across my shoulder blades within seconds. Nico splashed the wounds with cold water from a bucket. I felt feverish and sick to my stomach with pain but there would be no chance to lie down. After a bracing slug of wine from a goatskin, Nico and I were headed down the rutted track away from Leo's villa for the main trading road.

I glanced over my shoulder. In the dark I could hardly make out the large villa, but I saw the flame of a single oil lamp burning in an upper story window. A still, dark figure stood half-hidden by curtains.

So that was to be Leo's good-bye.

Nico and I travelled down the main road with difficulty. The moon was so new only the white marble martyrs' plaques along the road marked our way. We passed no more towns, only pathetic homesteads with feeble irrigation streams trickling through the night, feeding a brave checkerboard here and there of olive trees. Each precious tree was walled in and irrigated as individually as an only child.

For the first time in five years, I marched up a military road with no *spatha*, no *pugio*, and no knapsack or dangling cup. I shook with cold but my back burned. We left the paved road and started climbing hillier ground. The Circumcellions had hidden away from the towns and churches they attacked by retreating up into the foothills.

'There are niches and caves all around,' Nico said. 'No roads, only mule or goat paths.'

'How did you learn where they are?'

'They send out calls to the harvesters, trying to draw them off with promises of debt relief or freedom. They sent a kid to our farm this morning with a promise that they'd wait here for any takers.'

'What if one of Leo's pickers had really wanted to join?'

'No chance of that. He's hardly the worst boss.'

'Shush. Do you hear something?'

'Yeah. Over there.'

It was chanting and drumming. We crouched low and then for what seemed like a very time, we scuttled up a rocky goat path toward the sound until we came up to a jutting cliff. Lying down on our stomachs, we peered through the dark over the edge.

Camped on a flat, narrow plateau between two rocky slopes on either side, hundreds of Circumcellions were celebrating. Some sat in groups, pounding drums or drinking, others danced in circles and sang, flapping their rags and rolling their eyes in some sort of ecstatic parody of prayer.

Writhing and coiling their bodies around each other, they repelled me all over again. At that moment, the idea of infiltrating a nest of these vermin turned my stomach. Only the promise of freedom kept me pinned to the rocky promontory.

'They're sure to have sentries looking out for recruits,' Nico said. 'Probably somewhere down there,' he pointed to our left, 'behind those trees where the plateau breaks out into the lower valley.'

We slid back down the rocky path and felt our way in pitch darkness along the base of the hill walling us off from the revels. Rounding a slope, we spotted their campfires again, hidden by a natural barrier of brush and trees from the detection of any Romans passing by.

I shook hands with Nico and moved on alone until I faced the curtain of brush. Sliding down onto my knees, I crawled forward again, this time with face upstretched and hands clasped in supplication. For some minutes, as I got closer and closer to the camp, I wondered if their orgiastic trance meant no one would even notice me, much less apprehend me.

I pushed my way through the thickets and now saw the campfires burning straight ahead. This might be my only chance to get myself into their ranks but if they were too inebriated in their religious trance, I'd failed. My back burned hot with pain and I wanted to get off my knees as soon as possible.

I needn't have worried. Not every last one of the Circumcellions was off his head with drink and religion. I couldn't see much through the shadows on either side, but I was grabbed by the hair and my arms yanked forward by two men, both hooded and stinking. Their ragged fingernails cut deep into my muscles.

'Come with us, brother,' one said.

They pulled me to my feet. Lurching and stumbling, I half-hung, half-hurried between them but instead of joining the campfires, we skirted the celebrants and sidled along the rocky slope toward a darker opening obscured by overhanding wild vines.

It was a cave with a single campfire burning inside.

They tossed me forward onto the dirt.

'Another recruit, Juva.'

Beyond the flickering kindling, a black-eyed, bearded man of about forty looked up from a conversation with half a dozen other hooded men.

'Searched him?' he asked.

I was glad I'd taken Leo's advice and resisted the temptation to carry a hidden blade.

'Greetings, brother. Have you come to us with a pure heart, ready to offer your life to the true Catholic Church?'

'Yes,' I gasped. I felt genuinely winded and the welts on my back served as painful prompters of my story. 'I've been beaten for no good reason by a rich man for stealing a few olives off the ground. I'm sick of it all.' Without warning, I vomited right then and there near his fire.

My escorts turned my raw back to the firelight so this man Juva could examine my injuries for himself.

'You came alone? No one else heard the call of our martyrs?'

'I didn't wait for anyone else. They couldn't pay me enough coins to stay after this.'

'You leave your family?'

'Not really. We were pious, good Catholics. Gave offerings to the martyrs for the intercession of our souls. We despised the *traditores*. My father was a mule trader up in the foothills. My mother survived the massacres and then was caught and sold to the Romans across our Central Sea.'

It was easier than I expected. It was almost the truth.

'Those legs have done some miles.' Juva looked me over. The silence grew heavy. I'd answered as much as a common harvester might say. Any more questions from this leader might hint at suspicion.

'What do the pickers say about the fate of Stephanus?'

'The one in town?' I was stalling. It was a trap. Who was Stephanus? How could I risk an answer? Was Stephanus an assassin in the basilica? The tall priest who died in the wedding massacre? The short priest whose life I'd saved from the rampaging crashers? The man who had attacked the Commander back at camp?

'In Lambaesis, yes.'

Leo should have guessed these men would test me—they couldn't all be the slavering maniacs Paul and Macarius took them for. Someone commanded bands of fighters scattered from one end of the province to the other and they wouldn't choose stupid men to run their web of resistance.

I tried a bluff; 'There's no time to chat about Stephanus or anybody else in the hot fields.'

One of his companions spoke up. 'I don't like him, Juva. You're not interested in priests, picker? Yet you join a religious band led by Juva himself, a defrocked priest, our Captain of the Saints!'

Juva scrutinized me by the firelight. I decided to throw the last pair of dice in my hand—genuine fatigue and pain. 'My back is raw and bleeding. Is there any water to drink?'

Someone outside shouted, 'Another recruit! Glory to God!'

Thanks the gods Juva and his henchmen forgot this Stephanus and looked away from me to the mouth of the cave.

A genuine straggler to the cause had saved me from further questioning? I'd watch this new recruit and learn by imitating the genuine thing. I could have shouted hallelujah myself but instead I just lay down on the ground and hoped for them to dismiss me as no longer interesting.

Unfortunately, the other man they dragged limping into the cave just then was Nico. He gave me a helpless smile.

CHAPTER 7, CONVERSION

—THE CIRCUMCELLIONS' CAMP—

'You said you came alone. Do you know this man?' Juva erupted.

I glared at Nico. He was overconfident as well as clumsy. I had to take control of his stupidity before he ruined the whole mission. It was bad enough that he was supposed to remain behind as my contact with civilization instead of turning up like unclaimed army train baggage.

'I wasn't lying,' I spit into the dirt. 'He must have followed me.'

'Is that true, stranger? You look like a pampered house servant. Are you a recruit to our cause or chasing down a runaway for your Roman boss?'

Even Nico could see there was only one right answer to that. All the men in the tent except Juva brandished brutal clubs, the harvester's only weapon.

'I'm . . . a recruit and an eager one. This morning we heard rumors your camp was passing through. I waited until everybody went to bed. I followed this picker off the estate. I want to give my life to the Lord.'

'That makes four in one night,' Juva said to his men. 'A good harvest of souls. Take them out now and clean up this stinking mess. I want to sleep.'

We filed out under guard. To my relief, Nico and I were separated by Juva's men—they may have been Christians to whom purity of spirit was more important than social class, yet I couldn't help noticing that I was tossed down on the ground into a gaggle of unwashed field hands while Nico limped off behind them in another direction. The camp was crowded with bodies sleeping around little hills of fading ashes and embers. Wine dribbling out of abandoned bladders wound through the dirt right under drunken sleepers.

Around us, the rocky slopes echoed with the occasional squeals and grunts of sex. These were strange Christians indeed. In Roma the Christians preached chastity and denial. Here couples mounted each other in the open air scarcely sheltered by boulders or bush. The commonest soldier's camp slut would have been ashamed of these sisters.

The smell around the margins of the camp turned my empty stomach. These people relieved themselves only inches from where they bedded down.

I longed for the discipline of the soldiers' camp or the elegant routine of the Manlius household. You got used to blood and shit on the battlefield, but no Roman infantryman dozed off like an animal next to his own muck. Since I couldn't sleep, I watched from where I lay, trying to figure out the hierarchy, if any existed, among the hundreds of people falling asleep in their unwashed robes.

After a while, I got a loose handle on the social order of these wanderers. Many of the stronger, taller men lay down or squatted in a ring around the campsite's perimeter, keeping watch on some horses tethered near that curtain of brush.

A gaggle of loud young women, teetering with too much drink, bickered over places near the largest central fire. There was a tent of sorts alongside the slope against which I sheltered. It was just a worn carpet tied to four poles, under which two older men were cleaning burnt grain stuck to the bottom of large clay pots. With no water handy, they scrubbed with the sand at their feet.

I saw a couple of mules and some horses, but no wagons carrying supplies or water barrels. These people were more threadbare than the lowliest Berber tribe.

I suspected two things—tonight's 'celebration' meant that one or more of their number would be heading for martyrdom tomorrow and that the group had used up its food supplies with no mind for the coming days' meals. If they needed more supplies, I could trace who was delivering it and who was paying for it.

I lurched back to my feet and stumbled over to their lean-to of patched animal skins.

'I'm hungry. Anything left over for a newcomer? A crust will do.'

'Not a crumb, brother.'

At least these men were sober.

'My wounds need tending. Is there anyone here who can help?' By the dimming fires, I showed them the vicious marks across my back.

'It'll be dawn soon enough. Then go to the women on the far side of the camp near the cave and ask for Sophonisba. She carries healing herbs.'

'Thanks.'

'Get some rest, brother. Christ be with you.'

They'd saved a few disks of flatbread for themselves, and I would have preferred the comfort of food above Christ's solace but I averted my glance from their pathetic cache. Before I could get assigned to crucial supply lines or assist in Juva's cave, it was important I make friends and fit in, taking what little kindness came my way.

Then I noticed the man staring hard at me.

I had already made a mistake.

'Christ be with you,' he repeated, making the Sign of the Cross again. He waited. I imitated him, making clumsy work of it and nodded my thanks. He smiled and went back to his work as I stumbled away for the safety of the brush where the sentries had dumped me. What had become of Nico? Yet I had to avoid him if I wanted to make any headway.

At first light, I'd find this Sophonisba—not only for a cooling salve, but for information.

𐤋𐤋𐤋

The sun rose over the mass of sleeping men and women, revealing their dirty faces buried under hoods against the desert chill.

Picking my way around their makeshift circles, I stepped right over some of the revelers who had passed out. After dozens of such deviations and detours, I came across Nico's snoring face, an empty goatskin in his hand with wine staining his red sleeve. He'd found friends fast enough and needn't worry me. Even when he woke up, he'd be laid low with a hangover.

I approached the single women's side of the horde with more respect. When a woman of about thirty invited me to come forward, I turned my naked back, filthy with dirt and sweat, for her examination with some exaggerated reticence. It wouldn't do to assume every female Circumcellion was an amoral slut.

The woman guided me to Sophonisba, an old woman of about fifty. She sat in a circle of modestly dressed women mending clothes with clean hands. She wore no jewelry but I detected a deep rivet in the skin left by a heavy chain that must have laced her neck for decades. I guessed she'd once been prosperous and had now fallen on hard times. Perhaps the necklace had been stolen or sold. Perhaps she'd given it away in a fit of charity.

'Make yourself useful,' she ordered a slender girl of about sixteen in a plain white servant's tunic that hung down over feet shod in clean sandals. The girl smiled at me with such sympathy in her innocent eyes, my heart sank to think she might have been one of the women rutting under the rocks the previous night.

'Here, girl, fill this basin with water from Bomilcar's cask. If he gives you any trouble, tell him it's for wounds, not waste.'

'Where should I find this Bomilcar?' It seemed proof, if any were needed, that the girl was a newcomer, like myself.

'Past the cave and to the back of the food stalls. There should be some fresh water left. If not, then go into the cave entrance and ask to borrow some from the sentries. But don't bother the men inside.'

The girl started off, so energetic and eager to help, she seemed a misfit in this sea of louche ruffians.

'A future martyr, too?' I asked. 'She seems too young to give up on her future.'

'She arrived last night with an older girl. She has nothing to look forward to—unless you call it a future to be forced into the bed of a villain three times her age.'

Sophonisba broke off a stubby plant and rubbed its clear, cool juice across my back.

'Is she a slave?'

'Around here, we don't care who anybody was and we don't ask. We're all equal in Christ. Ten lash marks tell your story. You a thief?'

'Just disobedient. There are some things a man doesn't submit to.'

'The boss too fond of you? You're handsome enough.' The girl returned with the basin. 'Here's our water. Wash yourself.'

'Will there be food any time soon? I walked all night. I'm hungry.'

'We'll get more. Don't worry.'

'When do we go begging? Where?'

'Ha!' She had a wry laugh. 'You see these hundreds of people? You think a crowd like this survives on sacrificial orange peels? We get grain sacks to keep us going. Sometimes fruit.'

'But the townspeople call you cell-rovers, *Circumcellions*, because you hang around the martyrs' cells and shrines, begging for scraps.'

'We don't care what the colonials call us. We're mostly *cuzupitae*, harvesters—although some are thieves or bankrupts—and we call ourselves *agonistici*, fighters for the Lord. Juva is our "Captain of the Saints".'

'He's a compelling figure.'

'There are dozens of captains like him leading *agonistici* all over the Numidian plains.'

'Whatever we are supposed to call ourselves, we have stomachs. Grain must be paid for and if we don't go begging?'

'We rob the merchants' caravans and empty their barns. We liberate their slaves and their money. You'll have to help. There, you're done. Let that stuff dry and come back for more tomorrow morning. Christ be with you.'

'Christ be with you.' I reached into my pouch.

'No, no, I can't accept it. I'm happy to care for others. But it's kind of you to offer.' She pushed my pouch away. 'Perhaps someday I'll think of a way for you to repay me. Now go.'

Sophonisba had had enough of my questions. If she knew who was sustaining the band, she wasn't saying. I was reluctant to leave the old woman's circle. After last night's madness, her women's sewing circle seemed an oasis of sanity.

I caught up with the girl returning the empty basin to the sentries at the cave.

'Thanks. You're very kind to help me. I'm new here, too.'

She smiled, but looked at her feet as she walked, whether too modest to talk to a strange man or too repelled by my appearance, I couldn't tell.

'I'm Marcus. What's your name?'

'Kahina.'

'I got lashed so I ran away—from a big oil estate down the road that way, about five or six hours' walk back.'

'Which farm?'

'The Longus Farm. I moved with the pickers from field to field.'

She looked up at me with a little spark in her eyes. 'You talk a little —'

'I'm not much of a talker. Who are you?'

'Just a girl.'

Then a startled look flooded her eyes. She brushed past me and hurried through the crowd back to Sophonisba's side. After so few words, there wasn't much to make her so skittish. Still, something I had said rattled her.

'We're mobilizing!' One of the camp escorts from the previous night pushed me toward a crowd of men gathering at the end of the long camp where the shallow valley extended to that brush curtain, an easier exit to the main road than the climb Nico and I had vaulted the previous night.

Nico was left behind. He wasn't of much use with that foot in any attack. I could have kicked myself for my stupidity in not laming myself for show. Time was short and a twisted ankle would have kept me closer to the secrets of Juva's cave.

'Wear this,' the escort ordered. It was hardly a garment, just a long mess of woven goat-hair dyed black and fashioned into a hooded tunic that scraped my ankles. Judging by the jagged tear about breast level, it must have belonged to someone martyred on a Roman sword.

At least they'd washed off the bloodstains, but it still reeked of sweat and dung. It chafed me badly and was the last thing I wanted to wear over my lash burns. But all the men standing around me were dressed the same, except for the man Bomilcar, whose soft brown woolen robe was buckled tight by a fine example of barbarian gold handicraft. It was a shame I had to keep my bronze mirror hidden in my pouch. I reckoned this thug liked his vanities.

'We're taking a caravan of grain moving along the *Cursus* this afternoon. Here's your club.' He handed me an olive wood bludgeon.

'Is this all you've got?' I scoffed. 'Or don't those Donatist faithful in the towns want to arm their defenders properly?'

'Since when would a common picker know how to wield a blade?'

'We're not defenseless,' a smaller man said. 'We know how to use these well enough.' His words were distinct but his expression unfocused. He looked up at my forehead with an illuminated, glazed expression, like a drugged oracle virgin rattling off omens. His name was Capussa.

Leo had ordered me to get into a position of leadership fast. Moreover, I was starving and as anxious as any of them to seize that grain. It was about an hour's ride to their chosen ambush point. They knew their terrain, but once we arrived, I spotted two flaws in their plan. Our position was well hidden on a rocky outlook behind some desert scrub, so we had the advantage of surprise. But there were easy escape routes for the escorts and a level stretch of road if the first driver decided to make a break for it and dash off with the wagons to safety leaving the escorts behind to fight us off.

I suggested we split into two parties, with one hidden up the road to take the vulnerable wagon once we'd separated it from its defenders.

'No, they'll be easy pickings. We kill them all in one go. Chase them down to a man,' Bomilcar retorted.

It seemed like Bomilcar was more interested in engaging his gang in a wasteful fight than in grabbing the grain.

'I think this man is right. We divide up. We need the food,' said a young boy. The others' drawn faces turned on Bomilcar. He scowled at me in turn. He didn't like having his authority questioned by a newcomer, but he relented and sent a dozen of us around a farther bend ahead to take a driver if and when he made a break for it.

It took us about five minutes to reach the best position and we were in for a long and hungry wait. The sun was full in the sky before we saw a small grain convoy moving steadily toward the rise in the hills where we nestled under our smelly robes.

I recognized that tense hush before a real battle, shields positioned in mathematical precision to form the *testudo*, the signalers wetting their lips to sound the horns for the attack, the eagle standard visible even to the ranks at the back of thousands of men waiting to move forward in turn with relentless persistence—the whole might of the Roman military machine of which my master was a proud part.

However, these desperate men displayed fear, not confidence, with their expectant silence. After all, the unspoken assumption of this raid was that grain was only one objective— the other was a death perversely touted as 'martyrdom.'

We'd waited too long. I reckoned the delivery team had stopped roadside to escape the rising heat, but I was wrong. Just when I would have sounded retreat, we now saw with more clarity two closed ox-drawn carriages rumbling northwards. I'd expected flat wagons, but if they were using high-roofed carriages, it must be a big consignment—too big to carry off across the hills, even if we sent for the mules to meet us halfway.

To take the grain, we'd need to carry off the carriages too, and that would keep us on the road and vulnerable to arrest.

The ponderous oxen moved patiently along the paved, sand-strewn road toward Bomilcar's ambush. Two armed drivers rode at the front of each carriage and, on either side, a simple farmhand on a mule. That made only eight men to our dozen plus. It was obvious they hadn't expected trouble like us.

Bomilcar led the attack, but their descent down the slope was slightly too slow. As I'd feared, the first driver cracked his whip, leaving his escorts on mules behind to protect the second carriage. One of our band rode out of our hiding place screeching 'Laudate Deum' like a demon from Hades. There was nothing for it, but to follow through, even though the oncoming carriage had ample time to see our impromptu barricade of ghouls brandishing olive clubs from one side of the road to the other.

I reckoned the driver would chance his thundering oxen on the softer desert ground and drive his load right around us, but we'd made a deadly miscalculation.

He pulled the oxen up short and the doors of the carriage flew open. It was the Circumcellions, misled by myself, who had fallen into a trap—six more men armed with shield and sword, probably hired mercenaries with skills to match—set upon us. They were decoys to keep us from the cargo, but our battle blocked the road so no one could drive the second carriage—no doubt full of grain—past.

It was the kind of fighting I'd trained under the Commander for—close combat defending him from blades. I hated the running and thrusting with my legs caught in the damned skirt of my robe, but as soon as I got my hands on one of their swords, I'd be fine. So I aimed for the smallest of the men and dodging his sword parries, got a good whack at him below the knees. He went down, possibly with a broken bone. I wrested his weapon off him and went for one of the larger men in earnest.

Back down the road behind us, Bomilcar and his harvesters were facing a surprise contingent hidden in the second carriage as well. They were holding their own, but I was afraid we'd lose one of them at any instant to self-impaled martyrdom.

Even in that too, our side was frustrated. It became obvious that these guards were fending us off, but when I turned aggressive, they didn't aim to kill. The one I'd disarmed fled on foot across a wheat field. I suspected they were briefed to provide no new martyrs to the 'true' Church that morning.

But a strange blood thirst was upon me. I reveled in the play of metal ringing on metal. I was pressing two of them farther and farther from the carriage.

'*Laudate Deum*,' Bomilcar screamed to raise morale.

'*Laudate Deum!*' I yelled and the rest of Circumcellions joined in. I saw one of them fighting hand to hand with an armed soldier. He was faring well enough with his club, as he was the bigger and more determined. Then to my astonishment, I saw our Circumcellion toss aside his club and rip his robe open to bare his breast to his panting opponent. The idiot hesitated and prepared to pinion himself on the enemy's sword as he threw his head to the skies and screamed, '*Laudate Deum!*'

I shoved the fool out of the way and took on the carriage guard. Laying sword against sword, I parried his thrusts.

I kept our group on the offensive. We were pushing the convoy men hard. Another mercenary lost grasp of his sword to the swing of a club, but instead of picking the valuable blade up off the ground, the Circumcellion stuck to his religion's prohibitions and chased the mercenary off with his lethal swings. A third 'enemy' fled with his sword after his companion into the fields.

There was no time to ask ourselves how the main band under Bomilcar had fared but the tide of our standoff shifted when we heard the second carriage thundering our way under the reins held by one of our own hooded men. To my astonishment, the farmhands who had driven it into our ambush were putting up no more fight, nor were they pinned down inside the carriage where they rode. They jumped onto the ground around us and one of them grabbed the abandoned sword, brandishing it against the fleeing convoy driver.

'*Laudate Deum*,' he shouted, and flailed away as best he could against his former travelling companion.

He was a slave breaking for freedom.

For an instant, I felt a wash of sheer envy at the simplicity of this man's 'liberation' compared to the deadly bargain I'd struck for my own. He had courage and passion. If he hadn't dared to join the notorious Circumcellions before now, today was the day he'd seized the choice of immediate death under our bludgeons or martyrdom in heaven on another day.

Our reconstituted band overwhelmed the remainder of the grain's defenders. The guards were no army-trained fighters. They took off, scrambling away from the roadsides. Some dove into the wheat stalks and some through the wild brush along with their drivers and mule riders.

We had the grain and a new recruit, but not a single martyr. The fool who had bared his breast for the sword looked a little relieved, now that his fever of self-sacrifice had subsided.

'Everybody eats tonight,' I congratulated Bomilcar. 'I was wrong not to guess they'd have a trick up their sleeve. I'll do better next time.'

Bomilcar didn't look as pleased with me as I hoped. 'Lay down those swords,' he barked at the armed slave and myself. 'We're religious men and we don't ignore our Lord's instructions—drop them or I'll beat you to death to prove my club is as good as any Roman blade.'

So it was over for the day. With both carriages and some good oxen in our hands, we drove the grain back into the hidden campsite to cheers from the starving throng. As I arrived sitting next to the driver of the second carriage, I looked out from under my hood and saw Nico massed with the others, still wearing his servant's tunic, but limping along with the crowd to get his share of a meal.

If he saw my hooded profile, I don't think he recognized me. That made me hope that by staying separated, I could make headway in ferreting out the root of this movement as soon as possible.

Bomilcar headed off to the cave to report to Juva. I lingered alone not far from where I'd spent my fitful first night. I didn't even admit it to myself, but I was hoping for a glance of the soft-voiced girl Kahina.

She was impossible to spot. A bustle of women set to work pounding and sieving away at the grain, working in a team alongside the cooks to turn our catch into something digestible. I saw Sophonisba trying to prevent some rabid fools from guzzling the grain raw out of a split bag but not everyone could be controlled.

Their empty stomachs, not their hungry souls, were the problem. How much of this religious fervor was sheer poverty begging for relief? Would these penniless wanderers really take offense if Constans' gold coins turned their bare footsteps away from Donatus and into the imperial basilica? I began to wonder at Leo's belief in their fierce pride.

As I waited for my dinner, I saw that by wasting a day ambushing carriages, I'd missed a morning in the camp learning how information, money or other support reached Juva.

The consolation was that at least today's skirmish had won me membership, olive club and all, in their morbid circle. If I hadn't yet solved the mystery of who ordered this campaign, at least I'd taken a swift easy step in my conversion to the last 'true' Catholic Church.

It turned out I was wrong again.

One of the cave sentries searched me out with a message. 'You can eat your fill,' he said, 'but after that, go straight to the cave. Juva *especially* wants to see you.'

Chapter 8, Interrogation

—THE PRIEST IN THE CAVE—

It was sunset by the time I got my flatbread and it was cool enough to eat. I forced myself to make it last with sips of wine from a borrowed cup.

From my favored spot protected by a few scrubby bushes on the slope at the edges of the campsite, I kept my eye on the entrance of Juva's cave. I had hoped that at some point during the later afternoon, the man himself would emerge into the sun. Deep down, I would have felt more comfortable answering his invitation in the open air. Talking to him in his lair, a visitor felt trapped by those sentries and vulnerable to his whims. Buffered by the company of hundreds of followers, a man might look Juva straight in the eye with fewer qualms.

My nerves tightened when I saw what happened next. A middle-aged man wearing little more than a dishrag around his loins—a worker who by rights should have been sharing his gruel tonight with wife and children—had disappeared into the cave. It felt like a good hour or more before he reappeared, eyes glazed over and face streaming with tears, and stumbled back to his friends.

I understood better when a second man was summoned to the cave entrance, exchanged a few sentences with a sentry and disappeared alone through the dark mouth.

Unlike the first man, he wasn't gone for very long at all. He re-emerged wearing a radiant expression and whispering, 'I've been chosen. Juva has selected *me.*'

Some gawkers had been listening with curiosity near the mouth of the cave. Now they encircled him and gathered others to join in. They swallowed him up into their communal embrace. He seemed neither to see nor hear them as he walked away in their care and only muttered, 'Brethren, I am to be next. My family will be praised and my shrine will be worshipped for all time. *Laudate Deum.*'

So I was the third invitee. There seemed no point in postponing my own interview with their leader—not that punctuality seemed a high priority among Circumcellions—but a kind of hysterical excitement now roiled underneath the surface of the gathering, a quiet hysteria mixed with glee illuminated their faces and burned in their eyes. It might well simmer round the clock in the breast of the Captain of the Saints. It wasn't an emotion I could afford to inflame.

I cut a path against the tide of worshippers and announced myself to the cave's sentries. For all that I'd volunteered, they still seemed eager to rough me up.

'Here he is,' one said, tossing me down hard on the sand just inside the entrance. The night of my arrest, the cave had been lit up by a campfire and filled to its tiny dimensions with his trusted advisers. Now I crouched low not to hit my head on the low stone roof and worked my way along the bumpy wall until my eyes adjusted to the darkness.

I found Juva in the shadows at the back, alone. He rested on one hip and was reading by the light of a couple of oil lamps nested in the sand beside the edge of his worn rug.

Now I had a chance to notice his feet were soft and uncalloused and his fingers long and fine. His black beard was clean and combed. His tunic was well bleached. He may have been a leader of discontented laborers and religious fiends, but he was no savage himself. He squinted at the pages like one who had long ago strained his eyesight.

'Yes, here he is,' Juva said to himself. He kept his eyes trained on the book. I could judge only that it was in Greek. My peering over at his reading didn't ruffle him. I was, after all, an illiterate peasant to Juva. All the same, it was a private relief for me to see that someone in this hellish tribe could even read. Every Roman soldier could write his signature, and many could read logistics, commands and letters from home. And I've yet to meet an auxiliary who didn't enjoy defacing foreign walls with rude graffiti.

I doubted many outside this cave knew what their simple names looked like in ink or wax.

Still, I found it unnerving that Juva continued reading for many minutes without taking any more notice of me.

I heard the shouts and jests of the hooded masses outside finishing their bread. If the meal was done for the day, obviously there was still more wine. We heard an eruption of drums outside and the start up of screeching and handclapping by a handful of girls pounding their bare feet on the sand outside.

Yet the cave seemed as quiet as death.

'I thought this was a pious community. I wouldn't permit my sisters to behave like that,' I said. After all, why shouldn't I address Juva first? He wasn't my commander or even that goon Lieutenant Barbatio. We were all equal here.

'You should get used to that.' He didn't look up from his book. 'Ignore them. They're just pickers' women. They'd lift their skirts in the fields every day if their fathers and brothers didn't stop them. They join us for freedom, just as you do. You can't blame them if they prefer dancing and carousing to being harnessed by their husbands to the plough right next to the family mule. Besides, my converts want them.'

'It's shameful. Not all mountain women are whores.'

'Not all the women here are loose.' He flipped a page and continued to read a few lines, then turned his face to me.

'Sophonisba is a wise woman. It's not her fault her medical skill was taken for sorcery by city priests who feared her cures. She's saintly as well. Many of the maids follow her modest example. A few of them are even church *sanctimoniales*, still virgin, fleeing from the corruption of the imperial church.'

I couldn't help but hope that perhaps the girl Kahina was one of the untouched.

Juva stroked his beard. 'Bomilcar tells me that you picked up a Roman mercenary's sword to win today's fight. Don't you know that's against our creed and that we take our Lord's admonition to the apostles to heart?'

'I wasn't thinking, Juva. I knew you wanted that grain. I'm sorry.'

'I'm tempted to throw you out. Your right hand is creeping down your naked thigh where a weapon might hang. Does the thought of expulsion make you nervous?'

He slammed the book shut and sat up, crossing his legs and straightening his back. 'So I'm right in guessing you're trained to fight as well as harvest?'

'Life is tough in the fields. I've picked up a few tricks on the road. You said yourself, tribal rules fall by the wayside. Itinerants have to know how to protect virtuous women.'

'St Peter took up a sword in Gethsemane to cut off the centurion Malchus' ear. Our Lord stopped him from cutting off anything else but—' Juva lifted up a hefty cudgel lying at his side on the rug. He thudded it twice on the ground.

'—The Lord does provide. We wield our fathers' olive clubs instead, just as the Jews held their staffs as they ate the Pascal lamb. We call them our Israelites.'

'I'll try to remember,' I said. I had to divert Juva from talking about swords and training, and was afraid the next topic would be my proposed death.

So I prompted the conversation in another direction. 'I thought it was on orders of Father Donatus the Great . . . They say he performs miracles. Is that true? Does he come to us to preach? . . Is he your teacher?'

'The holy Donatus is a living saint, the purest of us all. I swear on the grey beard of our great priest, but no, he is not my teacher.'

'Who led you to this path of salvation?'

'I studied and was ordained in Carthago.' His voice turned sarcastic, 'I opposed the *traditor* Caecilianus as Bishop of Carthago! I lost my church when the court smashed all our altars to rubble. So,' he gestured at the walls around us, 'I end up with a cave instead of a nave! Sorry, a poor joke—'

'I . . . I need water.' I had to keep Juva talking to postpone whatever honorary martyrdom he'd scheduled for me.

'Get us some drinking water!' Juva shouted.

'Yet you command and inspire,' I said. 'The word travels and people join you with faith in their hearts.'

'Yes, we have survived. We control many congregations all over this troubled land.'

I thought of Leo's map with its triangles and circles. I mustn't forget that I was kneeling in this dirty cave to add more information to that map.

'You studied at the great schools in Carthago? But forgive me for saying, you don't look Roman any more than I do.'

'I consider that a compliment, picker. No, my father was a Greek doctor and my mother a Berber servant girl.'

'Should I call you Father? Are you still a priest?'

'Who decides that, picker?' Juva smiled to himself wryly.

'The Church elders in Roma—?'

Juva shook his head. 'Thirty years ago Constantine sided with the collaborators who survived the Diocletian lions and fiery stakes by renouncing our Lord. But many of our people weren't so weak. We died by the hundreds, in flames and by the imperial sword. And even lying in pools of our own blood, we never denied Christ while those cowards wailed and sobbed and handed over our vestments, Scriptures and chalices to the imperial whores of bishops.' He spat on the ground next to his rug.

'But peace has been declared. Toleration and love—that's what we Christians must follow, no?'

'You think we should tolerate their contamination of the sacraments?' He was aghast at my innocence.

I took the pottery bowl of water from his sentry and drank deep. The camp wine was bitter and the desert drier than a crone's dugs. I handed it to Juva who sipped only a little and washing out his mouth of grit and dust, spat the water on the ground.

'After three centuries, we, here in this downtrodden province, we are *all* that's left of Christ's *true* disciples. We are the final, hard, unyielding kernels of the uncompromised Catholic Church. We kneel to no earthly emperor. We hasten to worship at the feet of Christ in the next life.'

I felt my own life beyond was hurrying too quickly toward me, so I blurted out, 'But Romans are turning Christian! Surely they can be brought around to your view of discipline and purity?'

Now I'd angered him. 'Christians? Who seize our land? Drain away our oil and harvest our grain? Build walls pushing our people into the barren desert? Groom our children as slaves . . . and battlefield fertilizer?'

'The Emperor Constans—'

Juva threw his head back in hollow mirth. 'I didn't know you were a comedian as well as an ignorant ruffian! What do you know, picker, of the Emperor? He and his family are worse hypocrites than their father. Their Catholicism is a sham, but anyway, that dissolute Emperor Constans won't last much longer. His "official" priests are just . . . politicians.'

I had run out of arguments and claims on his attention and worse—to my surprise and discomfort—Juva had yet to say anything that I could fault.

I wondered what the Commander or Leo would argue if they were here in this cave, listening to Juva's bitter and knowing cynicism. Constans' reign had survived his elder brother's greed to steal a larger portion of the empire, thanks to our army's loyal defenses. But rumors of Constans' personal corruption was filtering down through army ranks, depleting the enthusiasm of fighting men who had given him their loyal sweat and blood.

Now, it was almost as if Juva was voicing hidden resentment and pride seeded deep inside my own soul. His words were like rainwater on parched land, bringing to unexpected life those twitches of resentment against the Commander, Leo and illiterate brutes like Barbatio. Such feelings were disloyal in a slave, I knew, but I couldn't help their quickening to Juva's heated conviction.

'I was about to be sold into slavery if I didn't bend to my employer's will, ' I improvised. 'That's why I ran.'

I dared not tell him the truth—that my mother and I had already been sold through a broker to the powerful Manlius family more than a decade ago. Still but it felt good to unburden even a distorted part of my story and enjoy the irony. Here I was, acting out the charade of a free man fleeing slavery rather than an army man's slave earning freedom.

Juva sneered at my hesitation. 'So *be a man*! Hate them as much as we do! We're all equal before God. Christ shows us the way.'

He paused and his eyes narrowed at he scrutinized my docile pose. 'You don't strike me as a fool like so many out there. You do know what I'm saying?'

'You mean equal before God *in death*.' I felt a humid chill off the cave walls.

'Do you believe in our Savior? Are you willing to die as He died for us on the Cross? Do you really want to save your soul . . . or as Bomilcar suspects, just your skin?'

So Bomilcar had betrayed me? He'd spotted my instinct for survival as well as my skill with the weapon and condemned me to his leader.

'First, I . . . I want to learn.'

'Learn what, exactly?'

I could hardly answer, 'The identity of the mastermind behind your rebellion.' So I fumbled out, 'The truth, of course.'

He looked at me with a cynical curiosity and waited.

'I mean, the pure truths that the traitors forgot when they handed over the sacraments, Juva.'

'Do you know the great Church father, Tertullian?'

I smiled. 'No. Nor do you. He died a century ago.'

Juva looked up at me sharply. 'That's a clever joke . . . for an olive picker.' Too late I remembered Leo's last-minute warning, resist *showing off*. 'So you know Tertullian came from Carthago. His father was a Roman invader, like your landlords. But his heart was with his people here, people like us. Tertullian wrote that a martyr's death day is his birthday! Do you agree, picker?'

The right answer eluded me. This was a birthday I was determined to skip. My life hung in the balance of Juva's regard. I couldn't exit this shadowy hole, shocked and muttering, 'I've been chosen.' My mission was to worm my way into his trust, but if I went too far in swearing allegiance to their 'true'

Church, I might soon end up like that deluded howler I'd killed at the basilica altar back in Lambaesis.

So I couldn't let Juva imagine I was already converted to the cause without reserve.

'I want to agree, but I don't understand, Juva. Why be fanatics, rushing into martyrdom?'

'Tertullian teaches us that it is wrong for a Christian to flee martyrdom.'

'Why not stay alive for the resistance? What does Father Donatus want? Surely he wants his followers to live and expel the imperial frauds?'

Juva smiled. 'Donatus yet again?'

'Aren't we Donatists?'

Juva sighed, as a father explaining a simple idea to a child. 'That name makes us out to be heretical followers. No, we're the Church of the Martyrs. We need martyrs because Tertullian teaches that martyrdom is the seed of the true Faith. Not everyone is called to the ultimate sacrifice, but our movement needs such seeds to bloom in this desert of half-hearted hypocrisy.'

His dark eyes burned straight into mine. My fears were right. If it wasn't Bomilcar who had fingered me for death, somehow that fool Nico must have given our game away.

'What's your name again?' Juva just wanted to make sure one last time that he was condemning the right man.

'Marcus.'

'Marcus, we need leaders to guide the martyrs to sainthood and men who aren't afraid to speak up. Trained fighters with guts like you. Half the people partying outside this cave are cretins.'

'Yes, I can fight.'

'I learned something from Bomilcar today. He had the impression that the caravan men had orders to defend their cargo, but not to kill. Surely they were better armed than our side. Yet they stayed on the back foot. Do you share this view?'

I thought for a minute and replayed what I could of the heat of the skirmish.

'The only man we would have lost was the one I saved. He tried to thrust himself onto the point of a sword today.'

'It's as I thought. The colonists are under orders to create no new martyrs to our cause. I have a better idea. I've singled you out.'

My stomach dropped to knees. 'I'm honored.'

'In a few days, we're going to lead a procession to the cliffs around Nif en-Nsr near Ain Mlila. There, God's rocks will kill the chosen souls.'

It seemed a strange and creative definition of martyrdom, but playing for time, I kept that opinion to myself.

'The Romans may try and prevent us. I need strong men to escort the weak. I've added you to our guard to help protect our funds,' he gestured to a small strongbox in the shadows behind him, 'as well as to protect our volunteers on their journey to heaven. Nothing must disrupt our path.'

'I'll make sure of it.'

My breath started filling my lungs again. So Nico hadn't squealed. Bomilcar merely wanted my sword arm wielding an olivewood club under his command. I would be protecting martyrs, not joining them.

It was a reprieve of sorts, but I was no closer to discovering who or what was sustaining Juva and the other Circumcellion cells with the contents of that strongbox.

Juva dismissed me with a wave of his hand. 'You can go now, but remember, I'm no a fool, Marcus. I'll be watching how you serve our Lord. Betray us and you die—and not as a glorious martyr—but as disloyal scum.'

Chapter 9, The Martyrs
Prepare

—THE CIRCUMCELLION CAMP, EVENING—

I stumbled out of the cave with a brow covered in sick sweat, clammier than any I'd felt in the heat of honest combat. Verbal jousting with Juva scared me more than I'd expected—and not only because I didn't want to follow those two men already saying their farewells to their fellow converts.

At least for the moment, I'd escaped that kind of 'liberation.'

No, the fear lay hard and heavy in the pit of my stomach because I understood these Circumcellions better than I wanted to admit. Of course, I couldn't condone their mindless violence at the wedding feast, but I could feel their righteous anger in being relegated to outlaws for standing by their beliefs and defending their people. All the way to the burning stakes, they're refused to compromise their principles or faith.

In short, they were stubborn as mules—like me.

There was no need for any formal announcement that we'd be marching north to the cliffs of Nif en-Nsr. Once the two 'chosen ones' told the manner of their coming deaths, the news raced through the camp. Already I could measure the sick agitation coursing through the faithful as they readied for the next stage of their struggle.

It was difficult finding my way back through the churning clusters and mini-camps that marked one group of

Circumcellions from another. Still, I was starting to recognize faces—not just Bomilcar and his toady pal, the little Capussa, but some of the more eye-catching wenches and biggest drunks.

I also noticed that Sophonisba's circle of devout women kept a distance from the rowdier converts who veered between bouts of celebration and sullen, petty quarrels over bread and firewood.

I decided to find Nico before we broke camp. It should have been easy to spot him—as long as he was upright. It was important that he get out of the camp, so we could set up the signaling before the Circumcellions migrated farther from the Longus estate. Leo would be wondering what had happened to both of us. I was reckoning that moving camp meant new contacts or fresh supplies from outside—clues to Juva's puppet-masters.

For a minute I thought I saw Nico's red shirt still bright amidst all these rags—but it turned out to be only a kerchief waved over the head of one frenetic dancing girl being taunted by an even meaner bitch.

I strained to remember how far through the crowd I should trudge to reach the place where I'd stepped over Nico's sleeping body, but when I thought I'd reached the right spot, I met only a trio of bearded toughs sharing a bladder of booze as they polished their 'Israelites' with oil.

I looked for a path up the rocky slope just above my own sleeping niche. From that height I might make Nico out in the crowd below. Instead, a hand grabbed my bare shoulder. I winced with pain.

'Your wounds have calmed down some.' It was Bomilcar and he knew how to hurt.

'I have Sophonisba's medicine in my pouch.' Her comforting salve nestled in the pouch next to Leo's vial of deadly poison.

'She's a good woman. Come with me. We'll talk with the others now and plan better than we did this morning.'

I wanted to appear eager. I followed the tall Numidian through the camp in the other direction. I'd resume my search for Nico after dusk.

Bomilcar had chosen three others as escorts for the procession. All of them were as tall, strong and young as me, but within minutes that shrimp Capussa had glued himself to us. That made five and a half of us.

Aside from our general robustness, we had less in common than the others might notice. They were all much browner than I and, even stripped down to my last cloth with wounds still red from the lash, I couldn't help noticing that I was in much better shape. Their hands were already those of old men—distended, buckled, broken and scarred.

I listened carefully to their grunts of welcome and kept my own words to a minimum. I still wasn't sure if my Punic dialect could fool a suspicious picker as well as it held up to the ears of a Carthaginian priest in a cave.

'We have all tomorrow to prepare to move out of here,' Bomilcar said.

I had no exact idea of our current whereabouts, nor even an inexact idea of how much ground Nico and I had covered from Leo's farm, or for that matter, the farm's position relative to Nif en-Nsr. I had a vague memory of the terrain we'd marched between the military camp and Lambaesis because any army man could calculate distance crossed at a set pace, calculating hours to miles.

But in our journey through the night to this hidden plateau, Nico's limp had been irregular and his direction unsure. Now, lack of familiarity with 'our own' terrain might show me up any second as an impostor.

'We'll hold apart, putting a hundred people in between each of us,' Bomilcar said. That told me he knew we had at least four hundred of these fools in our care. Our raid had brought in barely enough to feed two hundred for more than a day or two.

'How about a diagram to decide positions?' I suggested, drawing an 'x' in the sand, 'Here's the camp.'

Bomilcar nodded, and to my relief, his vanity took over. I figured anyone who wore a stylish buckle like his had a streak of ego I could drive a mule team through.

'It couldn't be more straightforward,' he said, drawing his plan in the dirt. 'We'll connect up with the military road running past from Lambaesis here,' he scratched a diagonal line starting slightly west of my 'x,' 'and head north toward Constantina, up here. We'll take a day to reach the west bank of the freshwater lake, here, where we'll make camp and the martyrs can take their ritual bath. Then another three or so days to reach the cliffs, here.'

'We don't have state road permits,' I said. 'We'll provoke trouble and arrests if we clog up the main transport road like that.'

'That's the idea, you moron picker,' Capussa sneered.

Bomilcar nodded. 'It's the fastest way to make a ruckus. We want the farmhands and village people to witness the sacrifice of our faithful. Some may even join us on the way.'

'Got enough supplies to make the journey?'

'No. That's another reason to take the imperial road—we'll get fresh water at the lakeside and beg food and wine off the villagers. When they hear we're escorting martyrs to the cliffs, they'll be willing to donate the price of admission for the show.'

'And the strongbox? Who exactly guards it? The procession will be hard to defend with so many stragglers drawn out along the road.'

Bomilcar swallowed and turned away, 'Leave the strongbox to me . . .'

My position turned out to be end man and I liked it that way. I could survey the entire line from the back and maybe signal to Nico the best good moment to make a run for it without being caught. Now that I was determined to get Nico out of the camp and into position, where in Hades was he?

The sun was setting over a scene of exhaustion as the excitement of the imminent trek subsided into a frenzy of packing. I heard arguments breaking out over the use of the animals at hand—our horses, mules and the oxen drawing the carriages stolen only that morning. I saw that places on the hijacked vehicles were already the objects of bitter jockeying between the camp bullies and Sophonisba, who'd left the safety of her women's enclave to lobby for places for the lame and sick.

And it was then that I spotted Nico, exaggerating his limp to hitch himself a ride.

'Where've you been?' he shouted when he saw me, disregarding any caution in the mayhem all around.

'What are you doing still here?'

'I'll be damned if I'm limping halfway to Constantina. Am I the only one who knows how far the hell that is? I'm guessing most of these people have never left the county.'

'It doesn't matter. You've got to get away from here, tonight. You've still got your piece of mirror, right?'

'Here somewhere. If some bastard hasn't robbed me in my sleep.' He fumbled through his belt pouch, 'Yeah.'

'You've got to escape tonight, and get word back to Leo. They're carrying a strongbox, probably full of coins. I'll stake my life those aren't pickers' donations.'

'So?'

'Just tell Leo that I'm tracking the box.'

'No.'

'No?'

'No, I can't'

'Why not?'

'You're the last person I'm taking advice from. Do you know what they do to people who try to quit??'

'What?'

'Look over there. No, not there, over there—the one poking around with the long stick.'

'The blind man?'

'They *blinded* him. Some of these bastards reckoned he needed to learn from the example of Saul, struck blind as he travelled the road to Tarsus. Ever heard of him?'

'Yes, I heard the story . . . but then he regained his sight and became St Paul.' Lady Laetitia's Christian lessons were coming in handy.

'Well, I don't suppose there's much hope of that happening this time,' Nico shrugged. We watched this pitiful man, buffeted by the unfeeling ruffians, hold tight to a rock for balance at the foot of the rocky slope that paralleled my own bedding-down spot.

'How did they do it?'

'He was a porter slave travelling with an oil shipment they attacked a few months back. He told me that when the Circumcellions "liberated" his wagon, he ran off into the hills. They caught him and said he needed "enlightenment." Then they rubbed lime and soda into his eyes. I've been making sure he got bread and water and trying to keep him from getting stepped on.'

'They can't have had orders from Juva to do that.'

'Who's Juva?'

'The so-called Captain of the Saints around here and don't you forget it. Keep your head down, Nico. He's the one who bestows martyrdom on you when you least expect it.'

'I guess you're right. I've got to get out of here. I just want to get back to my girl. I didn't have a chance to say good-bye. Anyway, I'm bound to be a drag on this march.'

'That'll give Juva all the more reason to expedite your trip to heaven. So *go!*'

Nico looked around him. 'There's only one exit pass out of this canyon and the sentries have it covered.'

'So when we get underway, limp like hell, team up tight with the blind guy as an excuse and slowly drop right to the back of the procession. I'll be the last guard on the trek but don't greet me. When the moment's right, we'll shove you into hiding, in some ditch or dune, and you lay low until the whole train of Circumcellions has crossed the horizon. I'll take the blind man's hand and he won't know what happened.'

'You think it'll work?'

'If it doesn't and they blame me for your defection, we're both in trouble.'

'All right. I want to get out of this.'

'And if you don't want to be spotted, lose the red shirt, okay?' I called at his departing back, 'Now where're you going?'

'Back to the dice players. At least they help the time pass. Maybe I'll win another bladder of wine, or better yet, lose my shirt,' he chuckled, pulling at his loud tunic. Last I saw of him, he was limping away and hailing the regulars at the heart of a knot of gamblers.

The bakers were busy, grinding the last flour for the next day's rations, while the camp settled down to what, I now assumed, was their nightly ritual of prayer on one side of the camp and lustful release in semi-hidden spaces. I braced myself for another night of sleep broken by the grunting and sighs of the promiscuous rutting that seemed a feature of the 'freedom' of these 'liberated' Christians.

It had seemed a day without end. Yet dusk fell at last. Lantern oil was as plentiful as food was scarce. A glow from dozens of nests formed by the Circumcellions at rest shone under a cloudless desert sky.

I laid my head on the ground, making myself as comfortable as I could. I pretended it was just another night on campaign. I was just outside the Commander's private tent, sheltered from the winds by my army-issue blanket and rocked to sleep by the familiar rhythms and subdued routine of army discipline. I drifted off . . .

'Picker! I need you!' It was Sophonisba bending over me in the shadows and shaking my shoulder. She was leaning so close to me, the aroma of medicinal herbs rising from her cotton *stola* bit my nostrils.

'I'm tired, woman, please, I must sleep.'

'You must come with me, now.'

'Tomorrow. I'll come tomorrow. Whatever it is, I can carry or pack a load for you tomorrow.' I put my head back on the sand and closed my eyes.

'You *must* come with me. *Now*, please.'

'What is it?'

'Yesterday you promised to repay me. Now you can. But come *quickly!*'

If I was dreaming, it was a painfully real dream, what with her claw-like fingers digging into my shoulders as if she'd never tended my lash marks only the day before.

I staggered to my feet. Still drowsy, I followed her ragged silhouette—and nearly lost her twice—as she darted between the sleepers. I assumed we were heading to the peaceful corner where the *sanctimoniales* worked their needles and sorted herbs, but no, the sinewy crone was leading me away from Juva's cave.

We threaded past one group after another in the opposite direction, crossing a hundred feet or so of plateau toward the roughest neighborhood of the camp where the sentries guarded the mouth of the enclosure and the smell of human piss and turds clogged my nose.

'There, look!' Quick! Stop them!'

She pointed into the thick of a roustabouts' gang. They were all drunk enough—that was obvious from their red faces, loud guffaws and unsteady lurching.

I made out through the lantern light the teeth-gritting, joyless lust of at least two couples humping in full view of the others, hardly conscious of their shame. I'd seen worse on campaign, though Roman army men treated their regular followers and mates better by far. I reckoned Sophonisba knew the ways of human dregs. Dignity was a luxury for their kind. I couldn't believe the haggard wise woman was so worried about the morality of debtors, drunkards and aged whores she would drag me through hundreds of people at midnight just to witness their degradation.

Only yards away, a gang of four or five men tussled over possession of a new tunic. Some of the dancing girls looking on were drunk enough to cheer their favorite's victory over this trifle, and it seemed safest to leave them to their petty pastime.

I shook my head and was about to turn away when Sophonisba cried, 'No, you must *save her!*' She pointed at two men farther back in the darkness well out of the lantern's circle of light—one was nearly a giant, burnt oak-dark by a life in the sun. His oiled leg muscles shone bare under a dirty robe hitched up around his loins and tied tight with a crude rope.

The other man was more sunburnt and fairer, wearing only a short tunic. Of the two, the smaller one was definitely worse off for wine. It was only a matter of time before he lost his quarrel.

'They're too drunk to know what they're doing!'

I peered closer through the flickering shadows. Their nasty squabble was a struggle over a slight, white shape—like a frail ghost—pulled roughly, back and forth, between them. They were fighting for the girl Kahina.

It looked far from a game to her. As wild-eyed as an animal in a trap, she was sobbing but too paralyzed to do much more than cry for help over the furious drumming and chanting around the small campfire that lit up the scene with a nightmarish ephemerality.

'All right, let her go!' I shouted at them. Pounding through the churned-up dust of their marked territory, I thrust myself between Kahina and the small man, reckoning that I'd get him out of the way and then reason with the giant. The little one hadn't seen me coming and it was easy to catch his arm and release his grip on Kahina with a powerful chop of my hand to the inner elbow. He lost hold of her and she tumbled into the arms of the taller drunk.

'Piss off.' I kicked the runt in the stomach for good measure, then turned around and warned the big one, but he was already backing off deeper into the shadows and dragging Kahina backwards underneath his thick arms.

'Sooner or later, she's going to die a martyr like the rest of us, so there's no reason to save herself for Christ,' he spat at me with contempt. 'That's not what *agonistici* ask of our women.'

'Let her go. She doesn't want you.'

'Here, they're free and equal, not slaves or servants. All that obedience and virtue is for farting *traditor* cowards and their whimpering priests,' he snarled.

'If she's so free, let her chose her man,' I yelled back, following his footsteps deeper into the darkness.

'The girl is new and doesn't understand our ways, do you?' He tried to kiss her face but she jerked her mouth away from his lips.

'She's *free* now. Let her go.'

The others took no notice. The fight had been won now. They went back to their mindless revels. I held my ground, wishing I had a weapon to level the field.

'Why rape a boring virgin when you can have a whore with tricks to please you?'

'This little tease needs training,' he growled, tightening his hold. At least my challenge had emboldened Kahina. Instead of shaking with fear, she had started to make the most of my distractions, twisting herself this way and that, trying to free the giant's hold on her. Already with one hand, he was hiking his loin-tied robe loose, baring his ready sex, and licking her cheek as she pushed back against him.

She was fighting him off the strength of a panicked animal trapped back in the Circus arena in Roma. I was frantic and couldn't figure how tackling him bare-fisted was going to free her. Any minute now, he would disappear with her into the black gloom of the wilds beyond the brush curtain and out of the camp's reach and beyond my tracking either of them until it was too late.

I heard pounding feet behind and turned to tackle the little drunk again, reckoning he'd decided to side with his wrestling pal in the hope of leftovers. Instead, it was the wild-eyed Sophonisba weighed down with one of the knobbed 'Israelite' clubs.

She thrust it into my hands.

The goon saw I was armed now, but using Kahina as his shield, also knew I couldn't get at him without hurting her. I was taller than most men, and I aimed to land an overhead blow on his shoulder, but he parried my swing effortlessly without losing his hold of his prize. He almost managed control of the club with one meaty hand but I lurched back and wrested it out of his grasp.

We squared off again, him inching backwards with her deeper into the black night. Soon all I could make out was the white of her dress, even though she struggled only a dozen feet ahead of me.

Then her eyes caught mine in one last desperate glance and she dug her jaw down and sank her teeth into his wrist. He bent his head down in pain, and I raced forward and caught his temple with one swift swing of the club from my right, knocking him sideways. Kahina yanked his bleeding forearm off her chest and raced past me for the safety of the camp.

Bellowing, the hooligan rushed at me, both arms outstretched to get me in his murderous grip. I dodged low to convert his charging force into my own, and brought up the club horizontally to hold it in both hands as a crossbar. I shoved it at his legs. I felt the club smack hard against his knees but I'd only slowed him down as he felt wood strike bone.

He took me around the neck from above with one mitt and was trying with all his might to snap my head back with the force of his palm on my forehead. I brought my right knee straight up into his groin and sent him back roaring and heaving a few feet away.

I still had the club but I wasn't yet used to its weight and timing. I longed for my stabbing little *pugio* and waited for his next move, gauging which way to swing the club, but as he charged me again, I turned it on its end, which I'd never yet seen a Circumcellion do, and jammed it hard right into his stomach as if it were a sword.

He folded over, hanging on to the wood and pulled it hard, trying to win it off me.

His groin must be killing him with pain, but he was willing himself to fight on through the shock. And my jab to the stomach had winded as well as surprised him. His type knew how to swing but weren't used to sudden thrusts.

'Break him, Stembanos!' someone cried. Lantern lights were moving toward us, flickering all around. A circle of rowdies had abandoned their warm fires to cheer us on and wager which of us would prevail.

Stembanos and I squared off at each other for another minute. He had height and strength while I had brains and a weapon, plus one great advantage—I was sober. When I weaved from side to side, he lost focus—he was seeing double from drink.

So I zigzagged toward him, left and right, and saw him squinting harder to keep me in his sights. If I could keep this up while avoiding his iron grip, I had a chance to take a decisive swing.

I kept at it, and at last, it worked—he lost patience and lunged for me. I dodged him and seized my best and only chance to send a clean blow down on the back of his head as he leaned past me. The club made a sickening thud. I worried that I'd murdered him, but he was just out cold.

It was over for the night.

The gamblers settled their debts on the spot and offered me wine from their skins. I shook them off and headed back into camp. I staggered into the enclave of boulders where Sophonisba and her women always bedded down. Neither the old woman nor Kahina was there.

I found them waiting across the entire mess of hundreds of people, sitting in the shadows where Sophonisba had woken me up half an hour before.

'You've beaten him?' Sophonisba asked.

'For now. He'll recover fast.'

'I know that Stembanos. He'll avoid *you* from now on.'

I waited for the two of them to leave me in peace and wondered why they'd waited for me in my spot instead of heading to their makeshift sanctuary right away. Kahina's dress was badly torn and she clutched at her cheap cotton skirt to cover herself from the desert chill.

'He'll leave her alone, too. Get some sleep.'

'Not if she's with us. He'll try for her again.'

Kahina kept her head face down in the shadows. Had I not seen it for myself, I would hardly have credited this shy young girl with daring to sink her teeth into Stembanos' flesh.

'She'd better stay with you,' Sophonisba ordered.

'I'm exhausted. I can't sit up guarding her all night.'

'She'll be safer with you,' Sophonisba insisted. Hiking up her long robe, she strode off with her *palla* pulled over her gray hair and her strong toes digging into the dirt.

'Why did Stembanos take you?' I asked Kahina.

'He thought I wouldn't care anymore as there's so little time left before we set off,' she whispered.

'What do you mean?' I croaked. My neck still ached from the bruises of Stembanos' strangulating grip. 'Why you? There are dozens of lusty women ready at his end of the camp.'

Kahina lifted her face to mine. In the darkness, her features seemed scarcely more than a change of shadows and shapes. Then someone with an oil lamp in hand padded past us, his feet churning up the soft pummeled ground. As his light flickered by us for a few seconds, her eyes glimmered up with both tears and relief.

'Didn't Sophonisba tell you?'

'Tell me what, Kahina?'

'That Juva has chosen me for *reditum*, too, to render my soul up to Christ. Within a week, I'll be lying dead at the foot of the cliffs at Nif en-Nsr—martyred by the rocks. Stembanos assumes that like all the other doomed women, I have no more reason to resist.'

'But it's suicide! Christians don't believe in suicide, no matter how many times these fools call it martyrdom!'

'No, the rocks will either kill me or not. That what Juva says.'

She spread herself down on the ground, laid her head next to my knees and closed her eyes, 'I'm so tired, I don't care any longer. In only a few more days, I'll be at peace with our Lord at last. But until then, I only want to rest.'

What horrible future had driven her to prefer the company of these outcasts ending in death on jagged rocks? All I knew was that I shared her desire for rest.

I hoped the next day would be more merciful to us both and slightly less eventful.

CHAPTER 10, ANOTHER'S BRIDE

—ON THE ROAD TO NIF EN-NSR—

The night stretched on and on, and yet I couldn't sleep.
After an honest battle, any imperial warrior, even a
lonely slave running military supplies and messages, lies down
and sleeps soundly on his bed of rank, justice, and discipline.

He hears the signal to sleep, so he sleeps. He hears the
orders to move and he moves.

I'd started this morning in a twisted skirmish fighting on
the wrong side of an ambush and then spent midday verbally
jousting with a defrocked priest spouting Tertullian. For a
rousing finish, I'd kneecapped a giant rapist.

Though the day had been full of strange things, the evening
was proving even stranger.

As I looked down at Kahina's slender brown body next to
mine, I faced a sweeter struggle—to fight off the urge to stroke
her long twists of thick brown hair bound with a length of
embroidered cotton. I smiled at her girlish vanities—not just the
cheap market ribbon woven by some peasant, but the square of
unbleached cotton she draped over her hair and shoulders as if
it were a wealthy lady's imported woolen *palla*. She had fastened
two bent copper pins over each shoulder as if they were costly
fibulae embedded with jewels.

Of course I'd had women. Even volunteer slaves in the
Roman army got their turn—always last, of course. Billeted in
small towns for the winter lull in campaigning, I'd wasted my
pocket change on weathered and toothless whores. Sometimes I

befriended a camp follower abandoned by her disgruntled cavalryman.

Sometimes I even found more than sex. There could be comradeship and humor and occasional affection and flattery. Before Gregorius' terrible wounding, I was told by one flame-haired troublemaker in Aquileia that I was 'as handsome as that arrogant Commander Gregorius—and younger and stronger.'

'Come on,' I blushed.

'If you wore his uniform and rode his horse, you would be twice as glorious as he.' She had promised she would follow me all the way to North Africa if I treated her well.

Then another man paid her more and she followed him to Sirmium instead.

A soft grayish-pink light peeked above the rim of the plateau's eastern slope. We had a long day of preparations ahead. I'd keep an eye out for that strongbox and notice which of Juva's lieutenants was entrusting it to Bomilcar's protection.

Unlock that treasure and you had the key to unlock this movement. If there was one strongbox here and hundreds of Circumcellion camps, then there had to be hundreds of strongboxes. Donations from olive pickers alone couldn't possibly fill them...Who supplied the boxes? Who refilled them?

I awoke from a short doze at dawn, just as the blinding curve of the sun cleared the ridge above us. The two cooks were patting and baking up flatbread on hot stones over a dung fire with a pair of Sophonisba's maiden assistants.

I watched them measure the dwindling water rations and count out dried figs into batches for distribution. I leaned on one elbow next to Kahina. She slept with one small hand clutching my ankle in her sleep.

⚶⚶⚶

The shapeless mass of hooded rags gradually took form as dirty, hungry people again. The looming hulk Stembanos was nowhere to be seen. I relaxed and waited as the Circumcellions regrouped for the day.

I now understood that what had struck my newcomer's eye as a whirling horde of unwashed madmen observed and obeyed a hidden ranking that favored Juva's lieutenants, sentries and holy women over the bankrupt debtors and drunks that festered along the perimeters. The well-behaved or weaker Circumcellions were looked after and the others were left on their own to hoard their own caches of food that they bartered and stole from each other.

Yet somehow this motley herd of homeless—like all the other gatherings like theirs across the Numidian province— claimed they were the last true Catholic faithful left in a corrupt, abusive Roman Empire.

What a strange ideas these Christians clung to! They threw themselves onto rocks or swords or into fires, then called it martyrdom? I'd learned from Lady Laetitia that the Christian religion forbade suicide. Yet didn't these fanatics provoke their own death by the most obvious means at hand?

And *suicide* as a route to their heaven? Even a slave like me, whose education was nothing more than literary crumbs dropping off the Senator's library table, even I knew different. Suicide to a Roman was the last resort of the proud or dishonored, of the sick man choosing a dignified end or a prisoner who wanted to cheat the Fates and their enemies of their capture and slavery. It was for when there was nothing left to those who'd failed their nation or were hopelessly abandoned in love.

The Carthaginian queen Dido had killed herself out of despair, falling on the very sword Aeneas left her as her Trojan lover's boat sailed out of sight toward Roma. Every Numidian knew the legend of Dido's tragedy. They didn't need Virgil for that.

But I didn't understand the philosophy of death espoused by Juva. What I did understand was the native fervor coursing through this crowd. I could even feel it taking root in me as I listened to the rough 'sha's' and throat-clearing 'h's' of their morning salutations and grumpy complaints. The slave's resentment was quickening in me, despite all my loyalties to the army and the Commander, despite all my memories of childhood in the Manlius clan where I'd been coddled as a slave pet and educated as if I were a whole man.

Even as she fell ill, Lady Laetitia had never raised her hand in anger or cursed me out of irritation when Gregorius spoiled me over her own nephew. Nor had she mistreated my humbled, discarded mother.

I had no cause to complain whatsoever.

Yet weren't these my people, just like my parents, simple farmers and mule traders ruined by drought? Runaway slaves and itinerant harvesters, all exploited by wealthy colonists clean and fragrant from their baths lined with mosaics and marble? I'd scraped their bodies clean myself—the Senator, his son and nephew—never asking myself what was right or wrong about with my servility.

But here, the echo of my mother's tongue, forbidden in the Manlius corridors and only whispered after nightfall each time I settled down next to her on that thin pallet, was softly evocative to my ears. Now those images of life in the back rooms of the Roman townhouse sprang to life as I listened to the chant of Sophonisba's women reciting their morning prayers.

If I wasn't careful, these emotions would cloud my judgment and drain my energy for the mission at hand.

Kahina sat up, still dazed from her sleep. 'I have only a few more days. I want to stay safe with you. May I march by your side today?'

'No, of course not. You'll be on display, along with the other future martyrs for all the villagers to admire as we pass. It's supposed to be glorious to show off your bravery and devotion. Don't worry. No one will trouble you.'

'You don't sound as if you believe. Aren't you prepared to die for our Lord?'

'Not quite yet.'

'Your voice betrays you. You're strong on the outside, but you mustn't be afraid to admit your fear to me. I'm so afraid of the cliffs and that last moment when I must leap. I'm afraid of the rocks below. I hope I die right away.'

'If you're so afraid, why—?'

'Because I think of what my life will become otherwise.' She avoided my gaze. 'I'm grateful that Juva gives me the freedom to choose Christ instead. Our Lord promises peace.'

'But you didn't really choose, did you? Juva decided for you.'

'He decided how and when but I came here of my own free will.'

'You're not veiled, like some of Sophonisba's companions.'

'You mean the *sanctimoniales*? Oh, they took vows when the priests consecrated them. Even Stembanos wouldn't dare touch one of them!'

'Because they're not as pretty as you.'

Kahina laughed. 'Who knows, under those veils?' She had a lovely smile showing even white teeth against plush brown-rose lips.

She turned serious. 'I'm a servant girl, but they treated me worse than a slave. My employer promised me to an old man with a cruel face and he gave my family money for my virginity.'

'Now they'll have to give it back.'

'I can't bed with that man. He wouldn't love me or know me or even stay with me. He wouldn't talk to me as you're doing now.'

'You could always bite his arm to get his attention. Stembanos won't forget that in a hurry.'

'He'd probably kill me if I dared.'

'So run away, fine. But why jump to your death?'

'Because it brings honor, not just to my parents and family, but to my entire village. It will make up for the money my family will have to pay back because I ran away.'

I shrugged a little. 'Honor?' My disdain riled her.

'Oh, yes! Sophonisba told me about the sainted virgins Maxima and Donatilla. Consul Apulinus tortured them during the reign of Emperor Maximian. That's almost fifty years ago and people still praise their virtue.'

Kahina's face lit up now. She might have been one of Lady Laetitia's fashionable society friends back in Roma, gossiping about some muscle-bound gladiator's victory. As she kept talking, it struck me that these martyrs were like celebrities here in the colonial backwaters of Numidia. Kahina had known little else of the wide world.

'Listen, Marcus. It's an amazing story. It started on the proconsul's imperial estate in Thurburbo Maius where he ordered his two magistrates to arrest all the Christians. It was past midnight by the time this official Apulinus had them all rounded up. He ordered the Christians to sacrifice to the pagan gods or be tortured and killed on the spot. Everyone was terrified, of course.'

'Yes, I can imagine.'

'Even the deacons and the priests fell flat on the ground and worshipped the Roman idols, all of them, except for Maxima and her sister.'

'So Apulinus tortured them?'

'Well, first he gave them time to reconsider, but Maxima said, "It is better for me to be condemned by you than to defy the one, true God." And Donatilla spoke up and she was even braver than her older sister. She said that Christ was with them and that the Roman official spoke for the devil. So he starved them for days and days and gave them only gall and vinegar to drink but they didn't give in, so he released them to think about it.'

'That was fair of him. I would have run away, like you.'

'No, they walked proud in the streets, quite in the open and everyone admired them. A third girl named Secunda, only twelve years old, jumped out of her rich parents' window to join them. And then he—'

'This official Apulinus?'

'Yes, Apulinus arrested all three girls again. They still refused to worship the pagan gods, so he had them lashed. But they didn't give in.'

'They sound too tough to believe. Do you think perhaps Sophonisba exaggerated this story a little?'

'No, no! Then Apulinus had them forced onto a bed of crushed shells and rubbed their naked bodies all over with lime, so they were all cut up and burning sore.'

'They didn't give up, did they?' I didn't know her well enough to cajole, but my skeptical tone provoked her all the same.

'No! No! It only made them stronger, don't you see? And then,' she puzzled for a few seconds, 'I think that's when he revived them with more vinegar and had them stretched out on the rack.'

'But the girls held out, right?'

'Of course, because the Lord was with them in spirit. Apulinus started to get fed up with the whole thing because he was only following the Diocletian Edict and these women weren't tired at all! So he put burning coals on their heads . . . and . . . I think that was when he threw them into an arena of starving bears.'

'I can't imagine they'd taste very good after all that lime and vinegar.'

She reared away from me in dismay. 'How can you joke like that? Now comes the best part of the whole thing. God spoke to the wild animals and as Apulinus looked on, the bears shied away and *refused to eat the virgins.*'

'Oh, Kahina, you want to be a famous martyr, but I don't think you really want to die,' I said. I hardly knew the girl, yet I felt like throwing my arms around her foolish shoulders. Instead, I just shook my head, saying, 'Kahina, listen to me, you can't count on any hungry bear or jagged rock to spare you.'

She shook me off with a coy twist of the head, saying, 'You must believe it. Because otherwise, why did Apulinus have to behead them, one by one? He'd tried everything else he could think of.'

The sun was full up in the eastern sky now. It was time to eat our bread and dried fruit and then help with the packing and loading. With reluctance, Kahina prepared to leave. She pulled her cotton square well over her brow to cover her hair and features. 'Stembanos is not the only man I must avoid,' she said.

I watched her as she set off across the camp to Sophonisba. Discretion and modesty came naturally to her, but I could still admire her graceful hips underneath the long rough tunic as she slipped unnoticed through the ragged crowd.

Bomilcar, Capussa and the others let me help load the carriages. All morning we worked, testing the oxen's harnesses, allocating cargo space and tying up meager belongings until the midday heat signaled a rest for everyone.

For what it was worth, I'd beaten Stembanos in an all-out fight and I was now accepted as a Circumcellion. I threw my heart into the work. I guessed that strong hands willing to haul and carry were of more use to Juva alive than martyred. Only when I saw that the strongest were taking a break did I rest in the shade under the belly of one of the stolen carriages.

The strongbox was never far from my mind. Surely it would travel in Juva's carriage or on a wagon at Bomilcar's side. For the moment, it was nowhere to be seen. Nor did Juva emerge from his cave to lift a finger to assist his followers.

But I saw two of his lieutenants leaving his cave, one carrying a pouch bulging with coins. The burly duo trotted out over the plateau and through the brush barrier on two mules, leading a third animal, all of them loaded with empty water barrels. I was tempted to follow them somehow, then and there, but I feared the trip might only lead me to some farmer with a full well and an empty pocket and betray my dangerous curiosity in the bargain.

The three men returned only at dusk, walking ahead of the three mules weighed down now with water for everyone. I spotted my chance. The money pouch wasn't totally empty. Without hesitation, I dropped the crude bundles I was securing for Sophonisba and followed the man as he made his way from the makeshift stable corner toward the dim light coming from the mouth of the cave.

'Good foraging, brother?' I hailed him and fell into step.

'Good enough. No one will die of thirst tonight and happily, not all of it is water.'

'Wine for the martyrs?'

'Wine for all who wish to take a sip in the Lord's honor.'

'Wine costs real money, brother.'

'Don't worry. We always find friends who give us a fair price or better.' He waggled the handle of the olive club swinging at his side with a sly smile.

I was thinking as fast as I could. I trailed right behind him into Juva's presence with no excuse other than that the cave was wonderfully cool and I was pouring with the sweat and stink of the camp.

'You're back, Hiempsal! Good!'

'Enough wine for a day or two and plenty of water to hold us until we reach the lakeshore. They promise more food for us on the road ahead.'

There was no ceremony in the way Hiempsal tossed the money pouch back into Juva's pale hand. I hung around, hoping to see what Juva did with it.

Hiempsal lowered his voice. 'I have worrying news.'

'Sharp-eared, as usual, Hiempsal. What have you heard?'

'Two high-ranking inspectors, civil officials, landed in Carthago. There are rumors they intend to—'

'Wait,' Juva lifted a hand to cut Hiempsal off. 'What do you want, picker?'

'To . . . ask you if . . . if it's time to pack your books and belongings, Father.'

'I have Isalcas to do that, but . . . yes, why not? He's busy elsewhere.' Juva waved a pale hand in the direction of the rear of the cave—his heavy books sat next to a folded pile of simple tunics and a clean woolen cloak. I found coils of cotton straps of colorful embroidery carefully set aside for binding the books into a secure bundle. I took my time untangling the strings and arranging the books by size.

'Officials, you said?'

'Yes, Juva. The season of tolerance is ending. Emperor Constans has issued an edict commanding unity of the two churches, forcing the religious pacification of all Numidia Militaris. These two commissioners are here to shove their "unity" down our throats. They're carrying trunkloads of alms for the poor and chalices of gold and silver for the churches but instead of sharing out equally, they favor the imperial churches over ours.'

'Contaminated gifts from a corrupted throne.'

'The Holy Donatus met them on the docks at Carthago. He told them to sail back to Constans with their dirty money.'

'Brave and gentle Donatus,' Juva said, shaking his head.

'Not that gentle for such a frail old man. He shouted, "What has the Emperor got to do with the Church?" and said that our people must emulate Daniel, who chose to face the wild beasts rather than accept gifts from a Gentile king. He's sending letters to all his bishops instructing them to tell all the villages to refuse these Roman donations.'

'He's right. These are poisoned bribes from polluted hands. To accept their aid is to submit to imperial occupation. You know, sometimes it's hard to overestimate Roma's blundering. On the other hand, Donatus should be careful. Hungry people are hungry first, and faithful second. It's dangerous to refuse assistance and not offer any ourselves.'

'Once we run the Romans out, there'll be enough to keep everyone happy.'

'What do people say of these two envoys?'

I kept on packing but was running out of books to stack.

'They say they're arrogant pagans who know little of Christianity and even less of Africa's holy martyrs or bitterness. I say they're two little turds shat out of the emperor's buggered ass.'

Juva heaved a sigh at Hiempsal's vulgarity. 'What's their route?'

'Carthago first, then the road heading southwest. Already, starving widows and children are waiting for them along the roads, claiming their handouts.'

'They've starting handing out the money?'

'Not yet. To get it, the people must attend Mass in the Catholic basilica where Macarius places this bust of the late Constantine on the altar like some icon.'

'Blasphemy!' Juva's hands shook. 'They tried under Taurinus and there was bloodshed but,' he stopped and smiled, 'they also made many martyrs. Now they try to subvert ignorant street people with their dirty coins. Then they'll move into the countryside and drive the Church of the Martyrs from all the parishes they can buy back. Without the protection of the peasants, we *agonistici* will be arrested, tortured and executed.'

'But this time the Romans promise peace. They're clever. They accuse the imperial priests of neglecting the poor. They say the Emperor wants to relieve the misery of his African people to expiate his sins.'

'Ha! Clever? Constans, the runt of Constantine's murderous litter, the catamite Constans aspires to be a better Christian than any of us?'

Juva and Hiempsal had forgotten about me, but there are only so many ways one can arrange a few books. After I'd tied up the bundles, I crouched in the shadows rotating them around in piles.

'What's their exact route after Carthago?'

'The trunk road through Theveste to Lambaesis, via Vegesela. They've got a small civil escort.'

'That's *very* interesting.'

'Why?'

'That the army keeps its hands clean. The soldiers are fed by the taxpayers and our taxpayers don't want civil war.' Juva pondered in silence as Hiempsal and I waited.

'Hand me that metal box back there, picker.' They hadn't forgotten me after all. I scrabbled on my haunches across the dirt under the low hanging stone roof, working deeper into the back recesses where the strongbox sat half hidden.

The priest unlocked it with an iron key hanging off his belt. Then to my surprise, instead of replacing Hiempsal's depleted allowance into the box, he opened the lid wide and grabbed out another handful of coins and handed the pouch back full.

'Use them freely but don't leave a telltale trail of gold,' he told Hiempsal. 'Tomorrow, when we head north, speed ahead of us to collect information sifting down from the coast. Are the Carthaginians obeying Donatus' boycott or feeding from the Roman trough? Are they filling those phony churches or steering clear? I've got to know more! We can play the Romans' game—and not with pathetic letters to the bishops—but using their own tainted coin.'

'All right, Juva.'

119

Juva continued, 'Listen to the gossip of the army veterans and their whores in the wine houses. Find out which way the army really leans and why they're leaving these envoys with a civil escort. Make contacts with any other *agonistici* raiding the marketplaces. Collect rumors from street beggars lining up to kneel and pray for bribes. They don't care whose portrait is on the altar—Constans or the Sun God's pet kitten. For one *solidus* you can buy almost anyone. I need to know which way things are going. Report back to me on the plains of Ain Mlila.'

'Certainly, Juva.'

I'd seen and heard more than I'd hoped. I scuttled out of the cave on Hiempsal's heels and headed back to Bomilcar's team, careful to show no more regard for Hiempsal's quiet preparations than those of anyone else in the camp.

Now that I knew who was Juva's spy, I had to make doubly sure Juva's spy didn't know me.

And I'd learned something from that strongbox. As I watched from under my lowered lashes—the way all good slaves and servants watch their masters for signals, gestures and moods—Juva's hand had sunk deep into the coins. The box wasn't filled with what itinerant priests would scrounge from random donations in rural churches—dirty, battered change given by gullible olive harvesters and devout widows.

No, the strongbox was piled to the brim with golden coins, all of the same denomination and sheen, all looking like they might have come from a single source. It might have been booty from a lucky raid, but I suspected something or someone else. Even if nobody claimed responsibility for the likes of Juva's violent beggars and drunks, this money said they must have a powerful backer all the same—just as Leo and his curious friend Apodemius feared.

It was urgent that Nico get word to Leo and the military that our caravan was heading northwards in a provocative display of sacrifice and resistance. If the Romans wanted to avoid another inspirational massacre and keep the oil deliveries moving to the ports of Rusicada and Carthago, they'd have to keep these factions from erupting. I wasn't clear how far Juva and his fellow Captains of the Saints might go to overwhelming

Donatus' peaceful boycott with a violent insurrection of their own.

Kahina was waiting for me in the dark shadows of my shrubbery nest with two portions of food. She'd spent the day hidden from the likes of Stembanos, working with Sophonisba preparing herbal paste for the sores of hard walking to come.

'I've decided to stay with you until the final leap,' she announced. It was not quite as decisive as the way she'd sunk her teeth into Stembanos' hairy flesh, but I welcomed her decision with a confused smile. No matter how much I worried about Kahina's plunge onto the rocks, I couldn't risk her marching alongside as the caravan trailed off ahead of us leaving me to secrete Nico out of sight.

'That's not possible. I can't guard the tail of the train and watch out for you at the same time. But you can stay here for the night if you feel safer with me.' I'd likely get more sleep that way than having Sophonisba wake me again for another brutal duel.

'If I only have a few more days, it's my choice how to spend them. Christ is not my bridegroom just yet.' She smiled and looked at me with life in her eyes. How much of 'love' had this innocent seen in service to her colonial masters?

'I'm sorry, Kahina. You're sweet and very . . .well, very beautiful, but we can't travel together. Everyone will look to you as the model of virtue and strength. You must march with pride like, what were their names? Maxima?'

'And Donatilla and Secunda.'

'Those three. They didn't hide their faces at the lagging end of a procession. They led the other faithful in song and prayer.'

'You don't want me?'

'I'm not sure what you mean. You're going to be fêted and celebrated as a virgin martyr for the entire route until we reach the cliffs of Nif en-Nsr. Isn't that what you want?'

'You know very well what I mean. The other women here have claimed their freedom as equals to men. I'm not shameless but I'm not a child either. Here, give me that salve.'

I handed her Sophonisba's supply of soothing salve and she stroked it across my back with her soft fingers.

'You think you can't show me such attention but you don't understand the *agonistici* love of life as well as Christ. They celebrate the glories of love, food and drink before giving it all up for our Lord.'

'I thought you wanted to emulate the virgin saints.'

'I hate drunks like Stembanos and the weak and stupid boys like . . . Anyway, I know the man I like as well as I know the ones I don't like.'

I admired the determined way she thrust her chin out at me. In her small stubborn way, she reminded me of all the determined Numidian women I'd known as a young child— driving their herds, pounding olives to oil and berating their lazy men.

But I could be just as stubborn.

'I'm sending you back to Sophonisba,' I decided, but I could no longer resist stealing a first and last long kiss.

'You cannot afford to send me away,' she said at last.

She nestled softly like a small brown fawn into the crook of my arms and leaned close. 'If you refuse my martyr's last wish, I might betray you to Juva.'

'Oh,' I scoffed, 'Juva will laugh at my stupidity and just find you a better and handsomer choice of companion.'

'I don't think so,' she murmured. 'Because if I betray you, Juva would make sure you leap to your own death at my side— but not as a martyr.'

She lit the oil lantern resting in the sand at our ankles and lifted the feeble flame up close so that she could examine my stunned expression.

'You see, Marcus, I could betray you at any moment . . . because I know who you really are,' she whispered.

Chapter 11, Kahina's Secret

—TOWARDS THE AIN MLILA PLAINS —

I bluffed, 'I'm just a picker. Nobody special.'

Kahina smiled through the flickering shadows, 'From a farm nearby?'

'That's right.'

'Which one?'

'I thought I told you. The Longus Farm.'

'The property of Leontus Longus Flavius?'

'That's right.'

'You're lying.'

'I escaped here with another man a few nights ago. Well, he followed me here. He's lost somewhere out here, but he'll vouch for me—if he's not dead drunk.'

'Oh, I'm sure he will, but that just makes two liars instead of one. You see, I was born near that farm. I've spent my entire life working for Leo, bathing and babysitting his two little brats when I was scarcely bigger than they were. When I was tall enough to work around the open ovens, I learned to bake. I've watched the pickers come and go each season. I've helped prepare their meals, served at their miserable tables, and put up with their pinching and dirty jokes.'

She sat up and spit out, 'I've never seen you pick a single olive. But I *have* seen you before!'

Then she burst into cynical laughter that didn't suit her one bit. I shushed her with the palm of my hand, but it wasn't necessary. The camp had finished its meal. The drummers and dancers were warming themselves up with rude gestures and flowing drink. I could see in the distance the lustier 'sacred virgins,' the true professionals, were already baring their breasts and rumps, dividing up partners for the night.

I tried to weigh where I stood and then recalled the sequence of events the night Nico and I were taken. It was clear enough—the other 'recruits' Juva had mentioned as I groveled in the cave that same night included Kahina. It was just bad luck.

I mustered a playful tone. 'Is this another of your fairy stories, then, like hungry bears that scorn delicious virgins? You imagine you saw something who looked like me, that's all.'

'You were parading across Lambaesis forum the day of the wedding massacre. I was standing behind the twins when Leo greeted you. You were wearing the livery of a Roman soldier and you were carrying a sword and dagger, but you bowed deep and kept your eyes lowered with respect.'

I took a deep breath. She really did know me—well enough to get me killed.

'But I didn't lower my eyes, ' she continued. 'You were the handsomest young man in your unit.'

I was no longer confused. I was trapped. I was hers.

'I can explain,' I said. 'I'm not a soldier. I'm a slave, a *voluntarius* assigned to my owner. The army's too tough. I got caught stealing. I was whipped hard and there was more of the same to come. I got fed up. I had no choice but to run.'

'And what if I tell Juva that you're runaway Roman property and not a picker?'

'He won't care,' I shrugged, 'As long as I fight and raid for him.'

'Juva might question you for the truth. Or the others might turn on you.'

I remembered the pathetic 'enlightened' blind man clinging to Nico's arm.

'Are you threatening me, Kahina?'

The drums beat louder now, pounding in time with the fear thumping in my chest. The wild-haired dancers were stamping their feet around the campfires to clapping and cheers. I could hardly hear my own voice and wondered if even our retreat from the general celebration might be cause for the mob's suspicion.

'No, Marcus, I'm making love to you,' she sighed and lifted her face for another kiss. I embraced her and returned her caresses and sighs. I laid her prone on the ground behind the scrawny bush that half-shielded us from view. It was to be a picker's marriage bed for Kahina, a girl who deserved soft feather pillows and cool silk covers. I could feel her own heart pounding as hard as the savage drums continued across the hundreds of yards of valley. The glow of dozens of rude little flames beyond us glinted off the crude brooches holding her tunic up at each shoulder.

But for all that those pins stayed fastened, my hands reached below her simple skirts and felt the softest skin above her knees. I slowly touched her round trembling thighs as I scattered kisses on her neck and ears. I was telling myself that I had no choice and that this was the only means to seal Kahina's lips and protect my mission—to do just as she wished. It was all I wished as a man and all I could do as a spy. I pressed myself gently forward, forward and as she cried out, I took her full, holding her tight and rocking her in my arms.

The drums urged us on our dance of passion. I lost myself in her little cries and eager thrusts. It had been months since I'd had a woman and never in my life one as young and fresh as Kahina. Her thick hair fell in a clean brown pillow smelling of herbs and wildflowers over our bed of dry sand.

She was indeed virgin, but hardly virginal. What had she witnessed—as we slaves and servants, we half-humans left standing by always do? What had she learned of love while her Roman master frolicked with his mistress in Rusicada or just ravaged his servants on his couch back at the farm? What private dreams were coming true as it was now her turn to give herself, just as she'd seen others do?

She was hardly out of childhood, but already used the wiles of a woman. She'd taunted me, threatened and frightened me, and now exposed me to her delicious whims.

As my reward, she charmed and teased me all anew. My lust was up. The drums wouldn't stop. I heard the chanting all around us and felt her breathing underneath me with her fingers exploring my waist, my hips and my groin. I stroked her, kissed her, and tasted her without knowing what I was doing. I stopped calculating the cost. Together we moved to those abandoned rhythms. I experienced a soaring joy surge inside of me. I was no longer earning my freedom. Well before time, I was already enjoying it.

☯☯☯

We dropped off to sleep as the music fell silent and the untamed noises of the camp's louche depredations subsided into snores. The campfires smoldered and sent wisps of smoke into the grey-pink sky.

I woke up just before dawn to hear the cooks grinding the last of our grain, stoking their makeshift oven, and patting out bread. It was the same routine as the previous morning, yet everything looked different to me now. Once again, Kahina lay nestled in my arms but now she was mine.

'It's time for you to join Sophonisba and the other women,' I whispered. 'You must march at the head of the caravan. Go now, before it's too late.'

'No, I'll wait until the crowds are up and moving. I don't want certain people to see me.'

'Cover your head again.'

'That's not enough. There is one who has eyes like a hawk, though he limps like a crippled mule.'

I jerked my head away from the morning bustle to stare at her. She was adjusting her long tunic behind the bushes and scanning the hundreds of jostling bodies scattered across the valley floor. 'Once everybody's up and yelling for their breakfast, he's less likely to notice me. It's easy then to veil my face under my shawl.'

I felt slightly dizzy as I tested her with a few well-chosen words: 'But you can always avoid someone so obvious—wearing that red shirt and all.'

'Yes, so far he hasn't caught me—'

She stared at me in turn. 'How did you guess who I meant?'

My heart plummeted as I put it all together. She'd come from Leo's estate and she could be none other than the missing girl Nico had been searching the kitchens and corridors for day after day, the girl he talked of, dreamed of, and wanted to say good-bye to—the girl he thought was off carrying the shopping bags for Leo's twins or helping with the laundry loads.

I pressed my eyelids in burning shock as I foresaw problems Kahina couldn't imagine.

'Why do you fear Nico?' I asked. 'Because you're his girl?'

'Of course not. Because he'll turn me in, of course. Surely that's why he's here? He's hunting for me. They're bound to want me back. I've been promised. The money has been paid.'

'To *Nico*? But I thought he was joking—'

'No, I told you, to a much older man.'

There was an awful silence between us and I could see her thoughts racing ahead of mine. What did she know? What was she not telling me?

She pulled her threadbare *palla* over her hair and grabbing the arm of a passing whore, she rushed off gabbling nonsense about spare water for washing to the bewildered passer-by. To any onlooker, the two women looked inseparable allies. I knew Kahina would wend her way safely in this fashion to Sophonisba's circle and hide herself away again behind their modest partitions of hanging cotton.

What a mess this was. I was no closer to tracing the power behind Juva's movement. Now I was falling for a servant girl promised to some nasty old man and worshipped by my only ally.

Everyone was ready for the march out of the valley. At last, Juva emerged from the mouth of the cave in a fresh white robe banded with red and gold stitching. He carried a long staff. Like Moses leading his flock, he rode in the front seat of his personal carriage ahead of us through the sheltering curtain of brush and into the open plains. He dared to lead us right onto the imperial trunk road open only to those holding transport licenses issued by the bureaucrats up in Carthago.

But there was no official traffic in sight as far as I could see—only small estates and odd goat paths crisscrossing the route of our straggling parade. As the hours wore on and the sun moved from our right across to our left in the sky, some of the weaker members of the camp lost pace. Our line stretched out to half a mile or more.

I slowed my soldier's usual speed by half down to the pace of the stragglers pulling up the rear. For all his lame foot, Nico was nowhere to be seen. Maybe he'd chickened out and hitched a lift with the other invalids chosen by Sophonisba. I couldn't spot him as I scanned the entire line as it took one curve around a hill or dipped to the bottom of a slope. I supposed he'd taken my advice and ditched the red shirt for a sack-like *agonistici* disguise. I sweated under my borrowed robe and cursed its layers of deep-bedded grime rubbing my scabs.

For all this, we made better time than expected. We arrived footsore and hungry at a village halfway to the promised lake just before dusk. The camp was strung out along the road opposite low walls marking off the mud hovels of faithful supporters. Juva stood on the driver's bench of his carriage and preached about purity and sacrifice.

I didn't take his words in—I was too busy searching the crowd of wretched faces for Nico. The sun sank behind the foothills. Its fading rays cast an orange glow on Juva's pale face as he presented Kahina and her two fellow martyrs-to-be to the impressionable audience.

'Behold these select, our *rediti!*' His words rang across the irrigation ditches and pitiful little workshops and dwellings. 'These souls offer themselves to the mercy of our Lord's grace and the will of his natural forces. These stainless spirits will make their final penance and find deliverance from the sufferings we all share! *Laudate Deum!*'

'*Laudate Deum,*' mumbled the miserable villagers, kneeling in the dirt alongside a low set of walls marking out each struggling olive tree.

Juva thrust Kahina forward, her face veiled and her feet covered with the day's dust. She reminded me of another veiled figure—the assassin who'd attacked the Commander, the very trigger for the trap I found myself in.

'We heard there are alms from Roma! Do you have money for us, Juva? Why shouldn't our children eat as well as pray?' a man shouted.

'Have faith in the Lord. He'll look after you. Refuse this money. It's a sign of your dependence and enslavement to their pagan hearts which hide behind the emblem of Christ!' Juva made the Sign of the Cross over their heads.

Then a local priest loyal to The Church of the Martyrs called the pilgrims to Mass. Dozens of filthy faithful led by Sophonisba's sisterhood stuffed themselves into a rundown barn they used as a church to watch as the foreheads of Kahina and the two men were anointed with holy oil at the foot of the altar.

Kahina stood dignified and proud, but kept her face modestly veiled, masking nose and mouth with the same borrowed linen wrap that covered her lush hair. She looked like a beautiful Greek statue, all drapery and form, looking down at her feet beneath her lush dark lashes.

I was sure that Nico had paid no attention to Juva's sermon or to the call to celebrate Mass, but was lost among the hundreds resting in the fields or knocking on doors begging for a little fruit or water. He might have realized 'his girl' was with us, within his reach, if he'd only stop thinking of his own gullet and safe escape.

For my part, I hadn't counted on a large reception from a gaggle of gullible hardscrabble Christians but it was luck for us. This stopover gave Nico a better chance to get away, I realized, as I queued with Bomilcar and Capussa for the unvarnished pottery bowls filled with a thin soup the villagers had mustered for our crowd.

Well after sunset, I spotted Nico's telltale limping figure leaving a circle of gamblers crouching over their dice behind one of the mule wagons. I managed to catch up with him jumping the queue for flatbread from a housewife's window down an alley hundreds of yards away from our camp.

'Forget abandoning the caravan in full view of the road. You can't afford to travel farther than this point. Here is where you can melt into the village and make your getaway and no one's the wiser.' I said.

'Good idea,' he mumbled through a mouth full of food.

'Steal a mule or a horse tonight and race straight back, parallel to the trunk road but keeping safely off it until you get back to Leo's junction. I still have my bronze mirror and I'll check for signals every night. We'll stop at the lake tomorrow so the martyrs can take their ritual dunking, then continue up to Nif en-Nsr. Juva is hoping to gather more followers as we go.'

'What do I tell the boss?'

'Tell him that our leader here, Juva, knows all about the Roman officials Paul and Macarius. Tell him that Father Donatus is shooting out letters to all his bishops calling for a peaceful boycott across the entire plateau. Tell Leo that Juva has dispatched a scout with a purse of gold coins to buy more information from army veterans and townspeople, and that he's trying to make contact with other Circumcellion leaders. Warn Leo there might be trouble for these emissaries, maybe even more violence than their sainted Donatus can control.'

Nico nodded, but I worried. It was too much and too fast for him to take in. I might be only a slave but I belonged to the greatest army on earth where we practiced obeying commands and logistics delivered on the run, or even in the middle of a full-blown battle.

Nico was only trained to take orders from wine stewards and laundry matrons.

'Did you understand all that, Nico?'

'Sure. Father Donatus is telling the people to stick it to the Romans but to stay peaceful. On the other hand, our cave ghoul Juva knows all about the Roman officials and he is buying more information up north and rounding up the other gangs to bash in some more heads. Right?'

'Uh . . . right.'

'First, I eat and get some sleep. I'll creep out when it's dark and quiet.'

'All right. And don't stop riding. Now I have to clear off before anybody sees us together.'

I was also relieved to think that within only a few hours Kahina would be free of Nico's threatening presence. She'd been lucky so far, since she'd spotted him right off and spent day after day hiding from him. After tonight, she need fear his tattletale tongue no longer. Nico could get home to the farm within the same three or four days that would see Kahina and me travel ever closer to Nif en-Nsr. The Commander would hear in time to warn Governor Silvester to take precautions and protect his imperial guests from an insurrection.

The oil barrels would keep on rolling toward the ports of Rusicada and Carthago.

Nightfall came again, and with it, the sweet assignation I'd waited for all through the day's boring march. With eyes searching over her veil, Kahina found me in the crowd. Together we slipped away from the hundreds of tired and dirty Circumcellions squatting and building fires along the edge of the trunk road facing the sullen village.

The villagers had listened to Juva, but for all their faith and devotion, they displayed nothing but hostility when we approached their doorways. We asked a farmer for shelter in his barn. He shooed us away with, 'Try the old churchyard, bums.'

We tried a tiny tavern but had no money for a bed and anyway, Kahina observed, even the innkeeper's wife was picking out lice behind her ears.

We followed their directions to the old church, but its timbers stood open to the night skies. No wonder they worshipped in a barn. This was nothing more than a charred and stripped-down ruin. There was no priest or deacon to receive us, nor even an altar left to mark where celebrants had once stood. When we saw a few bones sticking up from the earth, Kahina grew frightened.

'Marcus, this place is haunted.'

'It's just quiet. We're alone.' I drew her close.

She pulled away. 'No, we're not. I think this is the dead village of Octava.'

'Those victims were buried by the Donatists.'

'What do you know about it?'

'I only know the Romans' version.'

'I was a little girl when it happened. It was a very hot week when Leo ordered all of us servants to stay close to the house and not to leave the borders of his estate. Then we heard it was because of the rebellion led by two Numidian chiefs, Axido and Fasir.'

'You heard they had attacked Roman convoys?'

'Not at first. They seemed to be brave and good. They held their own courts in the countryside and overturned unjust debts and issued certificates cancelling loans. When debt collectors came to the markets as usual, to watch like vultures to see if our farmers sold enough that day to pay their debts, Axido and Fasir's men beat them off. But things grew more and more violent until they attacked landlords on the road and released their slaves by force.'

'So they were the first *agonistici*?'

'Yes, but their violent ways frightened Father Donatus. He always preached peace and Christian love and he couldn't control the uprising. They say that Father Donatus had no choice in the end but to appeal to the Roman authorities.'

'Donatus *requested* the Romans to suppress the uprising? He called for a crackdown on his own people?'

'Not a crackdown, that's not what he intended. He wanted peace. But the Romans took it too far. We were all terrified when Governor Taurinus sent his troops across the plateau to massacre the rebels. He ordered the Donatist priests to leave all the victims' bodies unburied in the sun for the dogs to eat.'

'And this is one of those villages?' The closer I looked, the more I noticed the bleached femurs and skulls barely covered by shifting dirt and brush.

'These bodies are only half-buried,' she whispered, burying her head in my robe. 'Oh, Marcus, I'm afraid to be a martyr.'

Private as we were there, Kahina refused to lie together among the dead. We returned, slinking under our head coverings, back toward the camp where we settled not far from a warming fire and indifferent strangers too worn out to drink or carouse.

But we were in the open. Kahina's modesty and my fatigue overwhelmed our urges to repeat the previous night. We lay in each other's arms, murmuring nothing much, and drifting off in a daze of illusory peace.

Then I felt a cold dagger point pressing the side of my neck.

'Get up, you bastard.'

Nico stood over us in the darkness in a Circumcellion's robe with the hood pulled low over his face.

'Where'd you get the knife?'

'I stole it from the bakery.'

'You may need it on the road. Get on a horse and get going,' I croaked, trying to get to my feet.

'Let go of her. She's coming with me.' He prodded the knife deeper under my ear and cut my skin, drawing blood. I was betting he didn't have the guts to go farther. I managed to stand up.

'She's staying here, Nico. She's not yours.'

'I know she's not mine. She's promised and I'm returning her back where she belongs.'

'To some villain of an old man? That's who I heard is waiting for her. You want that for her, Nico?'

'Is that what the little slut told you? "*To some old man?*" You fool! Yes! He's a monster with a crippled hand and half a face twisted around one eye like a Cyclops! But is that any way to talk about your own commander? The man who slew one emperor for the benefit of his imperial brother? The wounded hero of the Rhône? The military genius whose friendship Master Leo nurtures with gifts of pretty girls?'

'Nico, shut up!' Kahina jumped to her feet, grabbing at the dagger and slicing her hand on the blade. With a clumsy hop, he dodged out of her reach.

'Look at you, lying there, just like all these other whores! What are you doing with him? You were so proud! You were too good for ol' Nico, the cripple! I wanted to save you from being bartered like a rug or a couch that Roman brute just wants to sit on until he finds something even softer! I wanted to take you up north to Carthago. I would have taken good care of you there!' His voice was breaking with disappointment.

'Shut up, Nico!'

'No! You're coming back with me! If I can't have you, at least I'll get a rich reward as thanks,' Nico squalled with an agony that burst straight from his heart. He grabbed at the tail of her head covering, but she was too quick for him and yanked it back out of his hand. With one beseeching glance at my horrified expression, she gathered up her skirt and sobbing, dashed onto the dark plains beyond the light of the campfires.

'Get going!' I ordered him. 'There are more important things at stake than a servant girl.'

'You're right,' he answered. 'I'm heading back to the farm, just like you said. But when I get there, I'll tell the boss and his army pals how you know nothing and do nothing but waste your time screwing Leo's runaway.'

I grabbed him by the throat, nearly choking him. 'You'll give them my warning or you'll pay for it later.'

'In another lifetime, martyr boy—if you get one,' He wrenched himself free and disappeared toward the road, forcing his halting leg to keep pace with his frothing anger.

I was too stunned by the news of Kahina's bond to the Commander to chase her down. That was my fatal mistake. I should have hunted all night for her, but a lifetime's training isn't tossed over in an hour or two. By rights, Kahina and I both belonged to Gregorius, not to each other. She'd read that truth written all over my dismayed expression.

All morning, she stayed glued to Sophonisba's side and avoided my efforts to get her alone. No longer fearful of Nico's discovering her, she discarded her veil and marched off at the head of the procession with the dead-eyed look of resignation.

Her grave expression only made her more beautiful. This time the villagers were visibly moved by the sacrifice of the stoic maiden martyr. Women wept and tossed desert wildflowers into her path. Beggars with nothing to lose in that woebegone hamlet joined our procession.

The feeble song of our first day on the road grew into a more impressive chant.

I was still stuck with my position at the very end of the stream of pilgrims and hooded *agonistici*. If I squinted hard, I could just see Juva's carriage disappear and reappear with each bend in the road, followed by the mule-drawn wagons and proud ox-carriages.

It took a whole dreary day to cross that bleached horizon. By dusk, we reached the promised lake. Hundreds more peasants loitered along the shoreline to get a glimpse of the holy trio chosen for *reditum*. The atmosphere hit me as macabre. In their avid expressions I recognized the predatory ghouls who appeared after a battle to stare with fascinated horror at birds pecking out the eyes of the fallen, not all of them quite dead.

Juva himself took Kahina by the hand and she in turn held the next martyr in a chain as they went step by step across the wet pebbles and sand until they sank up to their knees in cool water. Their garments floated on the surface in billows around their waists.

I stood with the rest of the crowd trying to make out Kahina's expression as she was dowsed with a pitcher of water by Sophonisba and her attendants while Juva said prayers over her head.

The only prayer I murmured was the hope that she would come to me this evening and help me forget what lay ahead of us. Perhaps tonight we would find some peace and pleasure before her fatal leap. I waited and waited but she left me there squatting in the dark, waving away the offers of drink and dice games from Bomilcar and his mates.

As soon as the eating ended, the hellish dancing started up. This time Kahina was pushed into the center of the main circle. Reluctantly, she started dancing for all the *agonistici*, lewd and pious alike. Even Stembanos clapped along, his sweaty muscles gleaming in the camp light, admiring what he couldn't take for himself, but gleeful to see her lowered to the level of the others like him.

I scanned the crowd for Juva, hoping that his austere gaze would cast some sobriety over the celebration tonight, but he hid with his books in his closed carriage.

I stood on the edge of the circle and urged Kahina to stop her dance. I even reached for her and tried to put my arm around her, but she shook me off to the cheer of the rabble and fell to whirling more wildly than before.

It was a dance of despair.

As the *agonistici* crushed shoulder to shoulder in a circle tightening around her, she held her scarf above her head in each hand and imitated the sluttish, jutting hips of the older women she'd seen. I turned away. I couldn't watch her caught up in this frenzy, giving up to their herd-like hoots and cheers.

I pushed my way back through the hot crush of greedy bodies toward the outskirts of the campsite. I was desperate to cool off my temper on the lapping shores of the lake where the vehicles were hitched and the animals could drink freely.

Leo had said I didn't miss much. Although he'd flattered me in his study that day, I knew it was true. I was a watcher, an observer, but not from talent as much as sheer habit of survival.

Now, despite my distractions over Kahina, my eye caught a movement across the water. Perhaps it was a fallen tree drifting on the soft current or a family of flamingos wading on a submerged island off in the distance or even a very large ibis up past his bedtime.

But, no, the shape's movement wasn't random at all.

Through the moving shadows tossed out by the camp's scattered campfires and torches, I distinguished a steady form growing on the north horizon of the water. As it became larger and larger, I made out the lines of a fisherman's shallow skiff.

I waited in complete silence, crouching out of sight in a thicket of reeds. After about fifteen minutes, the skiff ground up onto the pebbles only fifty feet or so away from me. The fisherman dropped his single oar and lugged his craft up higher on the beach and almost clear of the water. He gave his hand to a tall, hooded figure who jumped neatly out of the boat and with that single leap, betrayed the swing of a club hidden underneath his robes.

There was no mistaking Hiempsal, the spy. He turned to help a second man seated farther back in the boat step forward through the craft and clear the shallows. Together they paid the fisherman to wait while they clambered past me through the reeds behind the shore and toward the campfires.

At Hiempsal's knock, Juva's carriage door opened to admit them. I saw the preacher's long pale hand reach out in greeting. Hiempsal and the other man mounted the steep carriage steps and disappeared behind the closed door.

All I could do was crouch among the humid stalks, hoping to catch sight of them again.

They talked for many hours while I brooded about Kahina and then dozed off, my head sunk down onto a heap of thick dry grasses. While I napped, a full moon rose over the lake. The surface of the water shone like molten silver.

Finally the carriage door opened and I shook off my doze. Hiempsal descended first, assisting his mysterious guest down the steps. They hastened back to the waiting boat. I could see them better now in the full moonlight, almost as clear as day. They jostled the fisherman on his bench to wake him up. As before, Hiempsal assisted the third man back into the craft with some ceremony and then they pushed off.

What good were all my tricks of observation when all I had to go on were dark and silent men covered from head to toe? I dared to move closer on all fours, through the reeds, hoping for just a glimpse of the stranger's face hidden under that generous hood.

And then, just as they dipped oar into still water, I spotted the stranger's hand that grasped the side of the boat as it rocked from side to side.

The hand did not belong to a Circumcellion.

On one finger, I saw an iron ring with a large reddish stone. I was determined to remember it—if I ever saw it again.

CHAPTER 12, LEAPS OF FAITH

—DUSK ON THE CLIFFS AT NIF EN-NSR—

The afternoon's blinding haze gave way to twilight's rose sheen. We were all, young and old, panting for breath as we attacked the last steep path zigzagging up from the barren foothills across the rock face to the highest plateau and the edge of the lethal cliffs at Nif en-Nsr.

Somewhere above me with the head of the caravan snaking up the narrow pass, Kahina must have already reached the crest of the ridge.

After her ritual bath with the other two martyrs, she'd ridden on a mule donated by the miserable town of half-buried bones. Sheltering in the shadow of Juva's carriage, she stayed well out of my reach. Admired from all sides now, she'd kept her face veiled and eyes averted.

In this way, she avoided me for two solid straight days.

It was just as well. I didn't know what I'd say. The moment Nico had screamed out the truth, she'd read my horrified expression—my loyalty to the Manlius clan was the very stuff of my heart, muscle and spine. To embrace a bride promised to my own master was a private stain on my conscience and possibly a capital offense under law.

Shielding my eyes from the piercing rays of the setting sun, I couldn't pick out her white-robed figure, but I did spot the bent silhouette of Sophonisba standing clear of the narrow path clogged with the procession of chanting *agonistici*. The old woman scanned the column winding up to where she stood.

I guessed she was looking for me down here. I was stuck, urging on the feeble and cowardly at the very end of the trail.

Had the crone suffered a sudden change of heart? Maybe now she regretted filling Kahina's head with nonsense about noble maidens and courteous bears that kept their claws and teeth off virgin flesh?

There was no turning back for any of us now. Kahina was doomed.

I watched my footing between the loose boulders on a mean gravel trail best kept for goat herders, not glass-eyed fanatics. With every step, I dreaded the moment I'd be forced, helpless and hypocritical, to kneel on the plateau and offer thankful prayers for Kahina's leap from the precipice. Or worse—to be ordered by Juva to collect her broken bones from the rocky plains hundreds of feet below.

We got the stragglers to the top at last. A broad plateau of green shrub and grass offered us soft rest.

A cheer of victory went up from the crowd as our last group completed the assembly. I gazed past the cliff edge and across the plain in astonishment. There were hundreds of us gathered again, some collapsing with relief in little groups, other already lining up for water to relieve their thirst.

But was it a miracle that during the arduous march, our numbers had multiplied many times over? I saw immediately that the Circumcellion masses had trebled, at least. It didn't seem possible, even if Lady Laetitia already talked about loaves and fishes coming out of nowhere. Then I realized that hundreds of villagers and herders' families, summoned by their priests to bear witness must have been waiting for us all day up here on the final stop.

There were makeshift shelters offering bread and wine studded across the wind-twisted shrubs and squatting men tending low fires roasting goat meat on spits.

If Sophonisba had been looking out for me before, she must be lost to me now among the masses milling around the square half-mile of wind-brushed grass.

I reeled with the macabre festivity of it all. Kahina's imminent death had become a carnival event for these illiterates gathered in the name of their Savior. It certainly couldn't have been the death of two disillusioned bankrupts that would draw such an eager audience. I sensed a sexual undercurrent running through the crowd at the lurid prospect of her broken white flesh and innocent blood exposed for everyone to see on the jagged rocks.

Kahina's predicament both repelled and frightened me. Hadn't she uttered, 'I'm afraid of the rocks below'? She wanted to be celebrated, admired and emulated, but nothing could convince me after holding her passionate body in my arms that this was a girl who wanted to quit life the next day.

I slept fitfully, crouching myself down into yet another hooded, anonymous hump of stiff black cloth like the hundreds of other penitents. I made sure I was within sight of the door to Juva's carriage. Long after all the campfires had died into smoking red embers, the oil lamp in the leader's window burned late.

I saw Bomilcar enter and leave the carriage while the moon was still low on the horizon. Then I dozed off. Hours later, I woke up at the soft padding of hooves on the ground. Under a bright moon, Hiempsal led Juva's spare horse across the last yards of the treacherous path and across the plateau. He handed the mount over to that drooling Capussa for brushing down. He strutted past me to join Bomilcar and Juva in conference. The murmur of their hushed debate was too tempting for me not to eavesdrop.

I scuttled toward the underbelly of the carriage and hoped no one would notice as I slipped between the wheels and out of sight. I leaned my darkened head against the inner rim of a front wheel. There was a generous crack in the vehicle's wooden planks just above my head. A strip of lamplight fell in the sandy grass not inches from my calloused foot.

'. . . delegation to negotiate an end to the beatings and terrorizing.'

'Their leader?'

'Bishop Marculus.'

'Hah!' Juva's disdain was clear. 'Before he was ordained bishop, Marculus was a *lawyer*, trained in pretty legal briefs to make underhanded deals with imperial magistrates!'

'He's venerated enough now as a holy father by his diocese.'

'I say Marculus is a fool! He thinks he can *mediate* the Roman bullies out of their rampage? This is civil war, not some paternity suit up in Carthago.'

I couldn't make out the next few sentences. Someone poured himself a drink. I heard the crackle of papyrus. Either Juva was writing something or Hiempsal might have delivered instructions—but from whom?

'. . . Beat and clubbed them on the way to the Carthago docks. Rowed them out to sea, then tied their necks and hands to barrels of sand and threw them overboard to drown. Half the city saw it from the shore. The Donatists up there are in shock. Now the Romans are saying that any priests resisting the unity edict are to be banished west into the desert—or worse.'

It seemed that Hiempsal had produced news that astonished even the most cynical Circumcellion.

'They'll regret that,' Juva murmured.

'Who were Maximian and Isaac?' Bomilcar asked.

'Two nobody clerics,' Hiempsal said.

'But they're dead now. So we can build them up into something more—much more,' Juva said.

Bomilcar said, 'Well, one thing's clear now. The Romans' pacification tour didn't stay charitable for very long.'

Hiempsal chuckled. 'Don't play the idiot! Did you ever believe it would stop with alms-giving? Wherever these Romans travel, they display the very same racks for pulling bones out of sockets and iron claws for flaying flesh that they just used up in Carthago.'

Bomilcar reacted, 'That can't be imperial policy! It must be the spirit of Satan returning to finish the job left forty years ago. The Church of Martyrs survived him then and we'll outlast him again.'

Juva sounded more bemused than disgusted. 'You're right, Bomilcar. Can Constans be so stupid as to order these two idiots to play into our hands? I don't blame the Emperor. And don't blame Satan either, Bomilcar. These two are just emissaries—far from Mediolanum. They've become bloated with their power. The August sun has gone to their heads and our sands have blinded them to their folly.'

Bomilcar was still shocked by Hiempsal's report. 'I can't believe they're resorting to torture.'

Hiempsal couldn't suppress his delight at the Romans' stupidity. 'They instill fear wherever they go. Now they order thousands of our faithful to unify at a Mass in the imperial basilica at Theveste and warn that those who stay away will regret it.'

Juva chuckled to his aides, 'It's a present on a silver platter.' He spit out a plum pit. It rattled across the planks, then fell through the crack in the floor and bounced right off my forehead.

Bomilcar broke into Hiempsal's gleeful reveries. 'What about these orders to join forces? Can they be trusted? Can we be sure the others will come? Did you consider this might be a trap, Hiempsal?'

'I don't carry bogus summons, you cowering desert gopher!' Hiempsal was aching for a real fight. He resented Bomilcar's caution. I couldn't see their faces, but their tones explained why the clever Juva kept these two rivals battling for his favor.

'Get to the point, Hiempsal. When? Where?' Juva asked.

'On the plains outside Bagae. Paul and Macarius still travel without military escort. By then we'll have thousands of armed *agonistici*. Emperor Constans will think twice about religious unity when he gets two heads delivered home with his next oil shipment.'

'A victory for us will force Constans to recall that pagan turd Governor Silvester and embolden all of Numidia to overthrow the Romans.' Hiempsal could taste victory already.

I had heard enough. I mustn't get caught. It was enough to know that Paul and Macarius were walking into a trap set by their own arrogance and brutality. I wasn't worried about Governor Silvester's career. But my own commander was part of the *limitanei* forces responsible for keeping the peace.

His career and the future of the Manlius family were both on the line.

I plucked some smoking dung pellets from a campfire, wrapped them well in fresh leaves and slipped them into my leather pouch. I scurried beyond the edges of the sleeping masses. I was searching for a safe spot to signal southwards. I recalled the upward journey had led us past a buzzard's nest in a crag along the cliff face. It was a space of about five or six feet across and three feet deep, located somewhere about ten feet below the edge. If I got the wrong spot from up here, it was a lethal drop onto the boulders below.

So I decided to approach it from the other direction and see if I could climb over to the nest from the path leading up to the plateau. I crouched and moved across the camp, hoping Hiempsal, Capussa and the other lieutenants didn't spot my departure back downhill.

It was almost impossible in such darkness, but I managed to find the curve in the path where I'd spotted the buzzard taking off. Clinging to the sheer face with fingers and toes, I worked my way across a treacherous span to land clumsily into the birds' niche. Two young buzzards woke up and sent up a caterwaul, pecking at my bare feet. I was half-minded to just push their nest over the edge. They thought better of me when I gave them the last crust of bread in my pouch.

The buzzards' home hung directly above the broad rough landscape perched high above the long imperial road. The land lay black in front of my toes but for a distant glow of a village fire down below about half a mile off.

I built a small fire of my own using twigs from the nest and sparking them by poking the last orange ember in my dung pellets with a straw. The black sky didn't fool me. I knew the desert well. If I didn't act fast, the dawn would soon cast its gray pall over everything, including my contact signal.

Nico and I had invented a crude code: One flash at regular intervals to say I was safe but had no news. Three flashes for 'I have information to pass on whenever it's safe to meet.' Five flashes meant 'Urgent, take any risk to make contact.'

It was a quarter of an hour before I'd got a strong fire going and devised a system of twitching the polished bronze to signal into the darkness. I signaled five flashes over and over with the mirror.

My shoulder grew stiff and I switched hands, signaling and stoking my flame into that chasm of darkness. We were so high on the plateau that I almost imagined I could see the Aurès peaks to the south scraping the dawn sky, but it might have been my exhausted imagination longing—for what? I couldn't say. If my sight failed me, so be it, but bleary-eyed, I watched the dark horizon for any signal of acknowledgement.

There was none.

What usually worked with the bright sun for soldiers signaling across the stretches of desert between fortresses didn't work as well using a mere fire into the black night. Still, the flames themselves must be visible, so I wrenched myself out of my robe and using it as a curtain, moved it back and forth in front of the fire, hoping that by making the light blink on and off, it would work better than a small mirror.

I changed direction slightly and kept signaling. Perhaps I'd misjudged our position. Nico had had time to bring others by now, if he'd travelled without stopping.

Still, there was no answer, which meant either that we'd travelled too far to be followed, which at our pace was very unlikely, or worse—Nico had betrayed me utterly and there was no one trailing northwards after us to see my signal.

The night's shade was shifting from black to navy blue. I heard the lowering bellows of the hungry animals above me. A flock of flamingos crossed the sky. I tamped down my fire. In the dawn I could get a safe toehold across the treacherous rock face and return up to the plateau to sleep like the hundreds of others.

I had barely returned and huddled down near a family of peasants starting their day when some damn soul started praying. The waves of pilgrims' voices taking up the chant reached me where I crouched at the perimeter of their madness. They sang of their love of God's creation, but underneath it, I detected a lust for destruction.

The song rose and fell as the celebrants gobbled down their humble breakfast and slowly gathered into an audience. They clamored for Juva, their 'Captain of the Saints.'

After a tantalizing delay, Juva appeared, for all purposes looking like the Savior himself—tall in his plain, clean robe, fine in his gestures and proud in his posture. He blessed them with the Sign of the Cross while holding in his other hand a harmless shepherd's staff of olive wood.

'Brothers and sisters! Remember the words of our Holy Father Tertullian. Christians do not fall into the foolish worship of emperors. We do better than that. We pray for the salvation of the imperial family. Christians can afford to be put to torture and death, because the more we are cast down, the stronger we grow.'

'Amen!' someone shouted from the audience.

'The blood of our martyrs is the seed from which our Faith grows ever stronger and more resolute.'

I scanned the expressions of the listeners—dirty and scarred, hungry and wan—standing nearest Juva's carriage. They pressed closer and closer now, like birds of prey moving drawn to his talk of blood and death.

'You know, true Christians, that the Romans Paul and Macarius parade through our countryside, bribing God's faithful to worship in their *traditor* Church, the Emperor's false church, just as years ago the emperors in Roma commanded Christ's followers to sacrifice in their pagan temples.'

'Blasphemy!'

'Heresy!'

Juva had them going now. 'Do you kneel and worship a bust of a mere emperor?'

'No!' Standing sentry in front of the wagon wheels, Bomilcar rallied their response with a thrust of his 'Israelite' club, and hundreds more voices echoed, 'No!'

'Listen to me, my brothers and sisters in Christ. Up in Carthago, the Roman envoys arrested and tortured the good priests Maximian and Isaac. They whipped them until their switches broke and so they changed over to lead-tipped scourges. They flayed them for all the city to see, shredding their flesh with iron claws! They stretched them on the rack until their limbs were loosed and the liquid flowed clear, right out of their joints! Then, so as not to outrage the eyes and inflame the protests of our brothers and sisters in Carthago, they carried the priests out to sea and drowned them with weights of sand tied to their innocent necks!'

'Avenge Isaac! Avenge Maximian!' Bomilcar gave the crowd their cues and the people answered with more passion each time.

'But wait and listen!' Juva rang out. 'The sea refused their holy bodies. The waves opened up and recoiled from these saints. The waters delivered them in a fiery turbulence right back to the shore where they received the burial of which they were worthy!'

People started shouting, weeping and crossing their breasts. You could feel their excitement rising in swells, but whether it was over Constantine's bust or the priests' vivid death, or maybe anger that Paul and Macarius' coins were slipping out from between their eager fingers, who could say? The clamor felt dangerous, like the sound of soldiers banging their swords on their shields just before the *cornicen* sounds the charge.

I elbowed my way closer to the middle of the crush, searching for Sophonisba or Kahina, but Juva's women devotees were keeping to themselves.

'Many souls have heard God's call up in Carthago. Are they more pious than you? Here, today, three souls answer God's call. They do not wait for old age or hunger or disease to take them. They risk their lives for God, as others have done, protesting the imperial occupation of our lands and churches, the military marching up and down our roads, the rape of our orchards and fields. These martyrs show us the way! Whether God chooses to receive their souls or not today, His Will be Done!'

'His Will be Done!'

I felt the momentum of the gathered faithful and knew the only thing that would satisfy them now was death—hot, red, violent death.

Kahina appeared from the rear of the carriage, along with the other two *rediti*. Juva had worked up the crowd's frenzy so well, a few people were racing ahead to lean over the cliffs where hundreds more rude spectators waited below. I could heard them praying for the rocks to receive the martyrs' blood.

I was not so sure now whether even Juva could control what he'd whipped up.

The hysteria was taking some as if by the shoulders and shaking them. The bolder of the two 'chosen' men raised his eyes to heaven. The tension had overwhelmed him. Shouting 'Laudate Deum!' he ran headlong past the gathered multitude. Before our very eyes, he kept running on and on, making straight for the cliffs. No one stopped him but many gasped as he took two steps right into the air beyond the tufts of brush at the edge. He dropped out of view, his cry of joy becoming terror echoing off the cliff and then ending in abrupt silence.

There was a distant cry from the voices far below, 'Laudate Deum!'

Now across our plateau, hundreds of avid faces turned to Kahina and the second man. Kahina stood with eyes veiled and hands clasped, praying with such dignity, none dared molest her final penance.

But the cowardly Circumcellion looked around, frantic for companions to hold him back. To my alarm, I felt myself being pushed from behind by celebrants caught up with emotion.

'We give you courage. Take us with you!' some lunatic cried to the hesitating 'martyr.' 'We can show the emperor we are not afraid of death!'

I was jostled and pushed forward by dozens of maddened and hungry men and women. Some were rushing like mindless cattle driven from behind me toward the cliff. Others fought in the opposite direction not to get swept up in the agitation.

People started screaming. Despite my efforts to resist the pressure from behind, the crazed faithful were moving dozens of us toward the cliff's edge toward our own death.

Crushed on all sides, I battled my way, fighting foot by foot, to reach the shouting gang of men and women who were taking Kahina up in their arms to propel her willy-nilly over the edge.

They tore her veil off her terrified face. I caught her eyes darting in all directions as she was lifted onto their shoulders into the air. I'm not sure she even recognized me under my hood.

I could see no other way—I lunged for her hem. Being one of the tallest in this crowd and wearing the garb of a Circumcellion, no one stopped me from gathering her skirts into my hands and wresting her from the clutches of the common villagers who acclaimed her. Lifting her up high on my shoulders, I shouted '*Laudate Deum*' until I was hoarse.

Screams rose ahead of us as hundreds approached the precipice, some of them willingly and many others not. Fools near the cliffs hoping to see the martyrs tumble onto the merciless crags were toppling over themselves.

If you've ever been to the Roman Circus when the chariot races go against the crowd and their champion is overturned and the gambling crowds lose their minds and trample cripples and old women in their outraged uproar out of the stadium, well, then you know how it felt.

Kahina's hands gripped around my ears as she struggled to keep her balance, but I couldn't tell whether she recognized me or not.

With each shove from behind, I threw my weight to the side and let someone fall forward past us, but there was more resistance from the side edges of the crowd than I'd reckoned. Luckily I could see over the heads of the horde whirling in circles of panic and pressure. With every yard forward, I was gaining two yards to my right.

Kahina must have realized by then that I was fighting to carry her free of the tumult. She began to kick with her right foot, making space for me to turn and roll some unfortunate behind into my place. We worked our way, second by second, twisting out of the way as best we could. Kahina could not have guessed my destination was the buzzard's crag, but I could only hope that a jump at that point would land us on straw and not broken bodies.

The screaming and shouting made it impossible to speak. At last we broke free of the suicidal stream. I dropped her to the ground and showed her my face. I grabbed her hand and to her confusion, dragged her on a diagonal forward and toward the cliff's edge.

'No,' she protested, pulled back, so I grabbed her waist and pulled her straight to the edge. Dropping onto my stomach, I leaned over and saw the nest another couple of yards along. The baby buzzards had fled.

She started to run back but I caught her and forced her to lean with me, holding her tight, right over the edge. I pointed to the crag below.

'I'm going to lower you down, then take the drop myself,' I said. And now she saw the buzzard nest and understood.

She gripped my forearms with her small hands and I eased her over the edge. She gasped as she felt her feet hang in the air. I prayed the crag was as sturdy as it had felt hours before. I let her go. She landed and I inched my weight over the edge. I swung dangerously too far. Kahina tried to catch my ankles, but she was too short. I had to let go and pray, but I landed just short of the drop.

Flailing bodies fell through the air—at least two dozen more—passing to the left of us as we huddled in safety. It was many minutes before the crowd above got control of itself and there were no more victims.

The faces of the people waiting below still looked up with fascination at the cliff edge to see if it produced more 'martyrs.' Others knelt and wailed in mourning at the corpses scattered at their feet across the boulders. The most despicable started robbing the bodies.

'They mustn't see us.' Luckily the buzzard family had left. We buried ourselves from sight using the mother's generous branches and grass.

It was a long day of waiting in the nest. The hot sun reached the crag and bathed the straw until the smell of bird shit and dead leaves seeped into our nostrils and stuck to our rough clothes. Even if we hadn't wanted to remain as still as the bodies bleeding on the valley floor, we would have been desperate to sleep. We dozed, fearful even in our dreams of rolling off the little promontory to our deaths.

Kahina was too public a 'martyr' to risk her returning to camp. I reckoned that if Nico had made it back to the estate, he must've turned my message around somehow. I realized that no one was coming for my information. As for the army, no matter how good my information on the ambush at Bagae, I'd be punished, if not killed by Kahina's family, if Nico told them I'd enjoyed the Commander's virgin gift for even one night.

The line between a slave and a 'complete' man was the one of the time-honored divisions that kept Roma's social order. I never questioned it. I had only hoped to escape it. Jumping off mountains wasn't a solution I was ready for but waiting on the crag that long day, I felt trapped and full of regret.

Perhaps I was not capable of freedom. Perhaps I would always be a slave in nature. In fact, I missed the simplicity of taking orders, taking care of and sometimes taking abuse from a man I relied on, heart and soul.

Kahina and I sat up to watch the daylight fade. We were stiff and starving. It was time to move.

'You'll have to crawl across that way and slip down the path in the dark,' I said. 'Where will you go?'

'I don't know. I spent my whole life on the Longus estate. All my people live around it. They will be angry, but there is nowhere else I can survive alone.'

'I can't be caught with you.'

She burst into tears. I held her as she sobbed. 'How can I travel the road so far with no idea of where I'm going? Shall I find another Circumcellion camp?'

'No, they're all gathering to make a stand. You won't be safe.'

'So must I go back to the estate? Must I be given to your commander?'

I couldn't speak. There was only one honorable life for a woman—marriage and children. The losers suffered what they got and Kahina was a lowly servant being offered second-best status, *conturbinum* as the official mistress of a high-ranking Roman officer.

I held her waist as tight as I could as she clambered in the last light over the path. She pulled her pathetic shawl back over her head. I closed my eyes and sighed with my own stupidity. I'd been so keen to get her a secure footing and out of Juva's reach, I'd forgotten to kiss her good-bye.

She knew now that my love for her was enough to risk my life. I hoped she'd carry that with her for the rest of her days. I watched an evening mist close in our crag. Before it was too dark to see anything at all, I grappled my own way back onto the path and snuck up to the plateau.

Most of the pilgrims and villagers had melted away, leaving bereaved mourners to grieve. Too many had died. The sport of watching others sacrifice themselves had become a cruel reality of identifying remains for burial. The original Circumcellions huddled around, watching them, shrouded in gloom.

For now I'd saved Kahina but had I just doomed us both? The answer came with the hour.

'Juva wants to see you,' Bomilcar barked at me as I finished the last of my meager breakfast.

CHAPTER 13, ALMIGHTY BLUDGEONS

—JUVA'S CARRIAGE—

I climbed the steep carriage steps and knocked on the door. Juva didn't get up from his seat, but with a wave of his white sleeve, he welcomed me in. 'Many have looked for you, brother Marcus. We thought you'd disappeared over the side, along with so many others.' He crossed his breast and sighed, 'Blessed be their souls.'

'Blessed be their souls,' I muttered and made the Sign of the Cross.

'Shut the door.' He looked at my disheveled, scratched face and hands. 'So you were indeed injured in the riot?'

'Just some scrapes.'

'We can't afford to lose you. There are testing times to come. We need strong bodies and fierce hearts.'

'Yes, Juva. I'm anxious to serve the Lord.'

'The Lord is watching us more carefully than ever during these troubled days.'

'Yes, Juva?'

'But we don't struggle alone. We're meeting other *agonistici* at a rendezvous point near Bagae. Do you know the place?'

'I've heard of it,' I said, although I was hardly about to say when and where.

'We need more transport to get our group there in one week's time. With harvesting going full on, the roads in that direction will be full of grain cargo and pack animals. I'm sending you back to the main road to take any Roman vehicles you can and drive their teams and wagons to the foot of this mountain.'

'Yes, Juva.'

My eyes scanned the carriage's long compartment out of which Juva had improvised his mobile headquarters. With its half-barreled roof, a short man like Capussa could stand up straight but even stooping. Even a tall man like Juva could still make a tidy work place out of its space. The oak floorboards were worn and broken here and there—I could see the wide space where the pit had fallen through—but the suspension belts were strong and the brakes reliable. With the wooden shutters open to the high breezes brushing the plateau, the rectangular space was airy and light.

I spotted the strongbox hidden under a crawl space under the driver's seat outside. Juva's heavy tomes were just as I'd tied them with strips of hemp linen and embroidered bands back at the cave. I resisted the military urge to stand at attention. I bowed my head instead and clasped my hands in imitation of Bomilcar.

'It seems the rabble below us have collected many martyrs' bodies. They are digging graves and engraving plaques for their shrines. It's touching the way they argue over who will have the privilege of washing and clothing the remains of our martyred virgin.'

'God bless her soul.' For once, I meant it.

'You were seen defending the girl against the depredations of some brute—'

'The good woman Sophonisba summoned me one night. The girl protested and—'

'Yes, yes, I know all that.' Juva waved his spotless hand in the air. 'Yet Sophonisba tells me this morning—well, in fact, she tells me nothing in answer to my questions. And that, picker, is unusual.'

'What is there to tell, Father?'

'I have heard from more than one of our faithful that no one can find the virgin's remains.'

I said nothing and kept my eyes averted.

He waited. There was a long silence.

He knew something.

There was a knock on the door and I leaped to answer it. I'd never been happier to see that creep Capussa's glazed expression, now looking up at me from the bottom step.

'The blind man wishes a word with Juva.'

'What does he want, Capussa?'

Capussa called up, 'He says he's abandoned, Juva, and no one gives him bread or water. There was a man here, some cripple who accompanied him on the march, but that man has disappeared.'

'Send the blind man in.'

Capussa pushed the sightless man up the steps. I cringed at the sight of his sockets with only bits of burned eye left covered in scars. He fell to his knees and laid his forehead on the planks. 'I'm ready to die for Christ, Juva' he said. 'And I'll starve soon enough for no one ensures my rations and the Good Samaritan who guided me before has left my side without even a farewell. I fear he fell to his death with the others.'

'Who took care of you before the cripple?'

'That holy martyr-carpenter who leaped to his heaven yesterday, God bless his soul.'

We all made the Sign of the Cross again.

'Tell Sophonisba I want a new guardian for you from among her *sanctimoniales*. We *agonistici* are fighters, even you in your weakened state. We aren't starved monks wandering like skeletons alone in the desert. We eat and drink God's gifts while we're in his world.'

'I will tell her, Juva, thank you, thank you.'

'Wait! Tell me, blind man, have they found the virgin's body yet?'

'No, Juva. They say she rode to her death right over the edge of the cliff on the shoulders of a tall and glorious Circumcellion.'

I was thankful that Juva's witness was unable to identify my tall and glorious self right then and there. But there would be other witnesses to betray me soon enough. I had to think fast and as an idea sprang to mind, I thanked Lady Laetitia wherever she rested in Roma right now for her constant Christian lessons and exhortations.

'Is this possibly a blessed sign, Juva?'

Juva's eyebrows shot up at my interruption, but I plowed on.

'The girl went over the cliff, but she can't be found. The reason seems obvious.'

'Obvious?'

'Yes. If the virgin's body has vanished while hundreds of faithful scour the rocks for her without success, then there's only one possible explanation. She was assumed, body and soul, into heaven, just as our Holy Mother ascended intact to sit at the Right Hand of God.'

Juva's mouth dropped open as he stared at me in disbelief.

'Praise be to God!' the blind man cried. He dropped to his knees on the carriage floor and then prostrating himself full, started heaving in tearless sobs of joy at Juva's feet.

'Praise be to God.' I intoned, falling to my knees next to him.

The priest's eyes narrowed at me. 'I must offer my prayers of thanks to the Lord in private. You may both be excused now.'

I aided the poor man to his feet and helped him back out the carriage door. 'We have a miracle!' he shouted to the crowd as he threw his hands up to the skies from the wagon steps, 'Our own virgin has been received by the Lord, body and soul!'

Within five minutes, his idiotic revelation was taken up by hundreds of gullible, filthy and ragged poor.

It was an excellent moment to fill my growling stomach. I trotted to the cooks' campfire for a well-deserved bowl of nasty soup. I felt rather satisfied with myself.

I should have known better.

Bomilcar and Hiempsal called me over an hour later. It would take us the morning to get back to the main road where we would rest and then ambush any small cargo train we might encounter.

I glanced around the chosen team and recognized the two sentries who'd delivered Nico and me that first night to the cave. They were both strong and simple, only there for the proven loyalty of their muscles rather than for their brains.

Capussa made a sixth. He was grinning and flexing his wrists around his club like a boy playing with a stick and ball. Two more ruffians were recruited—the loutish Stembanos, still limping, half-drunk as always, and wary of me, plus a lively youth named Niptasan.

We all shared a bladder of wine for luck or foolhardiness, depending on your mood, and agreed to descend the goat track to the plains in an hour. Bomilcar signaled me for a private word. We pulled our hoods far over our faces and melted into the anonymous crowd.

'I'm staying behind. I'm needed to keep order around here.'

'I trusted that you'd direct this attack, not Hiempsal.'

Bomilcar glanced in all directions. He gestured me to follow him to a cluster of twisted shrubs shielding us from the wagons' sightlines. He knelt amidst a gaggle of pious villagers tending their pathetic dung fires against the breeze. I crouched on my haunches at his side.

'I suggest you be careful today,' he said.

'It seems easy enough with seven of us. There can't be more than four wagon guards, maybe five. If they're driving closed carriages this time, we just back off. It might be another trap.'

'That might not be the only trap being laid today, picker.'

'What are you saying, Brother Bomilcar?'

'Juva doesn't trust you any longer but he's still sending you on this dangerous mission. In all the confusion of the attack, someone might be martyred *by accident*.'

'I see.' I looked him hard in the eyes. 'Why are you warning me of this?'

'Not all of us became *agonistici* because we were eager to fall on Roman swords before our time. We hate the Romans and their pagan church dressed up in Catholic vestments. The imperial church is as corrupt as its politicians. They've raped our lands long enough.'

'You're not a martyr, then?'

'I'm a rebel. There were two good men—educated and brave—Axido and Fasir, who drew up the cancellations of debt and documents freeing those who were enslaved by the colonists.'

'I know of them.'

'My older brothers fought under their leadership and lost, hunted down by the Third Augustan cavalry and sliced to pieces as they fled through the fields. That was seven years ago.'

'I've seen the bones.'

'So you know why we hate them. When we buried our dead, Governor Taurinus ordered the priests to have the bodies dug back up and left untouched to feed the birds and dogs. And his simpering priests complied.'

'So you follow Juva.'

'I follow him. I fight against *traditores* and sell-outs and the grandsons of Roman soldiers who were handed our land as retirement pensions while we were pushed out. But I'm different from some.'

'Different how?'

'I want my reward now and not in heaven. I think you're more ambitious than devote yourself.'

'Juva is ambitious as well as saintly.'

Bomilcar smiled and looked away to make sure we weren't overheard. 'Juva uses the innocent and employs the quick. He dreams of reinstatement in Carthago. We control more than half the churches already. We just need one last bold stroke to tip the balance.'

'That day will come.' Despite my loyalties, I half believed it.

'But you won't live to see it. You may have fooled Juva into thinking you're one of us, but there's something about you that's wrong. I've been watching you. You smell of different food. You look me in the eyes. You climb into Juva's wagon with a confident step. And you speak our dialect with too much care.'

I tried to laugh it off.

'Listen, picker. I'm not a sadist like Capussa. He's the one who blinded that poor driver with lime and vinegar paste. And I'm not a rapist on the lam like Stembanos. But I warn you, if you have an accident today, it'll come as no surprise to me.'

I sought out Sophonisba. Her silence under Juva's morning interrogation told me that she was cannier than any of us suspected.

'I've come for more ointment, if there is any left,' I said. 'This robe only draws out more blood.'

'Yes, your sores healed and then broke open with too much use,' she said, examining my back.

'More exercise today! There's cargo, maybe oxen or mules, to capture.'

'Come back tonight and show off your latest wounds,' she said as she swabbed my skin.

'You're a wise healer.'

'Is Bomilcar leading?'

'He stays behind to guard Juva's carriage.'

'I see.' She packed up her herbs and discarded the leaves squeezed empty of their viscous juice.

'Picker, take a kindly word of advice from an old woman who once knew love. Follow Kahina, not Juva, for the sake of your soul.'

'Follow Kahina? Forget that. When my martyrdom comes, I want it delivered on the point of a Roman sword and not under the heels of a hundred panicked peasants.'

She whispered low, muffling her message through the modest folds of her stole. 'Listen to me, picker. I tell you again. *Follow Kahina*, before it's too late.'

I left her with that advice burning into my heart. Whatever she had seen during the chaos of the stampede, she *knew*.

It was a beautiful day for a deadly ambush—a day for leopards to stalk gazelles or macaques in the high mountain passes and for proud Numidian fighters to make the Roman occupiers their prey on the plains below. Despite my loyalties to army and master, I couldn't deny the excitement of the hunt on such a day. I swung my nobbled olive club as comfortably as if it were my old double-edged *spatha* hanging from my sword-belt.

The dry air and blue sky filled my soul with more intoxication than any Circumcellion wine. I'd heard Sophonisba's hints and Bomilcar's warnings but felt strangely liberated by their hidden menace. I'd discovered a new curve in my road, a signpost of freedom beckoning my soul.

I intended to survive today's mission but I knew that wouldn't make me safe. Nor could I return to spying on a spy like Hiempsal who'd read my colors right. So I would throw my whole being into delivering the information I'd learned to Leo—that an ambush at Bagae on the Roman emissaries was brewing. With that, I'd win Leo's benediction and I would leverage his gratitude into a bargain with the Commander, giving his servant Kahina to me as a reward.

If the Commander kept his word and Leo was discreet, I would soon be released from my bond as a *volo*. I knew the fate of most freedmen back in Roma. They were petty shopkeepers or attendants at their former masters' behest, inhabiting a limbo world where they were no longer slaves but neither full citizens.

Selling sandals or washing tunics wasn't for me. On such an afternoon with the broad lands radiating all around me, I felt ready to stake a new life with Kahina here in Numidia among our own people.

It all felt so simple there on the plateau, assembling behind Hiempsal at the crest with the others, and then cutting between the boulders, one by one, in single file down toward the flatlands.

We navigated the track as the sun passed its highest point in a white-hot sky. Our 'Israelites' came in handy more than once as walking sticks to steady our progress under loose rocks and slipping gravel. The sounds of the camp above our heads receded and a patchwork vista of small farms and pastureland stretched below.

The tall mountain shaded us as we landed with relief on the valley below. Somewhere on the other side of the long ridge stretching behind us, villagers faithful to The Church of the Martyrs were carrying on with their blessings and prayers for Juva's latest souls 'rendered' up to Christ.

It turned out that the youngster Niptasan had been selected precisely because he knew this stretch of the plains. Hiempsal had asked him about the best spot for an ambush, someplace just within reach of an imperial relay station but well out of sight. We hoped to surprise the caravan at their weariest, hungriest, and least vigilant after a good long ride of ten miles.

As before, our silent vigil dragged through the restless hours of a summer's day. My lightheaded optimism died down with the heat and stress of pent-up violence. Hiempsal and Capussa kept to themselves behind a shed sitting back off the paved curb. I was happy to leave them to their devious plotting. Once or twice I heard the little creep giggle at some aside from his chief.

The rest of us scattered through the grove lining the road, camouflaging our hooded shapes by separating into groups of two or threes, crouching at the base of olive trunks.

At last I heard Niptasan signal with a birdcall from his position farthest forward along the line of trees. We made out a three-vehicle caravan, at first merely gusts of dry dust sent up under their horses' hooves, then three distinct farm wagons.

We ducked lower, covered ourselves with dead foliage and mulch and waited until we heard Niptasan's second whistle signaling that the convoy had reached the right position for us to surround them.

I was in the middle group to the front. At the jingle of harness disks, I buried my head just before the first set of ironbound wheels rumbled passed us over the paving stones.

Hiempsal gave the third signal for attack as the lead driver came within his shed's view.

'*Laudate Deum!*' he roared. Capussa squealed, 'Praise God, praise God,' then started up that frightening 'Ulululu,' cry I'd first heard while we cremated the assassin's body.

It was this cry that roused their savagery and blood thirst. I dashed out at the second wagon and saw none other than the stable boss Mastanabal drawing up his whip to lash my face. I was too quick for him and let the lash wind right around my club. I jerked my weapon toward me with a ferocity that brought him right off his feet onto the ground. He tried to get up but I punched him full in the face and knocked him out. It was forgivable payback for the hard lashes he laid across my back in Leo's barn.

I kicked him to one side with no further intention to harm him and raced to help Niptasan and his mate tangling with the double guard of the third wagon. How was I going to finesse an attack on men from the Longus farm without betraying my loyalties?

The two agile, fight-hungry Circumcellion sentries had made quick work of Leo's two old farmworkers. They'd bashed both men in the head before either one could even muster a defense.

We left them, brains draining into the paving stones and ran forward to help Hiempsal and Capussa and the rest finish off the job before another caravan stumbled on our crime. I'd been shocked to realize we were attacking a convoy belonging to Leo's farm and decided to keep a wary eye on Hiempsal and wrap up this raid as fast as I could.

I wasn't thinking, just fighting, yet given the morning's warnings, I shouldn't have been surprised at a thunderous whack on my right shoulder from behind.

It was I who was under attack, not from Leo's drivers or farmhands, but from that junior Niptasan.

So it was *Niptasan* who had been chosen as my secret assassin. His greedy leer told me he relished his deadly assignment from Hiempsal. An olive picker from birth, he was as quick with his club as if it had been grafted to his arm in the cradle. A lifetime of darting up and down ladders and trees had made him quick and strong. His eyes were alight with glee at my reeling expression, like the glinting eyes of a green-eyed viper under a rock.

'Traitor,' he hissed.

He was powerful but fought 'high' like the harvester he was, while my legs were trained to hold me 'low,' for stabbing with my short dagger from underneath a shield.

I dodged his wide swings, looking to lunge as the club swished over my head. Once or twice I nearly had him, but now he realized my game. He lowered the aim of his club head as he swung it back and forth with the deadly swish of a scythe topping dead cornhusks.

My only hope was to back him into a wagon wheel or a ditch, but he was too clever for that, sticking to the open road. All around us I heard the cries and grunts of men fighting for their lives.

So I took the only action I could think of, and here was where I had him. As a naughty child, I'd often snuck off to the Roman arena without Lady Laetitia's permission to see the gladiator *retiarii* work their nets. Pulling away from him for a moment, I yanked my robe right over my head and off, adapting it as a net with my left hand.

Using my club in my right to block his next swing, I whirled the dead weight of the cloak twice around my head into a lasso and flung its length in a coil around Niptasan's neck and yanked him forward.

I dropped the cloak and grabbed the club from his grip and slammed its thick end down hard on his forehead. His eyes bulged and then closed.

I moved on fast to tackle the next fight.

I was horrified to see that there was Leo himself standing clear of his horses, front and center in the road ahead of me. He was fending off Hiempsal's heavy club with his long sword and working his wooden shield forward, and forward again, to push Capussa backward into a roadside ditch. He'd come armed, thank the gods, and he was holding his ground.

The oil merchant could fight like a pro. One of Hiempsal's sentries already lay dying on the far side of the first wagon. His face was draining to the color of clay. A deep stab wound in his heart pulsed like two pink lips, unleashing towering spurts of blood onto the grasses. That was the work of the pudgy oilman's sword.

The lead driver from Leo's farm, a foreman I'd seen supervising the plowing only a few weeks before, was handling his own sword with the skill of a hardened vet and giving Stembanos a good fight. But I knew Stembanos' talent lay nowhere above his armpits so I wasn't surprised to see the driver feint once or twice to draw the Circumcellion's battered club away from his chest, and then ram his blade straight through Stembanos' thick thigh. Stembanos roared with pain and the foreman withdrew his sword and wiped it clean across the giant's neck as he lay writing on the ground.

In seconds, I saw only one course of action. It was now Leo, his foreman, and myself against Hiempsal, Capussa and the remaining sentry.

The sentry made an abrupt move for the foreman who returned a blow into the man's ribs. We heard a bone crack as he staggered on the road, face forward. I swung my club around in a half-circle and took the sentry hard in the side midriff. I punched him with a quick upward thrust of my fist and he reeled back and over. His eyes bulged in shock at my betrayal as he doubled over and the foreman looked across at me in surprise.

I got away with this before Capussa and Hiempsal had realized I'd changed sides.

Capussa was still ululating his head off, in love with the sound of his own beastliness, but I could see that the two-on-one was wearing Leo down. The foreman made for Capussa, but opened up a chance for Hiempsal to knock him off his feet with his club. The foreman staggered and fell. I made for Hiempsal from behind to separate him out from Leo's fight.

Crouching low, I charged at Hiempsal's side holding my club as a bar and slammed it into the small of his back. He jerked in pain around and faced me.

'Roman dog,' he spat.

I was fending off Hiempsal's blows when I heard Leo's cries for help punctuating Capussa's eerie wailing. It was all I could do to keep my focus on avoiding Hiempsal's deadly advance. I kept my own weapon clutched crosswise in both hands, blocking one blow after another when, without warning, his powerful club smashed through mine.

I stood there, holding two splintered pieces of olive wood.

He roared like a lion with victory, throwing his glance upwards, and it was all I needed. Like any trained Roman I rammed the shattered end of my right olivewood shaft into his belly. He gurgled and grabbed at the wood to pull it out, but I twisted it hard until he fell forward.

The second sentry had recovered and despite his wounded rib, joined Capussa. The two of them had overcome Leo's swift thrusts. Somehow, the sentry must have been dumb enough to risk the brute jabs of Leo's shield but he'd managed to burst through Leo's protection, leaving only loosened planks and leather straps hanging from metal fastenings.

I was only in time to see the sentry lunge on top of Leo and hold him face down while Capussa screeched and brought his club straight down on Leo's spine.

The trader's legs twitched as if a bolt of Zeus had run through them, but then flopped like a doll's as Capussa rolled him face upwards. I stumbled forward as I heard Leo scream. The sentry was holding his head and Capussa was rubbing his vile burning paste into Leo's face.

I dashed up the line of wagons where I picked up a sword in my path. I drove it down hard, piercing deep between the sentry's shoulder blades and as he went limp, I kicked him out of my way.

Capussa was still at his vile work. I raised my sword and thought of my Commander on his horse in full throttle charging the barbarian front. I risked a deep swing from the rear and bringing my whole upper body forward, I sliced Capussa's ratty little head clean off his shoulders.

Still blinking at me, it rolled across the road and landed in the irrigation ditch. The clear water soon streamed bright red with his blood.

I went to the front wagon and using my last dregs of strength, cleared its flat bed of half a dozen sacks of grain. I lifted Leo's broken body with care and settled him down. He moaned, but made no resistance. I adjusted him for the journey as carefully as I could. His legs wobbled this way and that, limp and useless. I stretched him out under the travelling cloak he had left bundled there and wedged his travel satchel under his head as a makeshift pillow.

The road was wide enough for two carts to pass and had reinforced paving. It was one of the empire's so-called 'slow roads,' a *cursus clabularis* built for heavy cargo traffic as well as officials and messengers travelling at high speed by horse.

That meant it was a double-usage artery of the province. Any man left standing with a bloodied weapon in his hand on a pile of wounded and dead in the middle of an imperial trunk road is rarely tagged the victim.

I had to move fast.

CHAPTER 14, LEO'S SECRET

—LATE AFTERNOON—

I had no use for the heavy oil cargo in the second and third wagons. I carried Leo's concussed stable boss Mastanabal and the foreman one by one over to the bed of the third wagon and drove it within view of the shed.

Hiempsal's stomach wound was not as bad as I'd thought. He was still breathing so I dragged him and the dead or semi-conscious bodies of the others by their heels into the high grasses lining an irrigation ditch running parallel to the road some twenty feet out into the fields. Better to let people think the *agonistici* responsible for the attack had got clean away.

I drove the second wagon and its horses off the road as well. I unharnessed them to graze in peace.

I left Capussa's head staring at the sky from the bottom of the ditch.

He hardly knew where he was—or what he had become of him. He groaned and clutched at the air like a newborn. He scratched away at his face, now less a face then a mess of whitened sores and festering pink burns under the evil paste that seemed to still eat at his flesh with a will of its own.

The sentry and Capussa had not only robbed him of his sight—they'd broken his back. And I realized that this was what they had planned for me.

Whatever my sympathies for rebels overturning crippling debts and slavery, a wave of sheer revulsion at Capussa's sadistic hobby multiplied my disgust for the Circumcellions' religious 'faith' a hundred times over.

I lashed Leo's front team of horses into action and steered them northward down the center of the Roman pavement toward the next transit stopover. The state-subsidized *mansiones* for change of mounts and relief messengers sat between nine and ten miles apart, but in the heat of the attack, I'd lost any sense of where we were. I had no way of knowing whether the next station was within a minute's or an hour's hard drive.

After half an hour of merciless whipping, I drove the team into a rough clearing beside stables standing by at all hours for courier and licensed commercial traffic. Two young stable hands caught sight of Leo and me—covered in blood and other men's wet remains. They dropped their currycombs and ran yelling back into the station for help.

My telltale Circumcellions robe still sat back on the road where I'd tossed it in the fight with Niptasan. Nearly naked, I lifted Leo's burning body in my bare arms as their shouts brought help running.

'Is that you, Marcus?' Leo whispered.

'Yes, Leontus Flavius, it's me.'

'Where are we?'

'A relay station. I'll get the name later. First, we wash out those burns.'

The stationmaster, a *manceps* who held a franchise from the government, came with three other men to make an improvised sling from a sheet. Laying Leo on that, we shifted him inside.

The tavern consisted of two plain-tiled rooms with whitewashed walls. Imperial taxes financed thousands of such stations dotting the *Cursus Publicus*. On the outskirts of Roma such stations could turn out to be luxury rest stops, complete with restaurants, comfortable bedrooms, shops and fine stables.

Here, the front room contained only a couple of rickety wooden tables for quick snacks while teams were changed over.

The back room had a couple of cots so that imperial messengers could grab a nap before continuing on. The food looked stodgy but reliable and the welcome was gruff, but professional.

Unfortunately, nursing wasn't on the menu.

The stationmaster's wife fetched fresh water and was about to apply compresses made of kitchen rags. I ordered her to boil the rags and the water first and get me lots of vinegar, the way I'd see Ari do it a dozen times in his medical tent. Even with combat raging less than a hundred yards from his surgical table, Ari's procedures stayed strict.

Soon I washed my filthy hands in a basin of steaming water diluted with vinegar until they raged deep purple back at me. Then I went back to Leo's cot.

He tried to turn onto his side. His agony got worse, not less, when he realized that only his upper torso turned on command. His twisting shoulders couldn't make his pelvis move.

'I can't feel my legs. I can't feel my bloody legs.'

'We've got to get that stuff off your face. Lie still.'

'I'm on fire. I want to scream.'

I thought of Sophonisba's healing gel. My pouch was still tied to the rough cord around my naked waist.

We swabbed his skin gently with the hot rags. He wailed in pain and we had to stop when we saw stark white flesh as thin as silk coming right off in our hands, leaving the muscle of his cheeks raw to the air. I dabbed Sophonisba's cool medicine on the few places I dared touch.

'Here drink some of this,' I said. At the bottom of the pouch was the vial of *herba Apollinaris* that was a boon to wounded soldiers. I mixed a few drops in a cup of watered wine and together the woman and I got it down Leo's gullet.

'I was coming to answer your signal,' he gasped.

'Nico gave you my message?'

'Nico wasn't in good shape by the time he reached the farm. We set off too late.'

What had Nico told Leo about Kahina and myself? Leo didn't say anything, so I guessed that Nico had turned out to be a more calculating guy after all.

'A strongbox of money?' he whispered.

'Yes, Leo, I saw it. Not some parish collection of random coins. It was a single treasure, a fund in imperial *solidi* that could only come from a powerful backer, a political backer with access to a mint, a moneylender or some imperial treasury. The priest who took me in is no saintly miracle-worker like that barefoot Donatus. He's a frustrated city boy with Greek and Latin, a wily politician in contact with allies leading other Circumcellion camps. He wants his Carthago parish back and the imperial priests driven right into the Central Sea.'

'The strongbox—any markings?'

'No. But he had a mysterious visitor at the lake near Nif en-Nsr. I couldn't see his face but he was smuggled in and out of the camp. He wore a heavy iron ring on his knuckles, fixed with a heavy red gem.'

Leo's whitened eyes stared blank at the ceiling, and his mouth twisted in pain.

'What about the attack on the Romans?'

'They'll ambush the two envoys at a place called Bagae. They're gathering quickly in the hundreds—hooded savages with clubs and empty bellies.'

Leo gasped in pain. We swabbed his face again with the gel but could do nothing for his eyes. They were burned away. I dared not tell him that but I was too late to catch him pawing his brow as I turned to swap the boiled cloths.

'Marcus, where's my face?'

'You're burned, badly.'

'I can't move. I can't see.'

'Yes, I know. We'll get you home somehow, soon.'

He might have slept a while, but it was hard to tell because his eyelids were so damaged. Perhaps all the time he was still thinking, what next? What now? I must have dozed off because he woke me from a slump on my three-legged stool.

'Marcus, you must know the truth. It's too late for the wrong loyalties.'

'Shh, you should rest.'

'I'll rest in good time. Listen to me now. Marcus, have you never wondered why the Commander fussed over you as a boy?'

'He's a good master. It's the custom in noble houses to keep slaves like amusing pets. He was kind to me.'

'You never wondered why you were sent to the study to read to Senator Manlius?'

'No one else had time.'

'Marcus, your mother never said anything?'

'She was lonely. I tried to amuse her when I could.'

'She spoke of your father?'

'Only that I was as handsome as he was and as good a fighter.'

'Think on that for a moment, Marcus,' Leo gasped. 'I never met your mother's husband. Was the mule trader handsome or brave?'

I chuckled despite myself. 'It was a woman's love talking, Leo.'

'No. It was honesty. Your true father was the handsomest man in our class and the bravest of Romans on horseback.'

An abyss opened up before me. I felt my mind falling into it, like a man thrown into a cold black lake at night and counting the seconds it takes him to reach the surface and breathe clean air again.

I heard my mother's voice echoing down memory's long tunnel. *Because you are my little mule, and that is how I have raised you. And you are good and strong. You'll travel far. And you are a clever fighter, like your father.*

So, after all, my mother hadn't lied. The poor, stooped mule breeder, cowed from war and invasion, was survivor enough to sell off the woman he couldn't keep and the child who was nothing like himself for profit—because the child wasn't his.

The clever fighter and father I resembled was the Commander.

'Your mother suffered from a broken heart. When you were just a tiny child, she rode on a slave driver's wagon into Roma. When she realized who'd bought her, the dashing officer who had bedded her years before in Numidia, perhaps she rejoiced for a day or two. Perhaps they even had a night or two of happiness before her dreams turned to a cruel reality.'

'They never—?'

'The Commander adored Laetty then and respects her even now. He paid for you both to come to Roma but when the time of your arrival finally came, Laetty's illness had set in. Gregorius was unable to acknowledge you out of respect for his wife's frailty. He abandoned your mother to her sewing chores in the slaves quarters almost as soon as you settled in.'

'My mother never said a thing.'

'Gregorius had bound himself not to touch your mother again, for the sake of Laetty's dignity under her own roof. Not all men are so disciplined, Marcus, and not all Roman wives so forgiving. Everyone in the Manlius house made their peace, but if there was a victim, it was your poor mother, left working the rest of her life away in the back room. She never belonged in the city. She swallowed her misery only for your sake.'

I couldn't believe it. Yet now everything made sense like the end of a Greek play when the oracle's prediction takes on a new and entirely unexpected meaning.

The childless Commander kept me a slave to keep me close. Laetitia's nephew Clodius, growing up in the great rooms below the Senator's study, was the designated Manlius heir treading the black and white mosaics of the salons for the eyes of all Roman society. Clodius preened and postured, always ready for the adoption that would give him many centuries' treasure in Manlius wealth and property.

And all the time, upstairs in the old Senator's book-lined chambers, I was the true, unacknowledged son. I'd been loved as a pet by the Commander, but educated by his doting and wiser father.

'The Senator's amulet—'

'—Retrieve it from my study. It looks like a little boy's trinket, but the Senator thought it was one way to protect you.'

'My dangers are too great for a pagan bauble. How can I go back now?'

'As a freedman, Marcus, as a freedman!' Leo rasped. 'It's too selfish of Gregorius to keep you hidden in slave quarters and service tents forever. I forced his hand before witnesses just to give you this chance. Deliver your information to Silvester in time to raise the alarm with Paul and Macarius and move the Third Augusta to Bagae. Claim your reward. Gregorius will have to free you!'

'Rest now, please. The sun's down and it's too dark and rough for riding, even by torchlight. We'll move you tomorrow morning.'

He shook his ravaged head from side to side. 'What use is a life without feeling, without sight?'

'Shh. Think now of the blind Senator and his books. I read all the "Greats" to him. You'll have to learn all the wisdom of those busts you show off in your garden.'

'Give me more herb, boy.'

I mixed more drops and wished I had some of Ari's more powerful opiates.

Leo sipped his wine. Pawing around for his senseless knees, he groaned again in despair.

'Did you ever read the Senator any Socrates, Marcus? What did the old man say about suicide?'

'That it's wrong because it robs the state of service,' I gave him more wine.

'Hah! You're wrong, boy!' His momentary pleasure faded quickly in his pain. 'That . . . that was Aristotle and he was only talking about soldiers and slaves. Their services are the rightful property of others.'

'Socrates also said no man has a right to suicide,' I retorted.

'—Unless.'

'Unless what?'

'Socrates said, "Unless God sends some necessity upon him, as has now been sent upon me." I'm right on that one, Marcus.'

'Please rest now.'

How noble he sounded in such a bleak hour! How wrong I was on that first day I met him in camp to think him just an oily merchant wearing too much jewelry! I'd seen soldiers suffer badly and others suffer well. But to banter about classical quotes while battling this searing pain—now this was a true Roman! Leo would last for many more years yet. If I could free myself from my bonds to the dishonest, possessive love of one man, I could devote myself to serving a more generous and honest one.

'I won't leave you, Leontus Flavius. Depend on me. I'll be your eyes and legs for as long as you live.'

173

'Oh, dear boy, that was why the crippled Commander wouldn't let you go, why he couldn't face your leaving him. No, I had greater things in mind for you. You remember the man in my study?'

'The traveller with the arthritic feet?' Shh, we'll talk of him tomorrow.'

The stationmaster's wife came in with fresh rags, but I waved her away. Leo seemed calmer now, distracted by our conversation.

'No, Marcus, listen to me.' I could hardly hear his whisper so I leaned close to his crusted lips.

'I'm listening.'

'That Apodemius is a powerful man, one of the most powerful in the entire empire. *Trust Apodemius in all things.* Do you hear me? When this is all over, *find Apodemius.* Send a message marked with an *apodemus*, a little mouse, to the Casa Peregrina in Roma. He'll tell you what to do.'

'The Castra Peregrina. I understand. Now please, get some rest.'

'Yes . . . Is that my vial you're using?'

'The herb you gave me.'

'Let me hold it. It was my wife's.'

I wrapped his fingers around the tiny blue glass bottle. With one finger, he traced the delicate golden filigree etching its neck. 'It once held her favorite scent.' He sniffed it and smiled through his agony. 'It still smells of my sweet Aemilia,' he whispered.

Then before I could stop him, he'd tipped the vial into his mouth, draining the entire contents all the way to the dregs and swallowing it down with gagging determination. His body jerked forwards and back. His chest convulsed, lifting him an inch off the cot and dropped back.

'May the gods forgive me.'

He was going from me and there was nothing I could do. He had left us all for the other world.

I covered Leo's body and sat with it in a daze for the rest of the evening. I slept in the room with his corpse that night.

My mind flooded with questions, all of them too late. Until now, all my loyalty and admiration had been for the Commander. If only I'd known Leo longer. How had he learned all these truths of my birth? How many more secrets had just died within that noble spirit?

The stationmaster's wife shook me awake. I looked outside and saw it was almost dawn.

'An imperial courier passed through earlier wearing the feather of urgency in his helmet. He changed horses and took some packed food for the road.'

'Headed where?'

'Vegesela, to those Roman emissaries from the emperor.'

'His business?'

'It's not our affair to bother state couriers on fast relay. But he let drop that he'd passed a team of farmers cleaning the road and clearing away the bodies of murdered farmhands'

I avoided her piercing eyes. 'Anything else?'

'Who attacked you?' She crossed her arms and waited.

'Hoodlums. Scum. We must bury this man and mark his grave,' I said. 'Our people will come back for the body and pay you for your care.'

'My man will see to it.' She waited. I rescued Leo's satchel from the wagon and was relieved to find his purse still bulging with coins. The station keeper and stable hands were probably honest men, but any of them might have helped themselves overnight. Neither Leo nor I would've been able to do anything about it. I gave her a handful of coins.

It was not enough to send her away.

She looked down at Leo. 'This merchant passed our way for many years on his way up to Rusicada port. He was always kind and generous to my husband . . . We never noticed you before.'

I gave her more coins. She whispered, 'The messenger brought more gossip.'

'I can spare no more tips from my master's money.'

'No, this is more than enough. One of your men, the stable foreman Mastanabal, survived. He says you were attacked by a band of Circumcellions from the hills. Magistrates' men are scouring the villages now for hooded runaways. Don't worry. This crime will be punished.'

She stood in silence, gazing down at my naked chest wrapped in a rough blanket of hair she'd salvaged from the manes of mules and horses. She eyed the lash marks striping my back.

'I'll need some clean clothes to wear under my master's cloak,' I said.

'I can spare you one of my husband's long tunics and torn trousers,' she said. 'I intended to shred them for pillow stuffing.'

I finished off dressing myself with Leo's shoes, belt, sword, satchel of travel papers and his pouch.

The station keeper and two of his boys chose a spot for the temporary burial behind the station and got to digging. I gave them a coin to place on Leo's mouth as 'Charon's Obol,' his fare across the River Styx to the land of the dead.

'Where will I find these magistrates?' I asked the stationmaster. 'I can identify these vermin.'

'They're coming soon, up the road from the south,' he said and avoided my eyes.

I suspected he'd sent for the magistrate's deputies to question me. I'd already waited too long.

I thanked him and pointed Leo's wagon southwards. I promised to return with some farmhands as soon as possible. I rattled along at a clip until I'd rounded a high bend in the road. I camouflaged the wagon under wild brush and mounted the stronger of the two horses.

I turned the horse off the paved route to follow a country trail and kicked him hard. He was fresh again and pretty soon I was out of sight of the imperial road with my back to the eastern sun.

Everything was different now.

I no longer felt satisfied by the prospect of simple manumission, left to count myself blessed as a humble freedman with a little 'setting-up' fund from the Manlius accounts and life in Numidia with Kahina. A sandal maker? A butcher's apprentice, perhaps? Or a bathhouse manager? *I was a Manlius!* I was a son of Roma.

I felt the speechless outrage of a young man discovering he had been robbed of everything before his life had even begun—dignity, name and fortune had been wrenched from my hands by a cruel trick of legitimacy.

I thought of all those long mornings of beatings, pinches and kicks from the spoiled Clodius, no older than I, but always the privileged citizen. I thought of all those evenings of running errands and playing the pet while the Commander and his army pals lounged and laughed at me from their soft dining couches.

And I saw with new understanding the sad smile on Lady Laetitia's elegant features as she watched me grow from the child she'd failed to bear into an olive-skinned copy of the man she adored.

I thought of the prostitute who had spotted our physical resemblance, saying that I was so like that handsome Gregorius whom I served.

And I thought of the Commander himself, sending me upstairs to his father for an education worthy of a Manlius, just so long as he could always keep his eye on the illegitimate shadow of the legal heir he didn't have.

And I thought of all the long nights I lay staring at the crumbling plaster of the whitewashed ceiling in the servants' quarters. I lay sleepless not far from my unloved mother on a mean straw pallet on the plain-tiled floor. My mother never smiled. She just endured.

Remembering all this, I rode hard west for hours, skipping any offer of water or bread from villagers as I passed.

I was the youngest of the Manlius patricians.

I was a Numidian slave.

I was an educated Roman with the blood of Republican senators and Gallo-Roman nobles coursing through my veins.

I was a bastard hidden in the kitchen.

Who was I?

I knew one thing for sure—I wasn't going to stay a slave one minute longer than I had to.

I aimed straight for the garrison southwest of Lambaesis. I carried intelligence that might spare two Roman torturers from a nasty death, but it was a furious mix of pride and confusion, not duty, that drove me along those dusty tracks.

One question obsessed me, going around and around in my head like a crazed charioteer. What would I say to my master—my *father*—when I saw him next?

Chapter 15, Branding Irons

—THE ROAD TO LAMBAESIS GARRISON—

I hadn't slept all night. Yet I made fast time, moving forward like a man heading into battle, fueled by nothing but nervous energy and sheer determination.

As the miles lengthened, I stopped my brooding and shoved fear and fatigue away to focus only on the road and the fading light.

Long after the sun had set, I came to my senses and noticed my horse was practically stumbling over his own hoofs. I kicked him, but he had the good sense to ignore me. Under a black sky dusted with thousands of stars, he was feeling his way down a path that widened out a little with each mile we travelled.

I was approaching civilization of some kind.

The padding of the horse's hooves on soft ground gave way to a clopping sound as its feet struck stone. I had stumbled back onto the imperial road. I followed it southwest, keeping to the soft siding. The horse's mood brightened with a flick of his mane. Animal instinct or memory reminded him of the comforts of a good relay station ahead.

He was right. We arrived just before the station shut down its kitchens. I stabled my horse and headed across the clearing pounded flat by decades of traffic. A closed carriage, stained a glossy walnut and sporting polished silver pommels shaped like rams' heads, announced some elegant customers were already inside.

The main room was smoky from cooking fires and busy with noisy customers. I took the last available table in the corner nearest the cooks' serving station and ordered a meal. It didn't take long for me to finish off my fresh flatbreads dipped in a spicy chickpea stew.

'Figs in honey to finish?' the serving girl asked. I paid for two bowls at once and slowed down to savor the sheer relief of it all. Now I had the leisure to observe a domestic comedy at the table next to mine. A matron in her early thirties was travelling with a teen-age girl and small boy, both children competing for an imperial-grade prize for battiness.

'Stop fidgeting with your hair, Julia and for goodness' sake, *eat something*. Nobody wants to marry a broomstick.'

'I hate this food and I hate my hair.'

'Its simple and elegant and you're going to keep it tied up like that all the way to Mediolanum,' her little brother taunted in obvious imitation of their mother.

The mother herself had taken great trouble with her appearance. I knew the tricks of a lady's toilette. In the privacy of our rooms I'd watched my desperate mother try cheap cosmetics she could never wear in public.

This matron frowned at her two children through a coat of pale powder that failed to camouflage years of weathering by the harsh Numidian sun. I recognized the berry-stain on the lips, kohl pencil on the brows and eyelids, and rouge that turned her cheeks bright orange under the yellow lantern flames.

But for all her attention to her looks, she lacked the graceful confidence of a genuine Roman society woman. She was wearing too much jewelry for her own safety, a sure sign she hadn't travelled north before. I took her for the wife of a commodities trader or self-made estate manager taking her children across the Central Sea to offload the teenage girl in marriage. It wasn't hard to imagine the clan of down-on-their-luck snobs in Italia lowering their noses just long enough to relieve this colonial child in a bad hairdo of her dowry.

'It's too old-fashioned. My ears are sticking out like a mule's.'

'People are old-fashioned back home. It's called breeding. After the wedding, you can dye it gold or cut it off, for all I care. It'll be your husband's business then, not mine.'

'Can I eat her figs?'

'No! Julius, leave her bowl alone!'

'You can have them.' The girl shoved her bowl over to her brother. 'One day you'll decorate a banquet table with an apple in your mouth.'

'Mama, she called me a pig!'

'Finish that up. We're going to bed.'

I thought of Leo's daughters and my amusement faded. They were about the same age as this girl heading off to be married in the new capital. Who would find husbands for his orphaned twins now? Who would protect their fortunes?

A stranger on the far side of the room caught my eye in the flickering shadows of his own table lamp. He tossed me a knowing wink. Maybe he supported a wearisome brood of his own back home. His threadbare tunic and cloak were unfastened at the neck. He'd patched his travelling shoes with mismatched leather.

I would have given him more thought, but there was a commotion at the door. Two road inspectors burst in on us and demanded drinks from the serving girl.

'Get out your permits,' one yelled around the room. They tossed back their free tots of wine as they watched us fumble through our belongings for road passes.

'*Evectio*? *Diplomata*?' The taller of the two came up to my table and held out his hand to inspect my travelling permit— whether an imperial passport or local road license.

I produced Leo's permanent license to travel the heavy-cargo *Cursus Clabularis* with the nonchalant confidence I knew Leo would have affected. Any merchant would have paid handsomely for it and renewed it on the dot as required. His oil deliveries depended on it.

The other inspector was busy chatting to the ragged stranger in the corner. I half-expected them to throw him out for illegal use of the services, but he produced a document. They examined it and then took him aside for a longer interrogation. Then they moved on to the matron just now leading her children up the stairs to their rented bedrooms.

'Madame, you can't go until we've seen your permit,' the brasher of the two inspectors shouted at her.

'Yes, of course,' she sighed, already halfway up the stairs. I felt a little sorry for her. We all knew she'd had an evening of it with her two offspring. She gave him her permit but the inspector ignored her impatient sigh as he took his time. She fussed with her Julia's hair as the officer checked its number against his lists.

'Forged,' he said. 'Just like they said. Pack up your stuff. You can sleep in your carriage and take the unpaved roads from here.'

'I will *not*! My husband made all the necessary arrangements and I'm sleeping in that bed upstairs!'

'They warned us one station back. We've got our records, and this permit number is for a license issued somewhere called . . . *Aquincum*?' He looked to his partner for help.

'Only the gods know,' the other inspector said with a shrug.

'It's a base up on the northeast border of Pannonia,' I said, despite myself, 'where Marcus Aurelius wrote his *Meditations*.' Then I stopped short. Leo had warned me, *don't show off.*

'Well, what do you know?' They turned back to the woman. 'And you've come all this way,' the brash inspector teased her.

'My husband—'

'I don't know what he paid, lady, but I know he was cheated.'

'I have two tired children with me!'

'Well, they'll keep you warm enough in that fancy vehicle parked out front.'

I kept my gaze averted, but I knew the stranger in the corner was trying not to laugh. Certainly the serving girl had moved with the efficiency of a Roman tavern bouncer at high season on a festival night. She was already dumping two matching overnight bags of expensive tapestry-work outside the front door.

The stationmaster offered another round on the house for the inspectors. They chatted over the back bar. The night settled down to the shouts and bangs of the kitchen staff washing out cooking pots and the last crackles of the dying logs on the oven hearth. Then the stationmaster invited the inspectors into the back room where no doubt they would be divvying up the 'little road dividends' of the day.

I was considering the difficult choice between one more nightcap or a third bowl of figs, when I felt one of the inspectors had returned to my tableside.

'Could I just see your permit again for a moment, son?'

'Sure.' I pulled it out for his closer inspection and smiling to show I was on his side, I also produced Leo's purse to contribute a few coins to the inspector's personal funeral fund. Obviously, the man's 'tips' had come up short that day.

'This license is made out to Leontus Longus Flavius.'

'Yes, officer.'

'The station master over there says you aren't this Leontus Longus Flavius.'

'Well, come to think of it, I'm not,' I joked. 'But I never said I was. You see, we had an accident on the road but time is money. I'm seeing some of his payments through.' I jangled Leo's purse invitingly.

It was an idiotic mistake. The flickering flames of the hearth flared up for a moment as the heavyset inspector stood there, glanced over at his partner for a moment and then leaned over my table.

I fought hard not to lose my nerve.

'Yes, there was an accident. But the cargo was abandoned and besides, aren't you headed in the wrong direction if you're delivering payments for the Longus estate?'

I shrugged. 'I do what I'm told.'

'You were involved in that incident, weren't you?'

I felt the other inspector lift me off my bench. With both hands, he ripped the cloth on my back in two, exposing my naked torso right there in the middle of the dining room. The lash marks still gleamed across my back.

'You were right, Festus. What was that description?'

'Tall, light-olive skin, strong limbs, bronze cast to the hair and lash marks. It all fits. He's the runaway slave from down near Lambaesis. There's a nice, fat reward out for you, slave boy.'

They fetched some ropes from their horse packs and within fifteen minutes had tethered my hands and ankles to an iron hitching post right next to Leo's horse.

ᚱᚱᚱ

The next morning they led Leo's horse for the long ride to a jail in Vegesela with me stretched over his back like a hog tied for the market. The jail was right off the main forum studded on all four sides with vendors' stalls and small open *tabernae* hawking snacks and drinks.

They dragged me down some dry, worn stone steps and along a passage to a bolted door outside the cell. They stripped me down of Leo's cloak, shoes, sword-belt, satchel and money pouch, and tossed me through the door. I found myself crawling through stinking, humid black depths illuminated only by a tiny grated window that framed cart wheels and sandaled feet passing by.

Just outside that single window, a laundry had placed their vat to collect the public's urine needed for bleaching tunics white. Passing drunks unable to take good aim streamed their yellow piss right into the jail and stumbled on.

As my eyes adjusted, I realized I was not alone. I ignored four creatures already wasting away in the dank reaches of the cellar's four walls and was grateful they ignored me. I tried to sleep in a corner in the dirt.

I kept track of time by keeping my eye on that single window giving us a glimpse of the Vegesela streets from the rats' vantage. Nothing but sandals, wheels, horseshit, urine and of course, rats. The only advantage it offered was the changing square of light that turned day into night and night into dawn.

The oldest of my jail mates looked barely able to stand because of whippings across his back and beatings that had weakened his aged joints. Each day at dawn, the other three prisoners helped this graybeard up from the spot where he'd crumpled into a hunched, broken lump. He led them in prayers to start the morning and at nightfall he blessed the moldy bread that served as our 'meal.' To my astonishment, he gave almost all of his food to the others.

On the third day, a couple of jail wardens threw open the ironclad door and rousted out all but the old man. The prisoners fought the wardens off like beasts in the arena, but they lost and were dragged off screaming and shouting.

They never returned. Something told me they hadn't been released for good behavior. I was more desperate than ever to get my information about Bagae to the Commander.

That first evening we two were alone, the old man seemed desolate without his fellow worshippers.

'Shall we pray together, my son?'

I shrugged. I had no other plans for the evening. I knelt next to him on the detritus of the earth floor while he made the Sign of the Cross and began to pray. I got the feeling that my presence comforted him.

He prayed a long time. A lot of it was in Greek, which I could read quite well, but had rarely heard spoken. For a while its novel sounds captivated my ears. He then switched to the elegant Latin of an educated man, not the colonial variety studded with provincial words and accents. He didn't expect a local slave to follow that either, but I said 'Amen,' when he paused.

Then my ears perked up.

'... for salvation in the next world by the blessings of Christ, our Lord and Savior. And for all the poor of our country and for the intercession of our Lord with the powerful and mighty ... and for the souls of the Roman officials, Paul and Macarius, that they might see the error of their chosen path and that they might see the peaceful way to true purity from sin and to unity of purpose before God . . .'

I listened more carefully now. All the while, I asked, why was this wretched old man praying for two torturers?

'What do you know of Paul and Macarius?' I took the risk of addressing him in Latin.

'Why, they're my persecutors, son. Everyone knows that. Paul and Macarius have dragged me through three towns already. They lashed me naked in the public forum of every one. And to think I went to them in peace.' He shook his head and sighed.

'Why?'

'Where are you from, boy? Weren't you in those crowds that watched the humiliation of this poor body? Why do you think I'm still here? They're waiting for market day tomorrow, when they'll get the biggest crowd of the month.'

'Who are you?'

'I'm Bishop Marculus, son. Every Christian who keeps the true Faith knows me from Carthago down to Theveste. Who are you? You speak Latin like a Roman gentleman, yet you know so little of events around us?'

Who was I to know? Should I try to explain? Even if there had been time, I was bewildered by my own identity and it seemed I might waste away here for months until someone back in camp stumbled across the true fate of 'my mission.'

'I'm a messenger from another part of the country. You prayed for Paul and Macarius, Bishop. Why did you do that?'

'Because I forgive them. What did our Lord say? "Forgive them, for they know not what they do." What sort of messenger?'

'It's too late now. Paul and Macarius will travel onwards from Vegesela after they're finished here?'

'If they finish with me here, yes. But I fight, boy! I fight! My stubbornness has slowed down their campaign.' He tilted his head and gave me a sheepish, toothless smile. 'I fear they're a little irritated with me. You see, I refuse to die.' His rheumy eyes lit up with satisfaction.

'Bishop, those two officials are walking into an ambush of Circumcellions—hundreds, perhaps over a thousand of them. These ambushers want to tear the province apart with civil war.'

'That's the wrong solution. It will only bring more misery and hunger. That's not the way, not the way,' he shook his head.

'I know. I wasn't here when they slaughtered Axido and Fasir,' I said. 'But I saw the bleached bones of Octava one night. And I heard of families cut down limb by limb under the orders of Governor Taurinus.'

'It was a time of daylight horrors,' the priest said. 'It was as if demons had been unleashed on us, stalking our people through the thick waves of wheat and hunting them down among the olive groves.'

'Governor Silvester doesn't want that again,' I said. 'I've heard him say it myself.'

'You have, son? Oh, if only I'd swallowed my lawyer's arrogance and gone straight to the Governor,' Marculus moaned. 'But no! I was too proud, the Bishop Marculus, famed for his elocution and rhetoric, from legal bench to pulpit. I thought I could talk the lamb's skin right off the wolf's back! And I led my delegation straight into the devil's own garden.'

'Help me get word to the army garrison south of Lambaesis. Help me prevent further bloodshed. The army has learned its lesson from the days of Governor Taurinus. It wants to prevent more bloodshed.'

Marculus glanced at the skin shredding off his empty hands as he stretched them out to me, 'I can't help you.'

'Then get the guards to pass a message?'

'They're comfortable colonists, child. You can't afford their prices.'

We retreated to our separate corners. I tried to sleep. From time to time, I heard him mumbling his endless prayers, while I was left with confused and frustrated thoughts.

'There is a way,' he cried out. 'They've promised that the good and saintly Donatus will be my confessor before the final torture to come. It is he who will administer to me the Sacrament of Penance.'

'Well, we need a miracle now. I hear he's the man to deliver.' I had not imagined the Romans would be that kind to the wise old man.

'Shush, boy. I know what you're thinking, that it's nothing more than a hypocritical Roman gesture. Nevertheless *Donatus will come*, I know it! I expected him before this time already. He's a living saint. We'll tell Donatus to alert the two Romans. They respect him. They'll listen to him!'

The next morning, we were both dragged out in chains to the busy Vegesela marketplace. I was there to witness the main and only event. We stood sagging in the bright sun as heralds moved through the market's alleys and stalls, calling all and sundry to the forum.

And then I saw them. Paul and Macarius came out of the basilica and stood at the top of the high steps overlooking the open space. Paul was the taller of the two, a stooping clerical-looking type more at home perhaps with notaries and scribes. Macarius was shorter, with close-set eyes over a snout-like nose. The African sun had blistered his thick lips white.

Escorts flanked them on either side, carrying purple-hemmed banners embroidered with the Greek letters Chi and Rho emblazoned on Constantine's shields before the Battle of the Milvian Bridge. The two envoys beamed down on the restless curious of Vegesela. At Paul's signal, a Roman aide in civilian clothing stepped forward with a shining chest of coins in his arms. He laid it on the topmost step.

'This the reward of peace, people of Vegesela!' Paul shouted.

'Take the Emperor's face off our altar!' someone shouted from the back of the crowd. 'What has the Emperor to do with God?' yelled another. It seemed that Father Donatus' rebuff had been taken up as a slogan across the countryside.

'Come into the church and worship with us,' Paul pleaded but the surly crowd was turning against them.

'Release Marculus!' they shouted.

I witnessed the dry smile of Macarius the Unifier become the true grin of Macarius, a sadist.

Marculus was wrenched by the two jailers away from my side and dragged into the center of the forum. I now saw that a stake had been fixed in place. Marculus was propped against it as the jailers started to bind up the old man with ropes. But he beat them to it and grabbed the rough pole with both hands.

He began to pray.

I'd seen whippings before in the army, lashings that left the victim bleeding away his life while his tent mates were forbidden to cut him down from where he dangled until he was dead. And I'd seen cruelty on the battlefield, when barbarians and even rebel Romans had pleaded for mercy from us—and got none.

But this was the first time that I'd seen a naked old priest wrap his own torn and bleeding fingers to a post so firmly that no one could have peeled him away even if they'd tried. Now I watched as this old man was flayed raw anew. Not once did he cry out from the pain but his lips kept up their constant prayer.

When he was just alive enough for the next and last town's performance, they stopped. He made the Sign of the Cross and collapsed on the pavement. The guards marched me behind him and tossed us both back into the darkness again.

'Donatus will come to hear my confession soon,' he whispered to me.

'Donatus is coming,' confirmed one of the jailers as he slammed the door shut.

And the great peacemaker Donatus did show up at last. He arrived when the streets were almost as dark and silent as our cell. The only sound through the little window was tomorrow's news sung through the streets by someone reading off a poster.

The poster said that tomorrow Paul and Macarius would provide another entertainment. A runaway slave had been matched to a warrant for his arrest. The next morning this 'Marcus' would be branded on the forehead with the letters FGV for *fugitivus*, as prescribed by law.

Shocked and terrified, I collapsed on the dark ground. Even if I won my freedom somehow, a man branded with *FGV* over his eyebrows lived forever among the *dediticii*, people permanently outside the law and civilized life and despised by all Romans. I couldn't exist like that. I just couldn't. I quaked there, numb with fear. Finally, overwhelmed by starvation and despair, I passed out in a faint.

So I didn't see Donatus at first. I was lying in the darkest corner, the only spot that drew heat from a pipe running up to baths adjacent to the prison wall. Marculus no longer cared what his body suffered. His hope and heart were already with his Lord.

I woke up to his cry for joy when the jail door swung open and Father Donatus slipped past me and knelt at Marculus' side. The holy man clasped his battered fellow priest and embraced him without a care for the victim's blood smearing across his robes.

They prayed together with backs turned to me. I pretended to doze on as Donatus heard the final confession of Marculus.

I waited until they finished and Donatus made the Sign of the Cross over Marculus' bowed gray head.

I hoped Marculus hadn't forgotten that I was there. How else was I going to escape the mutilation of the branding irons tomorrow if Donatus refused me a chance to deliver my message to the Commander *in person*? Surely he was powerful enough as a living saint and head of the Church of the Martyrs to wrest that small favor in the name of unity and peace?

'This is the lad.' Marculus pointed across the dark waste at me.

'The runaway slave?'

'An educated boy. He'll tell you of great troubles brewing and he carries a message of peace that may save many lives,' Marculus said. 'Take him with you, if you can.' Too broken to move, the old bishop gestured to me to wait in the light near the window.

The two priests bid farewell. Neither man betrayed a woman's sentimentality, but surely they knew Marculus was unlikely to survive another round under Macarius' whips. I admired their stoic faith in a reunion to come in another world.

Donatus could not bring his fellow priest a miracle but he did bring him solace beyond measure that night.

Donatus gathered up his dark cloak and felt his way step by step through the stony blackness across the uneven floor strewn with prisoners' filth. Just then, the guards passed outside our door. The jingling of their keys reminded me that Donatus had not come to interview me. Time was short and the risk of interruption high.

The moon cast a silvery light through the iron bars of our cell. It wasn't until Donatus moved into the ghostly illumination that I saw how the gentle visage he no doubt offered to parishioners could turn grave and piercing. Behind the fatherly beard and bent shoulders, I detected a penetrating intelligence.

How could I quickly sum up for this powerful saint all I knew about Juva's role in a disaster coming for the whole province? People said Donatus was good to the point of weakness, and that he had no authority over the cruel rage of the Circumcellions. But here was a chance to disarm their ambush within hours, with just a few words to Governor Silvester. He'd already appealed to Governor Taurinus for peace, but then he'd acted too late. I hoped he had learned his lesson from that disaster as well as the Romans had. He would be sure to act faster on my information this time.

But I felt faint and the thought of the hot brand pressing down on my flesh only hours from then made me dizzy. He extended his hand out to support me, as if I weren't a runaway slave. Gratefully, I reached out for the strength of his steady arm.

The moonlight caught the glint of a jewel. On his finger I saw a large iron ring studded with a massive garnet.

CHAPTER 16, A PRIEST FROM HEAVEN

—THE LAMBAESIS JAIL—

'What's your message, my son?' Donatus asked me in Punic.

I swallowed and looked away from his hungry scrutiny. I'd been within seconds of telling all I knew about the traitorous ambush at Bagae to its very sponsor and strategist.

'You almost finished in there, Holy Father?' a guard shouted.

My thoughts raced to absorb just how far the puritanical bishop's conspiracy went.

First there would be the maddened onslaught by thousands of Circumcellions hoods clubbing the Romans envoys and their aides to unrecognizable pulp. Donatus, this frail old man who cured the blind and halt, would disown and condemn the violence.

But he would stand aside as Governor Silvester's hand was forced to revenge the death of the imperial representatives. The impetuous Emperor Constans would order the army to wipe out the Church of the Martyrs once and for all.

And all this torture and bloodshed would backfire on Constans' churchmen. Hundreds more shrines would sprout up across the province. Popular outrage and grief would topple the delicate balance between Donatists and the imperial clergy clean over, tipping Carthago and all the imperial churches at long last into Bishop Donatus' ambitious lap.

And the strongbox of gold? There was only one explanation.

In their rampages on the basilicas, like the one during the wedding at Lambaesis, the Circumcellions stole chalices and reliquaries of pure gold. They delivered these to Donatus who had it melted down to buy spies and feed his Circumcellion militants.

Leo must have suspected it all along. Those weekly trips to moneylenders on the coast were part of his investigation.

I looked straight into Donatus' penetrating eyes.

'Unrest is brewing from village to village, Father.'

'Indeed. Is that all?'

'Paul and Macarius have angered many people by forcing them to worship an image of the old Emperor Constantine.'

Donatus was losing patience. 'Marculus said you'd heard rumors of a confrontation. *What rumors?*'

'Yes,' I nodded, my brain racing. 'The Romans are planning another purge, just like seven years ago. They'll use any excuse to mow down men, women and children in the name of cleansing the province of The Church of the Martyrs. We must avoid bloodshed.'

'We must avoid bloodshed. Is that your secret message?'

'Yes, Father. They say you work miracles. Marculus failed with words alone, though none doubted his skill. You must use the power of your prayers to persuade Paul and Macarius to avoid making more martyrs. These Romans should go straight north to Carthago and sail back to Mediolanum.'

He patted me on the shoulder. 'I'll see what miracles I can do but if I know these Romans, they only learn the hard way. Bless you. You may be a slave, but you're also a child of peace.'

The branding irons waited for me.

'Only a miracle can save me now, Father.'

'I'll pray for you tomorrow. And I will pray for Marculus. Tomorrow they take him to the citadel on the heights of Nova Petra.'

He left us there. I listened to Marculus groaning and twitching in his sleep as I watched the dawn streak the buildings lining the forum outside with pink light. Marculus' confession had given me one last desperate idea.

There was no escape for myself, but I had to make one last effort to get a message to the Commander.

The guards changed over for the day. I called one to the grate in our door and whispered, 'I've heard some die from branding. The irons burn too deep, it goes wrong, and the fever infects the brain.'

'It's not a stroll around the arena, boy.'

'I want to make my confession.'

'You had the top priest in there half the night.'

'He was the wrong priest. I worship in the imperial church.'

He started to slam the grate door in my face.

'You can't deny me this!'

'You're a slave, idiot! I deny you anything I want.' He bolted the opening shut. I was pitched back into the dark. The stench hit my nostrils all over again. I went to the tiny light of the grille and standing on my toes, peered out to see Vegesela came back to life and breathe in the air of the world outside.

First the sweepers and dung carts moved through the grayish shadows, then fish mongers from the north set up their stalls and bickered over positions with fruit and spice merchants. For these people, it was to be a day like any other. For me, it was to signal the beginning of a life spent marked like a field animal, like the mere object I was, for the rest of my days.

Even if the Commander protested the damage to his property, he was bound to arrive too late.

There would be no food that morning. Marculus was beyond caring and they'd be moving him soon, maybe to another town for another public humiliation by order of 'the unifiers,' maybe straight to that place in Petra Nova.

If they were waging a campaign of terror, I felt that terror now. I felt the unmarred skin of my forehead with my fingers and imagined the irons searing into my flesh, letter by letter. I knew the disgusted looks tossed at a *fugitivus* slave. I myself had glanced away in horror at those crude deep scars. A freedman with a face like that?

I heard the crowd milling around outside. The market was getting underway again. Soon enough, I heard the guards tramping down the stone steps for me, maybe two of them. They expected a struggle, even from a man faint with hunger and fear.

The grate swung open. A guard glanced inside to make sure he could see me well clear of the door. I heard the door unbolted and then a hooded man stumbled through, feeling his way. His robes were dusty from the road. I watched him pat his way along the walls until his sight adjusted.

In my misery, I turned away. I had no time or mercy to waste on Circumcellion scum, whatever his fate. But when I saw the stranger was going to disturb Marculus, I scrambled over and pulled him back by his shoulders.

He jumped in shock.

'Leave the old man alone.'

'I'm here to offer the Sacrament of Penance to one who is sentenced,' he said.

He lifted his hood and looked up at me. Even in the dim light of the window, I recognized him. He was the short bald priest from Lambaesis.

'I know you! Don't you remember me?'

'Who are you?' He recoiled from the sight of a nearly-naked man bruised and covered in dirt. Had there been any light to speak of, he would have also seen Leo's lash marks on my back.

'Don't you remember, Priest? The massacre at the basilica the day of the wedding in Lambaesis?'

'You're one of those vermin!' He spit on the floor at my feet. 'You should all be tied up and drowned for the hell you've brought our country—'

'No, no, I'm not a Circumcellion!'

'Then why do you remind me of that awful day? I've been brought here by fraud!' He made to yell for the guard, but I slapped my hand across his mouth and held him with all my strength.

'Listen to me! You and I were fighting together at the altar. The big priest was run through, then you were alone, the last one to defend the reliquary and those things in the—'

'The *sacrarium*,' he mumbled through my fingers, 'I wouldn't let you rats get those!'

'Not me, Father! You fended off those thugs by swinging the incense burner at them until I could get at them. Listen to me!' In my desperation, I wrapped my hands around his throat.

His eyes darted in fear. 'Has God delivered me to be strangled by your insane delusion?' he croaked.

He tried to call out for the guards again but I choked off his cry. How could I convince him now? What had he seen that day but a sturdy Roman escort in ceremonial get-up, the bodyguard of a high-ranking commander on display? My face had been clean and shaved, my cheeks covered in polished metal, and the details of my hair and body eclipsed by the anonymous blaze of empire.

How could he possibly know me like this? I had to think, even as I wrestled with him.

'Do you remember a little girl, Priest? A little girl who died? Answer me quietly or I'll strangle you. I have nothing to lose.' I gave him a chance to reply.

'There were so . . . so many children that day. So many stabbed and trampled. You vicious, murdering—'

'She had a little rabbit. On a string . . . no . . . it was a red ribbon.'

The priest was small but determination gave him strength, whereas I was hungry and worn down. I was losing my grip on him. I wrenched him tighter with all the force I could muster.

'You remember that child?'

'*You* killed her?'

'I tried to save her.'

'You're lying.'

'She died in my arms.'

'She died in the arms of a Roman soldier.'

'Look at me! I *am* that soldier.'

'Murdering scum. You saw us.'

'Her name was Thalia.'

'You lying fool!' He jerked his knee up, aiming for my groin. His robe was too thick and his leg too short to land a blow, but I had used my last ounce of strength. I knew I'd lost.

I dropped him onto the foul floor of the cell. He fell back, panting for breath and then laughed at me as he wiped the spit off his chin with his long sleeve.

'Stay away from me, Martyr.' Keeping his eyes locked on mine, he inched backwards toward the bolted door.

I relived it again—the broken *amphorae*, the wailing wedding guests, the fallen Circumcellions and their trampled victims—'No, wait, Priest! The little girl's name was *Tasia*! You said, "Give little Tasia to me." Could a killer on a rampage have overheard your exact words?'

His eyes widened and he leaned toward me. I brushed back my hair and tried to show him my features by the thin light of the window.

'Blessed Savior.' He made the Sign of the Cross. 'You saved my life at the altar that day.'

'Yes!' I crawled over to him in the filth. 'And now save mine and thousands of others. When they open that door, let me walk through it disguised in your vestments. I carry a message to the Romans' military camp, a warning of an ambush on their envoys. That ambush could pitch this whole region into civil war. This time it won't be dozens of children cut down. It'll be thousands, village after village, if I can't warn the garrison to position themselves around Bagae in time and prevent the attack.'

'Bagae? I don't understand. They're going to brand you within the hour.'

'Help me escape.'

'You're the soldier who was carrying Tasia to the Romans' doctor?' He peered at my face in the darkness.

'I'm Marcus, aide to Commander Gregorius—and a *voluntarius*, yes, a slave. But not a runaway. I need to get back to my garrison in time.'

'But they'll brand me in your place!'

'Don't be a fool. In the broad sunlight out in the forum, they'll know you immediately for the terrified little cleric you are.'

'No, they don't know me!' He was shaking. 'Vegesela is far from our parish near Lambaesis. There was no imperial priest nearby. All the priests around here are of the Donatist sympathy. That's why it took me so long to answer the summons.'

'Don't worry. You look like a well-fed priest—pale and learned—even without your robes. Now hurry!'

'Yes, all right. Here, here.' he said, bundling his way out of his outer robe.

I put it on. It was far too short for me, but it was my only hope. 'Give me your crucifix,' and I dropped its sturdy black cord around my neck.

I yanked the trembling cleric into the deepest shadows of the cell and pulled him down on his knees next to me. His skin was as white as a dove's. I was afraid they would see the difference between the runaway suntanned slave and this pasty substitute in an instant. I rubbed his back with dirt as he squirmed. We bowed our heads in the darkness, far from the window's gleam, as the guards returned.

'That's enough!' the guard yelled to us. I pulled my head deeper into the folds of his robe. The fabric reeked of incense and mutton stew. Covering my bent knees with folded sleeves, I held my breath and felt my heart thumping when the door swung open. I made a deep bow under my hood and scuttled on my doubled-up legs in a rush past the surly guard and hurried up the stairs while he bolted the door again. The jail's main entrance giving on to the busy street wasn't far from the stairs to the cell. So with a polite nod and the Sign of the Cross in blessing to the other jailor guarding the exit, I stepped into the sun and scurried off.

I knew the forum well from hours of staring at passing traffic through the grate for a bit of air and light. I passed the urine vat in front of the laundry and slipped immediately behind a man selling strips of lamb on twigs off a kettle-grill.

I'd left the bald priest shivering in his under-garment in the deepest recess of the cell. I was sure when Marculus awoke, the two clerics would have more than schismatic differences to debate.

☙☙☙

I had only minutes to escape. The marketplace was jammed with hundreds of people, many of them hoping to see me branded. They may have been buying bread or braid, but they all looked sinister to me.

In a way, they were all sadists—peeking from under their pretty caps, pocketing their wooden trestle toys, hanging up their flower bouquets and setting aside their bolts of cloth to stop and enjoy the sight of a man lose his humanity to red-hot irons.

What draws ordinary people to gawp at degradation and agony? Do they need to witness savagery unleashed on others before they can say, 'I'm grateful for this day, this life, this light. I'm so thankful that it wasn't me?'

Anonymous under my hood, I straightened to my full height only deep in the crowd. The long robe barely brushed my knees, but no one noticed. I brushed past all these commonplace ghouls with ease. A three-day harvest market day meant disruption, confusion, missed assignations, and careless distractions. It was the best time to hitch a wagon ride, borrow a mule or best, steal a horse and head straight for the garrison.

It didn't take long to spot three horses left untended outside a bathhouse. The stable boy had his back to me. He was collecting his midday snack from a nearby stall. Like any slave, I could detect the signs of restless hunger in a fellow servant's face, but this time, I wasn't serving in a dining room—I was thieving in full daylight.

I earmarked the strongest of the horses, deftly unhitched him and without disturbing the other animals, led him in a casual saunter away from the bathhouse and off into the maze of streets well out of the crowd's sight.

As soon as I found an empty courtyard, I sheltered there with the horse, holding my breath. No cry went up, and with any luck, the stable boy had carried on with his snack somewhere else or stopped to gossip outside the baths.

I felt secure leading the horse through the side streets until I caught sight of a few ripped warrants posted weeks ago calling for my arrest. The irony was that these had been posted merely as a cover story to convince any Circumcellions visiting the town that I was the real thing.

The ruse had backfired on me. I had to escape these streets as fast as possible. I continued leading the horse on a winding route through back alleys, craning my neck around each corner in hope I'd see the exit to the main road. I'd need food and rest on the way, and the only two safe stops en route to the garrison that I knew in this nightmarish landscape were the military offices in Lambaesis and the Longus Farm.

At long last, I reached the paths that paralleled the east-west highway restricted to *Cursus* traffic. I had studied that map in Leo's possession and I reckoned now that Lambaesis was about ninety to one hundred miles to the west of me. I could count on doing the trip in two days, but I couldn't trust my safety or hunger to any of the *mansiones* on the way, of which I estimated there would be at least four.

There would be more road inspectors looking out for Marcus the Runaway Slave.

For the same reason, I couldn't change horses when I reached the busy town of Mascula. Now I was a horse-thief as well as a runaway and had to avoid any place that might be filled with government men.

So I moved on until I reached a large estate and simply left my horse in the stable. I stole another while the stable boy slept undisturbed.

And then I rode hard, thinking of the army scouts I'd known who could cover sixty miles in a day. But they had used well-maintained roads while I followed goat paths, cart tracks, even animal trails, trusting that in Numidia's low brush and barren stretches, there were few destinations in the landscape other than the centers that stood between myself and safety—

the town of Mascula behind me, the famous baths at Aquae Flavianae and the city of Thamugadi.

I watered my horse only in the smallest native hamlets, whatever mere clusters of native houses around a well that I could find. I stayed out of sight of the *Cursus* traffic as best I could, sometimes working my way well clear of all road markings just to remain invisible to those who might be searching for me.

The night was closing in when I spotted a small landholder's orchard, and I considered taking a rest. Once it was dark enough, I crept onto his property and stole fistfuls of overripe olives off the ground below the trees. I was so hungry I swallowed more than one pit in my haste and just let the oil drip off my chin stubble onto the priest's robe.

'Get up,' someone said behind me. I felt a hard rod prodded into my back. It was the end of a mule whip.

I'd been so engrossed in filling my stomach, I hadn't heard the farmer sneaking up behind me. My horse, grazing a couple of dozen feet away hadn't noticed, either.

'What do you want here, Priest?'

'I'm hungry.'

'What's wrong with your parish that they can't feed you?'

'I got lost.'

'You're pretty far from Thamugadi, aren't you?'

'Yes, I've got to get back before dawn.'

He looked at the crucifix hanging around my neck, a silver-wrought piece that a state cleric could afford. 'Mind how you go. That way is full of Donatists.' He pointed in the direction I'd just covered.

I rose to my feet and thanked him, nodding and bowing with hands extending my blessing. I was nearly back on my horse when he called out, 'Hold on, there!'

I waited, one hand on the reins, reading to mount the horse and hear the rest of the man's opinions from the safety of my saddle. But he got to me first and clutched my shoulder with a powerful grip.

'Who are you?' His voice had lost all sympathy for a hungry priest.

'I'm just a priest, from west of here.'

'No, you're not.'

I waited. If he didn't have more than suspicion to throw at me, I was on my way. I made to hoist myself up, but he yanked me back down.

'I want to know what a thief is doing on my land.'

He pulled out a rusty *pugio* from inside his wine-stained tunic. I carried no weapons and in any event, as a priest I wasn't supposed to put up a fight. The speed with which he produced a weapon told me I might be dealing with a Roman colonist. But he didn't look like a prosperous descendant of the old legions in their rich villas around Lambaesis or Theveste.

This man was down on his luck, by the looks of his isolated farm with its unmarked brush yard behind the ragtag rows of struggling olives.

'So who am I?' I challenged him.

'I'm turning you in.' He grabbed me back from the horse and wrenched me around. He'd come prepared with a rope. He was working it loose now to tie me up to one of the olive trees I'd thought so welcoming only an hour before.

'Wait.'

'I'm listening.'

'You're right. I'm not a priest.'

'You stole those robes. They barely cover your knees and your shoulders are about to bust the seams open.'

'I'm a *volo* from the new auxiliary attached to the Legio IIIA. I'm just trying to get back to the garrison.'

'That's no military harness on your horse.'

'I got separated from my unit. I . . . borrowed the horse.'

'Like you borrowed my olives.' He wrenched my arm so tight behind my back, I thought he meant to break it. I would stay well put until he'd got help. 'Why would a *volo* travel in disguise on a rough side road like this?'

'You want money?' I struggled to get free of him.

'Who doesn't?'

'I can pay you.'

He patted me down with one free hand and found no coins. Leo's pouch was back in the hands of the Vegesela jailors. He laughed at me with contempt.

'The money isn't not on me. I'll make a deal. I'm a runaway slave. They tried to brand me back in Vegesela. There's a price on my head. So let me head west and give me a day's start. Then report my whereabouts to the authorities in Vegesela and collect for the information.'

'I could take you in right now and get the reward in full.'

'You won't.'

'Why not?'

'Because you're a freedman and you'll do this much for another slave.'

He threw me off in defeated disgust.

I'd guessed right. Nobody else would have to start from scratch in this rough patch of terrain, nobody else but a manumitted slave avoiding his obligations to a patron abandoned and far away.

When I reached the town of Aquae Flavianae, I took a risk and asked for directions. I was within just one more day's hard riding of Thamugadi and then Leo's estates. My second horse and I spent the early hours of that dawn resting in harvested fields, sheltering from the rising winds between sheaves of stacked wheat.

The air was growing chillier these days. The thick, sweet, grassy smoke of an ox-dung fire not too far away warmed my nostrils. I was starving. Trailing my way along the irrigation canals, I followed the scent and came upon some harvesters by the road. I traded my priest's leather belt and a bogus blessing for a hearty breakfast of olives gathered from the ground and the wing of a bird they'd trapped and roasted.

I started to believe I was going to make it. I was known at Leo's and even with Leo gone, there was a chance of finding shelter at the Longus Farm. Moreover, it was one step closer to getting word to the Commander.

Many precious days had slipped past me since Leo's death. I had to make sure the twins were all right. If Nico had passed my message to Leo, then perhaps I could also rely on Nico to see me safely through to the army. I needed protection until I got back to the Commander.

It wasn't easy to get to Leo's farm. Without his highway pass, I avoided the state road running due west. An unpaved road parallel to the highway was good enough for my horse.

At last I saw the silhouette of his villa in the distance. The sun was setting directly behind it, framing its elegant two stories and the two wings extending around the back garden. I knew the study overlooked this approach. If only Leo had been there to watch me cross the fields this time.

His study windows were dark but the women's wing was blazing with orange lantern light, so the twins and their servants were home. Before I announced myself to anyone, I was determined to get one important thing over with.

I slipped through the kitchen gardens, past the long empty tables where only weeks ago the harvesters had eaten their meager meals. The tables stood stacked in a corner. The teams had moved on. The house felt abandoned and only the occasional sound of women's chat from an open window cautioned me to be as quiet as possible.

I stole into the peristyle garden that Leo had decorated with his busts of famous men and that *lararium* housing the domestic gods he had trusted to watch over his motherless girls and their attendants. Both parents now lay dead. The *Lares* had failed him. What had Leo done to bring down such tragedy on his descendants?

Unseen, I tiptoed through the shadows along the walkway lined with carefully tended flowers and bushes. In the center of the garden, the marble fountain trickled its desolate melody. It was eerie to dodge from one column to the next. I was no burglar, though I felt like one. All I wanted back was the only thing I owned in the whole world.

I reached the unlocked study door, put my ear to the crack, heard nothing and lifted the latch. I slipped into the silent book-lined room and felt the loss of Leontus Longus Flavius all over again.

Here no doubt was where Nico had delivered to Leo the news of the conspiracy, the strongbox, and our destination at

Bagae. It must have been a sudden interruption. I read the signs that the trader had left the room in a hurry. Accounts and receipts were still scattered across his desk. In the window alcove, a half-finished goblet of watered wine stood forgotten next to a book still opened to Martial's playful, obscene epigrams.

I found a leather-upholstered stool and carried it over to the bookshelves. I got up and ran my hands along the dusty wood where stone-eyed Virgil waited. Yes, there was the rolled-up map of Numidia's religious schisms and there was my amulet from Senator Manlius, pushed to the back and invisible to any casual visitor.

I tossed aside the priest's heavy crucifix and threw the beloved cord around my neck with the absolute relief of the most superstitious pagan child.

I'd be all right from now on.

'Is someone there?' A servant whispered, afraid and hesitant, from the doorway.

I jumped off the stool and backed deeper into the corner shadows. She held out a small oil lantern to guide her steps into the room. She laid the lantern on a side table. With only that tiny flame lighting her features, she looked softer and more vulnerable than ever before.

I stepped out of the shadows and whispered her name.

'Am I dreaming?' Kahina whispered back as she saw me standing there.

I crossed the room and held her in my arms. 'Are you all right?'

'Oh, Marcus,' she sighed. 'No one harmed me. People were kind. I'm safe here for the moment, but the journey was hard. I'm still weak and unwell.' I held her even tighter.

'Leo's dead, Kahina.'

'We heard. Nico said you'd come back but, Marcus—'

'The twins?'

'Mastanabal hasn't got better yet, so the deputy foreman is in charge. He summoned the master's sister from Apulia for the girls. Until she arrives, their nurse and I must do our best for them. Marcus—' Kahina tried to loosen my embrace to take my face in her hands, but I shushed her and held her tight in the dark.

I whispered, 'Has anyone else come here? An old man, a white-haired friend of Leo's?'

'No, only Nico and Mastanabal are left and what good is Nico? Marcus, you have to leave now. Nico warned me—'

'Where's Nico? I don't care how angry he is with me. He's got to come with me to the garrison right away.' I let her go gently. She was right. I had to keep moving. Nico must be somewhere in the back kitchens.

'No, Marcus! No!' Her small hand held me back with the grip of a tigress.

'Let me get Nico first.'

'NO!

'What's wrong? Kahina, what is it?'

'What's wrong is *you*,' said a surly voice from the garden.

Nico came out of the shadows on the veranda from behind a column supporting Trajan's bust. He stood on his good leg with his bad foot fighting for purchase on a step below. His tunic was stained with food, wine and worse. He was too drunk to find his balance. He grabbed one of the columns to steady himself.

'How's your face now, *fugitivus*?' he sneered.

Kahina cried, 'I tried to warn you, Marcus! It was *Nico* who claimed all the credit for informing Leo of the Circumcellion conspiracy. He also told the authorities that you were on the run somewhere near Nif en-Nsr. Now he'll only turn you in again.'

'I heard they caught you, slave boy. Shine that lantern on his pretty face, Kahina.'

'You can't stop me, Nico. I'll reach the garrison. You can back me up or not.'

Kahina held her small lamp up to my unmarked face, 'Oh!' She swooned a little with relief.

Nico pulled out a kitchen knife. 'I see it's up to me to finish their job.' He went straight for my face. I was unarmed, but I saw the blade coming. Pushing Kahina back into the study, I swung around and darted down the steps. He stumbled after me and lunged again. I dodged, but he knew the garden better than

I did and was backing me into the base of the trickling fountain. Luckily I didn't trip over into the fishpond, but felt the hard angle of the marble against the back of one heel. I darted over into a clear patch of moonlight and drew him into the light.

His knife glinted silver and swished again past my stomach. I made a dash at him after his blade missed me by inches and I kicked out my foot to catch him under his good leg. He spilled forward and I kicked him once or twice, really hard, more to sober him up than injure him. He groaned.

'Get me a rope, quick,' I ordered her. We tied him to Trajan's column. He was still slouching there groaning half an hour later when I rode south in a clean set of clothes on a fresh horse.

I was going to claim my freedom.

Chapter 17, Sounding the Alarm

—THE GARRISON OUTSIDE LAMBAESIS—

If this was my homecoming with everything at stake, there certainly was no fanfare of welcome, only outraged sputters that I didn't stop at the palisades to show our guards a pass.

All they saw coming at the outer perimeter was an impetuous farmer on horseback storming security, hell-bent for the garrison's parade ground. I was lucky not to get an arrow in my back within ten feet of the first checkpoint. What saved me was my hail to Lieutenant Barbatio as soon as I got within earshot. By the time Barbatio had figured it out, I'd already thundered down the outlying rows of tents.

I was halfway toward Gregorius, off my mount and dashing up the main lane between the tents when I saw Albanus. His trousers and sleeves were as neat as ever. He'd attached a scrap of animal fur to his helmet for style, but he still looked like a metropolitan society boy.

He grabbed my tunic and nearly yanked me off clean my feet.

'You're back, slave! Where the hell do you think you're going?'

'Reporting to my master.'

'Not a good idea. Talk to the tribunes.'

'Let me go.' I jerked myself from his grasp. 'I don't need an appointment.'

He shrugged. 'He'll be angry. Don't blame me if you end up standing guard over at the Simitthus quarry for the rest of your days.'

'What do you mean?'

'The Commander's not himself.'

'Why not?'

'His old friend, that oil trader, caught it somewhere up near Nif en-Nsr. Those suicide thugs beat him to death on the highway. Apparently, it wasn't pretty.'

'The trader was a nice guy.'

Only the Commander would hear of my role in the disaster.

'Well, it hit the boss hard. We hadn't heard from you. We thought you must have been bashed in the head by now. He was about to ride over to check on the man's estate when the mail packet from Carthago brought more bad news from Roma.'

It had to be the old man. Something must have happened to the Senator.

'Seems his wife is dying? That's when he started drinking hard.'

My steps froze. This was a kick in the stomach. The Lady Laetitia was the finest woman I knew, after my own mother. She had coped so long with her palsy and fits that we'd forgotten that someday the illness might kill her. She went to mineral springs and prayed to her Christ. She swallowed herbs and fiddled with her diet. She had good seasons and sudden setbacks, but somehow we'd all fooled ourselves that her new God might be more merciful than all the old ones.

I saw her in my mind, that dear woman, more and more befuddled, mixing up her unguents with her bath scents. I remembered those expensive hair clips tumbling out of her braids because of the uncontrollable trembling. I pictured her, worried sick one minute that one of us would drop a plate from her glossy Campanian tableware during a banquet, and the next minute, tending our fevers and flus without a thought for her own welfare.

How could the Senator carry on now with only the shallow, selfish Clodius at his side?

Albanus read my expression. 'Sorry, that was clumsy. I guess you know her, too.'

'Yes. Thanks for the warning, Deputy. Where is the Commander?'

'He hasn't attended morning meetings for a couple of days.'

'Will he see Ari?'

'No. Just lives on Hamzah's stew.'

I made a face of disgust.

'I agree,' Albanus said. 'If his grief doesn't kill him, Hamzah's cooking will.'

I promised Albanus I'd take things slowly. I warned him that the Commander would want to muster a force after I'd talked to him. Dismayed, Albanus pulled me out of earshot as a perimeter guard unit passed us by.

'Listen, I know as the Deputy Commander in Training, I'm supposed to rally everybody here if the Commander is out of commission,' he whispered, 'but these tribunes all know Barbatio is the most battle-hardened veteran. Unfortunately, our lieutenant is . . .'

I suppressed a smile under my hood. 'Not exactly the brightest flame in Delphi?'

'You didn't say that, slave, and I didn't agree.'

'Sure, sure.'

'So, just get the Commander back on his feet, Marcus.'

I trotted onwards to the Commander's private tent. The first thing I spotted as I slipped inside was my pack carefully roped up and lying on the ground just inside the tent flap, with my back frame and other belongings leaning next to it.

The Commander was lying on his cot. The dead, angry half of his face was turned to the door. The savagery of his disfigurement struck me anew. It was the first time I saw him and thought, 'I'm this man's *son*.'

'Commander, it's me, Marcus, reporting from mission.'

The tent was stifling hot inside. He woke up from his drunken doze and turned the good side over to peer through the dusty sun motes filtered by the seams of his leather walls.

'What? Marcus? Who are you? Some priest playing tricks?'

I drew back the hood of Leo's short travelling cloak and knelt at the side of his cot. I dropped my head in my old salutation.

'Marcus!' He threw his arms around me with a fierce embrace. He reeked of nights of liquor and days without so much as a scrub out of his basin. The Hero of Aquileia was in a bad way, indeed.

I wasn't much more presentable myself. 'I'm reporting on my mission, Commander.'

'Your *mission*? Forget that for now. All I care is that you didn't get yourself killed by those madmen,' he said with a sour laugh.

'Nearly fell off a cliff once or twice.'

'Those bastards attacked Leo,' he said. 'Blinded him, lamed him and then poisoned him.'

'I was with him at the end. He died nobly.'

'Did he?' The Commander sat up, focusing at last.

'I know he was your oldest friend. You would have been proud to see the way he endured his injuries to the last.'

Gregorius ran his hands over his twisted features. 'I'm a little under the weather. But now you're here to help.'

Hooves pounded through the parade ground, cavalry returning from exercises in the desert beyond. At least the lower-ranked officers had held things together as far as they could.

'I've got the goods on the Circumcellions, but you have to act fast, Commander. Father Donatus has summoned all the Circumcellion gangs to prepare an ambush on Paul and Macarius outside a place called Bagae.'

'*Donatus*? No, that can't be. He's a peaceful moderate, a trusted ally who called us in before—'

'He plays the saint, but he's behind the unrest.'

'When is this?'

'They've been massing across the plains for a good week. I was with a band of a few hundred. There might be hundreds more gathered by now, even a thousand or more.'

'No, that can't be right. Donatus is that miracle-worker who denounced all the violence. He was the one who begged Taurinus to suppress the rebellion seven years ago.'

'But don't you see, Commander? Governor Taurinus didn't ask himself *why*. Donatus *wanted* the Romans to raze those villages and create more martyrs. I saw the bleached bones that Donatus dug up from burial on Roman orders. The Romans played right into his hands.'

'That's an unbelievably cynical—'

'And Donatus will be the first to condemn the ambush on Paul and Macarius and beg the army to crush the uprising. I *saw* him supplying the fanatics with coins of gold, cast from chalices and reliquaries stolen in church raids. I *saw* him sneaking into their camp. I *heard* his instructions repeated to their leaders. I *know* he is the one laying the trap.'

'*Donatus?*' Gregorius rose on stiff legs and poured a jug of water over his head into the standing basin.

'That saintly face of tolerance and compromise is all sham. He doesn't want *peace*—he wants to reclaim *Carthago*. He wants an imperial cleansing of the *entire* province that will backfire on us. He wants the throne to be so discredited by our heavy-handed brutality that the whole of Numidia goes over to the Church of the Martyrs in revulsion. And he's more than halfway there.'

Gregorius listened and took it in. 'Yes, knowing Constans' temper and immaturity, that's exactly what he would order to save his imperial baby face.'

'Roma will starve if he gets away with it.'

'It's the clever plan of a desperate old man.'

'He's grown powerful on the smell of martyrs' blood, Commander.' The memory of reading Horatius came to me. 'He laps it up for strength like that mythical bird, the *strix*. If we get to Bagae in time, Commander, we can take them out just like . . . just like Ari removes an arrow's barb—surgically.'

'Get the officers to the meeting tent. We'll muster the men we have and send signals to the centurions in Lambaesis for the regulars to meet on the official route outside the town gates.'

'Yes, Commander!'

We got our entire force on the road before dawn the next morning. That was a full complement of six hundred men marching and riding toward the mustered contingent of another five hundred waiting for us outside Lambaesis.

I was very proud of the Commander that day. Shaven and sobered up, in fresh uniform tunic and polished armor, he rode proudly under the eagle standard. His throat wound had healed well during my absence. His nose and cheek guards masked the worst of his scars. His one shining eye checked our lines.

There had been no time to talk family business back at the camp. To wait for him to raise it was deeply ingrained in me. It wasn't my place to mention the Lady Laetitia, my mother, or even the Commander's promise to liberate me. In the urgency of the moment, I was only a slave and bodyguard again. The proof of my success on the Circumcellion mission would be waiting for us in Bagae.

I would have to learn patience, which I tried to convince myself was the virtuous application of my stubbornness. And in a way, I privately savored my new secret status as son. I also prayed for Laetitia as we rode forward that morning and thought of the Commander's grief. While lying scraped clean, shaved and back in my bedroll, I'd decided that some things were too important to be rushed or bungled. And today wasn't the time to reorder my whole existence, but to prove myself worthy as a soldier.

Nevertheless, doubt crept in as we rode north. Who was I kidding? Was it really tact or patience that silenced me? The truth was that I feared Leo had been wrong. Perhaps the Commander wasn't protecting his wife's feelings and intentionally hurting my mother with neglect.

Perhaps he'd never known I was his son.

Perhaps I *wasn't* his son after all.

I even imagined something worse. Suppose that when I confronted him, he denied my blood link and punished me for audacity by exiling me to work the fields on one of the distant Manlius farms.

Wasn't I better off as his beloved bodyguard slave than his cast-off bastard? The doubts grew as my horse settled into the rhythm of the army's practiced 'fast pace.' I'd loved the Commander all my life, and I knew he was reluctant to see me leave his side. I'd witnessed his hesitation as Leo forced him into sending me into the Circumcellions' camp. Perhaps just delivering my information to make good on my manumission was enough business for the moment. I resolved to raise that subject again only when we spotted the enemy at Bagae.

Two and a half hours of following the smooth-paved road took us up into the foothills and to Lambaesis. The regulars of the LIIIA waited for us with their rows of oval shields sporting bright yellow bosses on a red-rust background stood. Their ranks assembled along the outer town wall made a breathtaking river of color against the sandy brown landscape around us.

It was now another three and a half hours' march at regular pace to the former garrison town of Thamugadi. We merged into formation and set off again, teaching the regulars a favorite marching song from the Belgica front:

Mist on rocks and darkness 'round
My girl just left me on the ground,
I lost her love playing' dice one day,
I miss that girl and I want more pay!

⚐⚐⚐

We hadn't done a forced march in months. No three-times-a-week exercises could take the place of a full day's travel under pressure. Just before dusk the lead horsemen spied the monumental arch Trajan built at Thamugadi two hundred and fifty years ago. We pushed our pace up to a trot, ignoring the city boys' fatigue.

The distant Aurès mountains glistened blue under the final rays of the sun. We gazed at the neat town settled by the emperor's Parthian pensioners so long ago. Once Thamugadi—not Lambaesis—had marked the Empire's southern defense from Berber attacks.

The men fell to digging the usual palisade and pitching our camp while the officers met in the Commander's tent with a delegation from Thamugadi. I was busy setting up with all the others when Hamzah came to say I should stand by to give my briefing.

A worried Albanus fetched me after a full hour of waiting at attention under the glow of a single torch. I was feeling wrung out by the day's long ride and rather cross about the wait on my feet. Too soon, I was forgetting that I was a slave used to nothing better and still might stay one for the rest of my life.

'What's been keeping them?' I almost hoped someone inside the tent overheard me.

'We've blundered,' the deputy whispered through clenched teeth. 'Turns out Thamugadi is one hundred percent Donatist. There are priests in there saying that nobody's going to attack Paul and Macarius. They haven't heard anything about Bagae. They resent being slandered. They're the true Christians who stood up to compromise and persecution during the Diocletian—'

'They're calling me a liar?'

'Slaves are called worse things, but I'm warning you, they've got the Commander on the back foot. Good luck.'

I entered the tent and nodded with respect to the group assembled on stools around the Commander's council table. The three Thamugadi priests stood out among the nondescript town councilors and our wary officers. They wore black robes and heavy silver crucifixes on their chest. Their black eyes pierced through me for the Numidian toady they believed me to be.

These were none other than the descendants of the Emperor Trajan's Parthian captives. Although they were 'Romans,' I saw an enmity even fiercer than any bitterness burning in olive harvesters' hearts. I'd overstepped my place in their world. I'd impugned not only their control of The Church of the Martyrs, but the very righteousness of their Eastern souls.

'Recount your information in full, slave,' the Commander ordered.

'Three weeks ago I joined the camp of Circumcellions under the command of an ex-priest educated in Carthago, one Juva, a so-called Captain of the Saints.'

I saw not one flicker of sympathetic reception.

'I witnessed many cruelties and depredations, even coerced martyrdoms. I overheard one of Juva's spies reporting the execution of two Donatist clerics in Carthago and heard them plotting an ambush on the Roman emissaries Paul and Macarius. Later I saw Father Donatus himself making a secret visit to this Juva while we were camped at the lake near Octava.'

At my mention of Octava, the three clergymen dropped their heads and slowly made the Sign of the Cross.

'I discovered the transfer of gold coins from Father Donatus, probably melted-down Church treasures, to the very gangs that he so vehemently denies supporting.'

'This slave slanders a holy man. What's his proof?' the oldest priest muttered to his civil escorts.

'Do you have any proof, Marcus?' asked the Commander.

'Only my eyes and ears, Commander.'

'Dismiss this scum. Let's go home!' one priest exploded.

'No,' the Commander replied. 'We'll send three scouts ahead to Bagae to verify his report. I'm authorizing them to negotiate with the Circumcellions, if there are any. If this rabble agrees to disperse in peace, we will guarantee them safe passage.'

The Thamugadi delegation glanced around to weigh their consent.

'I'll go, Commander.'

'Thank you, Marcus. Barbatio, borrow us two good sensible men and bring them here.'

I didn't know whether to laugh or weep when that lug Barbatio returned ten minutes later with our *mercatores*, still carrying surveying tools in hand from measuring out the dimensions of our camp. They looked understandably bewildered.

'Remind me of your names, men?'

'Linus, Commander.'

'Lepidus, Commander.'

217

'Yes, of course. I want you both, along with Marcus here, to rest up, then leave before dawn tomorrow for Bagae. You're going to be doing a different kind of surveying, Linus, so you'd better polish up your weapons and leave the measuring sticks at home. Marcus will explain.'

The meeting broke up. I wished I had the courage to warn the Commander to have the three priests watched all night, just in case they decided to send an alert to Bagae ahead of us but I mustn't second-guess his command.

I lingered in his private tent in case he needed anything, just as in the old days. But he knew me too well and when his good eye fixed on my flushed and troubled expression, he barked, 'Speak up, Marcus! I gave you a fair hearing. If you're right, we'll show those crows in crucifixes something, right?'

'My thoughts, with respect, Commander, are that if I'm right, you'll soon free me.'

He stopped shuffling through reports and with both arms on the tabletop, bent his head in silence. Hamzah interrupted to set up the evening meal, but the Commander brushed the old servant back outside.

A dead silence hung between us, pregnant with unspoken crosscurrents of hope and eagerness meeting refusal and grief. It occurred to me again that since Leo's death, there was no one left to force Gregorius to make good on our bargain—neither the Governor Silvester far away nor the subordinate officers who depended on our Commander for promotion. Only Gregorius himself could decree whether my performance had earned my liberty.

'I haven't told you about some bad news from Roma,' he said, at last.

'Deputy Albanus said the Lady Laetitia is seriously ill.'

'She's dying, Marcus.' He pounded a fist on the table in frustration and got up, pacing the tent like a lion caged underneath the Circus. I could feel his frustration at being trapped in Numidia when his wife was on her deathbed in Roma.

'Lady Laetitia always understood your duties as a servant of the Empire,' I said.

'No matter where I was in the world, she travelled with me in spirit. She was part of me,' he said, still not looking up. 'But she knew you were serving at my side. She said because of your loyalty and care, she never worried.'

I didn't like where this was heading.

'Soon I'll be more alone than ever.' He sat down again and put his head in his hands. I fought off the shock. I knew what he was implying. He wasn't prepared to grant my freedom. He had resented having it imposed on him in the first place, but now it was more than pride or stubbornness at work—it was panic at the idea of losing my reliable assistance at every turn.

I reached for my amulet under my shirt and held it hard for a minute to steady my temper.

'I'll prepare your wash basin.'

He was wrenching my loyalties. He said he was going to be alone, but he gave no thought to Kahina, promised to him by her family in Leo's employ for his comfort during this posting. And I was not supposed to know about that.

He was holding Laetitia's death over me like a blackmailer. He was shackling me to him with guilt and gratitude. Perhaps in the old days, when he was so handsome, godlike and strong, he'd played such tricks on others around him and they'd fallen under his spell. *How heroic he looks, but how much he needs me all the same!*

Now I saw the ugliness in his roundabout appeal and the way he cloaked his selfishness with lies about love. If he was capable of breaking our bargain, he was indeed capable of denying any paternity.

I prepared the hot water and towels for his wash as Hamzah served dinner. I joined the hapless Linus and Lepidus to explain our mission. We were to ride hard until we reached Bagae some thirty-five miles away. We would choose a surveillance spot for the army who trailed us by a day.

I fetched a bedroll to rest up with the two *mercatores*. Linus packed away his calibrating tools and handed over his kit with obvious reluctance to a young *tiro* attached to his corps. 'Take good care of these, you hear?'

Lepidus washed the dust off his spare trousers and hung them up to dry so they'd be fresh for the ride.

'I always heard that real scouts went on mission in plain clothes,' he explained.

'We go in uniform as far as I'm concerned,' I told him.

We dropped off to the sounds of the camp following Albanus' quavering orders under Barbatio's stern supervision. The Commander's reluctance to make good on his promise festered inside me and curdled my trust. He hadn't sided with the Donatist priests of Thamugadi, but he hadn't backed me unequivocally, even after raising me from childhood in the bosom of his household.

Well, he would learn the truth of my mission the hard way at the very moment I unveiled the hand of Donatus behind the Bagae mobs.

I only prayed that moment would come soon.

CHAPTER 18, NEGOTIATIONS

—THE OUTSKIRTS OF BAGAE—

'It's certainly not much of a town,' Linus said, eyeing Bagae's walls and angles from our hiding place. 'The mortar looks solid enough but the gates are hung about half a foot off center, I'd say.'

'With all respect, I'd rather you counted heads than dropped imaginary plumb lines,' I said. 'I'm relieved to see how few wagons are moving through those gates. I reckon not more than a hundred or so have come or gone since the sun came up. When you tell such a small group that a legion is marching their way, they'll probably see reason.'

'I do hope so. Should we wake him up yet?'

'No, give him another half hour.'

Lepidus was dozing through the midday hours, his long torso comfy on a soft bed of wild sage.

'But I'm worried by the number of wagons loaded down with grain sacks,' said Linus. 'That's enough for a small army.' I was counting people moving along the road and didn't pay much attention to sacks. Linus was no combat officer.

Lepidus woke up, brushing away the flies settling on his sweaty face. We had made excellent time, starting an hour before dawn. We finished off the last of our bread and dried apricots. The sun had cleared the eastern Aurès peaks and a nice morning breeze had brushed the plateau but now the breeze had dropped and it was hot.

We led our horses down to the main road with our weapons primed but sheathed and headed toward Bagae's main entrance. We dismounted and tried to melt into the straggling traffic of mules, wagons and people on foot.

We were within about fifty feet of the entrance, when to our astonishment, the heavy gates swung closed. We heard the grinding of wood and iron as town watchmen bolted the reinforced oak doors fast against us.

A few merchants left outside with us pounded on the gates in protest. I glanced at Linus and Lepidus to make sure they knew that presentation was half our game if we intended to negotiate peace. We had decided that Lepidus would be our spokesman as he was our senior man in every sense. I trailed Linus, keeping an eye on our rear for any interference.

A tall hooded figure appeared on the rampart of the Bagae walls just over where we stood and shouted down, 'Romans! Yes, you three! Tell us your business!'

Lepidus, always a measured man, stepped forward exactly two paces, touched his scabbard smartly and shouted up, 'We come in the name of Governor Silvester and the *Magister Utriusque Militae* in Carthago on orders of the *Comes Rei Militaris* of *Numidia Militaris!*'

'That's a fuckin' big mouthful for two orderlies and a shrimp!'

I saw Linus bristle with indignation.

'What's your business at Bagae, Romans?'

Our interrogator's voice seemed familiar.

'We come to negotiate peace on behalf of the Roman emissaries Paul and Macarius who approach Bagae. They bring alms for the poor, not violence.'

'Paul and Macarius are two turds shat out of the Emperor Constans' buggered ass!'

Now I knew who it was. I stepped next to Lepidus and lifted my helmet off to show him my face.

'Hiempsal! We come to prevent bloodshed, yours and those of your followers. Surely not all of you wish to become martyrs today!' I had suspected my blow to his innards hadn't finished him off and now he stood over me, today.

'Who's that down there? Hah! That bastard picker? We have some unfinished business with you, that's for sure. So they've made *you* a Roman soldier? That's the most desperate recruitment move I've heard of yet! Is the army now just a band of olive pit suckers?'

'You'd better let us in, Hiempsal. We've come to deliver a message to your leaders.'

The Circumcellion's expression darkened. He had no authority to refuse Roman messengers and he knew it. Somewhere down inside those walls there were town councilors quivering in their suede booties because disheveled gangs of religious outcasts had invaded their town. For the moment, the bullies gave the orders, but sooner or later, those councilors would have their say about what happened today.

Hiempsal glared down at us. 'As you come in peace, leave your horses and weapons outside.'

'I hope this is over with fast,' Linus said as we handed over swords and mounts. 'Their sewage pipes haven't been repaired in months.'

We harnessed out horses not far from the walls. I put my helmet back on and checked that my short dagger was ready.

The gates slowly opened again. The three of us were allowed through under the stares of dozens of guards. We started walking up the main paved boulevard toward the center of town.

Within seconds, a killing stench hit my nostrils and the realization of our true danger engulfed me. Me, the master observer! Linus' nose and common sense had been quicker than my eyes or sword. No plumber's laziness was responsible for this clogged up sewage. My head count from our place of surveillance must have tallied only the very last stragglers of a gathered army of sullen filth.

Hundreds upon hundreds of Circumcellions were camped within Bagae, eating, sleeping and shitting within these walls. Buzzing and humming with menace, the starving crowd parted like a black cloud of insects to make a path for us, drawing us step by step toward the basilica. We couldn't have moved in any other direction if we'd tried nor turned around in flight, as the hate-fuelled mob closed behind us and nudged at our heels.

We were trapped.

Lepidus proceeded first with lumbering dignity and shoulders erect. We reached Bagae's forum. Where there should have been market stalls and posters advertising bath discounts and acrobatic acts, I saw fresh graffiti reading, 'Death to Paul and Macarius! A pox on Roman churchmen!' A curse on Constans' pagan Mass!'

'I told you there was too much grain,' Linus muttered. 'They're provisioning up for a siege.'

'Thank you. It's too late now.'

'I do know my job, Marcus.'

'People of Bagae!' Lepidus shouted. 'We've come to meet your town council!'

'The council is indisposed,' said a confident baritone from the steps of the basilica above our heads. I looked up. There was Father Donatus himself, his high forehead exposed to the morning sun, and his fingers clasped as in prayer. I saw the garnet stone catch the light. He bowed.

Lepidus couldn't have felt the chill I suffered, watching those piercing eyes staring down at us. He'd only seen me once by moonlight in the deep shadows of a basement cell where my face was covered in dirt, sweat and worse. Did he recognize me in the bright sun? As far as he knew, that dangerous prisoner was now a branded slave, not a member of a military delegation.

I scanned the crowds around the basilica, checking face by face for anyone who might know me. I hoped Hiempsal had stayed behind at the gates. The rest seemed to be strangers. I was about to focus back on Lepidus who was asking for a private audience, when I spotted Bomilcar hanging back in the shadow of a wide pillar.

'The Legio III Augusta has answered a call to protect the Roman envoys from harm,' Lepidus answered. 'They cannot be ambushed unawares now and all your riffraff should disperse in peace. Our forces are marching to Bagae and will encircle the town by tomorrow.

'What you call riffraff is an army of righteous souls,' Donatus retorted.

At first I couldn't make out more than Bomilcar's jutting jaw and powerful shoulders, but he lifted his face up to Donatus at this point and now I saw his features clearly. Then he turned to gaze at us and his eyes locked with mine. I caught his nod of recognition.

His thin lips pressed into a tight smile. He settled a hand on his belt, buckled as ever with that fine chunk of Germanic cloisonné that would have done Governor's Silvester's wardrobe proud. He must be thinking back now, no doubt glad indeed that he had backed out of the attack on Leo's caravan. He would have realized when only Hiempsal failed to return that same day, that the plan to 'martyr' me had gone awry.

Yet he said nothing about me now to Donatus. He sensed the volatility of the crowd and as so often, stayed clear of uncertain situations.

Bomilcar, I said to myself, was a survivor.

'I see no reason to deal with you,' Donatus shouted down at Lepidus but in Punic for the delight of the crowd, forcing me to translate for my companions. 'What has the emperor to do with religion? What has the state to do with the Christ's representatives on earth?'

The restless throngs cheered their patron and pressed in on us in a tightening circle. Anyone could smell the free liquor on their breath and the reek of unwashed armpits and hair. Lice scuttled freely over their brows. Perhaps they were maddened by heat, itching or perhaps they were just hungry and impatient waiting for all that promised grain being sifted and measured somewhere in the belly of the basilica.

'We're offering alms ourselves. *Our* gifts are uncontaminated,' Donatus cried down at us.

He gestured to the interior of the basilica. 'We have grain and money for all who have come to us in humility and need. Our Church of the Martyrs feeds the faithful better than any Roman officials who demand that we whore ourselves before the emperor's image or be tortured for standing by our principles!'

'We welcome their tortures,' a woman in the crowd cried out.

'We should give them a taste of the rack and iron claws they used on Maximianus!' another woman cried. 'Let their blood run as the blood of Father Marculus fertilized the streets of Theveste and Vegesela!'

Rivulets of sweat ran down poor Linus' temples and dripped off the end of his cheek guards. Neither he nor Lepidus could understand the crowd's thick Punic dialect, but they recognized an ugly opponent without any translation.

'Martyr *them!*' the mob cried out.

Donatus hesitated and turned to one of his men inside the basilica. A hooded man emerged carrying a strongbox that the priest unlatched. He lifted the rounded lid to run a stream of his gold *solidi* through his fingers. Then he flung a handful of this treasure into mob, sending them scrambling.

'The Church of Martyrs relieves your poverty,' he cried, lifting his hands to the sky. 'And the Church of the Martyrs has grain for all!' If he hoped to deflect their savagery from us, the old man's device fell short. While dozens scrabbled around on the pavement to grab their share of money, the bloodlust of others was merely inflamed.

'Send the Romans back with a message they won't forget,' yelled one man.

'Wait,' shouted Donatus. 'We have abided too long by our Lord's admonition to refrain from swords and daggers. We are facing a formidable foe, the representatives of Satan himself. Look what I bring you!'

Three more aides emerged from the church, wheeling a small barrow piled high with stolen Roman weaponry, glinting in the sunlight.

'The Romans will die!' the crowd screamed. Whether they meant us or Paul and Macarius wasn't something I was going to wait around to find out.

'Go!' I ordered Lepidus in Latin. 'Now! Now!'

Linus was the first to spot an opening in the confusion and lowering his helmeted head, the little surveyor beetled his way straight through the confused masses. I pulled at Lepidus when

I saw there was an opening, but the honor of his assignment gave the senior surveyor pause. It was a fatal hesitation. I reared back as I saw him sucked out of my grasp into a swirling vortex of dust-covered hemp, clawing, pounding hands and screaming women.

I pushed back against the mob and forced an opening between two children in the crush. I spotted Linus escaping down a side alley and ran after him as fast as I could. Ahead of us, two mobsters rounded the corner. We pulled our daggers and to my shock, these weren't two Circumcellions sworn to the use of a club, but well-armed idlers out for a bit of brutal fun on the side.

We squared off and I got one with a stab to the stomach, while Linus held off the taller one with an agility learned, no doubt, climbing unfinished construction sites. Unfortunately, he took a bad slice to his shoulder before we'd convinced the pair of attackers that our skill would outscore their street smarts.

'Are you all right, *Metator*?' I pulled him to my side and slung him half across my shoulders. We searched for a roundabout route to an exit. Luckily, Linus knew by heart any Roman camp layout, the foundation plan for every decent-sized town in Numidia. 'Right, right again, left, now straight, keep straight, now right,' he panted, mapping out our zigzagging escape to safety.

Our twists and turns made no sense to me, but he had to be right. The sounds of rioting were receding. I kept glancing back in the hope Lepidus would make it out of the town and catch up with us somehow, but we had to keep moving.

'There,' Linus stopped, panting hard. 'We can get out there.'

We had run smack into a dead end. I looked in all directions with frantic bewilderment. Linus pointed down at the city wall.

I saw only an irrigation grate in the wall below my knees. I dropped down next to Linus and together we pulled at the welded iron. Half a dozen good tugs and sure enough, the bolts holding the grate to the wall came loose.

'How could you guess?'

'These grates are never fastened properly,' Linus sighed. 'It's a security problem in every town. Smugglers, tax evaders, petty burglars—it's a headache.'

'Thank the gods you're a surveyor.'

'I do know my job, Marcus. Go on, you first.'

'No, you. Careful of your shoulder.' His wound was matting his uniform red with blood.

I wriggled after him through the grate and just in time, grabbed the rim with one hand. Linus was standing to one side, holding out his hand to save me, for I was dangling over a precipice, my feet scrabbling at slimy grass for a foothold to keep from tumbling into the ravine of sewage some twenty feet below.

'Watch it!' he said.

'I tugged at the grass again and again until I got hold of some clean tufts on the other side and pulled myself free of the drop.

We set off, struggling through tall grasses lining the road heading away from Bagae. There was no risking a try at reclaiming our horses from the sentries at the front gate, but stripped of our helmets and dropping our armor, I hoped we could pass for a little man with a bad shoulder aided by his Good Samaritan friend.

Unfortunately someone from Bagae was already chasing us down. I heard the rumble of a horse and cart coming along the road behind us, moving too fast for a normal load.

I dragged Linus down into a ditch and pushed him against a bed of faded red wildflowers. His blood made a nice match.

It was too late. We'd been spotted.

We held our breath hoping the wagon would pass us by. Instead, it braked just on the road above where we crouched. It was a four-wheeled cask wagon hastily hitched to one of our own horses.

Bomilcar held the reins. 'Get in,' he barked. 'Get in fast.'

'You'll have to fight me first,' I said.

'With what, picker? You left your swords back in Bagae.'

'Take me on, first,' I dared him.

228

'I'm not fighting. I'm defecting. I've had enough. I lost my entire family seven years ago in a crackdown like this. If you're not lying, the Roman legion will wipe out that whole town. Donatus will enjoy watching every last man and woman become a martyr. I told you before. I'm no martyr. I'm not stupid.'

I wasn't sure at all if we could trust him. It might be a ruse to get us into his wagon and save him the trouble of chasing the two of us through the grasses.

'I'm not stupid either, Bomilcar. Donatus was about to claim his first three trophies and he's still missing two of them. You've come after us to collect, haven't you?'

'He's missing all three,' Bomilcar said, pointing behind him. I climbed out of the ditch and cast a glance over the back of the cart. Lepidus was curled up inside. He looked bad.

'What's he saying?' Linus called from the ditch.

'He's taking us back to our side,' I said. 'But he'll need directions,' I shouted down to the trembling surveyor.

Linus was swaying from rapid loss of blood. I dragged him back up to the road and managed to get him into the back of the cart. He fought back the urge to vomit as he squeezed down next to Lepidus' battered figure.

'Straight that way,' Linus spit out, pointing Bomilcar away from Bagae.

'We figured that much,' I joked.

'I do know my—' Linus whispered, but his ashen lips fell silent. He had passed out.

CHAPTER 19, *LAUDATE DEUM*

—THE CAMP OUTSIDE BAGAE—

The army had trailed us eastwards, passing on from Thamugadi double-quick. Within five miles or so of Bagae on the main route, we spotted our men pounding down palisades stakes. The mounted *ballistae* had examined a map and chosen their assault positions. The officers were discussing numbers and tactics, waiting for our news.

We cleared the half-finished checkpoint and steered Bomilcar's cart along the row of tents ending with Ari's surgery. With the help of horrified medical orderlies, we delivered Lepidus and Linus to the old Greek doctor's care.

The big surveyor hadn't survived our jostling journey, but we moved his body in anyway, for preparation for burial. Word sped around the surrounding tents that we'd taken casualties on reconnaissance. Soldiers were trotting up from all corners of the camp to verify the bad news. Linus and Lepidus had been two of the most popular men in the camp.

Linus had recovered conscientiousness but his face had drained to the color of putty. He was too faint to dismount from the cart by himself, so we laid him on a stretcher and then shifted him onto a surgical table. Ari was scrambling to boil bandages, needles and clamps for surgery. Assistants laid out the bottles of acetum and henbane.

Around the medical tent, some fifty soldiers of all ranks pressed in to get news. They exchanged ugly glances and their anger was finding its target in the hooded Circumcellion standing right next to me.

'Follow me,' I told Bomilcar. We two forced a passage through the hostile onlookers.

The Commander was waiting for my report in the packed council tent. Within minutes I'd explained to the assembled officers our shock at finding Bagae already crammed with over a thousand insurgents collecting food, money and arms from Father Donatus.

'Insurrection! Nothing less, *if* what you say is true,' the Commander said.

'It is true!' I protested. 'The Circumcellions outnumber us and for once, they match our weapons. Now we know how Donatus has been spending the coin from his melted church treasures. He's been preparing a long time to strike a Roman target that'll rouse the emperor's temper and provoke an all-out civil war. Those two officials are just the high-value targets he wanted.'

'We've alerted Paul and Macarius to divert from their route and meet us here but I need corroboration before I march on one of our own towns.'

'Unfortunately, the other two are in no condition to back me up!'

'We wait for the envoys to arrive,' he said.

'How can you be so sure they'll avoid the ambush, Commander? We have to move now.'

'I don't take orders from a slave!' he shouted.

Albanus' note-taking stopped mid-air and his face turned even whiter than usual.

'I was assigned this mission as a *volo* before witnesses,' I said, fighting to keep my voice even. 'I'm in the service of the Emperor. I've fulfilled my assignment. I've located and identified the regional head of one terrorist cell. I've identified the financial and political source of an imminent insurgency threatening the entire province of Numidia Militaris. Lastly, I've alerted my command to a threatened ambush on imperial representatives.'

'I need corroboration from a *citizen*,' the Commander said. 'I can't send men to their deaths on the basis of a slave's impressions.'

I reeled with disbelief at his insult. Commander Gregorius knew I was no liar. He had raised me in his own home. His own father had educated me.

He also knew the stakes if he acknowledged that I'd more than completed the job.

The truth sunk deep into my bones. I heard his stubborn denial of my success—the very success that was going to rob him not only of his property, but of the company of his own secret bastard.

He was as stubborn as I.

And then I knew from his determined expression, better than from any tale of Leo's, that I *was* indeed this man's son. Hadn't my own mother described me as stubborn as a mule and a good fighter, *like my father*? Now, he and I were angry mules locked in a battle over my freedom.

And when mules are mismanaged, they kick hard. I wasn't giving way.

'I've completed my task, Commander. I've earned my manumission.'

'Fetch that surveyor, Linus!' the Commander shouted to the sentries manning the tent door. 'I want his report!' He looked Bomilcar up and down. 'You have a prisoner, Marcus? Lieutenant Barbatio, hand him over to the First Centurion.'

'He's a defector, Commander. There's no need for Barbatio's manhandling. He's ready to assist us in every way.'

Gregorius shook his head. 'Another thing I'll have to see before I believe.'

The sentry returned and reported, 'Ari wants to see you, Commander.'

The old Greek's surgical apron, stark white only twenty minutes before, was now a gruesome blood-drenched sight.

'I regret to report, Commander, that the *metator* Lepidus is dead. The man Linus is gravely injured. He can't answer your summons. I'm not sure he'll even make it through the night.'

'Can we get any account from him of what they saw in Bagae?'

'No chance, Gregorius. He's not conscious. There is little more I can do for the moment.'

'Well,' the Commander shrugged with a less-than-convincing sigh of regret, 'I suppose we'll have to wait until this Linus recovers his wits.'

'With respect, we can't wait, Commander,' I broke in. 'We can't let the Circumcellions encircle us. They outnumber our force and they understand this terrain better than any man here. They're sure to know our movements. We have to keep the initiative while they're corralled inside Bagae. We must select the moment and keep the high ground for an unequivocal suppression.'

Ari stared at me—the docile, loyal Commander's slave. But he didn't realize what was happening to me. This was no strategic question we were arguing. The Commander was weaseling out of his bargain to free me. After all, Leo was gone. Who had the authority to challenge him? Who would care whether he reneged on his promise to grant me liberty?

No one.

There was only one more hope, the one last witness who stood right next to me.

'Ask *this* man who's behind the rebel gathering, Commander. He's *free*. He's a Roman citizen of the province.' I could hardly contain the contempt and outrage in my voice. 'Ask *Bomilcar* how and where they planned to ambush the envoys. Ask *him* what tricks they're playing on their own people in the hope that the emperor will take his revenge on all of Numidia for the deaths of Paul and Macarius.'

Bomilcar lowered his hood and bowed his bare head in respect.

The Commander looked the Circumcellion up and down. 'I don't speak Punic and I don't trust vagrants and turncoats.'

Ari spoke up. 'I'd give him a hearing, even through a translator. Many lives may depend on it.'

'I didn't ask your opinion, Greek.'

'No, you just expect me to patch up the consequences later.'

Albanus coughed and glanced a warning at the Commander. True to his job, he was transcribing the conversation onto his wax tablet. If there was no one senior enough to challenge the Commander, there was always the matter of imperial record.

'All right, all right. Tell him to speak up.' The Commander took his seat and waited.

So Bomilcar bowed and stunned us all by answering in broken street Latin that landed like hard stones on a slate floor: 'Father Donatus does not forgive the Emperor for his destruction of the Church of the Martyrs in past years, for the lost basilicas, for the massacres of Axido and Fasir and his followers, and for promotion of dirty coward clergy.'

The Commander's good eye burned with fury.

'Father Donatus will become bishop of Carthago. He makes miracles. He gives alms. He controls half of Numidia with talk of sacrifice and martyrdom.' Bomilcar laughed with disdain. 'Now I, Bomilcar, meet the Roman who will lose the other half of Numidia.'

'I am *not* going to lose Numidia,' the commander shouted and without warning, he jumped out of his chair and slapped Bomilcar hard across the face.

'Is this true about an attack on the emperor's two envoys?'

'Yes.' Bomilcar had not flinched.

'As a provocation for civil war?'

'Yes.' The proud Numidian locked eyes with the disfigured Roman. Grasping his jeweled buckle with both hands and throwing back his broad shoulders, Bomilcar dropped all pretenses at submission. Perhaps he'd seen too much of the Commander's temper. If he'd made a fatal error in defecting, he must have realized he now had nothing to lose.

'Is it true that this holy man Donatus has armed hundreds of your kind?'

'More than one thousand, as you slave had told you, and maybe even two,' Bomilcar held up two fingers to get through to the angry officer. 'We lose count.'

'Do you believe me now, Commander?'

'Yes,' Gregorius whispered.

'Then I have fulfilled my mission?'

He nodded and his mangled fingers clenched the reports on the desk in front of him into a crumpled ball.

'Then I am to be freed.'

I didn't ask. I stated my demand. The Manlius blood in me had surfaced, steeled by the admiration I'd felt all those years as a child. It overcame nineteen years of submission, years of standing invisibly pressed against the walls of the Roman townhouse and sleeping on the rough pallet in the back room. My Manlius blood, enriched by the Senator's education and Leo's faith in me, was ascending over Marcus, the Numidian slave.

'There should be documentation,' the Commander muttered, 'Deeds and other matters to attend to, but only once this is over.'

'No!'

It was Ari. We all turned to face the medic, still standing in his blood-smeared clothes. The Commander had forgotten to dismiss him.

'No more delay, Gregorius!'

The Commander looked past Bomilcar at the Greek slave. 'What are you still doing here? Get back to your duties.'

'I'm witnessing a wrong done to this young man.'

'How dare you!'

'How dare I? I, a physician trained in all the drugs of Dioscordes, the anatomies of Soranus and the practices of Galen, yes! I, the most educated man in this camp and I, *a slave*, respectfully remind you of the ceremony of *Manumissio inter Amicos*. There need be no delay!'

'And if I refuse?'

'The honor of your house—'

'Ah! What do you know of that, old man?' Gregorius laughed bitterly. 'All that is left in that house in Roma is another old man as foolish as you.'

'Then I speak now for that old man. I speak for all the old men who watch proud and powerful fools betray their principles and forget the lessons of what it means to be Roman!

Maybe I will never be a citizen, but I know a half-barbarian when I see one!'

The enraged old Greek spat on the ground at the Commander's boots.

He shook his hand still covered with Linus' blood at the Commander. 'I may be only property of the state, but I declare to you, Gregorius, that if you don't free this boy as you gave your word to do, I will not mend, bandage, stitch or save another Roman, even if you flay me alive.'

A low rumble hit our ears as the trembling old doctor finished his speech.

'Barbatio. Find out what that noise is. And bring back the senior centurions,' Gregorius ordered.

Albanus' stylus kept scribbling away at his minutes, '. . . senior centurions.'

'Stop that!' Gregorius exploded and swept the wax tablet from his deputy's hands, sending it sailing into the tent wall.

'You'll need something to serve as a *pileus*,' Ari said, calming his voice down to a normal tone. 'Any hat without a brim will do for the moment.'

I was breathing in shallow gulps. Was my life really about to change? I'd only heard of the *pileus*, the conical cap of the ancient Greeks signaling liberation. It was an essential symbol of release from slavery.

The Commander said nothing and stared beyond us. The rumbling noise was coordinated banging outside the tent, growing louder and louder.

'I think your Pannonian hat will be just the thing,' Ari said. His steady claim to authority held the Commander in its power. 'Albanus, please fetch the Commander's green felt dress cap and some shaving kit from his tent.'

The deputy stared wide-eyed at the Commander. My master didn't budge to stop him. The Greek cocked his head to signal the young officer out the tent door.

Barbatio returned with three agitated centurions in full combat gear.

'Haven't they finished the palisades yet? What in hell is that infernal pounding?' Gregorius stood up and rounded on his lieutenant.

'It's the troops, Commander. They're banging their swords on their shields, demanding you signal the attack on Bagae.'

'I gave no order to muster for an attack!' The Commander shouted.

'I know, but they're already in formation, Commander. They're enraged about what happened to the two surveyors. They insist on taking their revenge.'

We listened to the insistent pounding of more and more soldiers using their weapons against their rust-red shields bossed with a gold center as war drums.

Albanus rushed back with the Commander's shaving tackle. Hamzah was right on his heels with the Pannonian felt hat in his gnarled hands.

Barbatio and his three officers stood at attention, waiting for the Commander's orders to march out of our makeshift camp. The pounding was less spontaneous now, ever louder and more regular as the troops found their strength in a single thundering voice of wood and iron.

The Commander stood up and glared at Hamzah with his one blazing eye. His scars flared red and white with temper. The bewildered servant shook his head and thrust the hat into the Commander's good hand as if its soft felt were aflame.

'We now have six witnesses. I don't count, of course. Take off your helmet, Marcus,' Ari said.

I removed my helmet and stood at attention, my eyes focused on the folding chairs at the far end of the meeting table. The pounding behind us was louder now than the pounding of my heart. I could feel the tension rising from Ari, Barbatio, Bomilcar, Albanus and the three centurions—like a wall of grim-faced men pushing me through an invisible barrier into the unknown.

There was no time for a thorough shave but Ari's deft fingers worked back and forth across my scalp with the Commander's razor with as much expertise as he used sewing up a gaping wound. With each wide sweep of the rasping blade, the slave part of my soul was scraped clean away. Bomilcar lifted his jaw and watched with a somber expression as clumps of dark and curly hair fell onto my shoulders.

Albanus just stared, goggle-eyed.

The angry clamor outside the tent grew more furious as the minutes inside the tent passed in concentrated silence.

Ari wiped brushed away my stray hairs with the sleeve of his bloodied tunic and stood back to admire his work.

'Manumission Proclaimed Among Friends is one step away from slavery and one step closer to Roman citizenship for your descendants,' Ari shouted over the rising clamor outside. 'You'll be a freedman, a full human, and no longer the property of any man. Any children by a free woman will be born into citizenship.'

He turned to the Commander and said, 'In lieu of a staff, I'm sure your *spatha* will do.'

Gregorius took a deep breath.

'Are you sure you want this, Marcus?'

'Yes, Commander.'

'From now on, I can't protect you out in the world. If you fight, you ride in the very front lines like any new recruit. You must leave my side and make your own way. Are you sure you want this?'

'Yes, Commander.'

'You have no more access to my council and you have no more right to my favor or attention than the lowest infantryman. Are you really sure?'

'Yes, Commander.'

'I can offer you a modest start in a shop or trade somewhere—'

He choked off. For a moment I feared he was going to defy us all, cut the ceremony short, and evict us from the tent.

Instead, he reached for his sword and laid it on the table. He raised the Pannonian cap and placed it on my head. It fit me perfectly. He picked up his sword and laid the flat of it against my breast, pressing it with his disfigured fingers.

'*Liber esto*.' he intoned. 'Marcus Gregorianus Numidianus *esto*.'

I had a full name. Marcus of Numidia, freedman of Gregorius.

Free. I was free.

The doctor patted me on the back and the others followed suit. No one chortled or chuckled or laughed as one might expect on a normal day. Only Bomilcar embraced me before Lieutenant Barbatio took him outside to advise on Bagae's battle conditions. The centurions filed out.

'Shall I copy this onto a fresh record, Commander?' Albanus asked.

'Yes,' the Commander shouted and turning away, added, 'Now, all of you, get out!' But before we could all file out, a messenger pushed past us into the tent. His flushed face hinted the worst.

Gregorius barked at him, 'What is it?'

'News from Roma, Commander.'

The messenger re-emerged from the tent a minute later, and wiped the sweat pouring off his brow. All around us the soldiers' clamoring shields still beat harder and louder, making it difficult to take in what was happening.

'His wife,' the messenger said. 'They rated the message ultra-urgent.'

So Lady Laetitia was gone now, freed from her pain just as I was freed from mine.

'Give him a moment,' I shouted to Albanus over the deafening sound of the relentless shields.

'The second surveyor has died!' one of the centurions announced. 'The Commander must give the signal to march on Bagae! Either he gives the signal and keeps control or I don't know what will happen.'

The Commander emerged from his tent, his helmet cheek protectors swung down over his face and his weapons in place on a sword-belt strapped tight. He had managed the buckles and straps without me. There was no trace of grief on his face and his scarred lips were twisted into the cruel and confident smile of a Roman ready to fight.

'Road formation!' he barked at the rioting men.

Half an hour later, Felix put horn to lips and signaled our departure. I rode in a column far behind my former master, no longer his bodyguard, but a lowly cavalryman assigned to a secondary mounted cohort. For the first time, I trotted among the troops as an ordinary man under my own name.

But I travelled with a heavy heart, thinking the Commander had always been an admirable master, only to reveal a selfish and fearful heart as my father. He had needed bullying—all but blackmailing—before he would honor his word.

Perhaps it was for the best. Under Roman law, Gregorius remained my *patronus*, as all former owners remained toward their freedman. Ordinarily that meant I would set up as a tradesmen nearby or do some little services still attached to the Manlius estate but already I had decided—I would be different.

From now on, I trusted only myself and no one else to protect a future so hard-won.

We arrived outside Bagae and pitched camp not far from some Roman military ruins, now just roofless pillars and broken arches cutting the skyline and casting a melancholy air to our endeavor. It was one of Hadrian's temporary camps built two centuries before us, designed to last only for the decades it took to explore and expand the border southward.

We repositioned ourselves according to the signals given, in a fixed spread of shields, armor, daggers, darts, catapults, arrows, swords, spears and steady courage. The battering ram was assembled and prepared with confident dispatch.

We were confident. Bagae's walls had been built to protect the townspeople from small Berber raids, not an army of Romans. What's more, unskilled harvesters and bankrupts mixed willy-nilly among hundreds of local townsmen. Women and children in a small town shouldn't be any match for trained Roman soldiers, even Romano-African colonists who preferred unclogging aqueducts to marching at 'fast' pace.

At least, that's how I felt as our horses held steady behind the infantry straightening their darts loaded in slots along the back of their shields. I watched with the pure joy of comradeship as courage flowed from my bosom into every limb.

Then our forces climbed the last stretch and rounded a small hill. I saw Bagae again, its gates firmly bolted. I peered along the walls and spotted rows of black hoods manning the ramparts, towers and walls, the hatred in their posture clearer with every yard we advanced.

We moved closer until we could see their eyes. They sent up a horrible shrieking behind those gates and my courage stumbled just a jot at the force of their horrible chorus. Thousands were screaming '*Laudate Deum*,' but how many of them were unarmed peasants and how many of them waited with bludgeons and blinding lime?

Whoever they were, Bagae butcher or callous Circumcellion, they were telling us that we faced a suicidal horde who wanted very much to die as martyrs and rise to heaven on this day—and that they intended to take us along for the ride.

Chapter 20, A Servants' Entrance

—BAGAE—

On a signal from my centurion, I shifted my horse to the very front line of the cavalry's right flank and squeezed into position between two other junior riders. The Roman imperial army always protected its seasoned soldiers at the rear and the LIIIA was no different. If a first-timer like me panicked, I couldn't turn and run—the toughened cavalrymen had my back and would force my mount relentlessly forward into the thick of battle.

If I survived the front lines today, I'd be blooded and 'made.' If I didn't, the army hadn't lost a valuable, experienced man, merely an ex-slave who had made too much of his first and last day of freedom.

Army life promised many good things, but sentiment wasn't one of them.

I was always nervous at the start of any battle, but before this, my lowly status had kept me from the heart of combat. I'd ridden clear of the fighting, listening for Gregorius' call for a back-up weapon. Or I had relayed orders missed in the heat of battle to signalers and centurions or, as on that nightmarish day north of the Rhodanus, I had rushed the Commander streaming with blood clear of the ambush site, with only minutes to find a medic who could save his remaining eye.

Today I watched the Commander and his senior officers conferring at the center, far to my left. Albanus and Barbatio and the senior officers flanked my father as they conferred and adjusted the cohorts strategically. We had cut off the main road out of Bagae by forming a crescent wrapping itself from one of the front towers to the other with the central infantry just clear of the range of projectiles from the town walls.

Our order of attack was to soften up their defenses with missiles and archers' fire, then ram the gates open and drive our mounted centuries through the streets of Bagae, scattering their fighters and terrifying the town into fatal disorder as we rounded up the leaders.

I heard the familiar signal for the two-wheeled *caroballistae* to be shifted off their transport wagons and rolled forward to within range of the barricades but just short of their archers' reach. We saw the enemy's bows poised along the ramparts above, strings drawn and loaded. They took aim at us as we ignited flaming grenades to launch over their heads.

The wind sweeping the plateau picked up and licked our fires into a light dance. Our drums fell silent as we settled into place, ordered with a crisp '*Ordenem servate*' to hold our positions steady, our horses snorting as professional corrections were barked at us down the lines. Slings and tension belts were primed and cocked. *Optiones* trotted behind our lines, keeping stragglers in position and enforcing the silence essential to discipline and signals.

A welcome breeze cooled my perspiring brow under my simple round helmet. Opposite us, the town stood closed, inscrutable and braced. Then a gust hit our nostrils full on with a stink from within those walls. It was the whiff of panic rising out of the town.

The wail of a frightened child reached our ears. A woman shouted to someone with an ear-piercing screech. I imagined her anxiety multiplied hundreds of times over, spreading from soul to soul. A couple of villagers' mules brayed. Within those walls, thousands of innocent Thamugadi families crouched in terror as their Circumcellion invaders turned their home into a hostile fortress. What was the calculating Donatus saying now to assuage their terror at being trapped by his self-destructive campaign?

We had advanced to Bagae just in time. The Circumcellions were all still trapped inside, not laying in ambush for Paul and Macarius or encircling us with a stealthy stranglehold. Was Sophonisba in there among the huddled crowds? Were Juva, Donatus and the other leaders sorting out the innocent from the death-wishers or just leaving them all to share in their doom?

Now a row of our soldiers moved forward, dropped to their knees in the brush and shouldered their *manuballistae*, loaded and aimed. But before they'd finished adjusting their launchers and bolts, we heard a sharp and agonized scream from their group. They had fatally misjudged either the opponents' skill or their distance. One of their team dropped his wide wooden frame and rolled bleeding onto the ground. We saw a Circumcellion arrow sticking out just below his left shoulder. His blood sprayed the grass around him.

Our attack signal blared out and all our trumpets blasted out as one. The two-man *caroballistae* launched their iron balls at the upper edge of the front walls. Like maddened assistants to Zeus, the *polybolos* experts released their iron bolts with a whipping sound, delivering eleven deadly prong-headed missiles a minute. The fighters manning the city rim hadn't reckoned on our automatics. At least six or seven of them jerked backwards and dropped out of sight at the first volley.

My horse bucked and tugged under me. I felt as taut as a loaded catapult myself, but the animal seemed just as impatient—disciplined but panting with a pent-up urge to get on with the action. I was a beginner in the regular ranks of assault, but I was riding a veteran steed. He neighed and snorted, as if to show he loved the clamor of shield clanking onto shield in the overlapping *testudo* formation like a protective shell, while the danger and death rolled toward us.

I tried to calm him, but he shook his mane, chomped on his bit and jerked his head once or twice at me. We still had to hold, hold, hold, while the soldiers under their protective shell worked forward in coordinated strides across the exposed field. Another *testudo* formation also sheltered our mobile battering ram made of reinforced hardwood covered with hides. They wheeled it inexorably toward the Bagae gates, foot by foot, under a hail of arrows that bounced off their impromptu roof of overlapping rust-red and gold ovals.

Once or twice a man fell under the thud of a heavy chunk of marble or paving stone torn up from Bagae's streets that landed square on his shield. But we watched with pride as the wall of defense closed up any sudden gap and continued forward like a determined tortoise on dozens of legs, immune to all fear or deterrence.

My horse sensed my increasing impatience. He bucked again and this time nearly got his way under my sweaty grip. The man riding next to me grabbed my reins and wrenched him back into alignment. All the disapproval I suffered was a curt nod of his helmet. I nodded back but felt as anxious as my horse to get on with it.

The ram had reached the gates now. We'd lost fewer than half a dozen men to injuries. Armored orderlies braved the onslaught of missiles to clear the wounded from the path of our horses' imminent charge. Their ambulance wagons trundled casualties back to the triage tent.

Meanwhile we waited for the ram to do its ugly job. We watched as the men tightened their roof formation in case of hot oil or fired arrows released from above. We heard the first thud as the ram was swung back and the slammed against the gates. A scream of alarm went up from inside the town. We listened as again, and again and again, the ram's thudding head tried to force the gates, but always without success.

The delay and frustration opened the door to fear. The minutes passed and even an hour as the ram slammed against the Roman-built defenses to no avail. Our horses trampled the field into a cloud of dust as the afternoon sun dipped its orange rim below the Aurès' peaks.

Our light was sinking. Felix and his colleagues signaled retreat. A cheer of relief rose from inside the walls. The battering ram slowly rolled backwards again to well beyond the danger zone. We turned, cohort by cohort, to trot slowly behind our infantrymen along the road to the safety of our camp. There was a palpable frustration coursing through our ranks, soured from hours of anticipation and self-control.

We filed back into our camp to prepare for repositioning at dawn next day.

'There is a way into the town,' I told Albanus, catching him on the trot as we fetched our evening meal.

'Yeah, burn it down.'

'An irrigation canal empties sewage and waste through a sewage grate into a ravine running down the backside of the walls and over a precipice. It's the way Linus smuggled us out of there.'

Albanus turned to me with closer attention.

'I could guide you to it,' I offered.

'Could you find it again, even after dark?' he asked. It was obvious that for his part, Deputy Albanus very much hoped the answer was no. If he died in the Battle of Bagae, he considered himself too highborn for his corpse to be extracted from under a rusty sewage grate.

'I think so.'

'Trust a slave to know the servants' entrance.'

I stiffened. 'I'm a *libertus* now, if you don't mind.'

'All right, all right. I'll tell them.'

I followed right on his heels, but he turned and laid a hand lightly but firmly on my breast.

He repeated, 'I'll inform them, Marcus, *alone*.'

He was right. I had no right to go unsummoned into the council tent. I closed my eyes and took a step back at the irony.

Gregorius had warned me of this. My liberation meant exclusion from my former master's confidences and company. I was no longer his cherished 'spare eyes and hands.' Manumission from slavery meant demotion from all discreet access to the inner workings of the camp's leadership.

Slaves were nobodies—so slaves could be everywhere, like flies or fleas or lizards. We heard and saw everything while we stood by, unseen, unnoticed and unheeded.

Now I was a complete human but the lowliest man in the legion. So this was what it meant to be an ordinary soldier. I removed my outer armor and armor pads, and found a resting place along with all the other cavalrymen and ate my evening rations. I waited for my orders like everyone else.

Half an hour later Albanus found me watching some medical assistants toss dice made of bone. I didn't ask whose bone.

'I'm delivering your orders to try to unbolt the city gates, Marcus. But if there are too many of you, you're bound to get spotted. Four men, tops.'

'That's enough to slide the bolt?'

'Yes. You'll be killed the minute after but that's what heroes do, I guess.' Albanus looked at me with steady pity.

'Not if there's a stealth regiment ready to force the gates and rush them.'

'You're taking the Brit signaler—'

'Felix?'

'—and two senior infantrymen to speed the first unit inside.'

'What about my prisoner, Bomilcar? He knows the town a little.'

Albanus looked at me in disbelief. 'That bastard is in irons and he might just turn on you once he's back with his old mates. Obviously, you're safer with our men. I'll see if we can get the back-up unit in position by the time the moon is level with the Pleiades.'

'Fair enough.'

I got my grub and then rested as the camp settled down to await the next day's assault. There was nervous laughter and soft humming as soldiers polished their weapons with sand. I noticed the usual rattle of dice and the crackle of small fires to ward off the desert chill. One of the auxiliaries played a flute. I looked up at the stars and watched the moon rising toward the Pleiades against a black backdrop of a velvet sky.

Then I remembered Kahina and how her dark eyes had reflected the stars that night I'd held her in my arms and heard her sighs. I recalled the touch of her soft skin. I longed to press her against me one more time.

But so much had changed since the night Leo died. I had changed. I had learned I had Manlius blood running through my veins. The dream of staying a Numidian freedman watering olive trees in a backwater sanctuary belonged to the slave

Marcus dreaming of no more than freedom. To retire to obscurity now seemed disloyal to the ideals and stature of the old Senator, my grandfather.

I clutched his *bulla* on its cord and bid Kahina's memory farewell. Being freed was only the beginning of my life. In my Manlius heart I knew now there were many, many things I would have to do and lands I might have to cross before my destiny was clear to me.

'It's time,' the signaler Felix said, with a nudge of his boot into my hip. I shook off my doze. We located the two other men. One was a bearded Dacian auxiliary. Choosing Mucapor, whom I'd seen devour an entire roasted rabbit in one sitting, was a good start. I didn't know the other man. He was a Thracian Celt named Bitus, with calves that twisted like ropey sinews.

We four set off for Bagae in silence and darkness, keeping our horses on the soft verge of the paved road, making no sound but the occasional clink of a weapon or cough. After less than half an hour, we rounded the last bend and Bagae sat in front of us, its dark silhouette lit from within by hundreds of Circumcellions' fires, the glowing red core of an angry volcano.

We retreated out of sight and tethered our horses. We drew straws. Bitus was the man to stay back and keep our mounts ready for escape.

We three now set off. When we were within about three hundred feet of the town walls, we heard their chanting. They were serenading their unwilling town hostages with a mournful prayer. My stomach churned up its undigested stew. I stopped to vomit in a ditch. The other two watched me almost with envy as I returned to the road with a lighter step.

We trod through expansive wheat fields and rounded the northwestern corner.

The watchtower had been unmanned when Linus and I had slipped under it heading for the main road. Now its lookout platform shone with just enough torchlight to illuminate the ground below. Stealthy watchmen circled its tiny space and peered into the darkness through which we scuttled as flat as crabs toward the next corner of the town due north.

Once we slipped around that, we were in luck. The lookout windows of the back tower were unmanned. They overlooked that steep ravine that helped evacuate the town's sludge and debris. No one could have wheeled a battering ram or a *caroballista* across this choppy terrain so all the rebels' manpower was concentrated on the assembled Romans threatening the southwest gates.

We slid through Bagae's shit and rubbish, clinging to weeds rooted deep in their fertile beds. From this approach in the blackness, we always kept one hand on the chill walls of stone. We pressed our feet into the deep and secure compost.

But exiting by the grate turned out to have been a far easier trick than locating it from the outside, much less getting back in. Thick, hungry undergrowth swished at our waists and obscured our objective. Nobody said a word as we dragged our hands into crevices and over rough boulders waiting for a finger to locate the elusive opening.

Felix whistled low. He'd braced himself somehow next to the treacherous gap and with his left hand grasped the iron fretwork. I leaned over and we two pushed and poked our fingers through to the other side. We felt a large stone, rolled into place to seal up the access. It took us another ten minutes of kicking our toes and running our hands through filth to locate something for leverage before the Dacian Mucapor pulled a broken shovel handle out of its sucking grave of muck. We wedged it through the grate and leaned down hard from both sides.

The stone jerked free at last with a noisy squelch but I nearly lost my footing and tumbled into the ravine below. Only Felix was quick enough to grab my sleeve while I regained my footing.

We forced the grate back out of its rusty frame. Within less than two minutes, we three stood straight at last inside the walls of Bagae but it was some job getting Felix's signal horn through the opening.

I checked the moon. She had moved halfway to the *Pleiades*, the Seven Sisters constellation—eternal and indifferent to our danger while a sliver of a new crescent moon gave only the faintest of light.

The windows in the buildings around us were dark. The ground beneath our boots was littered with shards of discarded oil pots and broken lamps. Without Linus' ingrained knowledge of the town's layout, I was as lost as the next man but I guessed it was a neighborhood of workshops by day.

We focused our eyes on the roofs and courtyard walls to search across the orange and smoky sky for the outlines of the basilica's bell tower. We would use that to orient our way toward the forum at the center and then the southbound road to the gates.

There was no chanting now to pull us in the right direction. Why had they fallen silent? Surely more than a thousand Circumcellion militants hadn't dropped off to sleep only hours before a Roman assault? As eerie as the voices were, this deathly hush was far worse.

We snuck down a dark alley so narrow our hands could reach both brick sides to keep our balance on the broken flagstones. At the end of it, we stumbled into an abandoned yard of market stalls under sagging awnings. Only a few feet away on our right, a thick tapestry rug hung over an open door. The warmth of a stove and voice from within put us on our guard. We pressed ourselves flat against the wall just in time.

A handful of four or five dark-veiled women rushed into the marketplace. Their heavy cloaks lent the impression of one single secretive animal sliding along in the shadows. They were supporting a woman in their midst who was waddling and moaning—a woman in labor. These women were no less determined than ourselves to move undetected. They searched all four sides of the empty bazaar for some prearranged signal.

They must have seen something that eluded us for—always moving as one—they threaded between the stalls and aimed straight for where we stood.

We pulled our cloaks tighter over our polished armor and flattened our back against the columns lining the yard's perimeter.

The lead woman whistled from under her veil like a boy. The rug was drawn back. A hand reached out in welcome and one by one, the arrivals dove behind the tapestry into the building. We crouched and waited, fearful of startling them.

A single head peered out and checked that no one had followed her arrivals.

It was Sophonisba. She was sheltering women from the coming slaughter in this abandoned neighborhood. She glanced up and down the empty marketplace. Mucapor the Dacian drew his short *pugio*, ready to silence her, but I gently pushed his blade back toward its sheath.

We waited for five minutes or so, until there was a brief shifting of the lights within the women's refuge. We heard the pregnant woman moan in pain.

Felix's hand shot up and pointed against the night sky in the direction of the basilica tower peeking out at us from behind some roofs.

Now we slid as fast and low as hooded lizards to the walls of the empty alleyways, each one broader and cleaner than the last, passing the waist-high walls of manicured gardens and the higher walls of a few wealthy villas, then skirting public baths, shuttered bankers' offices and dodging underneath merchants' signs and awnings.

We pulled our hoods closer over our helmets and fastened our heavy cloaks firmly over the shoulders of our armor. The least glint of imperial weaponry meant detection and death. We reached the back of the basilica at last and prepared to separate and meet again at the gate, weapons hidden and drawn to eliminate the sentries. We counted on mere seconds to unbolt the barrier and raise the call for support.

I could only pray that the backup unit was lying close by, hidden well but primed to storm through. Yes, the moon had reached the Pleiades. Taking a deep breath, we slid along the tall cold wall of the basilica. It was unnerving, this silence from so many people camped around its corner.

We rounded the corner and stood, stunned at our next discovery.

The enormous square was empty. Cinders floated over small kindling fires that burned untended. Only a few slumped figures slept under a stall awning. A handful of sentries leaned and chatted, their backs to our approach.

Worst of all, the gates stood wide open as the very last of the Circumcellions slipped in file out of the town, unmindful of our astonished eyes.

'They're staging an ambush, encircling *our camp*,' Mucapor burst out.

'Felix? Felix!'

But Felix had already raised his *cornu* to his lips and blew the alarm signal. He blew and blew as we two dove back into the shadows, ready to dodge the sentries who were bound to hunt us down. Trying to get a carrying wind under his notes, Felix climbed stacking boxes to get up to a low wall and from there, still blowing, pulled himself up with his spare hand to the roof of a bathhouse.

Would our sentries hear his alert?

Shouts went up from the Bagae guards. They had spotted Felix and were after us. Mucapor was already running headlong back the way we'd come, in the direction of the marketplace where Sophonisba was busy midwifing the unfortunate pregnant woman.

I tried to drag Felix off his horn and back to safety, but I couldn't get hold of his heels. I fell back into the alleyway. Like Linus, this Felix knew his job but he was foolhardy to keep blowing like that. He couldn't be sure if the winds would carry his message all the way to our palisades in time for the army to rally against an ambush, but he sounded his instrument steady and clear, waiting for a distant horn to reply.

After seconds that seemed like minutes, we heard a faint horn signal back. Felix blew again. The only thing that could silence him was an arrow.

Unfortunately, within seconds that's exactly what I saw pierce deep into his temple. His horn rattled to the pavement beneath my feet.

I turned and ran for my life.

Chapter 21, The Priest from Hell

—OUTSIDE BAGAE—

Bitus still waited with our horses in the thickets. We tethered Felix's horse to Mucapor's and lurked in the trees to measure the speed and direction of the black column of Circumcellions slipping past the glow of Bagae, right past our hiding place, and onto the dark plains.

'The army should be repositioning up to the high ground north of the camp,' Bitus said.

'It's up to us to tell them. So we stay off the road and out of sight by taking some goat path,' I said.

The moon hung in the sky next to the Pleiades now. Before too long we found a rough but reliable track and galloped for a good twenty minutes. We kept our sights on the furtive evil of Donatus' file of torches, slinking like a black snake toward our troops. For better or worse, our horns had not slowed them down. Could they guess the crafty slyness of our experienced officers laying an ambush for the ambushers or had the failure of our battering ram given them a false sense of confidence?

Bagae sat on a cool plateau above the plains, and the Circumcellions were moving downward toward our installation on the lower land. We three kept our horses on the higher ground as much as we could, reckoning that was where we'd find our forces waiting.

We were right. They were so well disguised we nearly stumbled onto our formation. Only the sight of our helmets shining in the moon's glow saved us from getting a javelin through our breastplates.

Hundreds of LIIIA infantrymen were lying on their shields, invisible in the thick grass. Officers scanned the main road below, trotting past us as we moved up from about fifty feet below. Behind them, disguised by a tall bluff on the hilltop, the cavalry rested behind a brushy thicket.

Down below us, our abandoned campfires burned hard. A handful of decoy sentries stood at attention along the lengths of our palisades.

The fires died down and the sentries rested, heads deceptively lolling over their spears. From behind the serried ranks of our tents, the bell of a single mule left behind tinkled.

True to his breed, the pack animal had sniffed danger. Somewhere below us, Juva and his dark-hooded thugs were ringing our emptied camp in a tightening noose. We couldn't see them yet, but soon they'd be visible. There was a slight crack of gray along the night horizon now. Dawn was less than an hour away.

Our troops didn't make a sound. More than a thousand men lay in wait to kill another thousand.

The sky turned the color of slate except for a rim of pink lining the Aurès peaks. The waiting became almost unbearable as our officers conferred in whispers over how many crucial seconds would offer us both visibility and the advantage of surprise.

I raised my head slightly from the matted brush tickling my chinstrap. I now made out the wide ring of black forms ready to strangle the sleeping camp. If I could detect them, the moment must be close. They were less than a hundred feet from the camp's perimeter now. Any second now, they'd realize the settlement of tents was empty.

Our trumpets and cornets blasted as one. I leapt on my horse and with thirty other riders, moved into position behind our *decurio*.

The infantry adjusted their chinstraps, checked their shields and weapons and shifted into tight formation.

This time we weren't waiting for anyone to knock off an artillery expert—the cornets blew again, the order for us to give voice to the terrifying *barritus*, Roman-style.

I listened to hear what the password of the cry would be.

Raising their shields close to their faces to make the echoing effect all the more frightening, the men launched into a coordinated and chilling murmur.

'Christus victor. Christus victor.'

Victorius Christ. The Commander hadn't lost his insidious sense of irony. He was going to wage a battle of the mind as well as of the sword.

The Circumcellions' hoods jerked up, their eyes jumping from the quiet tents just within their reach to the thousand attackers appearing poised above them. They realized now that they were ambushing a ghost camp and the ghosts were about to descend from above.

Our war cry rose now by practice degrees, ever louder but regular and set to the rhythmic beating of weapons on shields. We didn't scream like the old Germanic barbarians who'd shown Roma the heart-chilling power of the *barritus* centuries ago. No, we were soldiers of the modern Dominate. We prevailed across the civilized world because of our discipline and skill.

The cornets' signal for the bombardment sounded. Within seconds, the *ballistae* launched a flurry of iron bolts that cut into the unlucky Circumcellions skulking closest to our hill. Dozens of perfect boulders fashioned out of hard-cooked clay smashed down on the enemy. Another volley rained down. Robed men screamed as they fell.

With the next volley, I saw one ball take off the top half of a Circumcellion's head, leaving his startled mouth wide open to the morning sun.

Fresh signals halted the launchers. As the dust cleared, we counted dozens of Circumcellions who'd just become 'martyrs.' Hundreds of other screaming fiends were dashing beyond the camp into the plains.

The signal for the infantry's descent blew next. The first ranks stepped forward in a seamless, formidable block facing the prostrated extremists.

I swelled with pride for the regulars of the LIIIA. Perhaps these city boys hadn't fought a civil war against a rival emperor. Perhaps they hadn't faced hardened Alemanni in a snowy primeval forest. Perhaps they'd spent their whole careers mending bridges, irrigation canals and aqueduct pumps while nurturing their grandfathers' tales of combat under Trajan and Hadrian.

Today these same engineers and desk-bound clerks showed what a lifetime of Roman discipline and exercises were worth. At the order, 'Lunge,' the ranks tightened and I saw no gaps and no crowding of the next soldier in the line.

It was a perfect Roman assault executed with terrifying power. Hadrian's soldiers would have been proud of their great-grandsons.

A fourth signal blew. That was ours! We spurred our mounts and went roaring down to the far side of the valley, as the rising sun lifted the night mist off the drying grass. I thundered into position as we regrouped a hundred feet behind the panicked militants. At our centurion's order, *largia ad ambas partes*, we turned to right and left, thinning our back rows while leaving no gap until we stood in a deadly circle cast around the rebels.

This time my horse obeyed me. Our riders stretched the line from east to south to meet our counterparts moving their horses in parallel formation from north to west.

We'd cast a loop around Donatus' noose and were about to tie the knot tight.

The Circumcellion leaders shouted in Punic to their panicked gangs who were flung across the far side of the camp across the plain but our *barritus* drowned out their orders. Circumcellions were running along their outer lines, urging they reconfigure for escape but it was no use. Only our horns could penetrate the deafening thumping.

I scanned the scrambling clusters of robed men darting back and forth. I searched for the tall, bearded man I was determined to capture or kill before sunset.

Wherever Juva was, there was no escape. The soldiers' chorus now reached a concerted roar as the signal to close in rang out.

I was racing toward the enemy now, in the thick of hooves and horse breath, my riding trousers slapping against his pounding flanks and my long *spatha* ready to cut the enemy down. I was flooded with memories of the past few weeks— Leo's broken agony, Kahina's terror above the cliffs of Nif en-Nsr, the blind man begging for his rations and even the bravery of the Donatists' true saint, Bishop Marculus, gripping his stake with faith.

Then I spotted my quarry, but a knot of Circumcellions blocked my progress. I stabbed the man on my right in the shoulder with a clumsy stroke that merely cleared him away as he grabbed for my reins. I yanked my horse to the left and rounded on a second man. Gathering courage, I swung my sword straight for his hooded neck. I felt the blade meet thick cloth and slice through into flesh. His head, half attached, wobbled loose and wide-eyed as he fell.

Now came a third man, crazed and fierce, readying his sword to slice through my calf just where it was exposed behind my leg guard. His weapon grazed metal, but I knew he'd seen where the protection stopped and I had only seconds to bring my sword down with a slice onto the elbow of his fighting arm.

I rode on now, dodging a fellow Roman who was running his sword straight between the shoulder blades of a fleeing Circumcellion with the unfettered glee of a boar-sticking huntsman. I reined in for a moment and looked at the chaos all around me.

I'd lost sight of Juva, but one of his cave advisers was overwhelming one of the Legio IIIA infantryman with the expert swings of his 'Israelite.' I rushed my horse straight for him, relieving my fellow soldier and swinging hard at the Circumcellion, setting him back on his heels for only a moment. He charged away toward other Romans and I pulled on my reins and rammed the rump of my horse flat again his back, sending the man tumbling to the ground.

The horse knew what he was doing and rounded immediately for a repeat assault as the man scrambled to his feet. This time my sword was quicker and I managed a deep stab into the man's upper arm. We rounded again as the sentry recognized me under my headgear.

'Traitor scum!' he snarled. It was Hiempsal. He swung his powerful club into my horse's rear left leg to lame him. The horse faltered under me, but the club had only bruised his gaskin, landing too high to break a bone.

I rounded on the Circumcellion again. I guessed his game. Once he had unseated me, I was lost. I had only one more chance as he swung back to break the horse's cannon below the knee joint.

I rammed my sword straight into his face, leaned down hard, and withdrew it. I kicked him aside without glancing down at the damage.

I rode on, still hunting Juva among the flailing robes, flying weapons and screaming victims. The Circumcellions had outnumbered us, but only a real surprise on an army of sleeping soldiers would have given them the needed advantage. I felled at least three more Circumcellions in my hunt for the defrocked 'Captain of the Saints.' The dry desert brush was churning up soft and red under my horse. The stink of entrails and blood filled our nostrils. Fear made men piss and shit as they fled in robes stained with blood and stumbled over comrades draining their last strength into the ground.

My horse dodged the fallen, some wearing rough Numidian robes and a few in armor. I tried not to give him trouble as he turned and twisted under me. I was determined to find Juva but no one with his features looked up at me in fear or hate as I slashed and trampled along in a fever of combat.

I'd hacked and battled my way hundreds of yards from my original position when something caught my eye. A handful of Circumcellions had realized that the best shelter from death was in the direction of our camp—not the perfect rows of tents, but beyond—in Hadrian's haunting ruins.

They were scurrying like rats into collapsed baths and ferreting themselves between fallen stone partitions that had once supported a row of narrow barracks.

I rode to the back of the crumbling stone walls and directed my horse's tread along the worn paving between broken pedestals and fallen dedication plaques. I tracked the last hooded figure I'd seen running through an open colonnade toward a maze of brick rooms still standing.

I took it slow. My horse's foothold couldn't be sure in the sharp rubble and I sensed that the Circumcellion sentry's blows to his flank still hurt him. I heard a noise behind me just in time to see a Circumcellion start out at me from behind a column, his sword poised to stab my horse behind the saddle.

I rammed the man hard on his shoulder, sinking my blade into muscle. He tumbled onto the broken stones.

'Juva!' he cried out in warning.

I pressed on, the sounds of the fighting receding into a dull hum of pain and conquest at my back. The old red paving stones cracked under the weight of my horse. A silence of decay and past glory enveloped my single-minded search. Now thanks to the fallen man, I could be sure this champion of cowards was hiding from me somewhere near.

With cautious, high steps my horse halted at each doorway, as I examined the dormitory corridor of the former barracks. I peered past each sunlit entrance into the cool shadows of the ruined cells. Perhaps it was a stench familiar to any soldier that drew me forward past the sleeping spaces, but as I passed the final doorway to face the final chamber where I was sure Juva was crouching, all I saw were the three walls of a latrine lined with empty toilet seats of pitted stone.

A deep ravine ran along the toilets, a long slanting ditch that had been filled, then sluiced, and filled, then sluiced with daily discipline to keep the camp free of disease.

I heard something scratching on stone somewhere above my head. I looked up and discovered Juva at last, his sandals struggling for balance on the parapet of a high rounded arch that had once decorated the camp's second story.

He held a wide, flat stone plaque over his head. He had hoped to drop it on me as I passed underneath but it was too late for that so he threw it at me. I dodged just as it plummeted toward my upturned face. It crashed a finger's width from my horse's leg on the ground.

'I've got you trapped,' I yelled. 'I'm taking you to the Commander.'

The late morning sun hovered low among a few clouds behind him. His tall narrow frame cast a silhouette against the sky as if he were one of Hadrian's statues that once decorated the arch but now lay broken at our feet.

Juva didn't answer me but turned and ran along the top of the arch and scurried down a broken wall that tumbled into a pile of rubble at ground level. I rode after him and saw him dashing straight down the long ruined corridor that led to the back of our tent camp. I moved after him, but could ride no faster than he could run, for fear of my horse catching his hooves on the piles of pottery shards and broken paving underfoot.

I reached the stone perimeter and moved onto open ground. Juva was hundreds of feet away from me, scrambling up a steep rocky foothill that sat to one side of the tent camp. I followed him to the base of the hill at a full gallop. I would reach him any instant now and I'd cut him down.

But the red boulders were treacherous and the upper half of the slope even more slippery and dangerous. My horse picked his way between and over loose, jutting rocks toward the final crest where Juva's back was gaining in distance from us with every minute.

Then Juva halted above and turned to look down at me. I kicked my horse to surmount the final yards up to the plateau where more even ground awaited us above. Behind and below us, the battle of Bagae still raged. My horse pawed the ground and bucked his head but I held the reins taut.

'Get off that horse and fight me, man to man, Roman,' Juva shouted. 'Coward!'

He stood there taunting me. His black beard was covered in red dust and his long white robe ripped below the knees.

A few yards behind him stretched an open vista of wild plains patched here and there by irrigated farmland. The martyr-maker waited for me near the edge of the cliff. He was taller than I was, though I was the stronger. I considered whether I risked tackling him and waited instead.

'Get down!'

I kept to my saddle.

'Coward!' he bellowed again, heaving and panting from the steep climb.

'No, Juva. I have no need to fight you. I'm offering you a chance to rail against the injustices of the Empire face to face with its representatives.'

He backed away from me.

My horse took a few steps toward him.

'You bastard Roman! You dirty spy!' he screamed.

'I'm letting you live, to put your case to the Governor.'

'He's as corrupt as any of them.'

'No more two-faced than your miracle-worker Donatus.'

'Why would you spare my life instead of slaughtering me now, along with all my followers below?'

'Just call me a true believer.'

At my kick, the horse took a few more steps toward him.

Juva saw he was trapped. He turned and looked out over the sheer drop behind him, then faced me again. 'You'll have to force me over this edge and I swear before Christ our Savior that I will take you with me,' he yelled.

'I prefer that you face interrogation under the iron claws and rack of the Roman emissaries. I don't intend to do you the favor of killing you clean. Martyrdom without true suffering would be doing you too much of a favor.'

I saw him shudder at the prospect of hours of agonized dismemberment and flaying at the hands of Paul and Macarius. He turned his back to me and faced the sky. Raising his arms wide to the breeze, he slowly brought his palms together in prayer. He walked right to the edge and seemed about to jump to his death, as he had forced so many of his faithful to do, but I saw him hesitate.

Then he slid right out of my sight. There was no cry or final prayer as he disappeared.

Behind me the clamor of battle still raged on but here, on this lonely promontory, my ears rang only with confusion and disbelief. My instinct told me that Juva was too much of a coward to leap to his death. I would have bet my life on it, but had he mustered the courage?

I dismounted and led my horse to the edge of the cliff and looked over. I sensed the priest had managed another clever dodge.

He was trying just that.

What I had thought to be a sheer and lethal drop turned out to be a vertiginous avalanche, a river of rolling red rocks and pebbles down which he was stumbling, risking his limbs rather than surrender to me.

I had to follow on foot, though I could see already that the surface of the slope was shifting and slipping out from under him with each step he took. He grabbed at the larger boulders, only to feel them give way and he teetered precariously as the ground collapsed and rolled downwards ahead of him.

I took a careful step onto the loose and pebbly incline and fought for balance. Nothing stayed fixed underneath my boot, yet I ventured another step at a safer angle and leaned into the hill.

Juva was already some thirty feet below me, rolling and slipping to safety.

I tried a third step and felt the rocks slide right out from under my boot. I pulled that foot back and about to lose my balance, I reached for a boulder just within reach, determined to keep after Juva, no matter what.

The huge rock supported my weight only for a moment before I had to let it go on tumble down with it. It bounced away from me, triggering more streams of clattering red rubble clouding into dust at the bottom far below.

Juva's white sleeves spread out in wings as he flailed his way down. He was halfway to the bottom. He was going to escape.

I took another step and this time, I felt myself slipping altogether. I grabbed another, heavier boulder, and for a moment I was steady but it gave way and rolled right out of my hands. I started to feel my boots slide right out from under me. I slowed my slide with fingers grappling and scratching for something solid and felt the skin torn off my fingers until I got purchase again. I tried one more step and felt the entire slope shudder underneath me.

There had to be a route around the foothill to catch his flight. I turned away and dashed upwards against the flow. With each step struggling upwards to the edge, I sent more and more of the rocks rumbling down.

Juva screamed as he glanced up from his own desperate progress just in time to see the entire hill giving way over his head, a tidal wave of broken stone roaring down on his upturned brow.

I slung one hand over the top of the slope and found my grip on sturdy weeds with roots clamped between the rocks even as my knees were pulled downwards. I battered my boots against the disappearing rocks until I had pulled myself back to safety and, gasping for breath, looked back down the slope.

I watched the avalanche slow down to a standstill until nothing moved. There was no trace of Juva below. Not the glimpse of a finger or the flutter of a white sleeve. His body would never be recovered now—not under all that tonnage of rubble.

I would have preferred to lead him by a rope around the neck into a Roman tribunal to declaim his righteous fanaticism to the provincial authorities. It would have prevented some crazy Circumcellion from suggesting that the 'Captain of the Saints' had been assumed body and soul into heaven.

But such 'miracles' couldn't be helped. I mounted my horse again and just as carefully as before, we navigated the stony hill and made for the mayhem below.

It was time to capture Donatus.

Chapter 22, One Man Too Few

—LAMBAESIS HEADQUARTERS—

The Battle of Bagae ended at dusk. A weary army of victors stared dazed and bloodied across a field littered with the defeated. Now it was time for Ari's men to work as feverishly as we'd fought.

His medical assistants hurried across the fields surrounding our camp, probing and testing the fallen for signs of life. They made their hard-hearted assessments in low voices, selecting those comrades who had a fighting chance for life from those with wounds too grievous to describe, much less bandage. Medics were exempt from combat, but all the same, I had never envied their job and less than ever today.

Our casualties weren't too numerous but that was small comfort to the wounded begging for water and rescue.

I rested for a few minutes on the slope overlooking the camp, well above the scattered bowels and torn flesh. Screams for help from the Circumcellions didn't distract our orderlies as they stepped over and around the enemy wounded to tend to our own.

If a hooded casualty grabbed at their passing ankles or begged for a drop of water, they shook them off and passed on in a hurry to save our men. Like Linus, Lepidus, Felix and all the other Romans who had fallen, they too knew their jobs.

Part of me wanted to scream in frustration, for I'd failed to unearth Donatus in the hours since Juva's death. I'd hunted and searched through the midday blast of heat that drove fighters into a froth of murderous savagery and long into the hours of the afternoon as the sun sank toward its western rest.

I'd scoured the ruins of Hadrian's camp and returned again to ride through the brush beyond the battlefield as my comrades chased down Circumcellion deserters to take as prisoners.

Our men roped the captives tight and rounded them up in a procession for presentation before Paul and Macarius. The two envoys had now arrived unscathed in Lambaesis and would decide their fates.

The signal to regroup echoed off the slopes in the dusk. We broke camp to march the legion's regulars back to their comfortable homes and families in Lambaesis. The wounded would remain with us. The doctor's tent was now overflowing with groaning soldiers. A second triage tent was thrown up with a corridor between them reserved for the assistants' bustling nursing.

We made the long and tiring march the next day, but Lambaesis' families cheered us from either side of the gates and along the main street leading past the basilica, baths and shops, stables and counting houses. We moved under the imperial arches festooned with dedications to soldiers long forgotten and past the armory to return the regulars' weaponry. We paraded past the paved terrace of the permanent military headquarters with its archive rooms, pagan chapels, and barracks and staff offices so long outgrown.

I wasn't ready for my shock as I marched back into the forum and spotted the two Romans Paul and Macarius standing on an elevated podium above us. The last time I'd seen their smug and vicious faces was in Vegesela as Marculus was flayed at the stake.

Now Governor Silvester stood beaming alongside them. He looked steamed pink from a recent bath as he chatted to Commander Gregorius, his *vexillatio* staff and their Lambaesis colleagues, their uniforms still smeared with the blood and muck of battle.

Our prisoners were bundled forward under guard in front of our assembled ranks. A large well stood in the very center of the forum, making it difficult for me see around to count heads, but it seemed that of the thousand-plus Circumcellions who'd set out from Bagae, fewer than fifty had survived.

'Which one of you is the ringleader Donatus? Show yourself!' Macarius shouted.

The prisoners hung their heads and huddled like thirsty animals around the low walls of the large well.

'Give us the priest Donatus!' Silvester said.

There was still no answer. The Circumcellions stood mute and cowed. We waited for many minutes. The Romans on the steps above our ranks looked tempted to abandon their demand. Perhaps Donatus had died in the massacre. Perhaps he'd never even been there. Perhaps his ambition had wafted him, like some evil spirit, off to freedom to connive for Carthago's altar another day.

'Can anyone here identify the enemy of Roma known as Father Donatus?'

I stepped forward.

'Speak, soldier!'

Commander Gregorius' good eye squinted down at me. He murmured to Silvester.

'Speak up, soldier!' Silvester called.

The ranks in front of me parted and I approached the Governor.

'Donatus wears an iron ring studded with a large garnet,' I said quietly to the military men and officials in front of me.

With this information, our soldiers started to work their way through the prisoners, yanking their hands out of their robes to examine their fingers, and all the while enduring the spit and curses of the Circumcellions without flinching.

'He's here!' a soldier cried out. He untied a hooded figure from the others and pulled him free from the cowering Circumcellions.

The prisoner was dragged up the steps to face Macarius and Paul and kicked hard until he fell to his knees.

'Is this bag of cotton rubbish Donatus, the Great, the miracle-worker, the last *pure* priest?' Macarius sneered.

The man protested, 'No! I'm not Donatus!'

'Liar *and* coward! You'll confess it soon enough.'

'No! I am *not* he! But spare me your pagan tortures and send me quickly to my God as a martyr for his True Church!'

'Not Donatus?' Governor Silvester asked. 'Then why do you wear his ring?'

'It was his gift, I swear it!'

I stood some ten feet from the man and knew that the voice, the hair and stance were all wrong. This quaking creature was not Donatus. Yet scanning the crowd of prisoners, I saw no tall, bearded man.

'You've made a mistake, soldier,' Macarius rebuked me.

'Rejoin your ranks, Marcus.' The Commander's visible anger chilled my bones. My face flushed with shame as the tired, battered soldiers stirred with disgust at my bungling.

I refused to accept their judgment of me. 'May I examine the prisoners, Governor? I've met the man and spoken to him. I'll know him.'

I approached the cluster of prisoners and rearing back momentarily from their stench, I parted them one by one, turning this short suspect to one side and that meager-fleshed man out of my path. I worked systematically, so that none would escape my scrutiny. I tossed back their hoods and shoved them cleanly away as I eliminated them one by one.

The last man at the back was clean-shaven and round-shouldered. There was no one left.

I'd failed.

I turned back to the officials but not before I'd noticed the last man smile. I caught his black, piercing eyes exactly as they'd met mine in the darkness of the Vegesela jail. I knew that harsh and penetrating intelligence.

I locked eyes with him. I had to make sure that this time there was no mistake. I pulled him straight by the shoulders. I jerked his hands out of his sleeves. On one hand was the telltale band of white skin where the garnet ring had long sat.

I dragged him to the foot of the podium.

'This is the priest,' I said and stepped back with a salute.

'Are you the heretic?' Macarius demanded.

Donatus fell to one knee and folded his hands into his long sleeves in prayerful silence. He raised his face to the Roman emissary and asked with equal force, 'And are you Macarius, who places idols on our altars and buys Constans his parishioners with dirty coin?'

'Shut up and answer my question. Are you Donatus?'

'I am he. I go willingly to your tortures as a martyr for Christ!'

'I'm not so foolish, cleric, as to make you the seed of a revolt that would spread throughout most of Numidia,' laughed Macarius. 'No, I'll send you into an exile that will pain you more than any martyrdom, an exile to the west where there are no churches, no Christians and no altars for your hypocritical rituals of whitewashing away Roman stain. You will suffer alone, under guard, addressing your sermons to Berbers and converting the desert lizards.'

'I *will* die for my Lord!' Donatus uttered, 'as will *you!*' He put his right hand back into his long sleeve and with a swift, gesture pulled out a dagger and lunged at Macarius, stabbing it deep into the envoy's lower gut. Donatus pulled downward with a merciless slice that sent the Roman's intestines spilling onto the steps in glistening coils of red and white.

Silvester and the Lambaesis officers gaped in astonishment as Macarius rolled to the bottom of the steps. The prisoners' guards sprang at Donatus. He evaded their clutches and plunged back into the group of supporters who received him into their arms with savage cries of, '*Laudate Deum!*'

In seconds, they had hoisted Donatus onto the walls of the well where he stretched out his arms as their hero. Smiling in triumph, he made the Sign of the Cross in blessing over their heads. Their ecstatic howls of vengeance fell silent as he disappeared from their very midst.

He had leapt to his certain death down the black oblivion of the wet stone tunnel.

***

'Will I ever see you again, Marcus?'

'Yes, of course, some day.'

Kahina sat next to me on the marble bench in Leo's garden with her hands folded in her lap and her face turned away from me. Her eyes brimmed with tears.

After a long silence, she said, 'First I saw you as a Roman soldier and then I knew you as a runaway. Then you told me you were a slave but I didn't understand the whole situation until Nico came back and told me the whole story. You were very brave to win your freedom that way.'

'I was lucky, too. And there were many brave Circumcellions, in their way. Bomilcar, for one. He has enlisted, of all things. And Sophonisba. I hope Sophonisba survived.'

'She said I should trust you. Now you say you're abandoning me to the very future I fled.'

'Because I know some things you don't. The Commander is a good man, a loving and stalwart man who does not betray a woman. I know that you'll be happier as the mistress of the Manlius townhouse than you could ever be as the destitute partner of a bankrupt freedman. I think it is for the best, Kahina.'

'Is a woman never free to make her own choices in this world?' she moaned. 'And anyway, I cannot go to him now.'

'He won't care whether you're virgin and he won't force himself on you, I'm sure. You'll come to see it as the best choice for your own good. Do you want to end up like the women in that camp, like the women you see married to nobodies like me? What if something happened to me? You might end up alone and struggling like Sophonisba.'

'You said yourself Sophonisba was a good woman.'

'Her reward was to survive Bagae, if that, and nothing more. Her healing skills are wasted on ignorant men.'

'I wish I knew where to find her. I might need her skills more than ever now,' Kahina sighed and shifted heavily on the bench. She moved her thin body as if it weighed her down. Since that night in this very garden when Nico and I had fought, I'd suspected she was ill.

'You don't look well, Kahina.'

She turned to face me. Her next words silenced all my easy assurances.

'I think I may be carrying your child,' she announced with a bitterness I knew would stick with me for years.

'You *think*?'

'It's far too early to be sure. That would take another month. But it's possible.'

I took in this news in stunned silence. I longed to embrace her and kiss her downy cheek but I dared not even hold her hand. Any minute now, the escort which had brought me along with the command staff to settle Leo's will and collect his archives of sensitive documents and maps would summon me back into formation on the winding drive fronting the estate.

My thoughts raced far beyond Kahina's anguish.

Any son of the freedman Marcus Gregorianus Numidianus would be lower than almost everybody but an actual slave. Even if Gregorius ever acknowledged me as his offspring, by law no *libertus* could claim a legacy retroactively. Otherwise Roma would be littered with freed bastards pulling fortunes out from under rightful heirs. The Roman fathers had seen the pitfalls of that many centuries ago.

But for the first-born of the Commander, it would be an entirely different story. A girl would be pampered, of course, but a boy! He would be the spoiled darling of the endangered Manlius clan, sweeping Clodius' greedy hopes for adoption right off the table. As Laetitia had never borne the Commander a child, this baby would be the longed-for heir to quell all the cocked eyebrows and lowered voices whenever the childless Gregorius rode down the Esquiline Hill.

It would be an irony fit for a Greek drama. Gregorius' beloved heir under Roman law carried true and honest Manlius blood in his—but only I knew better than anyone how or why. Kahina could be trusted to keep the conception secret for the sake of her survival and out of loyalty to me but only I would know the full irony of this miracle-to-be. The baby bringing the Commander so much delight in nine months' time would indeed be a Manlius, not his child—but his grandchild.

If the Commander had refused the opportunity to acknowledge me as his son when he had the chance, I would hear of his lifting up my own son in his arms in the time-honored Roman ritual of legitimacy with deep satisfaction.

I hoped with all my soul that Kahina's suspicions of a pregnancy would bear fruit.

'There's nothing we can do,' I said to her.

'Nothing, Marcus?' Her eyes pleaded for me to relent, to say I wanted her, desired her over any arguments for common sense or the interests of a possible child, but that wasn't so.

If there was a child, I wanted everything for him, not for us.

'If there is a baby, will you care for him above all else, if only for my sake?' I begged.

'It seems dishonest.' She thrust out her chin and stared at the garden. She wanted to fight me with every weapon her soul could muster.

'Oh, Kahina, it's more honest than you know. Someday you'll understand, perhaps. But for now, all I can reassure you is that your child will be entitled to all it will receive.'

'But I want to be with you, Marcus!'

'*Dis aliter visum*, the gods see our fate differently, at least for now.'

'How can I love this mutilated old man when I desire you?'

'Underneath those scars is a man I once knew to be handsome, happy, loyal, generous, brave and loving. He's free to marry you now, Kahina. You'll be like a queen to him, making up for all he sacrificed for the sake of his sick wife.'

I thought of my sad mother and her life of obscure loneliness.

'But it's so hard even to look at him!'

'You'll come to cherish him for his suffering as well as his power and courage. Please don't forget, ever, that the secret of this child comes first, no matter how strong our feelings now and no matter how loyal you feel toward him later. *You must keep our secret.*'

She nodded and wiped the tears streaming down her cheeks. There was nothing I could do to reassure her more. This was far better for her than the degradation she faced as my destitute mistress. She was young, beautiful and too vulnerable to the predations of her greedy Numidian clan.

In Roma, she'd be respected, doted on and even educated. When the birth time came, my child and its mother would have the finest Roman midwife in attendance and the best modern medicines to ease her pain.

'I'll think of you every night,' she whispered.

'No, Kahina, no, no! You mustn't think of me at all. I would have so far to travel before I would be worthy of you or our child. No, you'll become a true member of the Manlius clan. You must face each morning with care for our child and gratitude for his good fortune. You must honor your family's bargain and go to the Commander at night with a heart full of tenderness for his lonely years and courageous suffering.'

She lifted her chin and smiled a little through her tears. 'I suppose that's what a grand Roman military wife would do?' she said. She smoothed her thick hair back from her forehead with resignation.

'You'll be the finest officer's wife Roma has ever seen.'

She gulped back her sobs and rallied her pride a little. I recognized the feisty girl who had buried her teeth in Stembanos' arm. 'You think I'm a weak girl, just a stupid servant girl who wanted to be a saint. But I can be stronger than that. I'll prove it to you. Someday you'll come back to Roma and you'll see how strong I was. And no matter how much I love you, I'll turn my back on you, Marcus, just like you're turning your back on me.'

'I hope that day never comes.'

'And what will you do now, if you leave the army with no money, no family and no friends?'

'I'm going to do what Leo told me to do, Kahina, I'm going to seek out a great man who stands no taller than yourself, with white hair, arthritic feet and the sharp eyes of a quick white mouse.'

CHAPTER 23, *AGENTES IN REBUS*

—THEVESTE—

Leo's dying words to me had been, 'Trust Apodemius in all things.'

But where should I go? How could I find the old traveler? What if he'd forgotten me? What if he'd died?

I pictured in my mind once more the oil trader's large map of imperial and Donatist church centers. While Lambaesis had mushroomed into a boomtown watered by generations of army pensioners, Theveste was important for a different reason—it was the junction of eight imperial roads. Leo had pointed it out on the map as the true hub of provincial traffic.

So I went to Theveste. I sent a message to the mysterious Apodemius at the Castra Peregrina in Roma by way of a red wares merchant heading north. I wrote that Leo had died, that I'd finished my mission and been manumitted, and that I waited in hope of instructions.

I survived for twelve long and bitter winter weeks living off a pouch of borrowed change until I had nothing more to eat but what I could forage or beg. Even if I'd wanted to change my mind, I was too proud to ask for help from the Commander I'd so deeply disappointed.

In desperation, I wangled a job from an army veteran nicknamed Caesar in a rundown Theveste bathhouse. I was doing nothing more respectable than any slave up in Roma. At first it was hellish work, manning the furnaces below ground that kept the heat running through pipes under the steam rooms.

I stuck with this until I was promoted upstairs and as in the old days while a slave up in Roma, I found myself back at work with a *strigilis*. Only this time, I wasn't tending the muscles of the Commander or sinewy limbs of the old Senator, but scraping and scrubbing the oiled shoulders of flabby, sun-blotched men. I lived from day to day and couldn't save a single tip from what I earned. It all went to keeping myself covered and fed. For the first time I learned that freedom doesn't silence a growling belly.

As soon as boats left winter dry-dock and had resumed regular crossings to Italia, I sent a second message with a Sicilian cloth merchant who supplied fresh linens to the baths manager. I carefully traced a mouse on the packet, just as Leo had instructed.

I waited in vain.

Then I tried a third time with the wife of a bathhouse client. She was travelling all the way to Roma direct on one of the biggest grain ships headed for the port in Ostia. The packing stuff I used wasn't cheap *emporitica* and her delivery commission almost broke me, but unlike the other two couriers, she guaranteed hand delivery to the doors of the Castra Peregrina.

Again, I drew a mouse.

I was young, strong and far from final despair, but I was also smart enough to see the grim probability. Leo was a Roman widower stuck for decades in a North African colonial backwater, driving oil barrels back and forth to Rusicada and wiling away his lonely hours with some divorcée or widow.

He must have got used to telling tall tales of intrigue and influence to his paramour and in his last hours, he'd forgotten what was true and what was wishful thinking. He'd been delirious with pain. In *extremis*, he'd inflated his feeble-footed friend into a fantasy godfather to whom I could turn.

There was one very bad day just as spring brought warmer days and double the number of customers. While I was rinsing the wooden buckets of soapy water and squeezing out used towels for the laundry bin, I overheard a businessman regaling another about a military wedding he had attended months before.

'Imagine, a fresh, succulent beauty like her waking up for the rest of her days next to *that* on the pillow.'

'She did well for a local nobody! Who cares what he looks like? She's damn lucky he decided to make an honest woman of her and not just keep her as a concubine! Let's just hope that her luck holds out. He can't be that far from retirement. He might leave her and their baby here with a monthly remittance.'

The other man said, 'Even if he takes her back to Roma, she probably hasn't got more than ten words of Latin. He'll keep her and his brat hidden away on one of his farms.'

'Souvenirs of service, my friends, just souvenirs. But you're right. She had better meet the challenge or find herself shunned by the family's old friends. A colonial girl with no education or upbringing can look very different in the cold light of a Roman winter.'

I sank onto a stool at those words and nearly retched. I knew the truth of what the strangers said. I had been a fool to let Kahina go to Gregorius for the sake of our child. Why would a marriage ceremony on the edge of the Gaetulian desert mean anything to the Manlius family when the Commander's tour was over?

And then I did give in to despair. I was going to be a bathhouse attendant for a long time if I didn't get a better job putting my brains to better use. I gave up waiting for a message from Leo's vanished crony. I started offering my services around town as a bodyguard or bouncer.

A few days later, I got a bite. Caesar told me he'd been asked to send the 'tall bronze-haired boy' over to test for a job at the local amphitheater, keeping order between animal acts and for all I knew, cleaning out their cages.

'Dirtier work, but better tips from the ladies in the audience who fancy that sort of thing,' he said with a wink. I wasn't keen to go. The address was somewhere in the slums behind the theatre district. Within a hundred yards of my destination, the reek of the gutters alone nearly sent me back for an off-hours bath of my own.

'Upstairs,' a voluptuous dancer mumbled a greeting to me and told me to go through a warren of dressing rooms and offices. I reached the door of a low-ceilinged room filled with costumes and acrobats' harnesses. Sitting on a deep-cushioned couch in the shadowy corner, a dark-skinned man was already passing the time of day. He fingered his short brown pointed beard in thought as I came in. He looked like the kind of weathered handyman who kept things running backstage. Perhaps he was interviewing for the same job. Perhaps we might end up working together.

He grunted and seemed indifferent to which stool I chose. I nodded as a courtesy but I didn't feel very cordial. The squalor all around me was disheartening.

And there we both waited in silence. I had almost decided that I was better off at the baths where at least the surroundings were clean when the handyman spoke up.

'Tell me what you see, Marcus.'

I knew his voice at an instant, if I just then I hadn't spotted the carbuncled toes peeking out from under his oil-stained leather apron and the inky bunion on the middle finger of his right hand.

'I don't—! I would have taken you for a leatherworker or a cobbler! I am so relieved to see you, alive and well.'

'Yes, it's me, *Magister* Apodemius, alive and as well as the Empire that gives me breath.' He shook his head as if he doubted how well that really was.

'How did you...?' I gestured at his convincing appearance.

'Walnut oil and a pot of wagon wheel grease. And I might even have mistaken you for a bathhouse attendant,' he joked. 'Look at those pink fingers withered up like prunes! And you smell better than a virgin heading for her first market fair!'

And so we talked and talked and to my delight, we ate almost more than we talked. He ordered his favorite fish in *garum* sauce and then lamb stew, followed by dates, fresh breads and a pitcher of fine red wine. Halfway through the feast, he sat back and watched me wipe the bowls clean.

'Do you recall what Thetis said to Achilles in the passage you read to me in Leo's study?'

'Yes, *Magister*.'

'You may share more with our Greek hero than you think—a choice of two destinies, indeed. *Nostos,* returning to the safe bosom of the Manlius household as a freedman with Commander Gregorius as your patron, and perhaps a shop to run with a pretty wife and little kids?'

'Or *Kleos*?'

'Yes. Everlasting glory in the service of the Empire—no matter how heavy the cost.'

'You mean return to the army, *Magister*?'

'No, I am thinking of another service, the *agentes in rebus*.'

'Become an *agens*?'

'Yes.'

'Why me?'

'In his youth, Leontus Flavius was one of our most experienced *agens*. The Emperor assigns two senior men to each province. Many decades ago, Leo was one of two dispatched to Numidia Militaris. But he tired of the service and retired so that he could marry Aemilia, have children and live a normal life. But he never forgot his love of the Empire, our *schola*, and the adventures we shared.'

'Did the Commander know?'

'Perhaps some of it. Not all. We *agentes* don't discuss every aspect of our work outside the *schola*, not even with childhood friends.'

'He seemed so affable and open, not a man to keep secrets. But he kept them well enough. He didn't tell me until it was nearly too late that he knew me as a child.'

'He was always on the lookout for someone like you, Marcus—someone who watches and listens and what's most important, someone who *sees*. He observed your childish talent for mimicry, something that comes only with sharp eyes and quick ears. He thought we could use those skills. I don't think he was mistaken.'

'Does it mean I would be attached to the army?'

'An *agens* can be attached or at least work in tandem with military staff, but as a career track, it means leaving the army for good.

'I might have burnt that bridge already.'

He refilled my wine cup for the third time. 'You see, we agents are not *exploratores* or *speculatores*. We are neither internal nor external military security. We're not really military at all, though we borrow their ranking system. We report straight to the top, to the *magister officiorum* in the imperial court.'

Just then, I heard an army trumpet, calling some soldiers out on detachment into formation. I glanced out the window and spotted none other than Lieutenant Barbatio leading a mounted cohort. They'd be heading back in the direction of Lambaesis and our camp beyond.

Despite their weary expressions, the soldiers looked serene. Whatever brought them up to Theveste, they'd done their duty and that was that. They led a simple, uncomplicated life, and with their women waiting for their return in a day or two, they'd enjoy an uncomplicated reward.

For a second, I wanted nothing more than to call out to them, to run down those rickety stairs and out of the alleyway, and around the amphitheater. I wanted to race after those trotting columns, even to remain a slave at the very rear, rather than travel in this obscure and twisting direction with no one but a strange old man in disguise pointing the way.

But perhaps it was not so twisting as all that? Perhaps it was very straightforward.

'So an *agens* pledges his life and loyalty to the Emperor, *Magister*?'

Apodemius shook his head and smiled. 'Well, no, Marcus, it's not that simple.'

'Because there's more than one Emperor right now, right?'

'We serve no emperor at all. When emperors falter or even fail—for they are merely men after all—when their generals dare to usurp them or their courtiers turn corrupt, it's our service that is watching and guarding—perhaps nearby or in some far off corner of the Empire. It's our service that is shoring up the Empire against all these temporary follies.'

'But don't you answer to the Emperor's whims?'

'No. Under the law we're a separate *schola* of the palace and we serve only *Roma* itself. We fight day and night for its unity, its integrity, and its strength. No matter what we do, only the Master of Offices can question us. What's more, in the execution of our duties, we're immune from the prosecution of law.'

I leaned away from the table, unable to believe my ears. 'That's an open license for crime!'

'True, things can and do go wrong. We have to recruit very, very carefully. Our predecessors, the *frumentarii*, became no better than a law unto themselves. They abused their position. The wise Diocletian disbanded them.'

'I never heard of them.'

'We took their place. We even took over their headquarters.'

'But men are only human, *Magister*. From what I've heard, civil officials can only hope to advance by bribes and backscratching. It's the way of the world. The only way things are done. At least the army promotes people for the right reasons.'

Apodemius managed a tired chuckle at my naiveté.

I tried hard not to take offense. 'I didn't say that every soldier was perfect.' I broke my bread into pieces and crumbled them as I wavered. 'After I was freed, Gregorius harbored a deep bitterness toward me. Leo had twisted his arm into giving me up. The Commander couldn't look me in the eye, even to say congratulations. That's why I left.'

'I'll try to square it with him. He may even be impressed. As I said, we're very careful now about the men we recruit. We don't care about their station in life, their bloodlines or their past. We want men of character and judgment. That's why I'm here.'

'I'm honored, *Magister*.'

I wanted to ask Apodemius what he'd been doing and which of my messages had found him and where. But I knew it was better to listen. There was a sense around Apodemius that his time was valuable and that he should be somewhere else, doing something far more important than interviewing a freedman in a dressing room stinking of makeup and dancing slippers.

'I warn you, it may never become what you dream of! To the naked eyes of the world, *agentes* are nothing but messengers, couriers, escorts, and state budget inspectors. A few of us relay highly sensitive information while others spend years delivering quite ordinary mail. Some check licenses on the state highways or keep watch on the traffic passing through the relay stations. Many *agentes* stay rooted in humble posts and that's where you'll start.'

'You make it sound like a priesthood, *Magister*.'

'If you like—although we're no Vestals.'

His joke struck a bitter chord. 'What religion are we? We serve only one deity—the survival of the Empire, the only civilizing force on the face of the earth. Without the Empire, we all would fall into a dark chaos that even now creeps toward us on claws of hypocrisy, fratricide, perversion and spiritual confusion.'

'When do I begin?'

'Your first task will be to escort that envoy Paul safely back up to the court in Mediolanum and then report for training at the Castra Peregrina in Roma.'

Later that night I sat up in my wretched rented cubbyhole watching the lantern flame flicker and listening to the noises of the street outside my window. I fingered my old *bulla* on its cord and thought of the ageing senator back in Roma, blind and living with his memories, grieving his daughter-in-law's death and fingering the books he couldn't read.

I could not believe such a gentle old man would be hardhearted to Kahina or the child. No one in the Manlius townhouse had patted my head more tenderly or squandered more time on training my childish mind.

The *agentes in rebus*! Senator Manlius would have wanted this for me. When I reached the city, I would visit him before anyone else to tell him I was on my way to the Castra Peregrina and a new life. I would thank him for everything he'd given me and promise to serve the Empire he loved above all else.

Chapter 24, The Long Game

—ON THE ROAD TO RUSICADA PORT—

It would be a long ride up to Rusicada, even with a government pass guaranteeing use fresh horses and good food at the relay stations along the way. There were twenty stations on the 187 miles from Theveste to the coast and I'd be responsible for the safety of the emissary Paul for the entire journey. Our road passport bore my entire new name and rank—trainee agens, basic rider class. More than once, when Paul wasn't watching, I took it out of my pouch and gazed at it in disbelief.

My Roman travel companion was as pompous and pusillanimous as his partner had been ambitious and vicious. He droned on and on about two subjects close to his heart—how he would convince the Emperor Constans that blame for the whole debacle of Bagae rested on Macarius' torture rather than misguided bribes, and how he was sure his wife had been faithful to him during his absence in Roman Africa.

On the first point I could be persuaded, although both torture and bribes were bad for political loyalty. On the wife's reliability, I definitely had my doubts.

If being an *agens* meant suffering these days of imperial pretension and irritability, then at least I had the hope of better missions to come. Once I'd seen the uxorious Paul safely to the imperial court, I'd head straight down to Roma and my new quarters. Apodemius had supplied me with a letter of introduction to the training school at the Castra Peregrina.

'With the imperial court travelling between Mediolanum and Treverorum, you'll find Roma is feeling the Emperor's neglect, but the Castra will always be our home,' Apodemius had explained.

'And the Senate remains in Roma, *Magister*.'

'Well, for what that's worth,' he sniffed. 'But the *agentes* matter more than ever. The training's tough. Even if you succeed, trainee basic rider is at the very bottom of five ranks modeled on the cavalry. You'll count the hours of sleep on one hand. The competition for promotion is ferocious.'

'The army is tough, too, *Magister*.'

'Yes, but it's straightforward, even in a civil war. You get orders or you give orders. You fight or you die. You're going to learn that the machine of the Empire is a complicated beast. We have laws but no morals, allies but no friends, and successes but no congratulations.'

'It sounds pretty treacherous.'

'And yet it's the only civilization on earth worth protecting.'

Paul's repetitive blather gave me time to think as we rode north—about trust. Leo had entrusted me to Apodemius and I'd entrusted Kahina and our child to its future as an heir to the Manlius estates. If we were lucky, I'd survive and thrive as an *agens*. The Commander would keep patrolling the limits of the Empire and now that poor Lady Laetitia's suffering had ended, Kahina could go up to Roma with no damage to her predecessor's dignity or memory.

I also trusted that even if Clodius was an unworthy custodian, the old Senator reigned over the family's interests, blind but overseeing everything and protecting the ones I loved from malice.

We kept riding toward the Central Sea. My heart lifted higher with each morning we found ourselves closer to the coast. I felt like the hero Aeneas leaving his beloved Queen Dido behind in Carthago to forge a new future in Roma.

Most of all, I was determined to live up to what Leo had imagined for me. All those years ago, he'd watched me, a 'quick little bugger,' who prated and pranced to entertain his master's friends. How long had Leo kept in touch with his friend Gregorius, and kept his ears alert for news of 'the little slave,' just in case he saw a chance to put me to better use? Leo might have retired from active service as an *agens* but when it came to talent spotting, he'd played a long game.

Now I was going to play a game just as long.

Our horses trotted past the junction turning off to Bagae. Paul made no comment. Did the official even recognize the direction that led to a county still licking its wounds from his devastation?

Shortly after we'd cleared the jagged cliffs of Nova Petra, I spotted a crowd of peasants. It was well past the hours of sowing, so why were they toiling so late in the failing light? We slowed to watch them, strung out in lines across the field, sorting and passing heavy rocks with an energetic chant to make their task go faster.

I dismounted and led our horses to drink from the irrigation ditch gurgling next to the pavement stones. I sauntered over to see what construction kept these workers sweating past dusk.

Closer up, I could see how they fashioned the stones into a clumsy cylindrical tower without doors or windows. I couldn't see the point of working on such a useless mound after a tiring day.

'What's this, brothers?'

They fell back at the sight of me. Many of them scattered into the brush, dropping the stones as they fled. I was wearing the livery of a Roman soldier and they saw no brother in me, however familiar the lilt to my Punic greeting.

The bravest of them knelt before me, however, and pulled the cotton wrap off his weathered brow.

'It's a shrine to the good Bishop Marculus,' he mumbled.

'So he is dead?'

'They say he jumped off the cliffs of Diana Veteranorum late one night.'

'The man did everything he could to stay alive.'

'We believe he was taken out of the prison at Nova Petra and pushed to his death where there would be no witnesses.

With your permission, Roman, may we bear witness to his sacrifice?'

'Go on with your work,' I said. 'I knew Bishop Marculus. He was a brave man of true Faith. God rest his soul. Peace be with you all.'

'Thank you, thank you,' the worker bowed and smiled with relief.

I gathered up the reins of my horse, adjusted my Pannonian cap, and rode on toward Roma.

The End

A note from the publishers:

If you are enjoying the *Embers of Empire* series, please post a review on your blog or reading platform, e.g. Amazon, Goodreads, Shelfari, Smashwords and Library Thing.

Corrections should be sent directly to this address: eyesandears.editions@gmail.com

Would you like to know when new Q.V. Hunter novels come out? Just send an e-mail address to:

eyesandears.editions@gmail.com
subject: Q.V. Hunter Updates

Your information will not be used for any other purpose.

Thanks,
Eyes and Ears Editions
Editorial Department

PLACES AND GLOSSARY

agens, agentes in rebus—imperial state agents
ala—a cavalry unit
amphorae—large containers, usually ceramic, for wine or oil
ancilla—army sex partner
Aquae Flavianae—Hammam Essalihine, Algeria
barritus—battle cry learned by the Romans from the Germans
buccina—a spiral-shaped horn signaling changes of shifts
bulla—amulet given to child for the protection by the gods
Carthago—Carthage, now suburb of Tunis, Tunisia
caroballistae—wheeled catapults
cornicen—army signaler
cornu, cornua—a brass horn used for signaling troop movements in battle by the signaler, the *cornicen*
Cursus Publicus—the imperial network of state highways
Cursus Clabularis—Cursus roads constructed for heavy cargo traffic
decurio—squadron leader
delicatus—cherished boy, possibly indulged and sometimes, but not always containing sexual overtones
dediticii—conquered people, ostracized outlaws
diplomata—licenses issued for use of the state roads
emporitica—variety of Roman paper too coarse for writing and reserved for wrapping uses (derived from the papyrus plant)
evectio—passport for official travel use
exploratores—army reconnaissance men
fibula, fibulae—shoulder pins
fugitivus—runaway, fugitive
Lambaesis—near Tazoult, Algeria
lararium—shrine for household gods

Lares—the household gods

libertus, freed slave

manceps—franchise-holder managing a state relay-station

mansio, mansiones—state-sponsored guest house operated under franchises to service the *Cursus* traffic

manuballistae—shoulder-mounted catapults

Mare Nostrum—the Mediterranean, 'Our Sea'

Mascula—Khenchela, Algeria

Mediolanum—Milan, Italy

metatores—surveyors

mulex—snails giving a reddish-purple dye

nummus—Late Roman low-value silver-clad coin, continually debased from the monetary reforms of Diocletian

optiones—lieutenants enforcing centurion commands at rear

palla—shawl

polybolos—repeating crossbow

reditum—used by Donatists as term for rendering (the soul to God)

the Rhodanus—the Rhône River

sacrarium—basin and accessories used for baptism

sanctimoniales—attendants

schola—government ministry or department

Simmithus—Chim-tou, Tunisia, mined by the Romans for black lapis

spatha—double-bladed sword in Late Rome replacing the shorter *gladius*

speculatores—army scouts

strigilis, strigiles—tool for scraping oiled bathers

stola—overtunic

strix—an owl believed to feast on human flesh and blood in Greek and Roman mythology

reditum—rendering soul to God

Rusicada—Skikda, Algeria

taberna—tavern, usually open to the street or forum

testudo—a wall of shields held in overlapping formation to form a defensive front resembling the shell of a tortoise

Thamugadi—Timgad, Algeria

Theveste—Tebessa, Algeria

—THE VEILED ASSASSIN—

Treverorum—Trier, Germany

volo—abbreviated form of *voluntarius* and *voluntarii*, for slaves volunteering to fight for Roma in the hope of liberation.

HISTORICAL NOTES

History leaves us with the riddle of at least two fourth-century North African bishops named Donatus ministering in The Church of the Martyrs. Some scholarship is open to the idea that there was actually only one, but there is substantial suggestion that we shouldn't confuse the 'Great Donatus,' contending against an imperial candidate for the bishopric of Carthago with a second 'Donatus of Bagae' who was a militant participant in the battle of depicted here. The idea that there were two is supported by reports that while the Great Donatus was sent into exile after the battle, his lesser religious colleague was captured in the aftermath and died at the bottom of a well—either by his own hand or that of the Romans, depending on which side of the schism you believe. I have fictionally combined these two fates.

Constans' two emissaries, Paul and Macarius, were responsible for the public-relations disaster that happened in North Africa during the year 347 AD. History says that it was they themselves who appealed to Governor Silvester for military protection against the Circumcellion forces summoned as an army by Donatus of Bagae. Other historical figures in *The Veiled Assassin* are the slow-witted military officer Barbatio, (recorded years later as arresting the Caesar Gallus and then failing to send the young commander Julian the Apostate backup troops in Gaul), the master-spy Apodemius, (famous for interrogating the jailed Caesar Gallus before execution) Governors Taurinus and Silvester, the virgins Donatilla, Maxima and Secunda, and the martyred lawyer, Bishop Marculus.

Accounts differ, so I chose to work with records saying Constans issued an edict on June 29, 347 posted in Carthago around mid-August. Although Emperor Constans did send a Gregorius to suppress the Donatists, this historical Gregorius was a civil prefect and he arrived in Roman Africa two years before my story begins.

Similarly, I've compressed some events for the sake of fictional pace. Bishop Marculus was held and tortured by Paul and Macarius until November 29 of that year, and as with Donatus of Bagae, the historians and theologians debate how exactly he came to plummet to his death—the Donatists insist Marculus was pushed from a precipice while St Augustine and the official Catholic Church insisted later that he jumped.

Circumcellion resistance to the imperial Catholic Church varied in nature and scale over the course of a century. It really only expired with the Vandal invasion of North Africa via Spain in the mid-fifth century. The Circumcellions threw themselves into fires, off cliffs and onto the blades of imperial authorities, according to various accounts. Their use of lime and soda to blind their victims is in the historical record.

Interpretations of Circumcellion violence can vary with the historian's worldview. Nineteenth-century Protestants studied the Donatists as early anti-Rome church reformers. Some experts assign their suicidal 'martyrdom' to a cultural legacy ¹rooted in the Jewish tradition of the Maccabees while Brent Shaw answers any incredulity at the devotional 'stretch' transforming persecuted schismatics into suicide militants by reminding us of extremists' suicide attacks in our own times.

Some academics stress the proto-nationalist or anti-imperial determination of the Numidians over any religious motivation. Others view the Donatists as neo-Marxists seeking to overturn a class-ridden colonial society in pursuit of a community of equals able to redistribute North Africa's plentiful resources.

If North Africa was enjoying the height of its agricultural potential, thanks to more than two centuries of Roman irrigation and engineering, why were there so many disenfranchised locals in poverty and debt? Leslie Dossey's research on the regional economy shows that mid-fourth century Arica was at a zenith of agricultural success—prosperity on which Rome depended more than ever now that the Emperor Constantine had deflected the flow of Egypt's corn shipments to his new 'Eastern Rome' of Constantinople. It was the insatiable appetite of Rome's welfare society for olive oil and grain that shifted Numidian production away from a healthy balance of crops—including barley as insurance against times of drought—into overdependence on a few profitable export crops. This left smallholders more vulnerable to a single crop failure and increased the rate of debt among farmers working marginal lands.

I could find no contemporary accounts of what happened to Paul and Macarius after they ordered the execution, if that was what it was, of the Donatist bishop, Marculus. They fade from the records at Bagae, but Macarius leaves his name to 'The Macarian Times' cited in an argument decades later between St Augustine and Optatus over who behaved worse during these years, the Circumcellions or the Catholic Church? This is the main reason for my depicting Macarius as the crueler of the two imperial delegates.

The history of the Legio III Augusta that defended Roma's African territories against Berber incursions for so many centuries begins to fade in the early fourth century. The years of their glory came two centuries before this story, when they accomplished major engineering feats, including water tunnels piercing the Aurès range and massive stone military fortifications and roads. During their heyday these soldiers exerted a major engineering and cultural influence on the region centered on the former garrison town of Lambaesis. They were responsible for not only maintaining the excellent highway links, aqueduct lines and city structures, but added theaters, basilicas, social clubs and schools, many of which survive in ruined form today. We can even read detailed records of the headaches of one engineer, Nonius Datus, as he drove a tunnel through the Aurès range using local labor.

By the fourth century, most of the LIIIA were administrative and engineering staffers and totally integrated into the life of the colonial settlements and Roman culture. Although the early fifth century military registry, the Notita Dignitatum assigned to the LIIIA a shield of a yellow boss and circles on a rust-red background, scholars find no significant involvement of the legion in any major conflicts during the period of this story.

Nor are there any reliable records of the manpower attached to that standard. The Diocletian and Constantinian reforms had whittled down the size of legions and cohorts by as much as half compared to their second century counterparts. Within a few decades of Marcus' story, the LIIIA seems to have completely vanished.

Thus, I've sent the Commander Gregorius into Numidia as a combat-hardened *Comes Rei Militaris* of an auxiliary *vexillatio*, i.e. a regiment reinforcing the softening regulars who, apart from desert sorties to safeguard the Berber frontiers, have long settled into urban lives spent repairing and upgrading the civil infrastructure.

So it's not surprising that what sparse records of Bagae we do find tell us that the men chosen to negotiate with the Circumcellions were *metatores*, construction surveyors, rather than *exploratores*, plainclothes scouts, which any mobile field army in Roman Europe would have had on hand. History records that it was indeed the infuriated fellow soldiers of the injured surveyors who precipitated the attack on Bagae.

I could not resist taking one liberty with a colorful illustration of Roman army medical skill. The astonishing account of the successful removal of the arrow through the back of a soldier's neck comes not from the fourth century, but from the sixth-century historian Procopius describing this operation inside a medical tent during the siege of Rome.

Mea culpa.

ACKNOWLEDGEMENTS

A special acknowledgement to Prof. Brent Shaw of Princeton University, whose *Sacred Violence* provided the basis for 'Leo's Map' of Donatist and Catholic strongholds across Numidia.

For those who'd like to read the historical accounts of the Circumcellions, Donatists and their times, the author recommends:

Ariès, Philippe and Georges Duby, *A History of Private Life*, Vol. 1, From Pagan Rome to Byzantium, Paul Veyne, ed. Arthur Goldhammer, transl. Belknap Press, Harvard University, Cambridge, Mass. 1987

Alexander, James, "Donatism," *The Early Christian World*, Vol. II, Philip F. Esler, ed., Routledge, London and New York, 2000

Banaji, Jairus, *Agrarian Change in Late Antiquity: Gold, Labour, and Aristocratic Dominance*, Oxford University Press, Oxford, 2001

Barry, Robert Laurence, *Breaking the Thread of Life: On Rational Suicide*, Transaction Publishers, New Jersey, 1994

Beales, Derek and Geoffrey Best, ed., "Augustine on Pagans and Christians: Reflections on Religious and Social Change," Henry Chadwick, *History, Society and the Churches, Essays in Honour of Owen Chadwick*, Cambridge University Press, 2005, Cambridge, England

Benedict, David, DD, *History of the Donatists*, Nickerson, Sibley and Co., Pawtucket, Rhode Island, 1875

Boissier, Gaston, *Roman Africa: Archaeological Walks in Algeria and Tunis*, Arabella Ward, transl. G. P. Putnam's Sons, New York, 1899

Bright, William, *A History of the Church from the Edict of Milan, A.D. 313 to the Council of Chalcedon, A.D. 451*, Kessinger Press, 1875

Cagnat, René, *Les Deux Camps de la Légion III Auguste à Lambèse d'après les Fouilles Récentes*, Paris Imprimerie Nationale, Paris, 1908

Caner, Daniel, *Wandering, Begging Monks: Spiritual Authority and the Promotion of Monasticism in Late Antiquity*, University of California Press, 2002

Clark, Gillian, *Women in Late Antiquity, Pagan and Christian Lifestyles*, Oxford University Press, Oxford, 1993

Dossey, Leslie, *Peasant and Empire in Christian North Africa*, University of California Press, Berkeley, California, 2010

Gaddis, Michael, *There Is No Crime for Those Who Have Christ: Religious Violence in the Christian Roman Empire*, University of California Press, 2005

Gibbon, Edward, *The History of the Decline and Fall of the Roman Empire*, in 12 vols, J.B. Bury, ed. with an introduction by W.E.H. Lecky, Fred de Fau and Co., New York 1906, The Online Library of Liberty

Gotoh, Atsuko, "Circumcelliones: The Ideology Behind Their Activities," *Forms of Control and Subordination in Antiquity*, E. J. Brill, Leiden, New York, 1988

Grabar, Oleg, *Late Antiquity: A Guide to the Postclassical World*, Edited by Peter Robert Lamont Brown, Belknap Press/Harvard University Press Reference Library, 1999

Milman, Rev. H.H. *The History of Christianity*, John Murray, London, 1840

Neander, Dr Augustus, *The General History of Christian Religion and Church during the First Three Centuries*, Cosimo Classics, New York, 2007

Rubin, Ze'ev, "Mass Movements in Late Antiquity," *Leaders & Masses in the Roman World*, ed. I. Malkin & Z.W. Rubinsohn, Brill, 1994

Shambaugh, John E., *The Ancient Roman City*, John Hopkins University Press, Baltimore, 1988

Shaw, Brent D. "Bad Boys: Circumcellions and Fictive Violence," *Violence in Late Antiquity: Perceptions and Practices,* Ashgate Publishing Ltd. 2006

Shaw, Brent D. *Sacred Violence: African Christians and Sectarian Hatred in the Age of Augustine,* University of Cambridge Press, 2011

St. Optatus, *Optatus, Against the Donatists,* Bishop of Mileve, trans. Mark Edwards, University of Liverpool Press, Liverpool, 1997

The History of the Donatists: Dissent and Nonconformity Series, The Baptist Standard Bearer, Paris, Arkansas, 2001

Scarre, Chris *The Penguin Historical Atlas of Ancient Roma,* (French edition: *Atlas de la Roma antique,* traduit par Camille Cantoni, Editions Autrement, Paris, 1995

Smith, William, DCL, LLD: *A Dictionary of Greek and Roman Antiquities,* John Murray, London, 1875

Tilley, Maureen A., ed, *Donatist Martyr Stories: The Church in Conflict in Roman North Africa,* Liverpool University Press, Liverpool, 1996

Tilley, Maureen A., *The Bible in Christian North Africa: The Donatist World,* Augsburg Fortress, Minneapolis, 1997

Also: deepest thanks to the online communities of:

Romanarmy.com, Jasper Oorthuys, Associate Webmaster, and Jenny Cline, Founder,

LacusCurtius at the University of Chicago, webmaster Henry Thayer,

ORBISvia at Stanford University

Forum Ancient Coins and

Academia.edu

Any errors are my own and I welcome corrections.

ABOUT THE AUTHOR

Q. V. Hunter is the author of nine novels and two radio plays. Hunter's interest in classical history began with four years of high school Latin followed by university courses in ancient religions. A fascination with Late Antiquity deepened when Hunter moved to a two-hundred-year-old farmhouse in the vicinity of an ancient Roman colony.

Colonia Equestris Noviodunum was founded around 50 BC as a retirement community for Julius Caesar's cavalry veterans. It's listed as the *civitas Equestrium id est Noviodunus* in the *Notitia Galliarum,* (the fourth-century directory listing all seventeen provinces of Roman Gaul.)

Noviodunum became Roma's most important colony along the Lake Leman—with a forum, baths, basilica and amphitheater and its potable water supplied by an aqueduct running all the way from present-day Divonne, France. It belonged to a network of settlements radiating out from Lugdunum (Lyon, France) around the Rhône Valley and supervising the Celtic Helvetii who were settled in the area against their will after their defeat at the Battle of Bibracte in 58 BC.

As a result of Germanic Alemanni invasions in 259-260 AD, much of Roman Noviodunum was razed but it flourishes today as the Swiss town, Nyon.

Hunter is married to a self-proclaimed 'Ur-Swiss,' a descendant of those very barbarian Alemanni who settled farther north of Nyon in the Alpine lake region that gave birth to the three founding cantons of the Confederation Helvetica, i.e. Switzerland, in the thirteenth century. They have three adult children.

36507654R00195

Made in the USA
San Bernardino, CA
25 July 2016